Raves for *Frozen*

"A thrilling, beautifully paced skyrocket of a novel."
—Peter Straub, *New York Times* [bestselling] author of
   In the Night Room

"A relentless c[hiller] [that left me] gasping again and a[gain]
—David Mor[rell], [bestselling] author
   of *The Broth[erhood of the Rose]*

"A captivating nove[l] [of] cold and meticulous suspense,
Bonansinga's *Frozen* rings a bell that defines eternal evil
in all its manifestations, in fact spanning six thousand
years of the entity we call evil. This thriller is like no other
serial killer novel. It has everything—a unique setting, a
compelling lead character, a new twist on forensics, and
the latent evil of mankind."
—Robert W. Walker, author of *Absolute Instinct* and
   Final Edge

"*Frozen* will chill you to the bone! Bonansinga breathes
much-needed life into the serial killer genre while
simultaneously turning it on its head. With enough suspense, twists, action, and surprise revelations for a dozen
thrillers, *Frozen* is the must-read book of the season,
written by a master at the top of his game. Be prepared
to set aside a few days, because once you begin *Frozen*,
you won't be able to put it down."
—J.A. Konrath, author of *Bloody Mary* and *Whiskey Sour*

"*Frozen* will send chills down your spine."
—Barbara D'Amato, award-winning author of the Cat
   Marsala mystery series; former president of the
   Mystery Writers of America; former president of
   Sisters in Crime International.

FROZEN

JAY BONANSINGA

PINNACLE BOOKS
Kensington Publishing Corp.
http://www.kensingtonbooks.com

PINNACLE BOOKS are published by

Kensington Publishing Corp.
850 Third Avenue
New York, NY 10022

All Kensington Titles, Imprints, and Distributed Lines are
available at special quantity discounts for bulk purchases
for sales promotions, premiums, fund-raising, and educa-
tional or institutional use. Special book excerpts or customized printings can also be created to fit specific needs.
For details, write or phone the office of the Kensington
special sales manager: Kensington Publishing Corp., 850
Third Avenue, New York, NY 10022, attn: Special Sales
Department, Phone: 1-800-221-2647.

Pinnacle and the P logo Reg. U.S. Pat. & TM Off.

First Pinnacle Books Printing: August 2005

10 9 8 7 6 5 4 3 2 1

Printed in the United States of America

In memory of Joseph S. Bonansinga
1910-2003

Acknowledgments

To David A. Johnson, my best man and best friend, for introducing me to the story of the "Otzi" the Tyrolean ice man; to the Great Peter Miller for indefatigable artist management and advice; and to Michaela Hamilton for the longest streak of continuous brilliance I've ever witnessed in the editing game. Last but not least, a special thanks to the love of my life (and wisest critic), Jeanne Bonansinga.

PART I
UNDER THE ICE

"'Tis all a checker-board of Nights and Days / Where Destiny with men for pieces plays / Hither and thither moves, and mates, and slays / And one by one back in the Closet lays."

—Omar Khayyam, *Rubaiyat*

1

The Evidence Clock

That night, as the seventh murder unraveled in the storm-lashed shadows of a Colorado nature preserve fifteen hundred miles to the west, Ulysses Grove writhed in fitful slumber in his Virginia apartment.

The FBI profiler had not been sleeping well for months, each evening his mind racing with the minutiae of the six unsolved murders that had come to be known as the Sun City Series (named for the gated community in Huntley, Illinois, in which the first homicide was discovered). Each night, all the dead ends, damaged evidence, and motiveless signatures wormed through the profiler's brain like parasites eating away at his confidence. Sometimes these feverish ruminations fomented into actual flulike symptoms—and Grove would have to anesthetize himself in order to sleep. But on that blustery night, as the profiler seethed in his tangled, damp sheets, clawing at the edges of sleep, his molasses-brown skin shiny with sweat, he was completely oblivious of what was transpiring on the other side of the country, in the strobe light flash and thunder of a remote corner of the Rocky Mountain National Park—

—where an unidentified man was silently emerging

from a drainage ditch bordering a dense cathedral of spruce. He clutched a hunting bow in his arms, his gaunt, twitchy face streaked with lampblack. A rangy, middle-aged man with voices in his head, the killer fixed his cross-hairs on his latest victim through veils of black drizzle.

The snap of the bow was completely drowned by the hiss of rain on the treetops. The victim—a black sanitation worker with a massive belly straining the seams of his city-issue rain parka—hardly had time to glance up, as the whisper of the handmade arrow crackled through the foliage behind him.

The projectile struck the victim between the cords of his neck, nearly lifting him out of his clodhoppers and tossing him across the path. Droplets of arterial blood misted the undergrowth as the garbage man sprawled to the mossy ground, his vital signs closing down even before his body came to rest in the muck. The trash can he was holding tipped and rolled down the trail—a distance of exactly thirty-six feet, as the crime lab people would determine three hours later—making a noise like a death knell played on a tympany drum. The racket was so dissonant and loud, in fact, that it completely covered the sound of the killer's footsteps approaching from the shadows to the east. These were heavy, purposeful footsteps, *purposeful* despite the fact that the victim was chosen at random. For there was much purpose in what the shadowy figure was about to do to the body. What the killer was about to do to that corpse would not only provide the key to solving the Sun City case, but would also shape the destiny of the man who would ultimately track the perpetrator down.

The same man who, at the moment, far to the east, was wrestling with his own phantoms.

In the darkness of the bedroom Grove jerked awake at the sound of his cell phone chirping.

A recurring dream of mass graves and desolate rooms still clinging to his brain, he rolled over and fumbled for the phone, which was plugged into its charger (as it always was on weeknights). As an active field consultant for the bureau's elite Behavioral Science Unit, Ulysses Grove was not exactly on twenty-four-hour call, but pretty close to it, especially in light of the stubborn Sun City case.

"Grove," he muttered into the phone after levering himself into a sitting position on the edge of the bed. A tall, thin African-American with chiseled features and a runner's physique, he was clad only in boxers, his legs rashed with goose bumps in the early morning chill.

"Got another one," the voice crackled in Grove's ear, reporting the news in the kind of clipped, impassive drawl one might hear coming over the loudspeaker in a cockpit during wartime. Grove immediately recognized the source, as well as the import, of the words.

"Sun City?"

"Yeah, Colorado this time," replied the voice of Tom Geisel, the Behavioral Science section chief. Geisel spoke with the pained resolve of a Confederate general about to surrender an encampment.

"Colorado now," Grove said with a sigh, rubbing his neck, trying to wake up enough to put the pieces together. In the dim light his dark skin looked almost indigo. "Which means he's moving west, or at least northwest."

"The thing is, kiddo, we need to get on top of this one."

"I understand."

"Get it as fresh as possible."

"I agree, Tom."

"What I'm saying is, we need somebody out there ten minutes ago."

"I'm on it," Grove said, standing up. The floor was cool under the soles of his feet. "I'll catch the next flight out of Dulles, be there before the uniforms are done with their donuts."

Silence on the other end of the line.

Grove took a deep breath. He knew instantly what that silence meant. Geisel was worried. Not only about the ongoing Sun City case, and all the ugly fallout generated by twelve months worth of grisly crime scene photos leaking to the press, gripping the country in utter terror, not to mention all the angry citizen groups, outraged reporters, and righteous politicians coming down on the bureau for allegedly bungling the case. Geisel was also worried about Grove, who was starting to buckle under the weight of expectations.

The pressure was tremendous. Grove had been brought in on the case nine months ago, after the second murder, and had been able to offer basically no help whatsoever. The problem wasn't a lack of observable evidence. The killer was obviously an *organized* personality in absolute control of his actions, someone completely cognizant of what he was doing. But the *randomness* was what continued to stump everyone. Never before had Grove seen such a meticulous yet specific modus operandi and signature—the way each victim was hunted, dispatched, and positioned postmortem—all of it meted out to such a random sampling.

By the sixth murder, Grove felt as if he had sunk into an investigative tar pit, suffocating under the weight of the paperwork. Usually the bureau would get enough calls to engage its criminologists on a number of cases at one time, but the Sun City job would ultimately become a priority for Grove, a burning ember in his gut, then a white-hot poker in his brain that seared his waking thoughts and roiled in his dreams. Grove was not accustomed to failure. He had the highest success rate of any profiler in the history of the bureau. He knew it, and his peers knew it, and they knew *he* knew it. Modesty was not one of Grove's finer attributes. But the Sun City perp was threatening to drag the profiler down into the realm of mere mortals. Especially in light of the aspect of the killer's signature, which had not been made public: the undetermined postmortem staging of each body.

Geisel's voice finally pierced the silence: "I'm actually thinking that maybe we should send Zorn."

"Don't do that, Tom."

"Ulysses—"

"Zorn's a good man, don't get me wrong." Grove started pacing across the cool tile floor beside his bed, his scalp crawling with nervous tension. His apartment was just beginning to brighten with the pale, predawn light coming through the blinds. The minimal decor reflected the profiler's austere nature—a single, gleaming stainless steel armchair on one corner, a Scandinavian design lamp that looked like a huge inverted hypodermic needle. It was odd how Grove had removed all natural fabrics, wood, and round corners from his world after his wife had died of ovarian cancer four years earlier. It was as though her death had stolen all the texture from Grove's life, and left only hard, sharp, metallic edges.

"It's just that I've been on this one from the jump," Grove finally said. "I need to carry it through to the end. Don't take me off this one, Tom, I'm asking you not to do that."

There was a long pause. Grove gripped the cell phone tightly as he waited. Finally Geisel's voice returned with a tone of weary resignation: "Shirley will fax your ticket and directions. Get your ass out there and figure this monster out."

Special Unit Director Thomas Geisel hung up the phone and sat back in his burnished mahogany swivel chair. He ran fingers through his iron-gray hair and let out an exasperated sigh. He wondered if he had just made another critical error in judgment, sending a burned-out profiler back into the wet zone. Ulysses Grove was definitely cracking. Geisel could hear it in the man's voice. And who wouldn't be melting down under the kind of workload Grove had been carrying? Not only was the profiler weathering the media storm of Sun City, but he was also juggling at least a dozen other active cases. He was starting to get sloppy. His reports were becoming scattered. But Geisel just didn't have the heart to demoralize Grove by taking him off Sun City.

Geisel had been making an inordinate number of mistakes lately, and was starting to wonder whether the naysayers at the bureau were right about the Behavioral Science Unit. Maybe the unit had seen better days. With recent advancements in DNA analysis, as well as the proliferation of regional crime labs, the magic had gone out of the modern "mind-hunter." Some of the wags at the bureau had even started calling Geisel's outfit "the BS Department" . . . and who was Geisel to argue?

Rubbing his tired, deeply lined eyes, the director considered starting a pot of coffee. It was going to be a long morning, and there were many phone calls to make.

Geisel was still in his robe and pajamas, hunkered down in the richly appointed study of his Fredericksburg plantation house. The home reeked of money—much of it from the Geisel Family Farm empire that Thomas Geisel, as the eldest of four sons, had inherited—but the accoutrements of the house were solely courtesy of Lois Geisel, the director's long-suffering second wife. From the cozy country-couture furnishings to the impressive collection of folk art, the house offered a welcome refuge from the exigencies of the BSU offices at Quanitco, twenty miles north along the Potomac.

Geisel threw a glance at the in-box sitting on the corner of his cluttered Colonial-style desk. The box brimmed with documents, memoranda, and letters. Geisel often brought his work home, and lately his to-do list had ballooned out of control. Scattered throughout that stack of papers were at least a dozen memos from the FBI brass admonishing Geisel for not relieving Grove. For months, Geisel had been dancing around that same issue with management. Grove would prevail, Geisel assured them. Grove was the best they had. But in his secret, three-in-the-morning thoughts, Tom Geisel was starting to doubt Grove's invincibility.

At the bottom of that same clogged in-box lay a seemingly innocuous document that Geisel had been relegating to the lowest possible priority for weeks. It was a printout of an e-mail sent to the unit several months ago by a journalist at *Discover* magazine—the kind of thing that the unit received by the bushel every week. It was either some twenty-four-hour news channel requesting another talking head for some celebrity scandal, or some morbidly curious member of the media asking for a quote. Although it was rare that a pop scientific journal such as *Discover* would make contact with the unit, Geisel still saw no reason to take it very seriously. He certainly would be the last person on earth to guess that a four-month-old e-mail from some science geek would change the course of the Sun City investigation.

But Geisel had been wrong before, and, as he was about to learn, he would be wrong again.

In forensics there's a concept known as the "evidence clock." The clock starts the moment a murder is committed, at which time the hard evidence starts to degrade. Prints are mingled, DNA washes away, blood dries and flakes and vanishes. Even psychological evidence atrophies over time. Body positioning is changed, uniformed officers move things. It's an unavoidable aspect to crime scene processing . . . and nobody knows this better than the FBI profilers.

Which is why Ulysses Grove was in such a hell-bent hurry that morning to get to Estes Park, Colorado.

He didn't even bother to pack more than a single change of clothes. He brought only his overnight bag, his briefcase, and a threadbare Burberry raincoat that Hannah had given him for an anniversary present ten years ago. Ulysses could not bear to replace that worn-out coat. Very few people knew this aspect of Grove's personality: he kept things. He was not sentimental, but he secretly kept certain things. Like that plastic bottle of congealed lavender bath oil on the top shelf of his bathroom linen closet, the one that Hannah had used. For months after his wife's death, unable to cry, unable to let the grief come out, Grove had detected ghostly odors of that goddamned lavender oil in the towels, in dresser drawers, in his own clothing, until finally he filled the bathtub with warm water and half the remaining oil, and got in and cried like a baby for over an hour. That was nearly eight years ago, and Grove still had that bottle of oil.

Therapy hadn't helped much. One shrink thought Grove was processing his grief by immersing himself in his work, chasing down violent criminals with a holy vengeance as though the mere act of preventing further death would somehow compensate for the loss of his wife. Which was, of course, ludicrous. The fact was, Grove was a born manhunter.

From the moment he had picked up his first Conan-Doyle novel as a child, to his undergraduate studies in criminology at the University of Michigan, to his years as a noncommissioned officer in the army—first as an MP, and then as an investigator in the military's crack CID unit—Ulysses Grove had proved himself a natural. When he received his honorable discharge in 1987— only months after marrying one of his fellow investigators, the lovely and amazing Lieutenant Hannah S. Washington—Grove was snatched up by the FBI. Affirmative action had nothing to do with it (although the top brass at Quantico were secretly pleased to have such a brilliant, polymath black man on their roster). There was a simpler reason that Ulysses Grove had been on such a meteoric career trajectory: he got results.

Grove was the one investigator in 1990 who believed that Oregon police had the wrong man in the "Happy Face Killer" case. Following a hunch after seeing a happy face scrawled on a gas station restroom wall, Grove eventually led detectives to the real killer—a deranged long-haul trucker named Keith Hunter Jesperson. In 1996, working with Interpol, Grove helped catch Anatoly Onoprienko, a former Ukrainian mental patient and perhaps the most prolific serial killer of all time (with a record fifty-two confirmed homicides). Grove's discovery of a stolen wedding ring on the finger of Onoprienko's girlfriend helped close that case.

Then . . . along came the Sun City Killer.

The instant Grove saw the first victim last spring in that northern Illinois retirement village—the woman lying supine in a cornfield with a sharp trauma wound to the back of her head, her cold, dead arms crossed awkwardly against her breast, one skinny arm frozen in a position higher than the other—he was stumped. None of his tricks had worked. Like an artist wrestling with a debilitating creative block, Grove could not translate the patterns, could not extrapolate one scintilla of psychology.

He was brain-dead.

As dead as all the random victims frozen in their inexplicably baroque poses.

For most of the flight, Grove was vaguely aware of a young woman in a Colorado State University sweatshirt sitting across the aisle from him, pretending not to stare at him. Grove was accustomed to such lingering glances.

Most men would be delighted by such stares from women—but not Grove. His good looks were the bane of his existence, and it wasn't just the beefcake factor—the male equivalent to being a beautiful woman who perpetually struggles to be taken seriously. The deeper problem was that Grove didn't *feel* handsome. He didn't feel desirable. In fact, there was a lot about his appearance that he hated. He hated his tightly coiled, onyx hair, his sculpted, almost feminine cheekbones, and his long eyelashes. He hated his dark skin—a mixture of his deep black African mother and his caramel-skinned Jamaican dad.

On some level Grove probably overcompensated for all this self-loathing through a certain formality of dress. He never dressed down, never wore jeans or shorts or sneakers unless absolutely necessary. Even on his days off, he dressed in shirtsleeves and pressed slacks. His colleagues back at Quantico teased him about it, joking that he often looked like one of Lewis Farrakhan's Nation of Islam goons. Which irked Grove even more than the comments about his looks, since he also had issues with his own culture, at least in America. He detested militant blacks, and rap music, and gangster chic. He felt that his own race was responsible for all the black-on-black violence, and if there was one thing Grove understood implicitly, it was violence.

The plane touched down at Denver International a few minutes ahead of schedule, thanks to an unexpected tailwind. Grove disembarked in a hurry.

Nobody waited for him at the gate, none of the customary police liaisons or community relations people who usually escorted him to crime scenes. This was a stealth mission, unannounced to all but the primary detectives working the scene up in Estes. The evidence clock was already at eight to ten hours past probable time-of-death, and the evidence was deteriorating rapidly.

Grove strode through the glass doors into the fragrant

mountain air of the cab stand, his briefcase in one hand, his overnight bag in the other. It was late spring, and the rains had lifted, and now the Mile-High City was redolent with the perfume of a crystalline early morning. The sky was high and scudded with clouds, and the distant snowcapped peaks of Berthoud Pass, dappled with columbine, were visible on the western horizon of the terminal. But all this scenic splendor went completely unnoticed by Grove as he flagged down a Rocky Mountain airport cab.

He spent the two-hour cab ride north consulting his notes, saying very little to the chatty driver. He arrived at the crime scene a few minutes before ten, the morning sun slicing through the tops of the Englemann spruce that bordered the nature preserve like ancient sentries. A fleet of squads and unmarked bureau cars crowded the trail head. Clutches of men in sport coats and uniforms huddled here and there. Crime scene tape fluttered in the wind.

The dizziness started the moment Grove emerged from the cab. At first he figured it was the altitude. Or maybe his nerves, or his empty stomach. Or perhaps a combination of all three. He went around to the driver's-side window, paid the cabby, then carried his attaché and duffel bag across the dusty gravel lot. He was greeted near the tape by a sandy-haired man in a suit with a Colorado State Police ID tag dangling around his neck, twisting in the mountain breeze.

Grove identified himself.

"Made good time," the sandy-haired man commented, glancing at his watch, then offering a hand. "Lieutenant Jack Slater, CSP Homicide. Appreciate the fast response."

Grove felt light-headed as he shook the man's hand, then was introduced to the other primaries. The detectives gave Grove the typical once-over, their suspicious gazes masked by cursory nods and polite smiles. Normally Grove would shrug off such a cool reception. Local detectives, as a rule, mistrust government experts and high-paid consultants. But that morning, their baleful gazes made Grove's stomach clench and his head spin. He felt as if he were drunk.

They led him under the tape, then down a winding path through a grove of balsams. Sunlight filtered down through the canopy of branches and flickered in Grove's eyes. The pine-perfumed air was cooler in the woods, cleansed by the evening's rain. Gnats hummed in Grove's face. The ground felt spongy beneath his feet. His mind swam.

"First-on-the-scene was a state trooper," Slater's voice droned as Grove followed the group deeper into the forest. "He was checking on an abandoned garbage truck, found it idling a mile or so down an access road."

Figures appeared about a hundred yards ahead of them. Near a toppled iron trash can a couple of plain-clothes technicians were crouching on the edge of the trail, taking measurements, dusting for prints. Grove swallowed hard, the dizziness washing over him. He could barely stand. Nothing like this had ever happened to him. Sure, he had experienced dizzy spells before. But never at a crime scene. At crime scenes, Grove was usually a machine, focused with laser intensity. *It'll pass*, he thought, *it's just the thin air, it'll pass.*

The group approached the fallen barrel.

"The vic's just up ahead," Slater announced over his shoulder, pretending not to notice that Grove was lagging behind, coughing and weaving a little. "ME puts the initial time of death sometime between midnight and two o'clock in the morning. We're waiting for the initial—"

The light dimmed, and Grove staggered.

"Whoa! You okay, Professor?" Slater's voice sounded watery and distant all of a sudden.

Grove steadied himself against the trunk of an Englemann, the woods spinning around him as if he

were on a carnival ride. Through unfocused eyes he got
his first glimpse of the body ten yards away. It lay supine
in the leaves, a hefty man, posed like all the others, the
ham-hock arms frozen with encroaching rigor mortis
across the chest, one higher than the other. Blood trails,
blurred by the rain, fanned out from the corpse across
the moist floor of pine needles. Blood, as black as onyx,
pooled beneath the garbage man's head, apparently
the result of a sharp trauma wound. The same MO and
signature as all the others.

"Grove? You all right?"

The profiler tried to say something, but a veil was
lowering over his face. He staggered just before his balance went completely haywire and the ground came up
and slammed into the side of his head.

Then everything went black.

Black and silent.

The next twelve hours were an ordeal for Grove—
mostly because the doctors at Loveland General could
find no serious physical maladies. His heart was fine, his
circulatory system healthy, his brain scan normal. His
collapse, occurring in full view of a dozen hardened
lawmen, was the ultimate embarrassment for Grove.
According to the doctors, it was probably the result of
stress. Grove didn't buy it. Stress was a factor that he
lived with every day. And nothing like this had ever happened.

For most of the afternoon Grove sat on the edge of a
hospital bed in a private room, doing a crossword puzzle, waiting to be released. Every thirty minutes or so a
nurse returned to check Grove's vitals, which were con-
sistently normal, heart rate a steady sixty beats per
minute, blood pressure a tranquil one twenty over eighty.
Grove couldn't wait to get out of there. He wanted to put
the humiliation of passing out in front of a bunch of

coppers behind him, and he wanted to get back to work. But there was another reason he wanted out. His wife had died in a room just like this—the same gigantic contraption of a bed, the same faded drapes, the same rattling wall heater, the same bank of percolating monitors. Grove would never forget sleeping on that hard-backed armchair every night for over a month while his sweet Hannah was eaten alive by cancer.

Just before dinner, a voice crackled through the tiny loudspeaker mounted above the bed's headboard. "Mr. Grove, you've got a visitor—"

Up to that point Grove had been pacing in his ridiculous gown, the cool air on his bony black ass, but now he frowned and headed over to the door, wondering if it was Lieutenant Slater coming to pay his respects, or one of the boys from the state IAB checking in to make sure nobody on the force was liable for Grove's collapse. Grove peered around the frame of the open doorway and gazed down the corridor, seeing nothing but a bustling throng of white-clad nurses, doctors, and wheelchair-bound patients milling back and forth.

Suddenly a familiar gray-haired head appeared from around the corner of the nurse's desk, a man carrying his topcoat in his arms, a sheepish expression on his craggy face.

Grove's jaw dropped open. "Tom?" As Geisel approached, Grove felt his stomach seize up. "The hell are you doing all the way out here?"

"Can't a general visit a wounded soldier in the field?" Geisel grinned and gave Grove's shoulder a friendly tap, and all of it seemed a little forced.

"I'm fine . . . it was just . . . a fluky kind of thing . . . exhaustion, I guess."

"What do the doctors say?"

"They say I have the heart of a twelve-year-old."

"And don't tell me—you keep it in a jar on your desk

back at your office?" Geisel gave him a look, and the two men shared a nervous smile.

After an awkward moment Grove jerked a thumb at his room and said, "Come on in."

They shut the door behind them for privacy, and Geisel draped his topcoat over the back of the armchair, then sat down. Grove sat on the edge of the bed, feeling exceedingly self-conscious in his baby-blue robe with the little faded chevrons on it and his rear end sticking out the back. The two men shared some small talk for a few moments. Finally the silver-haired section chief rubbed his mouth thoughtfully and came to the point. "Ulysses, I'm going to need you to take some time off," he said.

"Tom, I know how this looks, but I promise you—"

"I don't care how it looks, I care about *you*," Geisel interrupted. "I need for you to have all your cylinders firing."

"I'm fine, Tom, I promise you, I'm fine."

"I understand that, kiddo. I do. I just think maybe you need to step back, take a breather. Maybe clear your head for a couple of weeks."

"A couple of weeks."

"Ulysses—"

"A couple of weeks and Sun City could be back in hibernation, you said so yourself."

Geisel gave him a hard look. "This is not up for discussion, kiddo."

Grove sighed.

Geisel reached inside his sport coat and dug something out of his inner pocket. "I knew you weren't exactly the type to go drown some worms somewhere," he said, unfolding a letter-sized document. "This thing came over the transom a couple of months ago, and I thought, 'Wait a minute . . . what a perfect way for Grove to get away from the case for a few days.' Here. Rather than me chattering on about it, why don't you just go ahead and read it?"

Geisel stood up and handed the document over to Grove, who glanced down at it. He had to read the entire document twice just to comprehend the context—

—never suspecting that buried within its lines was a revelation that would not only lead to the solution of the Sun City case but would change Grove's life forever.

2

Neolithic

Subj: **An interesting opportunity for a profile**
Date: 2/11/04 10:03:01 AM Pacific standard
      time
From: Mcounty@Discovermagazine.com
To: Tgeisel@BSU/FBI.com

Mr. Geisel—

My name is Maura County, and I'm a contributing
editor at *Discover* magazine. I realize that you're
a very busy man, and the last thing you would
want to do is humor a member of the much-ma-
ligned media (ha!) . . . but I thought I would take a
shot, albeit a long one. Allow me to explain.

As a staffer at *Discover*, and a regular contributor
to the archeology beat, I have been absorbed
lately with a recent scientific discovery in Alaska.
To make a long story short, last year, on April 13,
in Lake Clark National Park, a pair of hikers stumbled across human remains on the side of Mount
Cairn, about 500 feet from the summit. The body

was well preserved, as it had somehow fallen into a capsule of snow beneath a "driftless" glacier. For this reason it was deep frozen and protected from the elements.

Since that part of the state falls under the jurisdiction of the Bureau of Land Management, the body was placed into the custody of the local field office of the FBI. At first, it was thought that the body was the remains of a local climber who had been missing for a number of years, but then a quick-thinking investigator decided to call the University of Alaska in Anchorage and have somebody from the archaeology department come out and examine the body.

At that point, the authorities were beginning to think that they might have the mummified remains of a nineteenth-century climber, or maybe even somebody from an earlier time. But when Michael Okuda, an anthropologist from the U of A, finally got a look at it, excitement started spreading across the scientific community. Okuda could tell even from a cursory examination that the body was old. Very old. From the garb, from the tools found with the body, and even from the tattoos on its mummified flesh, Okuda guessed it was from the Middle Ages, maybe even earlier. But then the body was turned over to the university, and carbon dating was done. And the results were astonishing.

It turns out that the mummy—which has been dubbed "the Iceman" in the media—is nearly six thousand years old. An adult neolithic male! Dating back to the mid- to early-Copper Age! Needless to say, it is the oldest perfectly preserved human mummy ever discovered. Which brings me to the reason I am bothering you, Mr. Geisel.

The reason I'm writing is this: At first, it was thought that the Iceman had died of natural causes—perhaps had fallen or had become too exhausted at such a high altitude to survive. But recent MRIs of the body have revealed wounds in the mummy that could not possibly have been self-inflicted, and were not from an animal. That's right: the Iceman is a 6,000-year-old murder victim!

So here's what I'm asking: would you possibly be interested in having one of your FBI profilers look at the find, and possibly do a psychological profile of the Copper Age killer? It would make a fascinating article. I know our readers would love it. Of course, *Discover* would be delighted to pay all expenses. We could fly you or one of your people out to Alaska and do a major interview for the magazine.

Anyway . . . that's about it. I realize this is an unusual request, and I would certainly understand if you are too busy to fool with such a "dead" issue (ha!) . . . but if there's any interest on your part whatsoever, please don't hesitate to call or e-mail me at any time.

Best wishes—
Maura County, Contributing Editor
Class Mark Publishing
415-567-1259 (wk)
415-332-1856 (cell)

At first, Grove could not muster a response. Sitting on the edge of that hospital bed, he scanned the e-mail for a third time and wondered if it was some kind of a stunt. "You're serious about this," he finally said, holding the e-mail aloft between his thumb and index finger as though the paper were infested with germs. "You want me to go out there, play Indiana Jones."

"Think of it as a working vacation," Geisel offered with a wry smile.

"While Zorn works the Sun City case."

Geisel sighed. "That is so beneath you, kiddo."

"What is?"

"Paranoia, professional jealousy, whatever you want to call it."

Anger stirred in Grove's gut. "Jealousy has nothing to do with it, Tom. It's not about jealousy. It's about the case, it's about Sun City."

"Alaska is gorgeous this time of year," Geisel said. "Ever been there?"

"Mummies, Tom? Mummies now?"

Geisel shrugged. "I just figured it was the only way to get you to take a break."

"By having me go look at a mummy?"

"By having you work."

Grove pushed himself off the bed and tossed the e-mail onto the bedside table. It fluttered down and landed between a Styrofoam coffee cup and box of Kleenex, where a water ring instantly soaked through the center of it. Grove paced for a moment before pausing and looking up at his boss. "Feels like I'm being exiled to Siberia."

Geisel smiled. "Yeah, but the food's better in Alaska, and there's no language barrier."

Grove rubbed his face. "If I do this thing, if I go up there and do this nonsense . . . you have to do me a favor."

"Anything."

Grove paused, then trained his gaze on the older man. Geisel was more than a boss, he was a mentor, a friend. Ulysses Grove had never really had a true father.

When he was still in his mother's womb, his dad had vanished without a trace, leaving Grove's mother—a first-generation Kenyan who spoke very little English—to support her only son. Geisel was probably the closest thing to a father Grove had ever had. But perhaps most importantly, Hannah had always loved Geisel. The two couples had seen each other socially quite often, and the old man had always made Hannah laugh. When she died, Geisel had been one of the few bureau people who had shown up at the funeral.

Now Grove drew on this long history between them when he said, "I want you to promise me if the Sun City perp kills again, you'll put me back in the game."

After the briefest moment, Geisel nodded. "You got it, kiddo."

"Maura, you got a call on line one . . ."

Maura County sighed at the crackle of the amplified voice coming over the intercom of the *Discover* offices, interrupting her once again. She was in midsentence, vehemently defending her latest story pitch, when she felt herself balk at the distraction, like a pitcher on the mound staggering in the middle of a windup. She closed her eyes, slowly shaking her head. What was it this time? Another disgruntled advertiser? Another junior college demanding a dozen free subs for their science faculty?

"Better take that one," Chester Joyce urged from behind his massive Steelcase desk. The old editor in chief was hunched within the padded confines of his ergonomic swivel like a shriveled despot on a high-tech throne. His liver-spotted bald pate gleamed in the halogen office light. He breathed in halting, raspy wheezes between each sentence, almost like punctuation, his oxygen tank sitting on the floor next to him like a favored pet poodle, constantly hissing, constantly feeding air into his sickly lungs.

"In a second," Maura said, tossing her long blond tresses out of her slender face. She rubbed her small hands together quickly, as though warming them at a campfire, a habit she had when she was struggling or cornered or stressed out. "I need a definitive slot on this one, Chester, I need to hear it straight from the top—"

"Maura, the thing of it is, we're not—"

"It's a good story, Chester."

"I'm sure that it is."

"Then what's the problem?"

The old man rubbed his grizzled face. "The paleolithic diet, Maura?" He wheezed. "If you'll pardon the language, it just screams *Omni* to me. If I'm not mistaken, this is the twenty-first century."

Maura squelched the urge to scream. "All I'm asking for is a thousand words."

"A thousand words is a thousand words."

Outside the office, the amplified voice: "Maura . . . that call is still waiting on one . . . Maura County . . . you got a call parked on line one."

"Seven hundred fifty words," Maura pleaded, hunching forward eagerly in her chair. "Just a sidebar, that's all I'm asking."

After a long moment Chester Joyce said, "Let me think about it."

"All I'm asking is—"

He raised a palsied hand, cutting her off. "I said I'd think about it, now go answer your call."

Maura nodded tersely, then rose to her full five-foot-two-inch height. "To be continued," she said, then whirled and strode out of her editor in chief's office with fists clenched.

She marched down the hall toward her cubicle, wondering if she had just ruined her future at the magazine by mentioning Chester's promise to promote her to managing editor. She wasn't good at office politics. She wasn't a schmoozer. All she knew how to do was write and edit, and the only subject in which she had any expertise was science. But now she was beginning to wonder if her two master's degrees—one in physical anthropology, and one in geology—were quickly becoming useless appendages. Like a couple of vestigial tails.

Her cubicle sat at the end of the main corridor, a cluttered hive of books and dog-eared binders sandwiched between rows of fluorescent light-drenched layout tables. The ubiquitous drone of light rock music played endlessly in the *Discover* offices, and most of her fellow workers' bulletin boards were adorned with the banalities of personal backstories—snapshots of children, family pets, *New Yorker* cartoons, and jokey bumper stickers. Only Maura's cubbyhole reflected any sort of restless intellect. Photos of Stonehenge, Einstein, Egyptian mummies, and Stephen Hawking vied for wall space with obscure advertising placards from long-forgotten punk rock concerts and French lobby cards for old *theater du grande guignol* performances.

Maura settled into her chair and gazed down at the blinking light on her desk extension, girding herself for another tedious call from an advertiser. Dressed in a sleeveless sweater and faded, patched jeans, she was a small, sinewy woman in her late thirties with a mane of highlighted blond hair cut long across her face. One ear—the visible one—bore a row of sterling silver studs, and a tiny tattoo of a black rose adorned her neck. Her complexion was so pale the veins stood out on her slender arms like finely marbled china.

"Maura County," she said into the phone after punching the luminous button, expecting to hear the saccharine voice of some obnoxious media buyer.

Instead, a rich baritone filled her ears: "Ulysses Grove calling . . . from the FBI . . . Behavioral Science Unit."

Maura frowned. "Behavioral Science . . . um . . . this is in regard to . . . ?"

"The mummy? I assume this is the same Maura County who contacted the bureau a while back about a profiler?"

Maura sat up straight in her chair. "Oh . . . oh yes, um . . . thank you. Mr. Grove. Is it Mr. or . . . ?"

"Special Agent Grove is fine."

Maura stammered on the words: "S-special agent, um, okay, Special Agent Grove, um—"

"Ulysses is fine."

"Ulysses, great. Um . . . yeah."

"So . . ."

Maura sighed. "Ulysses, I promise you, I'm usually not this flaky. And call me Maura. I'm really sorry, it's been a crazy week."

"I've had plenty of those," the voice wanted her to know. Maura could almost see the weary smile on the other end of the line.

She felt a ripple of relief travel through her. She had never in her life dealt with a member of any law enforcement agency. Had never, thank God, been a victim of any crime. Had never even *talked* to a policeman. Hell, she didn't even like cop shows or mystery novels. And here she was, talking to Sherlock Frigging Holmes, and he sounded like a decent enough guy. "Anyway," Maura finally said, "as you can imagine, everybody in the field's buzzing about this Iceman discovery, especially because it looks like he was murdered. I mean, we're talking a perfectly intact Copper Age man here. *Discover*'s already done two full stories about it."

"I assume they've done DNA sequences on the mummy?"

"Yeah, well, see . . . that's where things get kind of complicated." Maura pushed herself away from her desk and stood. She began to move around her cubicle like a caged animal with the phone glued to her ear. "There's been a battle between the state of Alaska and the park service over who owns the thing. It's kind of a mess."

"Where is it now?"

"It's still at the University of Alaska. They've got a pretty impressive lab up there, and they're keeping him frozen. They thawed him out once to get samples."

"Bone and tissue, I assume?"

"Yeah, exactly." Maura nodded. "About a gram from his hip. Which was damaged when the hikers pried him out of the ice. The first analysis was sort of confusing."

"Let me guess," the voice said. "They got a lot of different sequences."

"Exactly, exactly. How did you know that?"

"We see that at crime scenes a lot. You try to do a mitochondrial test, but you end up getting a lot of different sequences because you're working with the surface. It's a lot like picking up a dozen different fingerprints at a scene because the victim's been handled so much."

"That's it, that's it," Maura said, still nodding. "That's why they did a second test, cutting away the outside tissue. When they assayed the core they got one clean sequence. And that got everybody excited."

After a long pause the voice said, "I suppose we should get together and take a look at the thing."

A spurt of cold adrenaline traveled through Maura's belly. She couldn't believe that this was actually going to happen. Screw the "Paleolithic Diet"—Maura County was going to win the damn Pulitzer Prize after all! But in the midst of all the sudden excitement was a momentary hiccup of doubt in the back of her brain. Something about the profiler's voice bothered her. This guy Grove didn't sound right. He was saying all the right words, but the *tone* of his voice sounded wrong. It sounded reluctant, maybe even a little sad. And for a brief instant

Maura wondered if she was about to involve the wrong man in this amazing, all-important, once-in-a-career project. But almost as quickly as the notion had crossed her mind, she brushed it off and said, "Great, fantastic . . . then I guess the next step is setting up a meeting in Alaska."

The voice said that sounded good.

The following Monday, which was the fifth of May—a mild time of year for Alaska—Maura County found herself waiting in the outer lobby of the Heinrich Schleimann Building, which housed the university's archaeology laboratory, on the northwest corner of the campus. It was a clear day, and the mountain sun was a sledgehammer, pounding down through the skylights and battering the carpeted floor with yellow fire. It was nearly three o'-clock, and the profiler was late, and Maura was starting to wonder whether he was going to show up at all. She kept thinking back to the sound of the man's voice over the phone that previous week: that weird reluctance beneath his words. Maybe this was all a big mistake.

Snubbing out her third cigarette in a canister near the glass doors, Maura continued to pace and worry. Her compact body was adorned that day in a very uncharacteristic corporate pantsuit—the pin-striped slacks creased so sharply they looked dangerous. Even her hair was sedate—pulled back, swept up, and pinned against her skull. She felt ridiculous in the conservative attire, but she was representing the magazine that day, and she wanted to make a good impression on Ulysses Grove. She didn't know what kind of man to expect.

From the sound of his phone voice, she had gotten the impression that he was middle-aged, white, probably midwestern. He had a friendly manner, if somewhat guarded, and his voice radiated confidence. But what about that name, *Ulysses*? It sounded blue bloody, pompous, and southern, and yet the voice had been void of any accent. Maybe Grove was one of those slick, Clintonian, corporate types from the "New" South. Maura knew the type all too well. She had encountered more than her fair share of arrogant bureaucrats in the world of academia. But this was her show now. This was her idea, and her article, and her magazine, and she would not let some cocky, middle-aged, white asshole from the FBI push her around.

She was finishing up her fourth cigarette, lost in her thoughts, when the tall figure entered the lobby through the revolving glass door.

Maura whirled. "Special Agent Grove?"

"Miss County?" the man said with a perfunctory smile, and came over to her with his hand extended.

"Maura, please, call me Maura," she said, and shook his slender, concert-master's hand.

For an infinitesimal moment, Maura had to consciously blink away the urge to gawk at him. It wasn't the fact that he was black (although that was part of it). Nor was it because he was so dapper and well put together in his Burberry coat and tailored suit, his attaché gripped at his side like an appendage. What made her stare for that brief instant was the lack of guile on the man's face. This guy was the antithesis of a smug bureaucrat. He looked like a visitor from another time, a nineteenth-century abolitionist or poet, his dark eyes radiating passion.

"Maura it is," he said, his face warming. "If you'll call me Ulysses."

"You got it," she said. "And I really appreciate you coming all the way up here."

"I just hope I can offer something."

"I'm sure it'll be fascinating. How was the trip up?"

"Had a little problem with connections, had to take a puddle jumper from Anchorage that felt like it was powered by rubber bands."

Maura grinned. "Welcome to Alaska."

"Quite a facility they got here."

She nodded and indicated the inner doors on the opposite side of the lobby. "Why don't I give you a little tour? I believe the project leader's waiting for us back in the lab."

Grove nodded. "Lead the way."

They crossed the high-gloss tile floor and vanished through the double glass doors.

The University of Alaska's Paleo-DNA Laboratory is the largest of its kind in North America. Housed in the lower levels of the Schleimann Building, temperature and humidity controlled, the facility rivals the Pentagon for length and breadth of security. Its endless labyrinth of fluorescent corridors and access tunnels spread across nearly a hundred acres. Any significant archaeological find in the Western Hemisphere eventually finds its way here to be dated, sampled, sequenced, analyzed, catalogued, studied, or exhibited. The university has priority over the lab's teaching facilities, but the facility's main purpose is research. Which is why the lab is infused with millions of dollars annually from corporate endowments. Every multinational from Exxon to Union Carbide has money in this place, and controversies regularly rage on campus among environmental groups fed up with the corporate hijacking of the scientific community. But the lab continues to run smoothly, partly because of the constant influx of dollars, and partly because of the iron-fisted management style of the senior analyst and laboratory director, Dr. Lorraine G. Mathis.

In fact, only moments after Ulysses Grove was introduced to the prim, fiftyish woman in the white lab coat, he could tell that she was a bundle of paranoia and passive aggression.

"We're going to be taking a left at the end of this corridor," she was saying, leading the group along a narrow, carpeted hallway of glass display cases filled with skeletons of various exotic mammals, birds, reptiles, and amphibians. "Which will bring us to the wet room, where the initial cleaning and sorting of archaeological remains goes on."

There were three other people in the group, hurrying to keep up with the bombastic Dr. Mathis as she marched along the corridor with the rigor of an SS officer: Grove, Maura County, and a young researcher named Michael Okuda. Thin as a razor in his lab coat, with delicate Asian features, Okuda was the first scientist to see the mummy on the side of Mount Cairn nearly a year ago. He had been summoned by one of the initial investigators, and had made the hundred-and-fifty-mile trip out to Lake Clark expecting to find nothing more than a frozen hiker from some time around the Carter administration. But the moment he saw that brittle, leathery corpse lying on a parkway near a ranger shack, he knew he had stumbled upon something epochal. He knew it from the desiccated animal skins still clinging to the mummy's spindly arms, and from the grass-stuffed hides around the perfectly intact feet, and from the primitive axe blade lying near the body.

Dr. Mathis paused in front of a secure door, fished in her pocket, and pulled out a magnetic card. "The problem with all this media monkey business," she muttered as she angrily snapped the card through the electronic lock, "is the condition of the mummy. The remains need to be stored at a constant twenty degrees Fahrenheit with ninety-eight percent humidity in order to maintain preservation. Every time he's thawed out for examination or sample extraction—or this kind of nonsense—the tissues dry and the cells break down further."

Standing behind the scientist, waiting to follow her into the lab, Grove noticed a number of things rippling through the group. The young underling, Okuda, glanced away for a moment as though embarrassed by his supervisor's gall. The journalist from _Discover,_ a nice enough woman in Grove's estimation, gazed down at the floor and let out an almost imperceptible sigh of exasperation. Grove assumed that the crack about "media monkey business" was aimed directly at her. Grove detested rudeness of any kind, and already felt a vague dislike for this pious administrator. But worse than that, the dizziness was returning. Grove's gorge was rising, and he felt as though the walls of the man-made subterranean cavern were closing in on him. He needed to get out of there as soon as possible.

The door hissed open, and Mathis led the group into a narrow room that reeked of disinfectant and something else, something subtle just beneath the surface, something like the sweet stench of rotting meat. The air droned with voices, beeping, and whirring centrifuges.

"We're the only facility in North America equipped to house such a find," Mathis blathered on as she strode through the crowded dry lab. Half a dozen researchers in white coats shuffled about electron microscopes, banks of computers, and tables laden with rock samples. None of them even looked up as the group passed, as though Dr. Mathis might snap a ruler across their knuckles if they showed such insolence. "We're set up for both radiocarbon and luminescent dating, isotope analysis, and fluorescence spectrometry," she went on. "We can also do nondestructive gamma analysis, which we've already done on the specimen's teeth and bone tissue, as well as DNA analysis."

Finally they reached a thick, metal door with a narrow pane of safety glass down the left side. A placard above the lintel read CAUTION—WET SPECIMEN CONTAINMENT—AUTHORIZED PERSONNEL ONLY.

Grove glanced through the screened glass but couldn't see much more than a narrow examination room, and maybe a part of a table or gurney in the center, radiant with halogen light. He glanced over at Maura County, who had taken a step back and now stood behind Okuda with a sheepish look on her face. She gave Grove a nervous yet encouraging smile. Grove smiled back. He liked this woman. There was a frantic sort of honesty about her that was refreshing.

Mathis reached over to a metal lockbox mounted next to the door, spun a few tumblers, and opened the lid. From inside the container she pulled out a couple of sealed packages. In one package was a sterile mask. In another was a pair of rubber surgical gloves. She handed the packages to Grove and nodded at them. "You have four minutes, Mr. Grove," she announced without ceremony or emotion.

The door wheezed open.

Ulysses Grove took a deep breath, set down his attaché, put on the mask and gloves, then went inside the suite.

He didn't need four minutes. He didn't even need four seconds. All he needed was one good look at that six-thousand-year-old corpse and everything changed. Everything rearranged itself inside Grove like tumblers in his brain clicking into some horrible new combination, altering his world forever, causing an icy rush of gooseflesh along his spine. He didn't make a sound, didn't move. All he did for several agonizing moments was stand there gazing down at that narrow stainless steel examination table in the center of that sterile room.

The Iceman lay there in a pool of silver light, a runner of gauze beneath him and the metal table. Even to an uneducated eye it was obvious that this was an ancient cadaver, the skeletal arms and legs sheathed in flesh the color of burnt tobacco, so old it looked vacuformed around the bones and tendons. The body was so well preserved its eyeballs were still intact—two over-done quail eggs gazing up emptily at the miracle-light of a future millennium. In life the mummy had been diminutive by modern standards—perhaps no more than five feet tall—with the prominent jaw of early Homo sapiens.

But in death, it had taken on an eerie tableau of a toy posed by a disturbed child.

Dizziness jumped on Grove again, and he reached for something to hold on to. There was nothing to grab—only the examination table—so he staggered slightly. Then he stood there, blinking away the bewilderment.

One time when he was only eight years old, a group of class bullies lured him into the school gymnasium at night, locking him in, and then proceeding to torment him with ghostly projections shone through skylights with a jury-rigged slide projector. It had taken the young Ulysses over an hour to overcome his terror and analyze the situation, eventually figuring out the source of the "ghosts." But during that hour, the utterly debilitating *confusion* had almost been worse than the fear. He hated *not understanding* something. And on that terrible night, especially during that first hour, he just kept on thinking, *There's an explanation, a logical explanation for this.*

He finally tore himself away from the mummy and turned toward the door.

The latch clicked, and he stumbled into the outer room, nearly tripping into Lorraine Mathis's arms. The scientist jerked away with a mortified look on her face. Maura County stepped forward with concern knitting her expression. "Ulysses, you look like you saw a ghost. What's wrong?"

Grove took another deep breath. He had to cope with another jolt of dizziness before he could speak. "The MRI . . . the one that told you it was a wrongful death."

Mathis frowned at him. "*What?* What are you talking about?"

"The MRI you did on the mummy."

"It was an X-ray actually," Okuda chimed in. "We're publishing a piece on it next month in *Scientific American*."

Grove looked at the young Asian. "Did it show a sharp trauma wound to the first cervical vertebra?"

Okuda stared at him for a moment, then shot a glance at Mathis, who was staring at the profiler. The silence stretched.

3

Puzzle Box

"It could have been anything—warfare, murder, a dispute over land," Lorraine Mathis commented as she scuttled back and forth across her cluttered office. She already had her coat on, and was banging drawers and turning things off and generally making "leaving" noises. She had apparently run out of patience for Grove and his sudden, mysterious interest in the Iceman's demise. "The anthropology part is all speculation, anyway," she added with a dismissive wave of her hand. "And besides, I thought that was *your* bailiwick, Agent Grove."

Grove sat across the room, near the door, his attaché on his lap, his hands folded on top of the briefcase. He hadn't revealed much about his stunning discovery in the wet containment room, but he could tell that all those present could sense his nervous excitement. "I'm just wondering what the pathology has been so far," he said with monumental deference in his voice, trying to tease as much information as possible from the harridan of a director. "After all, I'm used to getting to crime scenes a little sooner than this."

Mathis showed no amusement in her heavily mascaraed eyes as she buttoned her coat. "I'll have Michael make copies of the X-rays and the initial reports."

Grove told her that would be great.

She looked at him. "Is that it?"

Grove offered her a smile. "I'm wondering if there's anything else you can tell me about the victim. The Iceman himself."

"In regard to what?"

Grove shrugged. "I don't know . . . in regard to background, I guess . . . cultural stuff."

The woman sighed as she slipped on a pair of elegant calfskin gloves. She looked like an impatient mother waiting for her children to clean their room.

Maura County was perched next to Grove on a file cabinet, scribbling feverishly in her notebook. Okuda stood in the far corner, wringing his delicate little hands, taking everything in, looking a little shaky. The office was situated in the depths of the lower level, a four-hundred-square-foot swamp of paper and loose-leaf binders crammed into every available inch of shelf space. The stale air smelled of toner and ink and Mathis's acrid perfume, and the glare of the overhead fluorescents only added to the stolid, institutional quality of the place.

"I'm sorry, Agent Grove," Mathis finally offered, "but I'm just not in tour-guide mode at present. You understand. I've got a funding committee breathing down my neck, and hearings coming up in June with the BLM and the Association of Indigenous Peoples over who owns the remains. I'm sure you see how my thoughts would be elsewhere."

Grove managed another placating smile. "I understand completely."

She went over to the door and paused, tying a scarf around her gray-streaked hair. "I hope your visit has given you everything you need. I'm afraid that's probably the only time you'll be able to see the artifact up close. There's been far too many examinations, too many temperature fluctuations. My priority has always been with the find." She flicked a terse smile at the room. "Michael will show you out. It was a pleasure meeting you, Agent Grove."

"Same here," Grove told her.

The director swished through the door, leaving a slipstream of tension flagging after her like a contrail. The door whispered shut, and the room remained silent for a moment as the latch clicked.

Michael Okuda put his hands in his pockets and looked down at the floor.

"I feel like I've offended her somehow," Grove said to no one in particular.

Okuda shook his head. "Not at all. Look. She's really not normally this . . . brusk."

Grove waved it off. "It's okay."

"She's actually quite brilliant."

"I'm sure she is."

"Certainly she can be difficult," Okuda tried to explain. "And yes, she's mistrustful of outsiders. But her work's impeccable. Believe me."

Grove nodded. "I don't doubt it."

"She's just wary of outsiders coming in right now, with all the arbitration going on."

"Where does that stand?"

"I'd put my money on the Native Americans," Okuda mused as he crossed the room. He sat down on the edge of Mathis's desk with a depleted sigh. His hands were shaking. "They've got the state constitution on their side. We're trying to learn as much as possible while Keanu's still here."

"Who?"

Okuda smiled. "It's a bad joke, really. Couple of guys up in Carbon Dating—big *Matrix* fans—started calling him 'Neo' because of the neolithic aspect."

Grove was nonplussed, and Maura must have seen the look on his face because she stopped scribbling and said, "Neo was Keanu Reeves's character in *The Matrix* movies."

Okuda's grin lingered. "Yeah, and there was this joke going around the lab that the Iceman was just slightly more animated than Keanu Reeves. I guess the name just stuck. It's pretty sophomoric."

Grove asked if pictures of the scene were taken.

Okuda looked confused. "The scene?"

"The crime scene, the place where the Iceman died."

Okuda thought about it for a moment and said he wasn't sure but he might have seen some aerial photographs of that part of the glacier.

"But there were no photographs taken before the body was moved?"

"I think that's correct. There are sketches though."

"Sketches?"

"Yeah, the investigator from the State Police Homicide Unit, a guy named Pinsky—Lieutenant Alan Pinsky, I think his name was—he had the hikers draw sketches of the way the body was positioned when they found it."

There was a pause.

Maura looked at Grove. "What happened in there, Ulysses?"

"It's kind of a long story," he said and rubbed his eyes. His head throbbed. A dagger of a migraine shot through his temples.

"Do you mind if I ask how you knew about the sharp trauma wound? I don't think I ever mentioned that in the e-mail, and they discovered it after the articles came out . . . so you'd have no way of knowing about that."

Grove looked at her and wondered how far he should take this, how much he should reveal. He felt exposed, out of control. These were new emotions for Grove. He was supposed to be merely killing time here in this remote world of rutted roads and weathered boardwalks . . . but now everything had changed. Fate had slithered into Grove's world.

The sound of a secretary pecking away at a keypad in an adjacent office drifted through the seams of the door. At last Grove looked at Okuda. "Is there somewhere we can go, maybe a place we can talk?"

Night rolled in and flooded the hills and ice-crusted streets with indigo shadows.

The parking lot of the Marriott Courtyard—barely visible through the front drapes of Maura County's room—flickered in the cold, desolate light of sodium vapor lamps, which were winking on at odd intervals.

She turned away from the window and went back into the small bathroom vestibule where her overnight things were spread across the counter. For some reason she had brought along her makeup kit in its little imitation leopard travel pouch. The kit contained a couple of different lipsticks, an eyeliner stick, a box of Q-tips, and a disc of blush-on that she hadn't used in years. She looked at her pale face in the mirror. She felt ridiculous, trying to make herself pretty for her upcoming dinner with the profiler. She was a journalist, for Christ's sake, and Grove was her subject. Plus, the man was married. Maura had noticed his wedding ring only minutes after meeting him.

So why was she standing there, primping at the mirror like a high school girl on prom night? Whom was she trying to impress? A decade of failed relationships had reduced Maura to this—a desperate, needy woman looking for approbation in a world of fast-food relationships. In recent months she had even resorted to an Internet dating service with disastrous results. The last matchup was a creep from San Rafael rebounding from his second divorce. This loser had treated Maura to a live sex show at the O'Farrel, then a trip out to the Sybaris for a little light bondage and discipline. It was enough to turn a girl's heart into burnt toast.

She pulled her hair back in a tight ponytail and applied generous amounts of liner to each eye, trying to occupy her thoughts with the Iceman article. Grove's strange reaction to the viewing of the mummy—as well as his mysterious behavior afterward—had not only mystified Maura, it also excited her, intrigued her. Occasionally an assignment will crack open like a Chinese puzzle box, and Maura had a feeling this one was about to do just that. She wasn't sure *how* exactly, and Grove's reluctance to explain until they met at dinner that night was a bit maddening, but Maura's instincts told her that something important was unfolding.

Her gaze drifted over to the photocopy taped to the edge of the mirror.

When she had arrived at the motel earlier that day, she had spent some time organizing her notes and cassette tapes. She had brought along some Xeroxes of the mummy taken from her previous articles, and had taped a couple of the pictures around her room for inspiration. Now she gazed at that ancient face, and those parboiled, egg-white eyes gawking up at the black void of eons. There was something deeply disturbing about the expression preserved on that mummy's leathery visage. At first it had looked like terror to Maura, or at least a kind of shock, contorting the Iceman's features. But the longer Maura studied it, the more it looked like a sort of *knowing* stamped onto his face. But what did he know? What awful knowledge—

Maura jumped at the sound of knocking.

It took her a moment to steady herself before she made her way across the room.

"You ready?" Ulysses Grove asked her after she had opened the door and greeted the profiler with a wan smile. Grove's topcoat was buttoned to the neck, his collar raised against the evening chill.

"Let me grab my coat and my tape recorder," she

said, and started toward the bed, where her notes were fanned out across the cheap taffeta spread.

"Um . . . about the tape recorder," Grove said from the doorway.

Maura spun around. "Excuse me?"

"I'm going to have to ask you to leave it in the room."

She looked at him. "So this is off the record now?"

"Something like that."

She licked her lips. "Okay, but promise me something: whatever it is, whatever you saw in that lab today, you'll give me an exclusive on it . . . when you're ready."

After a beat, Grove smiled and said, "Let's go spend some of your magazine's money."

They walked across the street to a place called the Black Bear Lounge.

The broken neon Schaffer beer sign over the massive, worm-eaten oak door should have been a clue to Maura as to what they would find inside. It was one of those dark, moldy taverns that masqueraded as a restaurant—the kind you find in every American college town—with the butcher-block booths, Tiffany lamps, and peanut shells on the floor. A few antler chandeliers and crisscrossed snowshoes added local color. But mostly it was a place for coeds to come and pound some beers.

Okuda was waiting for them at the hostess stand. Grove asked the hostess if they could have a table in the rear. The peroxide-blond matron led the threesome through the malty shadows as the Rolling Stones pondered with thunderous volume why brown sugar tasted so good.

They settled into a booth in the far corner and ordered a round.

After the drinks arrived—a draft for Okuda, a glass of pinot grigio for Maura, a single malt scotch, neat, for Grove—Maura asked Grove if he was going to tell them what was going on, or if he was going to keep them in suspense forever, and Grove replied, after taking a sip of his Glenlivet, that the information he was about to give them was not for public consumption. He looked directly at Maura as he explained that it was highly irregular for bureau personnel to reveal the facts of an active investigation, and Maura felt a twinge of defensiveness. Not only was she a consummate professional when it came to discretion, but the chances of somebody in law enforcement actually *noticing* one of Maura's articles in *Discover* seemed fairly remote.

After a long pause Grove finally told them about a series of murders he had been investigating. Unlike most serial killers—who reflect some type of identifiable psychosexual need or fetish in their crimes—this guy, even after seven murders, was still a complete mystery, and one of the toughest cases Grove had ever encountered. Grove described the manner in which the killer apparently hunted his random victims, then dispatched them with some sort of sharp weapon, a spear or a sword. Then, in a low, almost pedantic drone, like a teacher informing students of their failing grades, Grove elaborated on the postmortem staging and posing.

"Good God," Maura uttered without really being aware of her own voice in her ears.

"It's a coincidence," Okuda blurted, his dark eyes shimmering and fixed on Grove.

Grove shrugged. "I'll show you the forensic photos from the last scene, and you tell me whether that raised arm, that supine position, and that wound in the neck—all of it—you tell me whether it's all just a coincidence."

"It's not possible, is it?" Maura asked.

Another shrug from Grove.

"What are we talking about here?" Okuda wanted to know.

Grove looked at him. "What do you mean?"

"Well . . . you're telling us you're investigating a series of homicides that have a similar—what do you call it?"

"Signature, pattern."

"Signature, right . . . which means, what, the victims ended up looking a lot like Keanu?"

Grove corrected the young Asian. "Not 'a lot.' They're identical."

A cold finger touched Maura's spine all of a sudden—the way the profiler said the word *identical,* with that cutting gaze, and those almond eyes set deep in that sculpted brown face. For years, Maura County had found refuge, and perhaps even solitude, in the protective coating of history. Pain and savagery were an abstraction. But now, all at once, this assignment had become more than mere petrified bones and frozen flesh. In the space of an instant, the subject had turned to the here and now, and real grief, and warm blood and electric shock. And the change rattled the journalist.

She glanced over at Okuda and saw the incredulous look in the young scientist's eyes. "I still don't understand how you can rule out coincidence," he said after swallowing a gulp of lager and stifling a belch.

"Technically you're right," Grove replied with another shrug, "but the truth is, in this business you follow everything out to its logical conclusion."

"But where's the logic here?"

Grove regarded the watermarks on the stained tabletop. "All we have right now is a connection, a visual connection, and that's all."

"Okay . . . so?"

"We might be dealing with some sort of ritual, some sort of cult thing that gets its inspiration from ancient man."

Okuda looked away for a moment, thinking, and Maura saw something glint in the young Asian's eyes. Grove saw it, too, but didn't comment. Okuda's hands were trembling again. Grove wondered how a young man with such pronounced tremors could do delicate slide work at a microscope or finesse a brittle, priceless artifact—regardless of whether the shaking was a simple nervous tic or some kind of reaction to the current turn the conversation was taking.

"On the other hand," Grove said, "you've got to look at the possibility of a copycat situation."

Maura perked up. "But how would anybody—"

"Pictures have been published, correct? Photographs, maps, diagrams. Shots of the mummy's position, the pose."

Maura thought about it for a moment. "What are you saying? Some sicko saw the Iceman in *Discover* and decided to recreate the death over and over again?"

"It's a possibility we have to look at."

Okuda looked up at Grove. "What else?"

Grove let out a sigh. "What else? Well, there's the X-factor."

"Which means?"

"The X-factor is a connection we haven't figured out yet."

"What other possible connection could there be?"

"I don't know yet."

"We're talking about the early Copper Age here," Okuda reminded him.

"I understand that—"

"That's six thousand years ago. Okay? They were just figuring out how to use the wheel."

"If you don't mind, what I'd like you to do is tell me everything."

Okuda looked at him. "What do you mean?"

"Tell me about that time, and this guy, this Iceman, who he was, tell me everything."

Okuda slumped as though he had just been asked to swim the English Channel with an anchor around his neck. "It's kind of a big subject, Ulysses."

Grove flashed his smile. "We're not going anywhere."

* * *

They went through that first round of drinks pretty rapidly as Okuda described what the world was like six thousand years ago. The bar began to fill up with rowdy college kids, as well as grizzled townies looking to drown some sorrows on a lonely weeknight. The jukebox seemed to get louder and louder with each banal pop song, and Okuda had to strain his voice to be heard. He explained that the consensus among archaeologists was that the Iceman was European, or at least a native of Central Asia, who had reached the North American continent across the Bering Strait. From the tools found near his body, chances were good that he was a mountaineer. Maybe some sort of itinerant.

At some point, the waitress returned to ask if they wanted to order food. Nobody was hungry, but they did order another round of drinks. After the waitress had trundled off, Okuda said, "He might have been a shaman, somebody who went from village to village, healing people . . . you know."

Grove looked at him. "A medicine man, is what you're saying?"

Okuda nodded. "That's why the Copper Age is such a fascinating period—anthropologically speaking—because basically, before then, there was no such thing as a métier or specialty."

"How do you mean?"

"People basically did everything for themselves before the Copper Age. They farmed, they took care of their kids, they built their own shelters, they hunted, they basically did everything. But right around four thousand BC, people started developing specialties."

"You're talking about occupations?"

"Exactly. One guy would come and build stuff for you, another guy was good at making tools, another guy could repair things. This changed everything."

Grove was pondering, swirling the ice cubes in his glass of scotch. "A traveling medicine man."

"It's all speculation, of course," Okuda went on, "but we can tell a lot from the artifacts that were found on him and around him. He was so well preserved in that snow capsule, we recovered a lot of stuff that just blew the lid off conventional thinking. Like the axe blade."

"What about it?"

Okuda's eyes practically twinkled. "Up until now we thought axe blades from that era were all primitive and flat, pounded on rocks. But Keanu's is *flanged*, with ridges, very advanced. It's like digging up the tomb of a medieval warrior and finding a twelve-gauge shotgun."

"Do you know anything about his language, his culture, his religious beliefs?"

"Again it's all guesswork, but chances are he spoke a language called Indo-European. Basically most European languages come from this parent language. In terms of religion, polytheistic is my guess, especially when you consider the tattoos."

"Tell me about the tattoos."

"They're not like today's tattoos, which are pretty much simple ornamentation—'mom' and 'born to lose' and whatever. Keanu's tattoos were located in hidden places like his lower back and on the inner part of his ankle. Which suggests—to me, at least—that they're designed to give him some sort of supernatural power or protection."

The waitress returned with the drinks. Maura watched Grove. The profiler was thinking, gazing off into the fragrant shadows, as the waitress awkwardly cleared the empties and replaced them with fresh drinks. The silence hung over the table like a pall, and for a long time after that, and throughout most of the remaining conversation, Maura found herself wondering what was going on inside Grove's head.

What dark vein had they tapped?

* * *

*The wind sluices down the dark corridor of skeletal trees. It
whistles past the shaman like a banshee howling in his ears.
He takes one step at a time, his grass-netted boots sinking into
the snow up to his knee. His feet are numb, and he can barely
see his hand in front of his face as he climbs the crevasse. He's
almost there. Almost at the plateau.*

He pauses to catch his breath.

*Gazing back over his shoulder, he sees the valley of larch
trees spreading off into the distance like a great animal skin
draped over the land. The sun lies on the horizon in streaks of
magenta and gold. The temperature is dropping. It will be dark
soon, and the darkness brings with it new dangers. He must
hurry now.*

*He hears the scream again. It starts out low, as always,
coming from a great distance, then rising in one great ululat-
ing howl that pierces the wind and echoes down across the valley. It is a primal death wail—half animal, half human—that
penetrates the shaman's marrow and shoots through his soul
like a sudden ZZZZZAP!*

"What!"

Grove's eyes jerked open in the dark room, his face
pressed against the pillow, the linens bunched at his
feet.

Pale moonlight seeped into his motel room from
somewhere off to his right. He shivered. The night-sweat
dampening his sheets had chilled in an icy, inexplicable
draft. He could still hear that keening sound from his
dream, the horrible shrieking, and the beating of his
own heart.

He lay there for an awkward moment, waiting for
blessed reality to drive the nightmare away. But something nagged at the back of his brain. He blinked. He
stared at the darkness around him. Particles floated in
the gloom. At first they appeared merely as spots drift-

ing across his sleepy, compromised vision. *Artifacts.* Like specks on the backs of his dilated pupils. But the more he gazed at the darkness, the more he realized he was witnessing something far more corporeal than an optical illusion.

Snow.

It was snowing in his motel room. Grove swallowed dryly and clutched at the bedsheets. He glanced around the room and realized the walls had vanished. His heart quickened as he quickly registered several indisputable facts: somehow, in some spontaneous shifting of realities, his tousled bed now sat in a snowdrift on the side of a great primordial mountain, a sheer granite cliff rising up into the night sky behind his pathetic little veneer headboard.

Grove sucked in a startled breath—the air icy in his lungs.

A neolithic moon shone down on the alpine wilderness around him like a sinister, luminous face; and a gelid, angry wind swirled around Grove's ludicrous, incongruous bed. His breath halted. The strangest part— the part that would be most difficult to explain to the uninitiated—was that Grove had experienced moments like this throughout his life, especially during times of great stress. Like the time when he was twelve and he saw a premonition of his best friend's death by a hit-and-run drunk driver . . . or that time in basic training when he awoke one night to find himself chained to the lower deck of an eighteenth-century slave ship. Over the years, Grove had learned how to suppress the visions with little physical tricks, like a person with Tourette's syndrome learning to bite his tongue or breathe more steadily.

Without thinking, Grove suddenly did the one thing that he had always done as a child when such visions plagued him at night: he closed his eyes.

In the blind darkness Grove felt—or perhaps *sensed* is

a better word—a sudden, atmospheric *whoomp*, followed by a great inhalation of breath as the air pressure in the room seemed to return to normal. When he opened his eyes, he was back in his cheap Marriott single smoker, dimly illuminated by the predawn light coming through the dusty venetian blinds.

Grove glanced around the room at the particleboard desk to his left, his suit neatly draped over the back of an armchair, the twenty-four-inch Sony mounted on a swivel to his right. He drank in all the insipid details like a seasick mariner gaping at the horizon line, clinging to the promise of dry land. He could see the tiny red night-light in the bathroom, and he could see his cell phone sitting in its charger near a tented pay-TV movie schedule. For some reason the sight of that little green dot glowing on his phone charger brought him back to reality. He let out a long, pained breath.

He sat up. Clad only in his underwear, he noticed his entire body was rashed with gooseflesh. His teeth ached. His head throbbed, and needles of sleep still numbed his bare feet. He glanced over and saw the digital clock radio on the far bedside table.

It said 3:11 a.m.

He let out another long sigh. It had only been a couple of hours since he had stumbled back to his motel room from the Black Bear Lounge. But he felt as though he had been on a long, arduous journey since then. *Now is not the time,* he silently scolded himself. *Put it away, forget about it. You got bigger fish to fry. You got a mummy with the same signature as an open case. Just stick with reality and do your job and forget the damn visions.*

But "vision" was a woefully insufficient word for what he had just experienced—something he had been experiencing off and on since elementary school. "Dimensional shift" was closer, although the sound of *that* phrase still rang a tad "woo-woo" for Grove's forensic mind. Perhaps "neurological episode" came the closest. Not that these crazy spells had ever been given a diagnosis. These visions would always remain the province of Grove's secret world.

He got up and got dressed. It was time to call Tom Geisel and tell him about the Iceman. But before Grove had a chance to punch Geisel's number into the bedside phone, he realized it was still a tad early for a phone call to Virginia.

Another placard tented on top of the TV promised guests a delicious continental breakfast in the lobby every morning from four o'clock until ten o'clock.

Grove went down to the deserted lobby and found a meager buffet set up along one side of the room that included miniature cereal boxes, a large plastic bowl filled with ice and small sealed containers of milk and orange juice, and a big stainless steel tureen of Seattle's Best coffee. Grove filled a Styrofoam cup with coffee and sat alone at a round table, reading the morning edition of *USA Today* while CNN droned through a wall-mounted television.

At nine o'clock Grove went back up to his room and placed a call to Geisel's private residence in Fredericksburg.

"So how's the mummy business going?" Geisel wanted to know after the two men had exchanged good mornings.

"The mummy business is good, actually," Grove told him. "Better than I thought."

"Excellent."

A long pause.

"Tom . . . are you sitting down?"

PART II
THE DOORWAY

*"There are more things in heaven and earth, Horatio /
That are dreamt of in your philosophy."*
—Shakespeare, *Hamlet*

4

Dark Side of the Moon

The innocuous high-rise stood on a peaceful street corner in the sleepy bedroom community of Reston, Virginia. Insiders called it the Annex, a massive conical pile of mirrored glass and iron gridwork rising up against the robin's-egg-blue sky. Soccer moms in SUVs and kids on skateboards clattered by its unmarked facades, oblivious of the grim proceedings going on inside, the gruesome slide shows and morbid death talk.

The bureau had moved its administrative overflow here in 2002, amid the paranoid post 9-11 funding boom, and nowadays the corridors buzzed with ceaseless activity. The Behavioral Science Unit had an operations office here, a six-agent group headed up by Terry Zorn.

"That's a helluva theory," Zorn was marveling in his corner office, leaning back on his swivel chair behind his cluttered desk, a wireless headset connecting him with Tom Geisel over at headquarters. Fluorescent tubes shone down on Zorn's meticulously shaved cranium.

"And that's all it is, Terry," Geisel's voice buzzed in the earpiece. "Matter of fact, I'm not even sure there's a theory involved. At this point it's essentially just an observation, an interesting wrinkle."

"I remember when they discovered that damn thing, I recall reading an article about it—where was it, maybe in *National Geographic?*"

"Anyway . . . that's the situation up there."

"What does he want, Tom?"

"He wants to work the case. He wants to play this mummy thing out."

"All right."

"It's my fault, actually. I sent him up there. Who knew, right? He's a good man, Terry."

"Damn *straight* he's a good man, he's a goddamn prodigy. If he said there's a connection between the Sun City perp and the Easter bunny, I'd believe him."

On the other end of the line Geisel let out a sigh. It was an exasperated sound, the kind of noise a coach makes when a game becomes hopeless, and Zorn secretly delighted in the sound. At the age of forty, one of the youngest profilers in the division, Zorn was a mover, a bundle of ambition, from the top of his stylish bald head down to his thousand-dollar lizard cowboy boots. Originally from Amarillo, with a bachelor's from Texas A&M and a master's from Yale, he still spoke with a faint drawl. Cops loved him. At crime scenes he played the good old boy sleuth to the hilt.

"I'm not saying I don't have faith in the man," Geisel finally murmured in a low tone. "For all I know, this mummy holds the key to Sun City. Just like Grove claims. What I'm saying is, we've had Grove on the case for twelve months now, and he's up there operating all alone, no other perspective. Do you see what I mean?"

"Y'all want me to go there."

"I know you've got a hellacious workload, Terry, and the review's coming down the line."

"Don't give it another thought, Tom. I'll be on the first flight out tomorrow morning."

"I really appreciate it, Terry."

"How'd you leave it with Ulysses?"

"He asked me if I could send help, and I told him I'd ask you."

"Outstanding, Tom."

"Which reminds me, Terry . . ."

There was a pause then, and Zorn waited. He knew the old man had a soft spot for Grove, and it was probably killing the director to undermine his golden boy. But it was also obvious to Zorn that Grove's days were coming to an end. The Great Ulysses Grove had finally blown a gasket, and was up there in the wilds of Alaska, picking apart some cockamamie fossil when he should be working on a rapid-response plan for the next Sun City crime scene.

Zorn said, "What is it?"

The pause went on for another beat. Another sigh. "Terry, I'm sending you up there in an official capacity of second banana on this mummy thing. You take orders from Grove. You're there to help. *Ostensibly*. But unofficially . . . I want you to keep tabs. Reign this thing back in. Get Grove back on track with Sun City, if you can. Bottom line is, you're my guy. You're my eyes and ears up there. Does that make any sense?"

Zorn smiled to himself. "It makes perfect sense, Tom."

Grove spent the rest of that day learning everything he could about the Iceman. He went to the graduate archaeology library with Okuda, and underwent a primer in early Copper Age man. He snuck back into the Schleimann Lab and took another look—albeit through layers of hermetically sealed glass—at the mummy. He took digital pictures of the thing and found himself staring for inordinate amounts of time at the Iceman's leathery face. There was something about that face, and those gaping, waxen eyes, that transfixed Grove. Maybe it was the nightmare he had had the previous night, or perhaps it was the matching victimology. But something about the expression frozen onto the mummy's face fascinated Grove.

He mentioned this to Okuda, who commented that he thought the expression cemented onto the mummy's face was a clue as to how the Iceman had died. Okuda believed that the mummy was a victim of human sacrifice. Copper Age humans worshipped many nature gods, including mountain deities, and believed in the significance of sacrificial offerings in order to affect the weather, the harvest, even the birth rate. This was known now, according to Okuda, because of the fossil record, and because of the tools, belongings, and implements that had been found alongside mummies such as Keanu. Plus, recent CT scans and three-dimensional computer imaging of the mummy's internal organs revealed that part of the liver and the heart had been removed postmortem (this was done through a ragged opening beneath his ribs, a wound that was initially thought to be the result of a fall). Okuda saw this latter discovery as further evidence of some kind of ritualistic killing.

After a brief lunch in the lab's cafeteria—the profiler didn't have much of an appetite and only had half a bagel—Grove spent several hours in Okuda's cramped private office in the bowels of the Schliemann Lab, going through reams of material on the tests that had been done to the Iceman. He studied the endless sequences of mitochondrial DNA that were extracted from the mummy's bone marrow. He went through all the X-rays and scans of the Iceman's presumably fatal wound—the sharp trauma injury that had sunk the hook into Grove. After placing a long-distance call to Quantico, the profiler had one of the bureau secretaries fax him a series of pathological reports on the Sun City victims. Grove began assembling visual comparisons between the ancient victim and present-day victims. The wounds were absolutely identical. The only anomalies were the missing internal organs. The Sun City victims, as far as Grove could tell from the forensics, were all internally intact.

No detail was considered trivial or irrelevant. Grove learned that the Iceman carried a strange object—a small piece of mossy fungus pierced by a leather band— that had initially baffled archaeologists. The fungus contained chemical substances now known to be antibiotic, which suggested to Okuda that the fungus was part of the medicine man's arsenal. Grove also saw elaborate clay reconstructions of the mummy's face, as well as meticulously repaired grass sheathes and clothing worn by the Iceman. Grove even handled the Iceman's hatchet, which felt oddly comfortable in his hand, well balanced and finely crafted. In a mystical sense, Okuda explained, each swing of the Iceman's axe partook of the sacred. To slaughter an ibex or chop down a seedling would be linked to some god whose own axe had helped bless the world. Or perhaps the act emulated some mythic figure who had ridden the land of evil.

Grove wasn't sure what he was looking for, but he had a feeling that the more he knew about the mummy's origins and environment, the better he would be able to reconstruct the Iceman's murder and ultimately draw whatever connections there might be to Sun City.

He worked through dinner that night, absently picking at a box of chop suey that Maura County had brought him from a campus eatery. The journalist had been regularly checking in with the two men throughout the day, giving them encouragement and asking if they needed anything. Grove was very subtly—almost imperceptively—becoming fond of the fair-haired, punkish young lady. He found himself joking with her. He found his mood brightening whenever she showed her face. And he felt the fondness reciprocated. She seemed to be worried about him. At around nine o'clock that night, for instance, she appeared in the doorway of Okuda's office with her hands on her hips and a sideways smirk on her face.

"You think maybe it's about time you knocked off for the day?" she asked.

Grove stretched, rubbing his neck. "Not a bad idea," he said. "Getting a little cross-eyed."

She asked where Okuda was.

"He abandoned me, he went home."

"C'mon," she said. "Let me buy you a cup of coffee, there's something I want to talk to you about."

They closed down the office, turned out the lights, and locked the door.

Maura gave Grove a ride back to the motel, and they found the coffee urn in the lobby still warm and still half-full of bitter, stale French roast. They sat near the front window, the lights of passing SUVs flickering through the glass and flashing off their faces, the muffled sound of tires crunching in the snow. Grove rubbed his weary eyes. "The truth is, I really don't know what I'm doing," he finally said with a sigh.

"Welcome to my world," Maura muttered.

He smiled at her. "You seem pretty buttoned down to me."

She laughed, and the sound of her voice—that goofy, hoarse chortle—touched something deep within Grove. He noticed a tiny fleck of gold in the pale blue iris of the journalist's left eye, and all at once Grove felt something that he hadn't felt since his wife had died, and it bothered him. He felt an *attraction* toward this waifish young thing, as sure and hot as electric current running through him, and it made him miss his wife all the more. "I've been accused of a lot of things," Maura said at last, "but never being buttoned down."

"You said you wanted to talk to me about something."

"Yeah, it's an idea. Maybe a new approach to all this. When you're ready to go public."

"Go on."

"It might be a waste of time. I don't know. But I have this idea. With your permission."

"I'm listening."

She lit a cigarette and blew a circle of smoke away from the profiler. "To be honest, I got the idea from the FBI Web site, of all places."

"Tell me."

"This database that FBI agents use? VICAB it's called?"

"VICAP," Grove corrected. "Stands for Violent Criminal Apprehension Program."

"Sorry, right. VICAP. Anyway. I was thinking. Why couldn't you create a similar database for ancient history?"

Grove told her he wasn't following.

"Okay. Let's say, just for the sake of argument, we could send out an e-mail or a letter or whatever to the entire archeological community."

"Is that possible? The entire community?"

Maura shrugged, took another drag. "I asked Michael Okuda about it. He said they had a pretty decent mailing list. Anyway. What if we solicited the entire community and asked them if they had any evidence of similar murders? You see where I'm going with this?"

Grove looked at her. "Why would you think we'd find similar murders?"

"I don't know. Maybe it's a hunch. Maybe we won't. I just thought it would be . . . you know. Kinda fascinating. What do you think?"

Grove got up and paced across the deserted motel lobby. The front desk was unoccupied, the murmur of a television set from the inner warren of offices barely audible. Grove thought of his nightmare. The eerie, visceral quality of it still clung to his brain. In the dream, *he* was the Iceman, *he* was a human sacrifice—a casualty of some cruel, inexorable fate.

At last he turned and looked at Maura County, who

still sat by the window, waiting for his answer with her gold-flecked blue eyes. Grove grinned at her and said, "I gotta admit, it *is* an interesting idea."

That night, a thousand miles to the south, just outside Las Vegas, on the edge of the high desert near the Moapa River Indian Reservation, the Mason Dixon Truck Stop sat in the nimbus of a hundred sodium vapor lights.

The cumulative illumination was so bright, so relentless, so pervasive, that the stars in the vast Nevada sky were not visible for at least a quarter of a mile in every direction. Mayflies the size of walnuts swarmed by the lights. They made ticking noises that were just audible underneath the sound of canned music blaring across the cement lot. A score of fuel pumps—twelve diesel, eight gasoline—stretched across the bleached concrete. A single vehicle sat at one of the gas pumps: a sea-mist-green Honda Odyssey. The driver, a forty-three-year-old mother of two named Carolyn Kenly, had just turned the engine off.

She got out of the car and strolled quickly across the lot toward the minimart and restaurant. Dressed in a denim sundress, she moved with the kind of nervous energy and purpose a lone woman acquires late at night, her gaze fixed on the entrance, her sandals snapping rhythmically. She vanished inside the minimart for a moment.

A moment was all the killer needed. He emerged from the shadows behind a garbage Dumpster, then strode across the radiant lot with his head held high and casual, his arms at his side. A tall, sinewy man with a long, gaunt face streaked with filth, he reached the green SUV and paused by the front quarter panel, glancing once over his shoulder to be certain no one was watching. His movements were precise and deft, despite the fact that he wore rags and smelled of BO and dried feces. The thing inside him cared nothing of hygiene. The thing inside him cared only of its higher purpose.

The killer pulled a folding Buck knife from the back pocket of his stained, torn khaki pants. He worked quickly. Kneeling down by the front left tire, he unfolded the blade and slipped under the chassis. The task required less than a minute. Thirty seconds at the most. The killer found the proper cable and severed it with a flick of the knife.

By the time the woman in the sundress had returned to the SUV, the killer had retreated back behind the garbage Dumpster, where his own vehicle, a stolen Mercedes SL-500, sat idling in the dark. He climbed behind the wheel. The interior of the Mercedes reeked of urine, spoiled food, and old sweat, but the killer hardly noticed it.

The Honda SUV pulled out of the truck stop and started down Highway 15.

The killer followed.

The next thirty minutes or so were like a dance. The killer hovered behind the SUV, his headlights off, keeping just enough distance between him and the target to remain buried in the darkness of the desert. The woman named Carolyn Kenly drove above the speed limit. She seemed in a hurry to get somewhere. The killer watched as the rear of the SUV began to fishtail, the broken cable doing its job. Taillights flared. The SUV rattled over to the side of the highway.

The killer performed the rest of the procedure with tremendous accuracy and aplomb. A half mile or so behind the SUV, he pulled over to the shoulder, parked, and turned off his engine. His bow, quiver, and tools were in the trunk. He gathered them up, slung the quiver over his shoulder, strapped the tool belt to his waist, and gripped the bow tightly in his left hand. Then he started toward the SUV.

The desert was so dark, and the sky such a riot of stars, it was like walking across the dark side of the moon.

It took just under five minutes for the killer to reach the disabled SUV and the frantic woman. The Honda's hood was up. The woman was inside the vehicle, raving into her cell phone to somebody, probably her husband, or perhaps the clerk back at the Mason Dixon Truck Stop. It did not matter. The killer found an egg-sized rock and hurled it at the rear of the Honda.

The noise sounded like a pistol shot, and made the woman jerk as though someone had slapped the back of her neck. She moved instinctively, throwing open her door and lurching out of the vehicle. She stumbled. The killer watched from behind a grove of joshuas. The woman still held her cell phone and still babbled as she staggered across the deserted highway and into the scabrous pasture to the north.

"What was that? What was that!" she stammered into her cell phone as she hobbled along. *"Danny, can you hear me? Danny, oh God, what was that? Danny, Dannnneeeeeee!"*

The killer closed in.

Loping across hard-packed sand, not more than twenty yards behind her, not even breaking stride, he reached back over his shoulder to his quiver as if he were scratching his back. He was getting good at this part. With one graceful movement, he plucked an arrow out of the sheath and brought it up to eye level, snapping the bow back like a spring. The sling coiled. He held his breath, aimed, and let one go.

The arrow whispered through the night.

It hit the woman so hard in the back of her neck that her body rose off the ground. A yawp burst out of her that sounded like the squeal of air being forced out of a balloon, and she tumbled hard. Her body folded into the dirt, a rag doll tossed by a petulant child.

The killer approached.

Carolyn Kenly clung to life for several minutes. Over the course of those minutes, as she gasped for breath, choking on her own blood, convulsing in the agony of a pierced vertebra, she thought of her children, and she thought of her husband of twenty-two years, and she thought of her dreams and plans that would never come to fruition. But mostly she listened to the muffled footsteps approaching.

The woman expired just as the killer came into view, pulling a pair of rubber-handled pliers from his tool belt.

Grove couldn't sleep again. He tried everything he could think of short of taking a sleeping pill—which he didn't like to do unless absolutely necessary—but nothing worked. He watched infomercials on TV, he paced, he turned the fan up on the heater in order to fill the air with white noise. All to no avail. The motel room with its burnt-orange carpet and hideous seascape paintings was the inside of a kettledrum, and Grove's heart beat its insidious music, pounding in his ear, keeping him awake. His mind refused to shut down.

A repeating series of images and feelings would not leave his brain: the vision of being on an ancient mountain in the snow, the fleck of gold in Maura County's eye, the day he found out about Hannah's cancer, the Iceman's contorted look of horror, the curve of Maura County's neck, a fragmented memory of the last time he had masturbated, when an unexpected tear fell from his eye and mixed with droplets of semen on his wrist. Finally, some time around four o'clock that morning, Grove gave up trying to sleep and got up.

For the next couple of hours—right up until the moment dawn pushed back the shadows and sent rays of early morning light through his venetian blinds—the profiler sat at the desk by the window, studying notes from the Iceman project and copies of X-rays and files from the Sun City murders. The clues were in front of him, buried in the documents, but the answers were still just out of reach. Like a word on the tip of Grove's tongue, a name or place just beyond his grasp.

At some time around six o'clock, Grove's cell phone tweeted, and when he answered it he was not at all surprised to hear Terry Zorn's impudent drawl in his ear. "Hope I didn't wake ya'll up," the voice crackled.

"Terry . . . no . . . I was up already."

"How's it going up there in the Great White North?"

"It's cold."

"Understand y'all got some kinda mummy up there."

"Uh . . . yeah, it's a long story."

"I'd love to hear it. Y'all want some company?"

"Yeah, great. Tom mentioned he might be able to tear you off the Baltimore sniper."

"I'm all yours, buddy."

"Great."

"Fixin' to get on the nine-oh-three outta Dulles, be touchin' down in Anchorage about one o'clock Alaska time. Any chance you could pick me up?"

"Of course. Be happy to. Give me your flight number."

Zorn gave him the information, and Grove told him to have a good flight.

Grove clicked off his phone and felt a slight twinge of nervous tension in his belly. He had worked with Zorn a couple of times in the past, and respected the Texan's abilities, but there was something about the man that had always bothered Grove. Maybe it was the subtle contempt just beneath the surface of Zorn's constant joking, or the faint spark of hostility behind the man's gaze. And that good old boy facade had always gotten under Grove's skin. Zorn was the guy who had started the running gag at Quantico that Grove looked like a member of the Nation of Islam. The two men had worked to-

gether on the Oregon Happy Face Killer case, and Zorn
had been a competent partner, but the jokes had really
gotten to Grove on that job.

Was Grove too sensitive? Was he inordinately touchy
about such things? He wondered sometimes if this tender-
ness was formed at an early age.

Ulysses Grove came from a place of clashing cultures, a place of dislocation. Raised in a working-class
neighborhood on the North Side of Chicago, he was
educated in the public schools, and tossed in with the
general population who valued conformity over indi-
viduality. But it wasn't easy for young Ulysses to fit in.
His Jamaican father, Georges Grove (né Groviere), had
become nothing more than a bad memory by the time
Grove was born, and Grove's mother, Vida, was not exactly Carol Brady. She would dress her son in multi-
colored *kitenge* tunics and dashikis, and send him to
school with tribal adornments. And on the rare occa-
sion that one of Grove's friends would visit the Grove
household, Vida served traditional Kenyan cuisine and
instead of providing silverware would make all the kids
use the traditional *injera*—a doughy flat bread the consistency of human flesh—to pick up their food. Grove
was teased unmercifully. But Vida was too proud to as-
similate, and kept draping her reluctant son in African
beads and sweet potato sacks.

All this cultural angst had much to do with Grove's
estrangement from his mother. Now in her late seven-
ties, the woman still lived alone in the same modest
bungalow in Chicago, surrounded by her gourds and
beads and tribal charms. But Grove hadn't seen her in
years. He said good-bye to that life in the late 1970s when
he left Chicago for the University of Michigan. And as
his assimilation deepened—first in the army, and later
at the FBI academy—his resentment toward his mother's

stubborn ethnicity only festered. Nowadays he tried to think about it as little as possible.

Which was why he was currently clicking nervously through the radio presets in his rental car as he cruised south on Highway 3 on his way to Anchorage International.

All he could find was either shrill country-western music or annoying right-wing talk radio, so he finally turned off the radio and concentrated on driving the Nissan Maxima through the canyons of granite rock-cuts that bordered the outskirts of Anchorage. The spring sun had broken through the clouds a few hours ago, and now the rugged landscape seemed to be thawing before Grove's eyes. The highway teemed with traffic, and Grove had to squint against the glare in order to see the exit signs.

A symbol of an airplane loomed on an oncoming sign, and Grove took the next exit ramp.

Ten minutes later he was pulling into the short-term parking lot adjacent to the terminal. He parked and took the underground walkway into the building. An escalator brought him up into the bustling noise and light of the terminal, and he consulted a piece of notepaper on which he had written Terry Zorn's flight number and arrival gate.

Grove found the Texan standing next to a phone booth, a suit bag thrown over his shoulder, his cowboy hat cocked at a jaunty angle on his bald head. Zorn was on the phone, making notes. His eyes lit up when he saw Grove approaching.

"One second, Tom, hold on," Zorn said into the phone, then thrust his free hand out at Grove. "There he is!"

"Hey, Terry," Grove said and shook the man's hand. Zorn's grip was firm and dry.

"Be right with ya," Zorn said to Grove, gesturing with a single finger, then he murmured back into the phone,

"I understand what you're saying, Tom, don't you worry, we'll get it minty fresh this time." Zorn laughed then, a conspiratorial sort of chuckle that, for some reason, made Grove look away. "We're already *at* the damn airport. All we gotta do is hop a commuter down there. All right? Sound good? We'll call ya from the scene. So long, Tom."

Zorn clicked off his cell phone and turned to Grove. "You feel like gettin' on a plane?"

"Excuse me?"

"Just got word from Quantico: Sun City's been at it again."

"Where?"

"Few miles outside of Vegas . . . C'mon." Zorn gave Grove a friendly slap on the back, then started toward the bank of departure monitors, adding over his shoulder, "I'll run down the details on the way."

Grove let out a sigh, then followed.

5

Victimology

They sat in the rear of the Alaska Airlines 767 as the plane roared heavenward, executing a steep banking turn toward the south, the harsh sunlight slicing through the porthole windows. Turbulence rattled the overhead bins and galley cabinets, and Grove held on to his notes.

Zorn sat on Grove's immediate right, scanning his notebook. "Jurisdictional issues aside, Vegas homicide's got the primary on it."

Grove looked at him. "And the dump?"

Zorn glanced down at his notebook. "Unincorporated area out in the desert."

"That sounds like the state police."

Zorn nodded. "Yeah, well, they don't have the juice the Vegas PD's got."

They rode in silence for a while until Grove finally asked who flagged the desert murder as Sun City.

"I guess the primary recognized the signature," Zorn replied, gazing down at his notes. "Captain name of Hauser."

"Victim's female, you said?"

"Right . . . got a positive ID . . . forty-three-year-old

white female, name of Carolyn Kenly, married, mother of two, resident of Henderson, Nevada."

"Anything on her sheet?"

"Nothing, no priors, lady's pure civilian. Seems totally random again."

Another stretch of silence. Grove could not get the face of the Iceman out of his head. Finally he turned to Zorn and said, "We're talking the cervical vertebra again?"

Zorn gave him another nod. "Looks like it. No ballistics, no murder weapon found. They already got their ME down there."

"Time of death?"

Zorn looked at the notes. "Let's see . . . sometime between midnight and three o'clock."

"Sharp trauma?"

"Yep."

"And the staging, the pose?"

"No details yet, but . . . yeah, looks like they got Sun City on their hands."

Grove gazed out his window at the ocean of clouds beneath the plane. Every few miles the cloud cover would break, and a vast maw of black mountains would come into view. Grove watched the rugged territory pass underneath the broken clouds, and wondered if he should have called Maura County to tell her about this impromptu journey. Technically he was not obligated to keep the journalist informed of his every move, but somehow Maura County had become more than a mere interview with some obscure science magazine. She had become an associate. Or perhaps *associate* was the wrong word. It had been so long since Grove had felt these kinds of feelings, he wasn't sure how to process them. All he knew was that the fair-haired writer, for better or worse, was lingering in his mind.

The rest of the flight to Vegas was spent mostly in awkward silence. Every now and then, Zorn would make a bad joke about the mummy, or Grove would ask about another aspect of the Vegas murder, but mostly they rode in silence. The flight attendant approached them twice—once to take their drink orders, and once to serve them dinner—but other than that, the remainder of the flight was fairly uneventful, despite the nagging feeling in the back of Grove's mind that Zorn had ulterior motives. There was a sharp edge to every joke, every comment.

The plane began its descent into McCarran International Airport around six o'clock that night, the dying light turning the horizon a brilliant display of pastels.

After a gentle landing, the two profilers filed off the plane and crossed the Jetway, immediately noticing the climactic change. The air was warm and blustery, a huge departure from the clammy chill of Alaska. They crossed the busy terminal, heading for the cab stand, ignoring the percolating slot machines at every juncture.

"Do you know if Tom urged the Vegas tactical guys to get pictures of the crowd at the scene?" Grove asked as the two men got in line for a taxi.

Zorn looked at him. "You think this guy's a spectator?"

"I think there's a lot of meaning here, a lot of ritual and ceremony."

Zorn shook his head. "I don't think he'd be dumb enough to hang around at the scene."

"It's not a matter of intelligence, it's part of the experience."

A yellow cab pulled up in front of them, the miniature billboard on its roof advertising the BARE ASSETS GENTLEMEN'S CLUB—ALL-NUDE REVUE. The two men slid into the backseat, and Zorn told the driver they needed to go to the Las Vegas City Courthouse where the Special Violent Crimes Unit of the LVPD was located. The cabbie—a Pakistani man in a baseball cap—flipped the meter down and rattled out of there.

On their way across town, skirting the neon canyons of the strip, Zorn said, "My take is, this guy's a craftsman, a pro, somebody who's very careful."

Grove was staring out the window. "But there's a deeper issue associated with it."

"Did the mummy tell ya that?"

Grove looked at Zorn. "Pardon?"

"I'm just messin' with ya, Grove."

A few minutes later they pulled up in front of the court building, a great limestone pile rising up against the pale desert sky. Windows blazed.

Zorn paid the cabbie, and the two profilers strode across the concrete apron to the entrance.

The lobby was deserted except for a pair of security guards flanking a metal detector. Grove and Zorn flashed their IDs, then passed through the detector and went to the end of the main corridor. A glass door marked LVPD SPECIAL DIVISIONS directed them into another reception area, where they were greeted by an elderly woman with thick glasses. Zorn identified himself, and the woman punched an interoffice number on her switchboard. She told the captain the profilers had arrived, and then nodded and hung up the phone.

"Captain Hauser will be right out," she told them, then went back to her typing.

Grove turned to Zorn and said under his breath, "As a matter of fact, the mummy did tell me a lot about Sun City."

Zorn looked at him. "For instance?"

"The murders are not improvised."

"You mean they're premeditated?"

"I mean there's heavy symbolism there, and it's relevant to the mummy."

"Yeah . . . go on."

"I don't have it yet—the connection—but I'm close."

After a long moment Zorn grinned. "Maybe you're too close."

Grove looked away. "Whatever you say, Terry."

Captain Ivan Hauser of the LVPD Violent Crimes Unit, a pachyderm of a man with a big walrus mustache and marine tattoos on his sun-weathered forearms, drove the two profilers out to the scene. The victim had been found in a field about fifteen miles northeast of town, near Nellis Air Force Base. The Kenly woman had either been dumped, or left for dead, about thirty yards north of the highway. Her body had been found by a rancher, out before sunrise to repair a nearby barbed wire fence. When the call had first come in, the dispatcher had sent a state police prowler to the scene. The patrolman got one look at the mutilated body and called the investigative division.

By dawn, the area was bustling with law enforcement and forensic people.

That was almost twelve hours ago, and yet, even now, as Hauser's unmarked Crown Victoria approached the scene, the number of crime lab vehicles and police cruisers clogging the half-mile stretch of desert highway had barely diminished. Scores of chaser lights danced on the horizon. Flashlights crisscrossed the distant landscape.

Zorn rode in front, in the shotgun seat. Grove rode in the rear, staring at the back of Zorn's cowboy hat, feeling ridiculous and small and alienated. The two men had been arguing the whole way out to the scene, and now the tension in the car was as thick as a noxious gas.

"But what if there's no connection?" Zorn wanted to know, staring out the windshield, his voice taut with anger. "What if this is just a fruitcake with a subscription to *National Geographic*? That's what I'm trying to get through that thick skull of yours."

Grove stared at the oncoming blue streaks of light. "There's a connection," he murmured.

"It's a goddamn mummy, Ulysses. A six-thousand-year-old stiff."

"The pose is identical."

"So what?"

"It's my experience, you follow everything out."

The Texan shook his head. "And while you're dickin' around up there in the twilight zone, the perp's headin' to Disneyland."

Grove wanted to put his fist through the back of Zorn's seat. "You want to say something, Terry, why don't you just come out and say it?"

"I'm saying it."

"Yeah?"

"Yeah, I'm saying it."

"No, I don't think you are. I don't think you're saying what you really think."

"What—are you profiling me now? You profiling *me*?"

"For the love of Gawd!" Hauser boomed suddenly. He yanked the car over to the shoulder and slammed on the brakes, the Crown Victoria scudding to a stop in a thunderhead of dust. "I been listening to you two boys mix it up since we left the courthouse, and I've just about had it. I thought you two were on the same team."

Zorn was staring out at the night, the blue light flashing off his face. He pulled a pair of rubber surgical gloves from his pocket. "It's all part of the process, Cap—it's how we do things."

"You gotta be shitting me," the captain said.

"Just say it, Terry," Grove urged from the backseat, digging in his own pocket for his rubber gloves. He kept them in a sandwich baggie.

"What do you want me to say?" Zorn was snapping his surgical gloves over his hands.

"Just say what you really want to say."

"This is ridiculous—"

Zorn opened his door and got out, flexing his fingers into the gloves. Grove followed. The captain stayed in the car to have a smoke, and perhaps enjoy some blessed relief away from the bickering FBI agents.

The two profilers crossed the highway, which was blocked off by flares, wooden sawhorses, and yellow crime scene tape flapping in the night breezes. They stepped over a dry creek bed on the other side of the road, then headed toward the pool of tungsten light thirty yards away. Technicians still swarmed around the broken rag doll of a body, an ambulance canted nearby with the door gaping. High-intensity lights mounted on C-stands shone down at the human remains.

As he strode toward the victim, Grove felt his gut burning with anger. "Why don't you just say it?"

Zorn paused, turned to Grove, then spoke in a low growl. "Okay, you're a joke. You're burned out, you're toast. You got no credibility anymore."

"I'm a joke. Is that right?"

"Yeah, that's right. Why do you think Geisel sent you on that stupid mummy hunt?"

"I'm a joke."

"Let's face it, partner . . . your days of slam dunks are over. You ain't helped clear a goddamn case in three years, and Sun City's turning out to be an embarrassment to the whole goddamn division. And this mummy thing now is just the frosting on the cake—"

"You want to take off, Terry, you want to go back home, that's fine by me."

"You don't get it, partner. Anybody's going home, it's gonna be you."

Grove laughed at that one. "Oh yeah? I'm going home? I'm going home now, Terry?"

"Yeah, that's right."

"I'm going home . . . and how many cases have you cleared lately, Terry?"

"Yeah . . . eat shit!"

"That's quite a *brilliant* re—"

Grove was about to say the word *retort* with about as much venom as he could muster, but something snapped the word off in his throat. He stood there for a moment, staring past Zorn toward the corona of silver light that illuminated the dark pasture. Grove could not move. He stared at the body lying in that pool of light on the hardpack fifteen yards away. He stared and stared, and felt the revelation turning in his gut like a worm. Zorn was saying something nasty under his breath, but Grove could no longer hear anything but the buzzing in his ears. He realized right then he had discovered the key to Sun City, the connection between the mummy and the present-day crimes.

"Grove? Hey! Grove!" Zorn barked.

Grove turned to the Texan and said very softly, "Get everybody back."

"What?"

"Everybody, even the ME—I want everybody back." Grove started toward the body.

Zorn hurried after him, grabbing his arm. "Hey! What's going on? You see something?"

"Get 'em all back," Grove said, approaching the cluster of people crowding the body, snapping his surgical gloves. A half dozen specialists hovered there: two plainclothes detectives from the LVPD, an ambulance attendant, a pathologist, an FBI evidence technician, and the medical examiner, a graying man in a white lab coat.

Zorn pulled his ID from his lapel and flashed it. "Folks, this is Special Agent Grove from the Serial Crime Unit, my name is Special Agent Zorn, and we'd appreciate it if y'all would give us a minute alone with the vic."

After an awkward beat, the crowd slowly parted, moving back as Grove knelt down by the body.

The woman's flesh looked like gray marble in the halogen light, her denim sundress spattered with a Rorschach pattern of dried blood the color of old rubies. Her eyes were still open and filmed over with a milky substance known to pathologists as adipocere. One arm was pinned behind her back, the other raised in the trademark pose of all the other victims, including the Iceman. It looked as though she were shielding her dead face from some invisible sun. Her neck was coated with dried blood. Grove carefully slipped one hand under her shoulder blades and turned her over.

The neck wound was identical to all the others, a ragged pucker the size of a half dollar. But that's not what Grove was looking for. He pulled a penlight from his inner pocket and thumbed it on. The delicate circle of light traveled down the woman's spine to the small of her back. Grove stared at the fabric of the sundress, which was torn and soaked in blood. With his rubberized fingertip he prodded open the rip. The same inexplicable flesh wounds crisscrossed the woman's taut flesh: perpendicular fissures already scabbed and crusted. Like all the others, these looked hastily produced by a serrated blade.

"They're superficial," Grove murmured to himself, tracing the wounds with his fingertip, then pressing down on them. The skin held like the head of a drum, confirming something Grove had already been told by over a dozen medical examiners. But up until now, the fact had held very little significance.

"What? What's superficial?" Zorn was standing over him, waiting impatiently.

Grove rose. "The difference between this victim and the Iceman."

"The hell are you talking about?"

Grove started toward Hauser's Crown Victoria, walking briskly. "It's all about seeing, observing the victimology," he muttered.

Zorn hurried after him. "What did you see? What's going on?"

Grove was peeling off his gloves as he walked. "We're gonna need to talk to the first-on-the-scene in Alaska."

"What in the good Lord's name are you talking about? There's no scene in Alaska!"

"When they found the mummy, when they took it out of the ice. The mummy's the doorway."

Zorn finally caught up with Grove and grabbed his arm. "What doorway? What the hell are you babbling about, Grove?"

Grove paused, gazing directly into Zorn's eyes. "The mummy's missing internal organs. Sun City victims are intact. That's the key. The exit wounds were never made public, they were never part of the *Discover* articles."

Grove turned and continued striding toward the captain's car when Zorn suddenly grabbed him. "Wait! Grove, wait. I still ain't followin'."

Again Grove looked into Zorn's eyes. "The guy we're looking for, the Sun City killer. He saw the Iceman."

"How do you know?"

"The internal organs were removed from the Iceman. That's the part the killer is getting wrong."

"Yeah so?"

"Because he couldn't *see* that part, he couldn't see it. It's all about seeing."

Zorn frowned. "You're awful sure about this."

"He was there, Terry. When they found the mummy he was there, he saw it."

Grove turned and strode toward the captain's car, leaving Zorn standing there in the flashing shadows, speechless.

6

Unseen Forces

Michael Okuda enclosed himself in the stall, the squeak of his hiking boot on the tile echoing in the deserted men's room. The noise made Okuda doubly lonely and jittery. He had decided to come to the lab early, before dawn, in order to get a head start on the busy work Dr. Mathis had given him—an entire Pendaflex folder full of mitochondrial test results that needed filing—and now he was starting to regret the decision. He could be home sleeping. Or better yet, he could be working on his own stuff—maybe finishing that curriculum vitae so that he could maybe find an appointment somewhere with at least a remote possibility of advancement.

He latched the stall door and sat down on the edge of the stool, his pants still buckled, his hands shaking, his leather portfolio still slung over his shoulder. He did not have to move his bowels. He reached into his pocket and pulled out a matchbox bound with Scotch tape and a rubber band.

Inside the matchbox lay a tiny glassine vial of heroin, which Okuda rooted out carefully and peeled open. He got his dope from a graduate student over at the chemistry building, and it was gourmet shit. Laboratory grade.

Okuda had gotten to the point that he couldn't function throughout the day without at least one pop, or maybe two. So far, he had been able to keep his drug use a secret, but discretion was getting more difficult every day. Mathis had walked in on him in the lunchroom the other day, and Okuda had been forced to dump about seventy-five dollars' worth of powder down the sink.

Thumbing through his portfolio, he found a stiff piece of plastic—a copy of one of Keanu's X-rays—and laid a tiny little snake of beige powder across its shiny surface. He plucked a hollow coffee stirrer from the matchbox, and greedily sniffed the dope off the X-ray.

A bolt of cold pushed down his nasal passage and into his throat. He had always preferred snorting the dope to smoking it or, God forbid, shooting it. Okuda hated needles. He sat back, resting his head against the wall, waiting for the buzz to calm him down and steady him. His hands trembled. Nervous tension knotted his gut. He gazed down at the X-ray on his lap, still frosted with powder. He looked at the milky, unfocused image of the Iceman's skull, the eye sockets like great gaping craters in some awful relief map.

From the moment the FBI profiler had started snooping around the lab and making connections between the mummy and the modern serial killer, Okuda had been exceedingly spooked. There was something going on now that was simply beyond his grasp, beyond the prosaic world of laboratory analysis and scientific method.

A noise out in the main corridor sent gooseflesh up Okuda's back.

It sounded like muffled footsteps, or maybe a voice, Okuda wasn't sure. The janitors roamed at this hour. It was probably a janitor. Okuda was just being paranoid and jumpy. He wondered how bad off he would be without the heroin. He wondered if the panic attacks would be constant, if his nerves would eventually send him to an institution. He had a therapist once who told him that he did drugs because his mom and dad were so judgmental and hard on him. First-generation Okinawans, the elder Okudas had always pushed their son to enter academic competitions—spelling bees, debates, essay contests—because that was what America was all about: competing, winning, beating the other guy. By the time the boy was a senior in high school, he had developed a full-blown ulcer.

The noise was outside the men's room now—hasty footsteps and a muffled voice.

"Michael? You in there?"

The sound of knocking made Okuda jerk. He dropped the X-ray, and the matchbox bounced off his lap. Adrenaline surged in his veins, and a Roman candle exploded in his line of vision, the buzz kicking in all once. He brushed himself off and swallowed hard. His mouth was dry. He took a deep breath and tried to blink away the shock. Who the hell would be looking for him at five o'clock in the morning?

"Y-yeah—who is it?" Okuda's voice was wobbly.

"It's Grove, Agent Grove. The guard let me in, said you were down here."

"Just a minute!" For a moment Okuda could not swallow, his mouth was so dry. He dropped to his hands and knees and gathered up the X-ray and the matchbox. He put the X-ray back in his portfolio and zipped it closed. Then he stuffed the matchbox back in his pocket.

"You okay?" the voice wanted to know.

"Coming!"

Okuda pushed the stall door open and went over to the mirror. His face was ashen. His eyes watered with the telltale glaze of a fresh dope buzz. Would the profiler recognize the druggy stare in Okuda's eyes? In a weird way, Okuda didn't really care. Was that the high working on him? Was that the false courage of a heroin surge? The Asian splashed some water on his face, dried off, and went over to the door.

"Sorry to barge in on you," the tall black man said after Okuda had opened the door. Grove stood in the hallway in his tweed overcoat, his hands in his pockets, his expression burning with urgency. His shoulders looked damp with rain. "I tried your apartment, then figured you might be working the early shift," Grove said.

"What is it?" Okuda asked, his own voice sounding meek and strangled in his ears. "What's wrong?"

"I need your help," he said.

"Anything."

"I need to know about that day."

"What day?"

"When they found him."

"Keanu?"

"That's right, I need to know who found him, who saw him first."

Okuda thought for a moment. "They were . . . hikers, I guess. They were on vacation."

Grove's eyes burned. "I need everything you got, names, addresses, phone numbers—I need to know about every single person who was on that mountain that day."

Okuda shrugged. "We got files on it . . . you might also want to talk to the cops."

"Mind showing me what you've got?"

"Come on," Okuda said, pushing past the door and into the hall.

The Asian led the profiler down a deserted corridor, past mazes of cubicles, light tables, electron microscopes, and examination areas. Known as the "dry lab," this area encompassed much of the basement level, and now sat completely empty, dark, and silent. Okuda's buzz had completely kicked in by that point, and the shadows seemed to pulse with a weird kind of energy. Energy radiated off Grove as well. Okuda sensed it like a red wake curling behind the handsome profiler. The man's expression was fixed and set, almost like a pitcher about to deliver a fastball on a full count.

Turning a corner at the end of the main corridor, Okuda remembered the diary. "You know what?" he said over his shoulder, snapping his fingers. "There's a document you might want to check out."

"What kind of document?" Grove was striding briskly along behind Okuda.

"A park ranger there that day, she kept a journal."

"A journal."

"A diary, yeah, we used excerpts in our presentation to the Royal Academy last year."

"And you've got her entry from that day?"

"Yes, absolutely, that's what I'm saying." Okuda nodded as they marched along. "We've got her journal entry from the day they found the Iceman."

They turned another corner and headed down a narrow side corridor bordered by unmarked doors.

Grove looked intrigued. "This is a private journal?"

"What do you mean?"

"It's personal, right? It's not an official logbook, or job-related thing."

"No, no. This is a copy of a girl's personal diary. She was pretty freaked out by the whole thing. Here we go." At the end of the hall Okuda paused in front of a painted iron door with an elaborate magnetic lock. He dug in his pocket for his wallet, found the little magnetic card, pulled it out, and swiped it through the lock. The door clicked, and Okuda led the profiler into a dark archive room.

Fluorescent lights stuttered on, illuminating a musty chamber of interlocking shelves brimming with hand-labeled binders, bound reports, and dog-eared old volumes reaching up to the acoustic tile ceiling fifteen feet overhead. A single shopworn conference table cluttered with index cards sat in the center of the room. The worn carpet was the color of old mustard. The air smelled of mold.

"If I'm not mistaken, that journal is still in the ID bin," Okuda muttered, more to himself than Grove, as he crossed the room and knelt down by a row of black vinyl binders packed as tightly as a huge tin of sardines.

"ID bin?"

"Interdepartmental . . . here we go." Okuda felt pleasantly giddy as he pried one of the binders out of its row and opened it. He saw the telltale labeling on the first page, a series of coded numbers over a Xerox of a freehand signature. Okuda smiled. Contrary to popular myth, heroin addicts are not antisocial creatures who nod off in shadowy opium dens with needles sticking out of their arms. The heroin high is so transformative, so monolithic to the central nervous system, that the junkie cannot help but become a hail-fellow-well-met. It's only when sobriety kicks in a few hours later that the addict wakes up in hell. "I believe the first ten pages or so are from that day," Okuda said as he handed over the binder. "The ranger's a young lady named Lori Havers. Can't tell you much about her . . . except that she was assigned to the Mount Cairn trailhead, which was the area in which the mummy was found."

The profiler opened the binder and started reading.

"If memory serves, I think she came from Denver, had a master's degree in social work, something like that," Okuda went on. "She left the ranger service shortly after all this happened. I think she moved back to Denver. Feel free to take a seat." Okuda gestured at the conference table. "Take all the time you need, and use the interoffice phone to call me if you need anything, just dial eight-two-one."

The profiler nodded a thank-you and sat down at the conference table.

His eyes never left the pages of the diary.

March 19

*What happened today . . . it started like any other day
and it ended like a dream. But I feel like I should get it
all down on paper before I start forgetting stuff. So . . .
here goes.*

*It was about 6:45 in the morning and I was sitting
in my ranger shack and I think I was actually reading a
newspaper and having my first cup of coffee of the day. I
should mention that I heard them before I saw them.
That much I remember really well. I heard this intense
bickering over the sound of the creek and the birds. I heard
this man and woman bickering. I couldn't tell what they
were arguing about, but they were mad. You could hear
the anger in their voices. Mostly it was the woman, rant-
ing and raving at her husband.*

*I looked out the shack's window and saw them about
a hundred yards away, at the trailhead, where the birch
trees clear, a middle-aged couple with this big object between them. At first I thought it was a big cocoon or a
wasp nest or something. It was dark and oblong shaped
and it had sticks at each end. I grabbed my walkie-talkie
and rushed out of the shack.*

*And I'm going, "Excuse me! Excuse me!" I remember
my heart was beating, because I could tell they were trying to remove something from the park—whatever the
hell it was—and all I could think of was the strict guidelines they hammer into our brains in training about not
removing any natural flora or fauna from the park,
and I'm going, "Sir! Ma'am! EXCUSE ME!"*

*And here they come—this wealthy couple in their de-
signer hiking garb—and I start telling them they can't
remove anything from the park, regulations and all that,
and this lady starts yelling at me!*

*"You don't understand, you don't understand," she
kept saying, huffing and puffing as she dragged this*

thing toward me. She looked exhausted, lugging her end of the thing with veins bulging in her skinny neck.

I have to pause here for a brief aside: usually this kind of woman would make me want to wretch—up here with her designer hiking gear and straight-off-the-rack hiking boots, scared to death of breaking one of her manicured nails—but this woman looked rattled. She looked like she had just seen a ghost and it was immediately putting me on my guard.

Another aside: it had been a mild winter in Alaska this year—and was turning out to be a warm, wet spring—so the ground around the trailhead was really soft and moist. And I remember this thing they were carrying made a splat when they dropped it on the parkway in front of my shack. And the lady's going, "I know we probably shouldn't have touched anything, but I couldn't see leaving it up there, you know, so sue me, I'm sorry."

Her husband was this big geeky guy in this stupid velour coat who looked like he wanted to scream but didn't have the guts. And he just stood there in a sort of daze.

Finally I took a closer look at it and realized what it was.

It's hard to explain, but staring down at that leathery thing, that corpse or mummy or whatever it was, I could not speak for the longest time. I couldn't move. I couldn't do anything but stare. I know I'm supposed to be a professional and all that, I'm supposed to be trained to handle emergencies, but Jesus God, they never said anything about human corpses in the Fisheries and Wildlife Handbook. I don't even think I took a breath. The look on that thing's face!

I had no idea what to do. I tried to think. But all I remember is staring at that shriveled, brown body at our feet and not being able to formulate any thoughts whatsoever. They told me where they found it. Actually it was the husband who found the thing. And when he told me where he found it—by the 10k trail marker—I was even more puzzled. That part of the trail is one of the most traveled areas on the mountain. It's like this crossroads where the beginner trail gives way to the intermediate. I'd guess about a million people have been over that spot since the park opened back in '27. Nearly eighty spring thaws. And it's this idiot who finds the thing!

Finally I told the two of them to go ahead and have a seat in my shack, and I would be right with them after I called the cops.

I'll never forget that couple: Helen and Richard Ackerman from Wilmette, Illinois. Later I found out all about their rich midwestern lifestyle, their dogs, their cars, their sailboat, and all that nonsense, as I was trying to piece together the chronology of their discovery. But anyway, I finally got them safely tucked away in the shack and then I took out my cell phone and dialed the sheriff's department.

The only person on duty at the sheriff's department at that time of the morning was this young deputy named Nick Sabitine. I knew Nick from county softball games. He was a decent guy, kind of shy . . . anyway . . . Nick was also kinda fond of looking over the shoulders of detectives. I guess he had written a number of memos to his superiors requesting future placement in training programs. Anyway, needless to say, when my frantic call came over radio dispatch that morning, Nick Sabitine's ears perked right up.

The deputy made the drive up to the trailhead in less than 20 minutes. By the time he got there, I was a bundle of nerves, trying to simultaneously keep the gawkers away from the body while keeping the Ackermans from tearing the ranger shack apart.

Taking one look at the body—especially the expression on its face—Nick got everybody out of there and cordoned off the area with yellow crime scene tape. He put the Ackermans in the back of his prowler (which wasn't easy, I have to say), then he called in the crime lab.

Another thing I should mention: Nick had no proof at that early stage—other than that hideous expression on the mummy's face—that this case was anything other than an unlucky climber or a hiker who had wandered off the trail and into a ravine. Any suggestion that there was foul play involved or whatever would not come until about an hour later, when Lieutenant Alan Pinsky, a detective from the Anchorage District 7 Homicide Squad, showed up at the scene.

Pinsky showed up around eleven o'clock, I think it was, and he totally took charge. I don't know whether this guy has some kind of Napoleonic complex or what. He's a little guy, totally bald, but he's a powerful personality. Dressed in his Columbo trench coat. With those little cunning beady eyes. Anyway, I'm not complaining. He treated me with nothing but respect and courtesy. But he took charge immediately.

I remember him saying that he thought the body might be the last missing member of that climbing team that got stranded a couple of years ago. I also remember the little detective's eyes sparkling with interest as he knelt down by the corpse and looked it up and down.

I told Pinsky we were keeping the folks who had found the mummy in the prowler.

Pinsky looked up at me and he goes, "Do you think they found this poor schmuck's johnson up there?"

I went, "Huh?"

And Pinsky says, "His penis, his cock." And then he pointed at the mummy's groin.

Pinsky examined the body for a few minutes, and then he told Nick to call the college, the one in Anchorage, the one with a department of physical anthropology.

By that point Nick already had his notebook out, and had his ballpoint pen clicked, and he was writing like crazy.

So then Nick goes roaring off in his cruiser, leaving Pinsky and me to deal with the crowd of hikers gathering on the other side of the tape, and also with the Ackermans, who were, by that point, following me around and yelling at me.

I watched Pinsky handle everybody like a pro. But he had his hands full with Helen Ackerman, who, by that point, was in no mood for another interview. She had some kind of nail wrap or facial or whatever scheduled for that afternoon at the Eskimo Village Resort in Anchorage, and no little "Jew" detective was going to keep her cooped up in this hideous shack one instant longer.

Another aside: this lady was the vilest kind of anti-Semite, which was ironic, since, according to their interview, she had married a Jewish man. God, it takes all kinds.

Anyway, Pinsky finally got so sick of her that he told the Ackermans they could go. The Ackermans left in a huff, the husband following the angry wife like a lapdog, and Pinsky and I sat on the hood of his car for a while, talking about whatever. I got the feeling that even then, just sitting in the sun, chatting, the little detective was getting information out of me. He was a real pro, this guy.

The dude from the university arrived 45 minutes later. Michael Okuda was his name, a young Asian guy. He exchanged greetings with Pinsky and me, then carried his little backpack over to the thawing body.

Pinsky and I stood close by as this guy knelt down by the body and studied it.

Finally Pinsky goes, "What do you think?"

And the young guy mumbled something without taking his eyes off the body.

And Pinsky asked him what he just said.

And this Okuda guy looked up at us and went, "Holy shit." I swear to God that's what he said. Those are Michael Okuda's exact words. And he proceeds to tell us this body is really old.

Pinsky asked him how old.

And he goes, "Old-old."
And Pinsky looked at the guy and said, "Like a hun-
dred years . . . what?"
And Okuda goes: "Like freaking neolithic old."
And that's basically how it all started.

Grove looked at his watch. It said 9:07. He closed the binder. He had been sitting in the archive room for nearly an hour, reading and rereading the ranger's diary. He had a knotted feeling in the pit of his stomach.

The phone was sitting on a file cabinet across the room. Grove went over and dialed 8-2-1, and after a single ring Okuda's voice was on the other end.

"The Ackermans, Helen and Richard," Grove said into the phone.

"Who?" Okuda sounded sleepy.

"The hikers, the people that found the Iceman."

"The Ackermans . . . right."

"How do I get in touch with them?"

After a pause Okuda said, "I'm sure we've got their contact information somewhere around here. Gimme a minute, and I'll bring it in."

"Great, thanks."

Grove hung up the phone and went back over to the ID bin, checking for any other possible sources. He crouched down by the tightly packed rows of binders, tilting his head so he could read the sideways labels, which were mostly cryptic interdepartmental code such as PALEO-3-XX-ID and PERSONAL EAX-4-O3 and QUANT-OX. His gut burned, and his head swam with dizziness. He hadn't consumed anything other than coffee since he had returned on the red-eye from Vegas the previous night, and he hadn't enjoyed much sleep. Was that why he kept having these damned spells? He needed to eat something, and he needed to talk to Tom Geisel, and he needed to talk to Maura County. But all that would have to wait because he was on fire. He had found a doorway into Sun City, and he had that amazing, delicious, secret feeling that a criminologist sometimes gets when a break is imminent. But this time, more than any other case he had worked on in the past, he sensed the strange clockwork of unseen forces at work.

He had first noticed it the previous week, when he had gone out to Colorado to profile the forest preserve murder, the dead garbage man, and the dizziness had washed over him. He had not mentioned it to the Denver doctors, but the fainting spell had been accompanied by a rush of something much more inchoate than dizziness, something like a transmission of images, maybe even fragments of memory, coursing through his brain, far too rapidly to grasp onto anything. He had noticed it again when he had first glimpsed the Iceman. A flood of images slamming through his mind's eye. But now, as the mystery of Sun City unfolded like an onion being peeled, Grove sensed something inexplicable catalyzing events, as though each successive layer was revealing something *underneath* the truth.

The sound of knocking pierced his rumination, and he looked up from the bin. "Yeah, come in!"

A thin, bald, suntanned man appeared in the doorway, a sheepish look on his slender face. "The kid said I'd find you in here."

Grove found himself staring at Terry Zorn. "What the hell are you doing here?"

"We need to talk."

Grove stood up. "I thought you were staying in Vegas to work the Kenly case."

"Yeah, well, I got to thinking."

"Is that right?"

"Those things I said to you, about being a joke, about being washed up and all." Zorn paused, licking his lips, glancing around the room as though he were having trouble putting it into words. "I just wanted you to know . . . I meant every goddamn word I said."

Laughter burst out of the Texan.

Grove rolled his eyes.

Finally Zorn got himself under control and said, "Okay, so y'all got something cookin' in that big brain of yours."

"What do you want, Terry?"

"I want to help, I want to work the case." Zorn's face hardened then. "I'm sorry I got uppity on ya. That was wrong. But I'm with ya now, and I want this guy as bad as y'all."

Grove looked at him. "You're serious now."

Zorn shrugged. "You got a theory, let's run it down. Let's do some detective work."

"No more bullshit?"

Zorn gave him an "honest Injun" gesture.

"And I'm still the lead on Sun City?"

"Always."

"And you're going to back me all the way down the line?"

"It's a privilege to work with ya, Ulysses, really."

After a long moment Grove pointed at the ID bin. "Okay, here's the thing: I think the probability is very high that the Sun City perp is somewhere in that file. I won't lie to you, Terry, it's gonna take a lot of thumb-work, a lot of reading, but I think he's in there somewhere."

Zorn grinned at him. "Then let's get busy and find the murderin' son of a bitch."

7

Breaking Open the Dark

Later that morning, alone in her motel room, scrolling through her e-mails, Maura County came across the following message from her mother:

Subj: hello sweetheart
Date: 3/17/05 10:12:57 AM Pacific standard time
From: Irenemcounty8@aol.com
To: Mcounty@Discovermagazine.com

Honey, I'm just following up on that little talk we had last week (the one about fixing you up with a nice man—ha!) I saw Roger Simonton in the A&P yesterday and he told me about his boy Carl being almost done with law school. (Hint-hint!) I understand the young man goes to Loyola University in Chicago and spent last summer working in the Peace Corps with the Jesuits in some god-awful place in the South Pacific. He sounds like such an interesting boy and the best part about him is he's single! Wouldn't it be nice to have a lawyer in the family? Ha-ha! But seriously, honey, I would

think you would have so much in common with
this boy with your love of rocks and old bones
and history and things. In case you're interested
his name is Carl Simonton (a good Catholic boy!)
and his phone number is (312) 986-3411. I'm not
pressuring you, honey. I'm just passing along the
information. A mother worries, right? Anyhoo, I
hope you're taking those calcium and glucosamine
pills. Remember all the osteoporosis you have to
look forward to. Just kidding. Ta, honey!
Love,
Mom

Maura laid her head on the edge of the motel room
desk and let out an exasperated sigh. Dressed in a ratty
pink Go-Gos sweatshirt, her hair pulled back into a
tight ponytail (in lieu of a much-needed shampoo), she
felt like screaming. On top of all the stress of the Iceman
project, she still had to contend with constant dispatches
from her mother. She adored her mom but sometimes
wanted to strangle the woman. Reaching for her pack of
cigarettes, she pulled out the last bent soldier from the
package, lit it up, then pressed the Reply icon on her
e-mail desktop and quickly pecked out the following response:

Subj: re: hello sweetheart
Date: 3/17/05 11:19:12 AM Pacific standard time
From: Mcounty@Discovermagazine.com
To: Irenemcounty8@aol.com

Dear Mom—
Thanks for your concern but I've decided to run
away and join the circus. I've fallen madly in love
with the human torso and we've decided to get
married. His name is Wolfgang Cockenlacher, and
he's such a neat guy—he's a practicing atheist

and leans a little toward necrophilia in his sexual preference, and of course there's the lack of limbs, but nobody's perfect, right? He's determined to make an honest woman out of me! We're registered at Madam Xena's House of Pain and Adult Book Emporium for wedding gifts—or feel free to send money in small unmarked bills. We're looking at a spring wedding (mostly because that's when Wolfy gets out of jail on that totally unfair morals charge brought against him by the bearded lady). Ta-ta!

Love,
Maura

Maura snubbed out the cigarette in a soap dish overflowing with butts. Her motel room was designated nonsmoking, but she didn't care. She was a tangle of nerves lately. Especially with the mummy project going in such a completely unexpected and disturbing direction. Maura wondered what her mother would say if she knew her daughter was actually developing a schoolgirl crush on an obsessive black FBI profiler—a man who also happened to be *married*. Maura hated herself for even noticing the ring on Ulysses Grove's finger. What the hell was wrong with her? Was she that desperate?

She glanced across the room at the cluttered bedside table. Amid the bottles of moisturizer, baby oil, and Chap-Stick—the Alaskan spring was playing havoc with Maura's fair skin—was a stack of files at least six inches deep fanning across the table, most of it background on famous mummified remains found through the ages that she had asked one of the editorial assistants back at the magazine to fax to her in Alaska. She got up, went over to the table, and rifled through the files. Finally she located the baby-blue plastic folder that Okuda had given her the previous evening, and inside it she found the e-mail list of leading archaeologists. She returned to her laptop with the list under her arm.

She began typing the following e-mail to be copied to all the research institutions on Okuda's list:

Subj: Fwd: An open invitation to the archeological community
Date: 3/17/05 11:33:07 AM Pacific standard time
From: Mcounty@Discovermagazine.com
To: patelfossil48@Dukeuniversity.edu

Dr. Patel—

Your organization was referred to me as a potentially excellent resource for an unprecedented project that I am currently researching. I realize this is a completely unsolicited request, and if you are too busy or unable to participate for whatever reason, please accept my best wishes. But if you are the slightest bit intrigued, please read on. . . .

You are probably familiar with the Mount Cairn Iceman discovered a year ago in Alaska's Lake Clark National Park. This adult neolithic male, carbon-dated back to the mid- to early Copper Age, is the most perfectly preserved find of its kind in the history of the field. But the most interesting aspect to this discovery is the apparent cause of death.

At first, it was thought that the Iceman had died of natural causes—perhaps had fallen or had become too exhausted at such a high altitude to survive—but recent X-rays of the body have revealed wounds in the mummy that could not possibly have been self-inflicted. Experts suspect a "wrongful death."

Murder, human sacrifice, or some other version
of foul play.

Attached you will find diagrams and analysis showing the exact position of the body, the injuries, the
cause of death, and a fascinating addendum written by an actual FBI profiler, speculating on the
signature, modus operandi, and possible motives
of the Iceman's killer.

During the course of writing a series of articles on
this subject, I have come up with an idea inspired
by the FBI's database of modern serial crimes.
Dubbed VICAP (Violent Criminal Apprehension
Program), the bureau's database is used to cross-
reference and inform the investigations of current
unsolved crimes. Since the Iceman was killed
6,000-plus years ago, why not develop a similar database for the ancient world? Why not
create a sort of VICAP program for the mummy
record?

This is where you and your organization come
into the picture. I would like to invite you or a rep-
resentative of your organization to report similar
causes of death you have observed in the archeological record from the last six millennia.

You do not have to concentrate only on the Copper
Age. Any era is appropriate. What I am looking for
are causes of death found upon examination of
mummified remains—or in the fossil record—
that match or at least approximate the attached
MO.

I should also add that if you are located anywhere
near the Bay Area—or are planning to visit this area

in the near future—please let me know as we can make accommodations for you and your staff to visit the DISCOVER offices. A sort of miniconference is planned for the near future, so if you are interested in attending, please let me know.

Thank you in advance, and all the best wishes—

Maura County, Contributing Editor
Class Mark Publishing
415-567-1259 (wk)
415-332-1856 (cell)

The FBI agents kept Michael Okuda hopping throughout the rest of that day. The profilers wanted contact information on the dozens of people who had come into close proximity to the mummy during those frantic days immediately following its discovery—including the hikers, the ranger, the deputy, the detective, any stray onlookers who might have left their names and addresses, the lab driver who transported the remains to the U of A, and even the research assistants who had helped clean and prepare the specimen for analysis. On top of all that, the profilers required a private, dedicated room with a single, isolated phone line. The room was no problem—there were plenty of deserted cubbyholes in the lower levels of the Schliemann Building—but the isolated phone line was a bitch. Okuda had to run a fifty-foot duplex cable into an archive room and steal one of Dr. Mathis's extensions behind her back. The lab director wanted nothing to do with Grove and Zorn, and had made herself scarce that day, which was fine with Okuda. He didn't need the added stress of having Mathis looking over his shoulder all day, asking him where the hell those mitochondrial test results were, while he tried to make the FBI guys happy.

But as the afternoon waned, the stress started pressing down on Okuda. The line of dope he had done that morning had long since worn off, leaving him jittery and nauseated. He couldn't eat. He had trouble concentrating on Grove's myriad of questions, and he found it difficult to focus on the mitochondrial readouts. One particular question gnawed at Okuda: what did Keanu's tattoos mean?

Grove had inquired about this repeatedly, and it seemed like such a non sequitur. If Grove was pursuing a garden-variety copycat, why worry about deciphering the tattoos? Did Grove think the copycat had somehow *translated* them? And what made this all the more troubling for Okuda was the fact that the meaning of the tattoos was a subject over which he had agonized *himself* for months. Years ago, on a postgraduate fellowship at Harvard, Okuda had worked with the infamous Archimedes Project—an international group of scholars dedicated to collating dead languages and symbols into a workable database. Okuda had been a whiz at symbology and pictography, especially those of pre-Sumerian origins. But the strange markings on the backs of the Mount Cairn mummy's knees continued to perplex Okuda, and haunt his dope-fueled dreams:

Those jagged petals, which had always reminded Okuda of tiny arrowheads, most certainly meant something trenchant and inexorable, perhaps even primal, to the Iceman. But they continued to remain elusive. Which was why Okuda was so intrigued by Grove's keen interest in them.

By late afternoon, the young Asian was exhausted. He told the profilers they would have to come back the following morning because the lab needed attention, and Okuda had made plans for the evening. Thankfully, Special Agent Grove found enough mercy in his heart to stop for the evening. Okuda liked Grove. The other guy, Zorn, was a difficult prick, but Grove seemed like a decent human being, thoughtful and cultured. After the profilers departed, Okuda hurried into the southwest lower-level men's room and snorted enough dope to anesthetize a rhinoceros. By six o'clock that evening, the lab was nearly deserted and Okuda was in the mood to relax.

He didn't feel like going home to his pathetic little studio apartment, which was located in the depressing student ghetto of Hausman Flats, so he called Wendy Hecht, his girlfriend, a grad student working on her PhD in physical anthropology, and he invited her over to the lab to hang out and maybe watch a movie. They did that sometimes. There was a plasma screen in the staff lounge, and a stack of DVDs, and Okuda knew how to disable the mag lock so they could have some privacy from the prying gazes of passing janitors.

Forty-five minutes later, Miss Hecht appeared outside the ground-floor loading dock entrance. A bosomy Jewish girl of indeterminate age, she wore denim and flannel, and carried a narrow brown paper sack containing a bottle of Quervo Gold tequila and a couple of lemons. Okuda gave her a sloppy kiss and led her down the rear stairs into the secure area, breaking several cardinal rules of laboratory security protocol.

They were hurrying, hand in hand, down the central corridor toward the lounge, like naughty children, when Miss Hecht whispered, "Any chance for a lowly doctoral candidate to sneak another peek at the Schliemann's crown jewel?"

Okuda didn't even break stride. "My dear, if you want me to drop my trousers you just have to ask."

"Very funny. C'mon, Mikey, is he out of the freezer today?"

Okuda sighed. "Yes, he's still articulated, and yes, you can take another look, but just for a second."

He ushered her around a corner, then hustled her through the dry lab. They tiptoed through the wet containment wing until they reached the door of Keanu's chamber. They gazed through the thermo-glass like two kids staring longingly through a toy store window.

The dark, leathery shape lay prone on the table, arms like cinnamon sticks, skin like bark. Centuries in ice will burn a rictus of a grin into a face—a curing back of the lips. The specimen looked to Okuda as though he were smiling at the ceiling. Another thought flickered across Okuda's mind: *he looks different.*

"All right, the peep show's over, c'mon," Okuda whispered, gently tugging at his girlfriend's arm.

"Hold on a second."

"C'mon, *now.*"

Okuda dragged Miss Hecht and her tequila out of the wet containment wing, then hastened her back down long, empty corridors buzzing with dead fluorescent light. They reached the lounge and glanced over their shoulders, ever the mischievous children checking for parents. The lab remained as silent as a coal mine.

"That's better," Okuda purred after securing them inside the cozy little lounge filled with plastic armchairs, bulletin boards, laminate cabinets, and the odors of stale smoke and burned coffee. They got out paper cups and poured some tequila and bit into lemons and giggled and tongue-kissed. A few minutes later, Wendy Hecht wandered over to the large-screen TV and started going through the loose stacks of DVDs. "Oh my God," she exclaimed suddenly, selecting one of the DVDs. "What an appropriate title for this dreary place!"

Okuda was zoning out on the sofa. "Don't do this to me," he murmured.

"Let's watch it." She giggled, loading the silver disc into the deck above the TV.

A few seconds of black, and then the telltale opening of an old black-and-white Boris Karloff chestnut was flickering and popping on the huge screen. A cardboard cutout pyramid rotated toward the screen, and then the big ominous title dripped into view: THE MUMMY.

"Not this again," Okuda groaned.

"Hush!" Miss Hecht trotted back to the sofa and settled in next to her boyfriend, and Okuda put his arm around her and shook his head as the old Tchaikovsky music warbled on the ancient soundtrack.

They drank tequila and sucked on lemons and watched the musty old tale of a group of archaeologists from the British Museum who unearth an Egyptian mummy called Imhotep. Ignoring the warnings of occult experts, the scientists defy the alleged curse and break the seal on the infamous "scroll of Toth," inadvertently reanimating the remains. The monster, played to the hilt by Karloff, shambles around the film in filthy shreds and baleful glares, terrifying everybody in his path.

Okuda had seen the movie about a dozen times over the years, at Harvard, at work, at various parties. But *this* time, when the first big shock scene came on-screen, Michael Okuda got very quiet and watched. Maybe it was the dope working on him, or the exhaustion, or something else, but Okuda watched the part where Karloff first opens his eyes, and slowly unfolds his ragged arms, and all at once Okuda got the feeling he was on the verge of figuring out the Iceman's tattoos.

A mummy reaching down and gently, almost tenderly, run-

*ning a petrified fingertip along an ancient scroll . . . insane
laughter coming from somewhere offscreen.*

"Michael? Mikey— You okay?"

Okuda snapped out of his momentary fugue state
and stared at his girlfriend. "Yeah . . . I'm fine. I just have
to make some notes."

The conversation that would forever be thought of
in Grove's mind as the first significant break in the Sun
City case took place the following morning in a small
conference room in the lower level of the Schleimann
Building. The room, a musty confine of forgotten ar-
chives, appeared to be the repository of a decade's
worth of corporate detritus. Stacks of cardboard boxes
rose to the ceiling on one side of the room, while reams
of documents bound with rubber bands covered the
oval laminate table in the center of the room.

Throughout most of the conversation Zorn sat on a
metal cadenza in the corner of the room, listening,
while Grove circled the table like a restless predator cir-
cling its prey.

A woman's voice sizzled through the tiny housing of
a conference speaker sitting precariously on a pile of
manila folders: "Can I ask what this is in reference to?"

"It's in reference to the discovery of human remains
on Mount Cairn a year ago—"

"Oh God."

"Excuse me?"

Shuffling noises on the other end. "For God's sake,
how many times do I have to go through this?"

"I'm sorry, ma'am, but we're just, um, gathering information at this point."

"There's no more information left to gather."

"I'm sorry?"

"I answered every question that annoying little detective could think of—what was his name?—Pinkham?"

"Pinsky?" Grove offered.

"That's it. Jesus, I talked with that old Jew at least half a dozen times last year."

A glance between Grove and Zorn. "I apologize, Mrs. Ackerman, if some of this seems a little redundant."

A sigh. "Oh, for heaven's sake call me Helen."

"Helen it is."

"Why are you people still torturing me?"

Grove measured his words. "The truth is, Helen, there may be something we missed that day that might help us with another case."

"That stupid goddamn mummy has been the bane of my existence."

"I promise we'll make this as painless as—"

"What possible difference could it make to anyone what I was wearing at the time or what direction the wind was blowing or what I had for breakfast that morning?"

"I know you've probably heard this before, but any detail no matter how minor might be helpful to us."

After a pause: "Go ahead and ask me your questions, get it over with, I got a Junior League meeting in an hour."

"We'll make it quick, I promise." Grove looked at his notes. "Now according to Detective Pinsky's logs, you and your husband, Richard, were taking a hike when you stumbled across the Iceman?"

Through the speaker: "For the umpteenth time, yes, we were out early because we wanted to make it to the summit before the afternoon showers rolled in because we had heard from the concierge at the resort that the sunrise was lovely but you had to hurry to get up and down before the rains came, so, yes, we were on our way up the trail when we found that hideous, disgusting frozen bag of bones."

Grove made a note, then glanced up at the speaker box. "Can I ask who saw it first?"

After a moment: "What?"

"The mummy, I'm wondering who saw it first that morning, you or your husband."

"Like I told the detective, Richard saw it first. At least I *think* he saw it. What difference does it make? When I finally saw what he was fooling with I thought it was a coat, like somebody had left a leather coat up there. But then I realized, who in their right mind would leave a gorgeous distressed leather garment up on the side of a mountain?"

"So your husband saw the mummy first?"

"What did I just say? Yes, for God's sake, Richard saw the thing first."

Grove leaned closer to the speaker. "May I ask what you meant when you said you *think* he saw it?"

An exasperated sound on the other end. "Here we go again. Okay, look, for the last time . . . I didn't see a thing at first. All right? Richard tripped over something, and I looked, and there was nothing there. I swear to God there was nothing there. No stump, no rock, but Richard's on his ass, and he's staring at this empty trail."

A beat of silence.

"Would it be possible for us to talk to Mr. Ackerman today as well?"

Another pause. "Are you serious? Are you kidding me?"

"Is there a problem?"

A flinty laugh spewed out of the speaker. "Let's see, is there a problem, let me think . . . um, yeah, I think you could definitely say there's a problem with putting Richard on the phone today."

Another glance between Grove and Zorn. Finally Grove told the woman to go on.

Through the speaker her voice sounded as taut as a high-tension wire. "If you two clowns did your homework you would know that my husband went out for a pack of cigarettes about a year ago and never came back."

Grove and Zorn looked at each other. Silence gripped the room.

Grove's pulse quickened.

Maura sat alone at a corner table in the Mariott Courtyard's crowded coffee shop, picking at a soggy BLT sandwich, absently going through her notes for an article that she was not sure she would ever publish, when she noticed a familiar figure out of the corner of her eye sweeping past the hostess stand, lugging along a suit bag and briefcase. Dressed in a smart Burberry overcoat, Ulysses Grove looked distracted and harried as he stood there for a moment, scanning the bustling restaurant. Maura felt a faint stirring in her chest when their gazes met. Grove's eyes lit up as he came over to her.

"There she is," he said, coming up to her table and giving her his warm, open face.

"You leaving us?" she asked.

"Yeah, um . . ." He nodded at her barely touched food. "I'm sorry to interrupt your lunch, but you mind walking with me for a second?"

She closed her folder. "Not at all. I'd love to, I was done anyway."

They left the restaurant, then went out the closest exit into the raw wind of the Alaskan midday. Grove told her he was on his way to the cab stand, and Maura had to practically trot to keep up with him. They strode along a weathered boardwalk that wrapped around the front of the motel, quickly sidestepping slow-moving guests and bellhops laden with luggage carts. Grove explained that there had been a break in the case, and he was going to be flying to Illinois that afternoon with his associate, Special Agent Zorn, to conduct an interview, and he needed to ask Maura something before he pursued this particular lead. Maura said she would tell him whatever she knew.

"These folks that discovered the Mount Cairn mummy," he said, loping along.

"Right." Maura nodded, remembering the phone conversation she'd had last year with the wife. "What was their name? The Ackermans?"

"Right . . . so, anyway, what I'm wondering is . . . you interviewed them for the article?"

She nodded, hurrying to keep up. "Yes. The wife. I spoke to her briefly on the phone."

"Did you notice anything—you know—out of the ordinary? Strange?"

"*Strange?*" Maura thought about it. "Not really. She was a little . . . how do I put it?"

"Bitchy?"

Maura grinned. "That's the word I was looking for."

"Anything else?"

Maura shrugged as she walked. "Not really. She just gave me a thumbnail of what they were doing when they stumbled upon the thing."

Grove nodded as they approached the circular drive in front of the courtyard. The cab stand was busy. Grove paused, waving at an airport van waiting for him at the bottom of the drive about twenty yards away. A man in a Stetson hat stood outside the van, leaning against its rear quarter panel, reading a newspaper, presumably also waiting for Grove. Maura assumed that the cowboy was the mysterious Agent Zorn with whom Grove had vanished a couple of days ago.

"There's something else I wanted to mention," Grove said in a low, conspiratorial tone. He seemed exceedingly distracted, anxious.

"Sure, go ahead." Maura waited in the wind.

"You're cold, we'll talk about it later."

"No, please—go ahead."

He rubbed his chin nervously. "I'm not good at this kind of stuff."

"Just say it. Anything. It's okay."

He looked at her. "I lost my wife to cancer four years ago, and not a day goes by I don't think about it."

"Oh my God, I'm sorry." Maura's brain suddenly flooded with contrary emotions. "I'm so sorry."

"The thing of it is, I need to get on with my life. Hannah would have kicked my ass, would have wanted me to do just that."

Maura had no idea where this was going. "She would have been right, too."

"The thing is, what I wanted to ask you is, after all this is over . . . if you might want to—I don't know—go have some coffee or something."

Maura was nodding like crazy. "Absolutely, yeah . . . coffee would be nice."

"Excellent, excellent," he said, awkwardly backing away from her as though he might trip over his own feet. "I'll be in touch, take care!"

He turned and made his way down the walk to the waiting van, and Maura watched, her eyes stinging from the wind and unexpected emotion welling up inside her.

8

Ghost in a Three-piece Suit

"Should be up here on the left." Grove glanced up from his MapQuest directions and studied the tasteful split-rail fencing running along the road. They had just made the fifteen-mile journey from O'Hare International Airport through a violent spring storm, but now the rains had lifted and the night had become crystalline and shiny.

"I'm in the wrong goddamn business," Zorn offered as he pulled the sedan over to the curb in front of 2233 N. Linden Avenue.

They found themselves in a world of graceful Victorians and old manicured trees. Gaslights dotted the parkways. Raindrops pinged off copper gutters. Everything had the patina of old money.

The Ackerman house was a massive Queen Anne with a wraparound screened porch and more roof pitches on it than an eighteenth-century hotel. Most of the shades were drawn. Gaslights burned along the cobblestone walk. Grove and Zorn put on their suit jackets before climbing out of the car, Zorn clamping his cowboy hat down over his gleaming pate. They traversed the vast lawn in silence, ultimately ascending the wide steps to the huge oak front door.

The bell sounded like something from the belfry at St. Mary's Cathedral.

"Yessuh?" A plump black woman in a pale blue uniform peered out at them from behind the enormous door. "Help you with something?"

Grove introduced himself and his partner, then told the maid they were here to see Mrs. Ackerman.

"She expecting y'all?"

"I believe she is, yeah," Grove said with a smile.

The housekeeper let them in, then told them it would be just a minute.

The two men waited in the spacious foyer as the maid vanished within the depths of the first floor. Grove glanced around at the mansion's interior, marveling at the burnished quality of the place, the rich furnishings. The air had that museum-quality odor that old mansions get—a mixture of must, wood, oil, and rich spices. A gigantic hardwood staircase dominated the entryway, sweeping down from the second-floor gallery. Grove could just imagine Helen Ackerman coming down those stairs during a party in her Versace or Donna Karan like a general about to survey her troops.

Grove knew this area—Wilmette, Illinois—from his childhood.

He had grown up ten miles to the south, in a much seedier part of Chicago known as Uptown. Uptown kids never came this far north. Uptown kids played street hockey in litter-strewn alleys and joined gangs and grew up hard and mean. The ones that didn't end up in jail usually became factory rats or city workers. Once in a great while they might join the military, and maybe even go to college on the GI bill. And maybe, just maybe, once every million years or so, an Uptown kid might make it all the way to the top slot at the FBI's Behavior Science Unit.

The murmur of a voice could be heard from somewhere within the house, perhaps the housekeeper summoning her mistress on an intercom. Grove thought of his mother, who was roughly the maid's same age, and certainly from the same socioeconomic rung. Vida Grove still lived just south of there. In fact, she was down there at this very moment, somewhere in the canyons of condos and tenements along Lawrence Avenue, huddling in that same stuffy little apartment in which Grove had spent his formative years. She was probably busily making some kind of hideous African stew on that ancient potbellied stove. Grove remembered warming his hands over the embers of that stove on cold winter mornings. He remembered the cold wafting up the back of those awful hand-dyed dashikis she used to make him wear to school. Over the years Grove had successfully blocked all that out of his conscious memory. He had completely excised it from his life, and that was why he was perfectly comfortable with visiting the Chicago area on business and not even considering calling his mother.

"I hope we can get this over with in a hurry," said a voice from across the vestibule.

The men turned and saw Helen Ackerman standing at the base of the staircase in a cranberry velour warm-up suit and a scarf tied around her graying head. She couldn't have been more than five feet tall, but she had a regal sort of bearing with her patrician nose and eyes gleaming like black cinders. Her bracelets jangled as she moved. "I've got a Pilates class tonight at the civic center that I cannot miss," she added as she approached the two fellows dripping on her foyer floor.

"Appreciate you seeing us, Mrs Ackerman, on such short notice," Grove said, offering his hand. "Special Agent Ulysses Grove."

Helen Ackerman's hand was bony and cold. "Interesting name," she said as she shook Grove's hand. "Ulysses . . . what is that, Greek?"

Grove smiled. "We're not sure what it is." He indicated Zorn. "This is Special Agent Zorn."

Zorn took off his hat, gave her a smile, and shook her hand. "Terry Zorn, ma'am, it's a pleasure."

"I suppose we might as well sit down," she said with a pained sort of surrender, then called over her shoulder to the housekeeper, "Alice! Coffee, please! In the sunroom!"

She led the two men through the richly appointed living room and into a breathtaking, glass-encased solarium situated off the rear of the house. A jungle of exotic plants perfumed the air. Rain ticked overhead on leaded windows. Helen Ackerman gestured toward a pair of armchairs, then flopped down on a wicker love seat near a cluster of fichus trees.

"So . . . let's see . . . you haven't seen your husband since last April, is that right?" Zorn asked after the men had taken their seats across from her. The Texan had his hat cocked casually on his knee.

Grove inwardly cringed at Zorn's bluntness. Grove thought they should finesse the information out of the woman, but Zorn thought they should get a little tough with her, maybe do the good-cop/bad-cop thing. The two men had argued about the approach all the way in from the airport.

"That's right," she said with a furtive nod. "And good riddance, if you want to know the truth."

Zorn looked at her. "You and your husband were having marital problems?"

"That's putting it mildly."

Grove chimed in: "If this is getting a little too personal, stop us . . . but could you tell us the nature of the problems?"

The woman ruefully pursed her lips. "My husband didn't exist."

"Excuse me?"

"He was the invisible man around here . . . a ghost, the ghost in the three-piece suit."

Grove pulled a small tape recorder from his briefcase, then looked up at the woman, indicating the recorder. "Do you mind?"

She waved an okay.

Grove turned the tape recorder on and said, "Do you mind elaborating on Mr. Ackerman being a ghost, as you say?"

"You want me to elaborate. Gee, okay. How about this: what kind of man goes limp after a minor little surgical procedure, gets a prescription for Viagra, and never uses it?"

There was a pause, a glance between the two men, and then Grove looked back at the woman. "Your husband had health problems?"

"He was as strong as an *ox*." She bit off the word *ox* like a child taking foul medicine. "He was also a hypochondriac, and oh my God, when they finally found that teen weeny little blockage in one of his arteries, it was like his wish had come true . . . and we're not talking a massive coronary here. It was totally curable. Big deal. They put a little tube in you, they Roto-Rooter it out. No problem. But not with Richard. Oh my God . . . you would have thought they cut his penis off. Of course he hadn't used *that* in years, so I guess it didn't make any difference."

After a beat Grove asked what Richard Ackerman did for a living.

"He crunched numbers for Deloitte and Touche," she replied with a sour look on her narrow, surgically tucked face. "Numbers, accountants . . . who cares anymore? He's gone. I get the house when the papers come through, and he's gone."

Grove measured his words. "Can you tell us about that day? When you found the mummy?"

She shrugged her skinny shoulders. "What about it?"

"Your husband was the first to stumble across the mummy?"

A thin smile crossed her face. "You could say that, yeah, he stumbled all right."

"Something funny?"

She gazed off at the rain-spangled glass as though remembering something hilarious. "He'd get these things in his head," she murmured. "Out of the clear blue, he'd decide he's going to run in the Chicago Marathon, or he's going to swim a mile, and he just goes overboard. With the outfit and the training and the equipment . . . so pathetic, a fifty-year-old man behaving like this. Anyway, we're on this cruise up in Alaska, and he decides he's going to climb this mountain—"

"—Mount Cairn?" Grove asked.

"Yes, yes, Mount Cairn, it was Mount Cairn this, and Mount Cairn that, for a week I have to hear this nonsense. And he's training on the ship, doing these ridiculous exercises, and eating raw eggs, the idiot. And I'm saying, 'Stop with the eggs already!' So finally he gets me up at four o'clock in the morning, and we drive out to the park, and we start out on this stupid climb."

"This was a technical climb you were trying?" Zorn asked.

She looked at him. "A what?"

"A technical climb, you know, with the axes and the pitons and the ropes?"

She waved her hand. "God no! An old lady could make it to the top of this thing. You walk the whole goddamn way. They had a business meeting up there for Mary Kay Cosmetics, for Chrissake, but my moron of a husband spent thousands on all this equipment, and that morning he drags me out of my warm bed, and he's got me out there in the pitch-dark. And he's bounding along, right? Like he's Sir Edmund Hillary, with this idiotic walking stick, and I'm bringing up the rear. I'm

covered in mud and I've ripped a hole in my brand-new
Eddie Bauer fleece jacket, and Richard is ignoring me,
ten paces ahead of me. And then he trips, and it was the
funniest thing I have ever seen, Richard tripping like
that—Mr. Big Time Mountain Climber—I mean, God,
it was so funny. His walking stick goes flying and he falls
on his ass and he slides about twenty yards or so. And
I'm just laughing my ass off. I remember the tears were
streaming down my cheeks, I was laughing so hard. I
don't know why that struck me as being so funny. But it
did. God, it was funny. That idiot."

She paused, and Grove asked her what happened
after that.

Helen Ackerman's smile faded. "The rest is not so
funny. I mean . . . when I figured out what he had
tripped over . . . *Jesus.*"

Grove said, "You're talking about the mummy? He
tripped over the mummy?"

She shrugged. "I guess."

Grove glanced at Zorn, who was staring at the woman,
waiting. "Go on," Grove urged the lady with a gentle
nod.

She rubbed her makeup-caked eyes. "Oh God, it
sounds so melodramatic. The eyes play tricks. Okay? It
was the thin air, or it was menopause setting in, I don't
know, but the thing is, I couldn't see the thing until he
crawled back over to that spot on the trail and touched
that thing. It was like seeing frost forming on a window."

Grove asked what she meant by "frost forming."

She was silent for a long moment—overcome by the
memory of watching her husband hunkering down
over a mummy that was visible, initially at least, only to
him—as Grove's tape recorder continued rolling, recording the leaden silence.

9

The Opposite of Divine

"So he crawls over to this slushy patch of trail, and he's staring down at the ground, and I can't see a damn thing. I mean, I'm probably as close to him as I am to that chair over there, and I'm wondering what the hell he's looking at. And he says something. I can't really hear very well at this point. I mean, the wind is blowing, and it's snowing, and it's freezing cold. But then he reaches down like he's going to stick a finger in a socket. I mean he's got that look on his face. That look that little bratty kids get when they're about to do something naughty . . . you know what I mean?"

The tape recorder sat whirring softly in the center of an oval meeting table in the conference room of the Restin, Virginia, Annex Building. The room was just large enough for the table, half a dozen swivel chairs, and a small cadenza at one end from which assistants served coffee and Danish pastry and documents.

Suddenly Grove's voice rattled out of the tiny speaker:

* * *

"What do you think he was saying?"

Helen: "I have no idea what he was saying. I mean, to this day, I've never figured out what it was he was mumbling when he crawled back over to that spot and looked down at the ground. It might have been just a moan or something. You should have seen the look on his face though. I never asked him about it . . . but it gave me the creeps."

A pause then.

Four people sat grim-faced before the tiny recorder, listening to the playback. Grove and Zorn, each in his shirtsleeves, sat at one end of the table. Tom Geisel was at the other end, chewing on a pen, his feet propped up on the corner of the table. Next to Geisel was Natalie Hoberman, a steely-eyed woman in a gray suit dress whom Geisel had recruited years ago from the Sexual Crimes Task Force. Hoberman was one of the top brass at the Serial Crimes Unit, and was a trusted sounding board on difficult cases. Grove had always got along well with her, despite her enormous ego. At the moment, Hoberman had her arms crossed across her chest as she listened skeptically to the playback.

Grove: "So when did you finally see the mummy?"

Helen (after a pause): "What do you call it when you see a flower growing real fast? In one of those hideous, boring nature films?"

Grove: "Time lapse?"

Helen: "Time lapse! Yeah, it was like that. I see Richard reaching down and touching . . . something . . . or nothing . . . but then there was something. It's hard to explain. Like an ice cube melting in reverse. I see this disgusting frozen thing, and it's taking shape right there in the slush, and he's poking at it, and I think I yelled at that

point, I think I told Richard to get the hell away from
the thing, it could have rabies, it could be crawling with
germs or whatever. He just looked up at me with this
weird expression on his face. God, he was a strange bird."

Grove: "Can you describe the expression? When he
looked at you?"

Helen: "I don't know. It was like, I don't know, like . . .
he had seen a ghost."

Grove: "And what happened then?"

Helen: "He climbed to his feet like he was drunk or
something, and he stood there staring at me with this
bizarre look on his face."

Zorn's voice: "And what did you do then?"

Helen: "I went over and saw it was a body. I guess I
went a little nuts. Never mind the look on my husband's
face! The look on that dead thing's face was . . . it was
horrible. I mean, I'd never even seen a dead body for
real before, and even though it turns out this thing was,
you know, this prehistoric man or whatever, I just kind
of freaked out."

Grove: "Go on."

Helen: "Well, you gotta understand, I didn't want to
be there in the first place. Okay? And now this! I mean,
I never would have dreamed in a million years we had
stumbled upon anything valuable or rare or important . . .
or whatever. First thing that crossed my mind was, this
was some drifter or homeless guy, or maybe somebody
from that Indian reservation who had wandered off
drunk and frozen to death."

Grove: "So what did you do then?"

Helen: "I insisted we go back, I insisted we take that
hideous thing back down to the trailhead and give it to
the cops." A brief silence then. "Look . . . I know we
probably shouldn't have moved it. They told us we actually damaged the thing, and then they kind of threatened us in this really slimy way, like somebody was gonna
sue us or something. That asshole detective—Pinsky—

he told us we actually broke its thing off in the ice when we pried it out. Which is totally ironic when you think about it."

Zorn's voice: "Its 'thing'?"

Helen: "Its thing—its prick, its penis—which by the way was stiffer than anything Richard could have come up with. And we broke it off! Me and my impotent moron of a husband . . . whose own schwantz hasn't worked in years!"

Another pause on the tape, accompanied by a series of uncomfortable shuffling noises and wry laughter from Helen Ackerman.

Natalie Hoberman spoke up. "Turn it off for a second, Ulysses. Please."

Grove reached out and snapped the Pause button.

"Does it get any better?"

Grove sighed. "If you just listen—"

"Let's hear them out, Natalie," Geisel broke in. "We're all working for the same thing here, and right now, this is all we got."

Zorn leaned forward and gave Grove a friendly slap on the back. "Hey, amigo, why don't we fast-forward to that stuff about the husband turning up missing?"

Another sigh from Grove as he picked up the tape player and fiddled with the buttons for a moment. Chipmunk gibberish squealed from the speaker as he fast-forwarded through a couple of minutes of the recording, watching the counter. At last he reached the section on Richard Ackerman's disappearance. He put the recorder back on the table and pressed the Play button. Helen's voice squawked at them.

". . . and it was the same thing when we got back home. Barely said two words to me that week after we got back. He was like a zombie, wandering around, bumping into things. Drove me crazy. He didn't go into the office, didn't go golfing, wouldn't see any of his friends. Usually just sat staring out the window. It was like he was in a deep depression or something."

Grove's voice: "Didn't you ask him what was the matter?"

Helen: "I didn't want to know. We stopped talking to each other years ago, and this was just another one of his idiotic mood swings. I always said he was bipolar. His therapist babied him like nothing you ever saw. I always thought he was on the wrong medication."

Zorn: "What about his firm? Didn't they call? Didn't they wonder where he was?"

Helen: "He was a senior VP with an army of ass-kissers covering for him. We got a few calls from Deloitte, which I don't think he ever returned. I mean, I think I heard him say maybe two words that whole week. You ask me, I think he finally blew a gasket. Or maybe had some kind of stroke. Or whatever. What difference does it make? He's gone now."

Grove: "Tell us about that."

Helen: "What do you mean?"

Grove: "His disappearance . . . the details, the circumstances."

Helen: "I woke up one morning and he was just . . . not here anymore. It's as simple as that. And to reiterate a point I made earlier: who gives a damn." (Pause.) "Wait a minute. Hold on a second. Why are you people so interested in Richard? What did he do? What did that sick fuck do now?"

Grove: "Nothing, nothing at all . . . we're just gathering information at this point, Mrs. Ackerman."

Helen: "Whatever you suspect him of, I'm sure he's probably guilty."

Grove: "Anyway . . . you were asleep when it happened? When he vanished?"

Helen: "I don't know, I guess . . . I literally went to bed a married woman . . . and when I woke up, I was single, alone in my own house. Simple as that."

Grove: "Did you hear anything in the night?"

Helen: "Nope."

Grove: "And when you woke up, did you find a note, or signs of any disturbance?"

Helen: "Nope . . . nada, nothing. The place looked like he had never even been there. His clothes were still hanging in his closet, sure, and his lucky coffee cup with the golf tee on it was still sitting upside down by the draining board . . . but that was it, those were the only signs he had ever even existed. And I threw all that crap out the next day."

Zorn: "Did you a file a missing person report, ma'am?"

Helen: "Are you kidding? The last thing I wanted was for somebody to find that idiot and drag him back home, I was delighted he was gone. I think his sister Phyllis filed a report, maybe a week or two later, I'm not sure. I've never been very close with his family. They all live in Detroit . . . Bloomington Hills, very preppie. Ivy League types. Total assholes. I'll give you their numbers, if you want to waste your time talking with those—"

Click.

Grove snapped off the player and looked at Geisel. "This is our guy . . . this is Sun City."

Geisel frowned. "You got DNA on the guy?"

"We got a hairbrush that survived the wife's scorched earth campaign . . . yes. It's on its way through the lab over at Arlington as we speak."

Hoberman was clicking her nails on the table. "And we've got DNA from the scenes?"

Grove nodded. "We've got a smorgasbord from the series, but I'm pretty sure we're gonna find a match."

"Shoes?"

"She threw out his shoes, but we got a heel impression from the Colorado scene that suggests a big man, a man Ackerman's size and weight."

Zorn spoke up. "Tell them about the tools and the tool belt."

"Tools?" Hoberman said.

Grove explained that Ackerman kept a little workshop down in his basement, very anal, everything neatly labeled, hanging on a Peg-Board. "We saw his tool belt was missing," he said with a shrug. "As well as a favorite pair of needle-nosed pliers and a linoleum knife. Which could easily match the Sun City pathology."

"Sounds pretty circumstantial," Natalie Hoberman said after a beat.

Across the room, Zorn flashed a smile. "Sweetheart, if I had a nickel for every conviction we've gotten on circumstantial evidence I'd be rich enough to take *you* out."

"Please don't call me sweetheart."

"Okay, children, let's get specific here," Geisel broke in, putting his reading glasses back on. He gazed down at the briefing document that Grove had written up for him. "We're basically basing this theory on a shared connection that Ackerman and Sun City have with the pathology of the mummy, the Iceman. Is that correct?"

Grove told him yes, that was more or less the case, then Grove pushed himself away from the table, stood, and went over to the window.

The iron-gray sky hung low over Restin, the spring breezes blustering through the elms and high-tension wires. A hundred miles to the south, tropical storm Beatrice was currently lashing the low country with hundred-mile-an-hour winds. For the past day and a half a ceiling of clouds had shrouded the entire state of Virginia, with the promise of rain in the forecast.

For just an instant Grove gazed through those blinds at the overcast day. A faint moaning noise rose and fell outside the pane, the breeze telling tales of primordial winds and flashing skies. Grove felt another dizzy spell teasing at the edges of his equilibrium. He grabbed the edge of the window to steady himself, then blinked away the faint sputter of artifacts on the back of his eyelids like flickering sunspots. *Not now,* he thought, *not in front of these people.* Finally he turned back to the room and said, "It's not just a copycat situation."

Geisel looked at him. "Excuse me?"

Grove went back over to the table and stood there with his hands in his pockets. "That's what I thought it was at first. The flaw in the pathology, the fact that Sun City left the organs intact. But now I'm not so sure. Ackerman's the guy all right, but what he's doing, the *meaning* of it . . . I believe it goes deeper than just replicating something he saw. I don't know what to make of the time lapse talk, but I'm telling you this thing goes deeper than 'copycat.'"

There was a pause then, a few eyebrows raising around the room. Hoberman glanced over at Geisel, who had resumed chewing on his pen. On the other side of the table, Zorn studied the patterns in the carpet. At last Geisel said, "You want to explain?"

Grove gestured at the little tape player sitting mute on the table. "It's in the behavior, Tom. It always is. I don't know exactly what's driving it yet, but it's in the behavior."

Another uncomfortable pause. Hoberman spoke up. "What do you want, Ulysses?"

He looked at her. "I want bulletins at every squad, in every wire room, on every onboard computer in every trooper car west of the Mississippi."

A pause, Geisel chewing the inside of his cheek, thinking it over.

Grove went on: "We got photos, we got deep background on Ackerman . . . I'd like to distribute the materials throughout the central and western regions. He's dealing with some pretty heavy dissociative behavior, he ought to be fairly easy to spot."

Hoberman kept tapping her nails. "What about money?"

"What *about* it?"

"Did he take any with him? Did the wife notice anything missing?"

Grove nodded. "He's got money, yeah—a lot of it. He had two private accounts that are showing heavy activity the day he disappeared."

"I wish *we* had some of it," Geisel said. "The guys on the third floor are killing me over budgets this year. I'm going to want DNA linkage before I write off on all this."

"Should have it by the end of the day."

Hoberman said she wanted to go back to the mummy, back to the reason why this wasn't a basic copycat situation.

"Okay, look," Grove said, beginning to pace across the end of the table, pushing down the emotion, the urgency squeezing his guts. "I realize how it sounds—all mystical and woo-woo and everything—but the behavior as related by the wife smacks of a classic psychotic break . . . and more."

Hoberman asked what he meant by "more."

"I'm still working on that part," Grove replied.

"All right, fine, so it's a work in progress," she prodded, "so give us a progress report."

Grove looked at her. "What we do over the next few weeks, our next move is huge."

"Why is that?"

Grove stopped pacing. "Because I think we're all part of Ackerman's delusional universe. Even *us*, the bureau, the shit we do."

"And what makes you think that?"

Grove shrugged. "Call it intuition, a gut hunch . . .

whatever. But that's why I think we ought to be at the next scene with a complete tactical unit. If one should occur, God forbid . . . I think he'll be there. He needs to see the aftermath, experience it, be a part of it."

Geisel shifted restlessly in his chair. "Ulysses . . . you know if there's any gut hunches I would put complete stock in, it would be yours."

"Tom, I—"

"The kind of resources you're talking about, the paperwork alone would choke a mule." Geisel shook his head, running fingers through his graying hair. "If you could just give us a little more, tell us about this hunch."

Grove wondered how far he should take this with them. He took a deep breath, then let it out with a sigh. "The reason I feel this way . . . is mostly because of the way *I* felt when I first saw the thing."

Dead silence.

"I know how it sounds," he went on. "I can't understand it myself. But there's something deep beneath the surface behavior here, that's all I can tell you. I got a taste of it when I first saw that mummy . . . when I realized it was the same signature as Sun City. The look on that face. You've got photos in your reports, you can see what I'm talking about."

"Ulysses—"

"I get paid to make judgment calls," Grove continued, pacing again. "They're all judgment calls. Subjective opinion. Maybe it's an empathetic thing here, I don't know, I really don't. But I think we should continue working up in Anchorage, and I think we should get the word out on Ackerman. Because Ackerman's our guy. That much I'm positive about. He's our guy. And that's the only part that really matters. Right?"

Another pause.

"Am I wrong about that?" Grove asked the room, getting very little reaction. "Do we have anything better than this guy? Do we like anybody else here?"

Silence.

Grove felt his pulse quickening. They had to agree with him. They had to give him what he wanted. They basically had no choice.

A thousand miles away, just outside Portland, Oregon, the man who was once Richard Ackerman lay on the floor of a squalid motel room.

Sobs shuddered through his lanky body like jolts of electricity, making his broad shoulders tremble and his grizzled face contort with agony. Faint mewling noises puffed out of him every few moments, but mostly he cried silently, convulsively. There was little pain in his weeping. It was the last remnant of his conscious mind, his last shred of humanity fighting the thing inside him.

"No, I won't," he sobbed, arguing with the voice in his head, his breath raising tiny puffs of filth off the shopworn carpet. "I'm done with it, I'm done, I won't do it again."

The voice begged to differ with him and calmly explained that he would continue to kill again and again and again and again and again until he found the right one, the right victim, the chosen one—

"No! No! Noooo!" Richard Ackerman howled in agony, pounding his fists against the floor. His fists were large, the size of gourds, but they were also knotty and rawboned. The hands of an aging artisan. These were hands that had once danced over calculators and spreadsheets, serving captains of industry, shaving millions off the corners of corporate income tax returns, now reduced to the bloodstained, psoriatic, leprous claws of a homicidal maniac.

The voice inside him ebbed suddenly, giving him temporary respite from the constant pressure on his brain. "Okay, okay, okay, I can deal with this," he uttered into the carpet. "I can beat this, I can."

He swallowed the horror and the poisonous metallic taste in his mouth, then struggled to his feet. He lumbered over to the mirror. He wore a torn flannel shirt, half the buttons missing, the front flayed open to reveal sagging, stained pectorals. Streaks of finger-painted blood and feces crisscrossed nipples haloed in gray hair. He looked at his face. Two hollow, sunken eyes buried in wrinkles stared back at him. His iron-gray hair, once meticulously coiffured by the finest Michigan Avenue stylists, now resembled a fright wig.

For a brief instant he considered bursting out of his motel room, running through the streets covered with the Nevada lady's blood, screaming at the top of his lungs for somebody to stop him, stop the thing inside him from killing again. But as quickly as the notion crossed his embattled mind, it dissolved into a caul of agony. Richard Ackerman wrenched himself away from the mirror and began prowling the edges of the room, wringing his hands, a lab rat pacing the confines of its maze.

In this state, it all seemed so clear, so obvious, so excruciatingly *pathological*. He realized he was sick. He was very sick. In some ways, he had been sick since he was a child in Cincinnati, and had secretly tortured the neighborhood pets and the errant raccoons that had wandered onto his stepfather's vast property. And all the boarding schools and private universities and political string-pulling in the world could not change the morbid images of blood and flesh that had haunted Richard Ackerman's fantasies and dreams since he was a kid. But now, all this secret deviance had come to a head. *His* head. Somehow he had managed to acquire this diabolical personality as if it were a virus or some exotic bacteria he had ingested from eating tainted food. And when it waned—as it was currently doing— he could almost think clearly.

He realized he should turn himself in. He should be in an institution where he couldn't hurt anybody. But he also knew that these thoughts would soon melt away in the acid bath of the entity's will. The entity would awaken again, erasing all knowledge and memory of his past, and get him cleaned up and fit and ready again for the Work.

The thing inside him had a shape, a color, and a texture—it was black and papery and malignant, like a face made of charred parchment. It was ravaged by a cancerous sickness, and it burned in him like a feverish furnace. It was an engine that powered his body, made him move with savage stealth toward some cosmic purpose that he could not begin to understand. He sensed it was old, very old, *ancient*, and it commandeered his body with the meticulous precision of a master puppeteer, but he was not certain about the mechanics of it. All he was sure of was that the entity was growing progressively dominant.

Soon there would be nothing left of the Old Richard Ackerman. He would have fewer and fewer of these intermittent spells of normalcy and would ultimately shrink inside himself like a tiny hard seed . . . until there was nothing left but the New Richard leading him toward some horrible objective. But even in this fleeting moment of insight—this fading state of awful self-awareness— the Old Richard Ackerman knew precisely when and where that black, silent, noxious energy had first overcome him with the abruptness of a lightning bolt.

Crawling.

Crawling . . . on his hands and knees, his face raw from the wind. Eyes stinging. Hard to see. His back wrenched from the fall, the pain screaming. He keeps crawling. Keeps crawling. He has his sights fixed on that dark object ten yards away.

That dark thing is not what it seems. That dark, leathery, brown object is important. It has shown itself to him for a reason.

He keeps moving steadily toward it. A few inches at a time, back up the ice-crusted slope. His gloves are wet from the fall, his fingers stiff with cold. Closer. In the swirling cloud of powder he can just barely make out the object. At first it looks like a pile of clothes or a tattered brown garbage bag half buried in the ice. Closer still. His flesh crawls. His ears ring, terror clenching his guts.

The thing has a face. It has a face, and spindly arms, one raised high and frozen in an awkward position. And a pair of withered brown legs crossed at the feet. Like Christ. Like Christ on the cross. But this figure is the opposite of divine. This figure is a sad, forlorn, bundle of desiccated skin, frozen into the rind of a glacier.

He approaches it and looks down into its ancient, cadaverous face.

A sudden urge wells up in the man—the urge to touch. Equal parts revulsion and fascination, it is accompanied by a convulsion of chills. The man's hands shake, his chin trembling. He has harbored this secret compulsion ever since he was a child. Touching things that he's not supposed to touch: an oil painting in a museum, the innards of an electric toaster, the smooth mons of a neighbor girl's vagina. Now it is irresistible. He finds himself reaching down to that scorched black face.

He touches the papery skin of its jaw.

Something like icy electric current suddenly sparks off the mummy's flesh—ancient eyes snapping open. A surge of cold, black, electric voltage floods into the man, a soundless gasp puffing out of him.

The man jerks backward instinctively, as though recoiling from a live electrical socket. The radiant yellow pupils of the corpse peer up at him now, a smile tugging at the corners of the mummy's face. Except it isn't a smile. It is a grimace—an ageless, eternal, omniscient death rictus—and it widens, and widens, until the mummy's mouth becomes a doorway, a portal into a black void.

The modern man tries to scream, but no sound will issue from his lungs, as a tidal wave of dark energy courses through him . . .

. . . baptizing him, inundating him, changing him.

10

Behold the Hunter

Grove hurried down the steps of the Restin Annex Building, fiddling with his umbrella, Zorn at his side mumbling wisecracks about how well the meeting had gone, the rain coming down in sheets, the wind buffeting them. Lightning popped overhead. Grove smelled ozone and angry seas as they reached the street and hustled toward their car, which was parked in the staff lot just west of the building. Thunder cracked a hole in the sky to the east, rattling the air.

As they reached the car and climbed in, the noise of the rain practically drowned the sudden trill of Grove's cell phone. "It's Maura," he announced with thinly concealed delight as he pulled the phone from his inner pocket, glancing at the display.

"Who?" Zorn was wiping moisture from his bald head as he settled in behind the steering wheel.

"The journalist, the one from the magazine." Grove thumbed the Answer button and said into the phone: "Is this the famous Maura County?"

"Mighty cozy with this lady," Zorn murmured to himself, starting the car, then pulling out of the lot.

Grove heard Maura's trademark husky voice greeting him on the other end of the line: "Hey, stranger. How goes it with the Ackermans?"

"Long story, very interesting," Grove told her, deciding to keep the details to himself for the time being. "You back in Frisco?"

"Yep, and I got news."

"You got news."

"Yep. Something's happened. And you're not going to believe it."

Grove glanced out at the rain. "To be honest with you, at this point I'll believe just about anything."

After a pause: "Not to be melodramatic, but it's just something you gotta see to believe."

"You've got my attention," Grove said. "Tell me what happened."

"Let me ask you something first." Maura lowered her voice as though worried someone might be eavesdropping. "Is there any possible way you could come here? I mean right now. Hop on a flight and come here today?"

Grove glanced over at Zorn, who was dying behind the wheel, wanting so badly to hear the other end of the conversation. "You mean San Francisco?" Grove said into the phone.

"The magazine'll pay. It's four hours *tops* from O'Hare. Right?"

"That's true, Maura, it's four hours from Chicago. The problem is, I'm not *in* Chicago anymore, I'm at Quantico, in Virginia. What is going on? What is this about?"

Another pause: "You remember that invitation I sent to the archaeologists, the one I attached to your last e-mail?"

"Sure I do. Your prehistoric VICAP idea."

"Exactly . . . well, I got some replies."

Grove listened to the mysterious silence. "And . . . ?"

"Ulysses, I don't mean to be such a geek about this,

but it really is impossible for me to explain it over the phone. You've just got to see it."

Grove sighed. "Hold on a second, Maura." He turned to Zorn, who at that point was pulling the unmarked government sedan down an entrance ramp into bustling highway traffic. "Terry, old pal," Grove said, "how would you feel about taking a side trip to San Francisco with me?"

Zorn's face twisted into a lascivious grin. "Grove, Grove, Grove, Grove, Grove . . ."

Somewhere north of the Columbia River, after the sun had dissolved like a melting yellow lozenge on the jagged spires of the coastal range to the west, and the shadows had reached across the dirt roads and switchbacks of north Portland like long emaciated arms, the puppeteer again took control of Richard Ackerman.

It happened just north of the mercurial gray waters of Vancouver Lake, amid the rolling patchwork of deforested suburbs and strip malls that made up rustic metro-Portland. Ackerman was hunched over the wheel of a '97 Buick Regal which he had just stolen out of a salvage yard parking lot, acting on pure compulsion after seeing the door open and the key in the ignition, not knowing exactly where he was going or how he was going to get there.

Stealing a car was another first for Richard Ackerman. Over the past twelve months he had either driven his own automobile—which he had abandoned in an Iowa forest preserve last fall—or had taken buses and trains. Now the white lines ticked under the grimy carriage of the Buick, the vapor light flickering in Ackerman's eyes as he grimaced at the car's odor, that greasy, stale smoke smell, the radio tuned to static, his head tuned to static, his central nervous system humming like feedback from a broken tube amp . . . when it happened. The cold metal hand gripped his spine, straightening him in his seat. His teeth cracked. And those great, blackened, papery eyelids opened once again in his brain, looking out at the world through the eyeholes in Ackerman's skull.

Ackerman shrank inside himself and watched his hands and limbs flex and jerk and curl and straighten. It was like watching a factory manufacturing movement, the puppeteer stoking the furnace of Ackerman's synapses, sending inertia down through his vessels and into his tendons, through his cartilage and into his marrow and muscle—*twitch-twitch-whirrrrrrr*—and the thing kept getting better and better at moving Ackerman around, telling him what to do, commandeering his body and soul. Hands welded white-knuckle tight on the steering wheel, eyes shifting like insects, the New Richard yanked the Buick down an entrance ramp and entered a sleepy outlying village.

Barton, Washington, is a little rusted barnacle of a town—not much more than a few hundred double-wides, ramshackle cabins, and pocked Airstream trailers—clinging to the banks of the Lower River. The Buick roared down the asphalt two-lane that ran along the water's edge, the blink of red reflectors like a vermin's eyes in the headlamp glare, endless columns of birch woods sliding by in the darkness, the night sky screaming overhead, scarred and insane with constellations. The thing inside Ackerman convulsed with hunger, a silent howl drilling through his ears. The thing had to feed. It had to hunt and feed and complete its mission.

A neon sign loomed up ahead in the fog bank of dust: REGAL MOTOR INN—VACANCY—COLOR TV—HBO—GO, BLUE DEVILS—GOOD LUCK AT THE STATE CHAMP'SHIP!

A yank of the steering wheel, and the car zigged across the shoulder. Ackerman's hiking boot snapped down on the brake pedal, and the Buick zagged into a narrow parking place in front of the motel. The car jiggered to a noisy stop, nearly taking out one of the wrinkled metal guardrails in front of the building, raising a cloud of debris in the night air.

The engine died.

Silence returned to the lot, and the New Richard sat there for a moment. Hands still vise-gripped around the steering wheel, heart still pumping, eyes still working back and forth like arc lights. The front window of the motel's office was ten feet away, a pair of figures sitting in there, the blue glow of a television set apparent in one corner, painting the dim lobby in shifting ghosts. Somewhere in the distant hills the screech of an owl scraped the night sky.

Right then, the New Richard decided that the man and woman in that lobby had to die.

The duffel bag sat on the Buick's rear seat—hastily tossed through an open window during the commission of the theft. It contained the quiver and the tool belt. The New Richard got out of the Buick, opened the rear door, dug out the duffel bag, put it on the ground, and tore open the zipper. Hands busied themselves with straps and buckles and graphite shafts and razors and oxidized tools.

As he worked in the shadows, preparing his instruments of death, Ackerman's hound-dog eyes filled with tears. The tears tracked down his face and mingled with the drool gathering at the corners of his mouth and the bottom of his gray-whiskered chin, then dripped across the front of his torn flannel shirt, saturating the fabric. The thing inside him wept as well. It wept silently as it worked, the great shimmering dragon eyes welling with tears of agony for all the innocents, all the sacrificial lambs. Its ancient mission—soaked in blood and anguish—could only be completed through death, mayhem, and devastation.

The New Richard slung the quiver over his back and tucked the bow under his arm. He tossed the empty duffel back in the car, then strode across the front of the office to the entrance. He appeared to be an ordinary customer arriving for the night—a sportsman, perhaps, just in from a duck hunt on Hayden Island. He entered the lobby through a glass door and instantly smelled sputtering radiator heat, burned coffee grounds, and faint traces of disinfectant.

"Evenin', sir," said a voice, tugging the New Richard's gaze across the room to an elbow-high counter behind which stood a gray little man in a threadbare cardigan sweater. The innkeeper wore thick, horn-rimmed glasses and looked to be about a hundred and fifty years old. "Any luck out there tonight?"

The New Richard reached for one of the arrows when another voice rang out.

"No bow-huntin' allowed this early in the season!" The voice was feminine, old, and gravelly. The New Richard looked over and saw the obese woman sitting in an armchair in front of a console TV tuned to CNN, a bent aluminum walker parked next to her. She sported multiple chins and a faded floral-print housedress. The undersides of her arms jiggled as she wagged her plump finger in the stranger's direction.

"Aw, put a sock in it, Evelyn!" the innkeeper barked at her.

The old woman sneered: "Them game wardens'll bust you just as soon as look at ya!"

"Be still now!"

"Just tryin' to help—"

"Would ya let the gentleman check in already!"

From over his shoulder the New Richard plucked an arrow from the quiver, then brought it down hard against the bow. The bow creaked as it was drawn back. The other two barely noticed this strange creature standing in their lobby, about to take their lives.

"I ain't stoppin' him!" the old lady crowed, ignoring the stranger.

"Please shut your pie hole!" the innkeeper shouted back at her.

"*You* shut your hole, you old cocker!"

"I'll kick your ass right on outta here, you think I won't!"

"Stuff it, Pete!"

"You think I won't?"

The thing that was once Richard Ackerman suddenly called out in a garbled, booming voice, "Turn around!"

Their voices cut off immediately. The innkeeper stared. The fat lady stared. A long beat of silence then, the only discernible sounds being the drone of CNN, and a moth, ticking against the front window, trying in vain to escape. The New Richard smiled sadly. "Turn around, please."

Late that night, alone in his forlorn apartment, amid the scattered notebooks and tented dictionaries, clad only in his underwear, Michael Okuda realized he was down to his last half bag of dope, so he decided to work the rest of the evening as straight as a judge. (In Anchorage, heroin cost eleven dollars a bag—although Okuda, on his paltry assistant lab-manager salary, was forced to buy in bulk. A bundle of ten bags usually set him back seventy-five dollars. Hoarding became a way of life.) Which was probably why he experienced the epiphany.

At first he thought it was the dope fading on him— he had snorted a half bag that afternoon, and by two o'clock that morning he was beginning to zone out. He could barely see the flip chart that he had positioned in front of the sofa, nor could he read his chicken scratchings that passed for notes. His vision began to blur and fracture everything into pairs. Which was when the discovery happened.

He was trying to concentrate on the repeating symbols scrawled in felt tip all around his living room—renderings of the mummy's tattoos, the little sharp petals that made no sense whatsoever—when they started to sprout doppelgangers, ghostly doubles in his wavering field of vision that swam and oscillated as though passing under a milk glass—

—and all at once he was reminded of the old "floating hot dog" phenomena from the fifth grade: Killing time in Mr. Gibbons's civics class, fascinated by optical illusions, little Mikey Okuda and his pals used to get a huge kick out of pointing their two index fingers at each other, and looking directly over the tips, and seeing the tiny little phantom "hot dog" floating between them. The hot dog appears because the focal point of the eye is crossed at that range. But now, so many years later, the adult Okuda was looking at a similar illusion floating only inches away from him on his wall, and it was making his gut stir with the strangest feeling.

And that's when the revelation jolted through his weary brain center, touched off by that vague, cryptic linkage that had been rattled loose by an image in an old Boris Karloff movie: *a mummy reaching down, gently running a petrified fingertip along an ancient scroll . . . insane laughter howling offscreen.*

The tattoos, when viewed in Okuda's drugged double vision, revealed a secret inner structure: they were cryptographs! Symbols for words! Sumerian probably! *Words that could be translated!*

A linguistic breakthrough for a junkie cryptologist,

even an amateur one like Okuda, is more sobering than an IV cocktail of caffeine and adrenaline.

He jerked forward on his ratty sofa, knocking over a box of Cheez-Its. He grabbed a ballpoint. Writing madly, alternately flipping pages in his dog-eared Oxford Compound Sign Dictionary, he translated the symbols into elemental Sumerian: *en-nu . . . en-nu-un . . . en-nu . . . en-nu-un.* Hooray for heroin, the anthropologist's best friend! Okuda didn't even realize he was both giggling and shaking.

When he had the phrase cold, he paused and stared down at it, cuneiformed across the notepaper like a bloody ink blot. The giggling stopped. He needed to call somebody right away. Mathis? God no. The bitch would scoff. Or worse: she'd take credit for the breakthrough. Okuda got up and paced, his skinny legs trembling. He stopped and thought about it some more, chewing a fingernail.

Maybe *Grove* was the one he should call.

The New Richard sat on a shopworn sofa in the blood-spattered lobby of the Regal Motel, staring emptily at the console TV, which was still droning in the corner, its screen misted with arterial spray. Head cocked as though hearing an ultrasonic whistle, the pliers gripped in his big hand, he watched a banal advertisement for the Amazing Kitchen Magician while the bodies of the innkeeper and the old lady lay cooling in puddles of dark fluids on the floor in front of him. The arrows rose out of their necks like signposts. Bloody drag-trails fanned out from the innkeeper's corpse.

There was much work left to do. The bodies had to be posed, and the arrows removed with the pliers like all the others. Removing the arrows was the messy part— like cleaning fish—as the tips were always embedded in the gristle and sinew of the upper vertebra. But posing them was a transcendent experience for the New Richard. Like taking communion. He would raise the right arm into its ritual position, then step back and pray in a language long forgotten by denizens of the current era. Someday the cycle would close again. The vessel would return, the sacrifice complete.

At that moment, however, the process seemed daunting to the thing inside Ackerman. Operating Ackerman's body had gotten laborious, gummy and slow, like a machine with sand in its bearings. A faraway pain throbbed in Ackerman's chest, the angina constricting his vessels, tightening his joints. He had a weak heart. The New Richard wondered if Ackerman's body would survive the rigors of the mission.

Ignoring the unexpected frisson of pain, the New Richard rose and went over to the first body, kneeling down with the rubber-handled pliers. He was about to clamp onto the end of the arrow and start working it out . . . when he stopped. Something coming out of the television had pierced his consciousness. Eyes tracking over to the TV, head turning like an automaton, his gaze found the screen.

CNN was playing softly. At the moment a blond anchorwoman addressed the camera: "An FBI spokesman offered a statement earlier today regarding the Sun City killings. After a twelve-month-long investigation, the suspect at this hour remains at large, as well as a complete mystery, leaving authorities scrambling for answers."

The New Richard focused suddenly with laser intensity on that television screen.

The TV flickered with file footage of FBI headquarters, a reporter's monotone accompanying the image: "As the entire western United States reels from another senseless killing in the Nevada desert, FBI profilers are seemingly grasping at straws for clues and motives . . ."

The New Richard froze and watched the broadcast cut

to shaky, handheld footage of a handsome black man in a tailored suit hurrying down stone steps, trying to elude the prying gaze of the camera.

"Even renowned criminologist Ulysses Grove, the man whose analysis led to the arrest and ultimate conviction of the Oregon Happy Face Killer back in 1990, is apparently stumped by this disturbing series of random murders . . ."

Pop!

The revelation struck the New Richard like a lightning bolt piercing the top of his skull, sending jolts of high-voltage recognition down through his marrow, the message transposing itself into a daisy chain of ancient languages, until it burst forth in the tongue of the current place and time. *Behold! Behold!*

"Agent Grove! Can you comment on the stalled Sun City investigation?"

Snap!

The New Richard jerked backward with the sheer power of the realization, a black hole imploding down in the nucleus of his being, sucking everything into it, distorting time and space, until the entire motel lobby seemed to contract like a great eye, like a huge black iris shrinking down around the membrane of that flickering cathode ray tube.

"Sorry, folks, I have no comment, no comment, you can address all your questions to FBI Community Relations, but right now I have nothing to say."

Boooooommmmmmmmmmm! The television screen imploded into a single, dreamy, grainy close-up of the chiseled ebony face of Ulysses Grove. A great onyx god sculpted by some divine artist. And the puppeteer inside Ackerman stared at it, and stared at it, and stared at it.

Grove found Maura County waiting for him in the lobby of San Francisco's Hotel Nikko.

"C'mon, you got to see this," she said, leading him over to a bank of elevators. They boarded one of the posh enclosures—the accoutrements echoing the rich carpet nap, deep green color schemes, and elegant brass fittings of the hotel's central hallways. Maura pressed the button for the BR level. "Never seen anything like it," she was saying as the doors rattled shut, "in almost thirteen years of working in this racket."

The elevator rose, and they stood there—just the two of them—in the awkward, intimate silence.

"So how was your flight?" Maura asked him, mercifully breaking the silence.

"Um . . . you know . . . uneventful," Grove told her, his hands in the pockets of his herringbone jacket. His head spun. More than ever, he felt like a human pinball, bouncing back and forth across the country at the whim of the Sun City case. He had arrived in the Bay Area around dusk, less than an hour ago, and already had that flaky, dissociated sensation of the overtraveled. Terry Zorn had come along on the trip, but had elected to check in with the Frisco field office first, before joining Grove and the journalist later at the Hotel Nikko. Now Grove felt oddly tongue-tied in the elevator, alone with Maura. She wore a sleek black turtleneck and black jeans that set off her milky complexion and pale blue eyes. Her hair was pulled back in a tight ponytail, and Grove felt his gaze drawn to the back of her neck. The compulsion made him feel guilty and jittery. "So what am I about to see, anyway?" he finally asked her.

"Sorry about all the mystery," she said with a tepid smile. "It's the journalist in me, I guess."

"How do you mean?"

"A perpetual fear of burying the lead."

The elevator stuttered to a stop, and the doors opened, revealing the stone planters, gold sconces, and mirrored panels of the ballroom level. Grove followed the journalist out of the car, then down a carpeted corridor bordered on either side by meeting rooms.

They passed the Muir Room, the Juniper Room, the Larkspur Room, and the Madera Room—all empty, all dark with chairs up on round tables and spaces glistening with metal polish and carpet cleaner. "So what *is* the lead here?" Grove asked as they strode briskly along. The journalist was moving so quickly, so excitedly down that corridor, that Grove thought he might have to start trotting in order to keep up with her.

She thought about his question for a moment, licking her lips. "I'm really not sure, I was thinking you might be able to figure it out for me."

"I take it you got some responses to your e-mail?"

She gave him a look. "Um . . . yeah."

"Evidence of similar deaths over the years? Bodies with similar pathologies?"

She nodded. "You could say that. Yeah. I think you ought to just see it with your own eyes."

"Let's take a look then."

"Right up here." She indicated the end of the hallway. "Last door on the left."

Grove followed her, preparing himself for another encounter with a cranky archaeologist like Lorraine Mathis, or perhaps a dozen dusty old professors sitting around a table, pontificating about clay pottery and arrowheads. They approached the last door, which was closed, a placard marked in gold inlay reading REDWOOD ROOM.

Maura paused for a long moment in front of that door, her hand on the knob. Grove stood behind her, waiting. He got the feeling this pause was for dramatic effect. Finally she glanced over her shoulder and uttered, "You ready for this?"

"Sure," Grove said with a nod. "Lay it on me."

She nodded back at him, then opened the door and ushered him inside.

Grove was engulfed in chaos.

The noise was tremendous, at least a hundred archae-ologists, maybe more, talking, arguing, milling about a banquet room that was far larger than Grove had expected. Round tables crowded with people stretched in all directions. The ceiling rose up at least twenty-five feet high, with dozens of chandeliers shining down on the throngs. Every conceivable nationality seemed to be present—Arabs in full headdress, Hindi professors, men with turbans, Asians, African scholars with dashikis and traditional headgear, and even a Muslim woman with a black burka shrouding her face. Grove had to step back and scan the whole length of the hall just to take it all in. And the longer he looked, the more he realized what he was looking at.

Flip charts and dry boards faced many of the tables, many of them displaying hastily drawn stick figures, victims, mummies, and fossilized human remains, most of them lying supine, arrows pointing to neck wounds, diagrams of entry vectors, blood trails, pathologies, and little stick-figure arms posed in supplication identical to the Sun City victims. Some of the attendees were standing at the charts, pointing things out to their colleagues, voices rising in spirited debate. Hands wagged and heads shook, and Grove stood there for a long moment, taking it all in, unnoticed by most present.

"Oh my God," Grove finally muttered, his scalp crawling with gooseflesh.

Maura looked at him and nodded very slowly, almost sheepishly. "Exactly."

PART III

CARRIGAN'S CYCLE

"There is no explanation for evil. It must be looked upon as a necessary part of the order of the universe."
—W. Somerset Maugham

11

Cornucopia

While Grove and Maura huddled in a banquet hall on the West Coast, holding court well into the night with a room full of archaeologists, an FBI laboratory on the edge of a marine base in Virginia ran test after test on genetic material recovered from both the crime scenes and Ackerman's house in Wilmette. They had several strands of hair from a brush and a bathroom catch basin, as well as blood chemistry reports from Ackerman's angioplasty at Chicago's Northwestern Hospital three years earlier. They also had an array of trace tissue samples from the various scenes—a flake of dandruff, a particle of skin, a single hair, and a damp spot on the body of Carolyn Kenly believed to be saliva. They had a partial fingerprint as well (authorities in both Colorado and Nevada believed that the Sun City Killer operated without gloves, judging by the smudged print found on a button), but they had yet to gather enough of a sample against which to make a comparison.

The *genetic* "fingerprint" was another story.

The lab in Virginia discovered that the killer was a "secretor." This meant that the perpetrator's blood type and genetic information could be determined by bodily fluids other than blood. From that tiny spot of saliva found on the Kenly sundress, technicians extracted a perfect multilocus DNA pattern. This strand, which under a microscope looked like a tiny bar code, became the reference standard to which Ackerman's genetic information was compared. The hair sample taken from the Wilmette house matched perfectly. The test was run three times before the call was made to Tom Geisel in the middle of the night. Geisel spoke briefly with the head of the lab, a German woman named Sabine Voerkrupper, before getting dressed and initiating a nationwide manhunt.

Years ago, the police called it an all-points bulletin. Usually dispatched and transmitted over squad radios, the bulletin announced the crime, described the alleged perpetrator strictly for investigation purposes, and authorized arrest on "reasonable belief." But in the early twenty-first century—an age of constitutional ambiguity, political correctness, and rampant litigation—extraordinary measures had to be taken to ensure airtight legalities during the course of a cold pursuit. Especially in cases involving a prolific nationwide serial murderer the magnitude of Sun City.

Reaching out to local police departments has always been problematic for the bureau. Detective squads often accuse the FBI of scooping cases, sending out press releases before a crime is solved. And some cops even accuse the bureau of adding police-solved crimes to the FBI's clearance reports. But at the same time, local authorities are integral to the bureau's tactical operations. Regional investigators know their territories, have critical informants, and live on the streets. This is why a special unit called Reactive Crimes was established in the late 1960s to act as a specialized conduit between the bureau and local cops.

The Reactive Crimes Unit was designed to react to

crimes that have already happened, such as bank robberies and motiveless spree murders, and maximize assistance and cooperation from individual police departments. Within this unit, a special squad known as UFAP (Unlawful Flight to Avoid Prosecution) had become the central command post for complex manhunts, handling all the bulletins, dispatches, communications, and logistical aspects of the physical pursuit.

At approximately 2:30 a.m. on that restless night of revelations, Tom Geisel placed a phone call to the director of UFAP, and briefed him on the latest developments of the Sun City case. He faxed him the case files along with all the materials Grove and Zorn had amassed on Ackerman. Within an hour, jpegs and PDF files zipped across Internet servers to hundreds of regional violent crime units. E-mails flooded FBI field office terminals. High-priority messages sizzled across phone lines, and dispatches crackled over radios. Photographs of Ackerman landed on the desks of every police captain or lieutenant in the western United States. Most major metro post offices received bulletins. Memos went out to every tactical unit. Even bounty hunters got calls.

Before the sun rose on the West Coast, Richard Ackerman was, as the old shamuses used to say, "number one on the hit parade."

"Hold it down for a second, please—*please!*"

Ulysses Grove made a halting gesture with his hands, palms out, silencing the crowd of scientists. A few whispers trailed off in the rear, but mostly the hundred or so archaeologists settled and waited, the light from the chandeliers reflecting off bespectacled, expectant faces.

The profiler stood before them at a blackboard, his jacket off, his sleeves rolled up. His briefcase sat on a podium next to him, lid open, exposing its contents—a Blackberry Palm Pilot, notebooks, cell phone, tape recorder, rubber gloves, case folders, and a Polaroid camera. Not readily visible was a lucky key chain that Grove's late wife, Hannah, had given him years ago as a Valentine's Day present. Grove kept the trinket tucked into a pocket in the lining of the briefcase—a tiny magnifying glass on a two-inch spindle, attached to a worn leather pad. The word *Sherlock* was embossed in Old English letters across the little pad. Grove was not sure why he carried the thing with him. He was not superstitious. He just felt better having it in his briefcase at all times.

It was nearly dawn, and Grove had that wired, shaky, wrung-out feeling one gets after a rough night of work and too much coffee. Maura County sat behind him on a stool near the blackboard, her black turtleneck smudged with chalk dust. She had been keeping notes for the last hour or so, trying to keep track of it all, trying to make sense of all the data, but it wasn't easy in this room full of clashing cultures and egos. At the moment, the board reflected in hastily scrawled bullet points the common causes of death among the remains:

- fatal wound—near 1 vert.
- undetermined pose
- supine pos. at death
- organs miss.

Terry Zorn stood by the door, arms crossed, nervously chewing his lip, his cowboy hat hanging off the doorknob. He had wandered into this hornet's nest around two o'clock that morning. Around four o'clock they had brought in another silver urn full of Starbucks, and the attendees had sucked it down like dying patients receiving plasma. But the truth was, nobody really needed coffee to stay awake and alert and engaged. The exchange of information was more than enough to spike their collective adrenaline, the pattern repeating itself over and over.

Among those assembled that morning was Dame Edith Endecott, a blue-haired Scottish crone from Oxford who had discovered a perfectly preserved mummy in a bog outside Edinboro, dating back to the fifteenth century—same signature, same neck wound, same pose. Also present was the flamboyant Dr. Moses de Lourde, a fey, anachronistic old southerner from Vanderbilt, who had been involved in unearthing a two-thousand-year-old murder victim from a mound site at Poverty Point, Louisiana. There was also the dapper Indian gentleman, V.J. Armatraj, a professor at the University of Delhi, who had led the team that discovered the "Year Zero Mummy" high in the Italian Alps, a frozen specimen with evidence of a fatal neck injury dating back to the time of Christ. Adding to the din was one of Saudi Arabia's infamous intelligentsia, Professor Akmin Narazi, who had amassed data on dozens of discoveries over the last five thousand years exhibiting evidence of wrongful deaths, many of them practically identical to the Mount Cairn Iceman.

Some of the scientists present already knew of the repeating pattern. They had corresponded with each other about it, drawing very few conclusions. But none had suspected such a pervasive repetition down through the ages.

"I need everybody to calm down and focus on one thing right now, the *link*, the connection," Grove told the room. "What is the common ground here?"

"Is it not obvious!" Professor Narazi barked from across the room, his dark, olive eyes glittering with anger. He was a compact little brown man in his midsixties with luxurious silver hair.

Grove looked at the Saudi gentleman. "Sir?"

"We've given description for hour upon hour," Narazi snapped at him. "Is it not obvious the pathology of the specimens is similar? What more is there to say?"

"Ostensibly, you're right, that's all there is to it,"

Grove said, "but I'm looking for a deeper connection, something psychological, cultural—"

"Dear sir." Edith Endecott spoke up, interrupting Grove with her soft burr. Her pear-shaped form was clad in an elegant navy blue dress, her cat's-eye glasses riding low on her long aquiline nose. "There is perhaps a feeling among my distinguished colleagues that you've not been forthcoming. No offense to Miss County or to her fine publication . . . but surely you've not been grilling us all night for a mere article of general interest."

Grove sighed, then gazed across the room at all the impatient faces. He glanced at Zorn, who said nothing, just nodded. It was time to tell them. "Okay . . . look," Grove said finally. "I'll admit we're dealing with something a little more . . . specific."

The Scottish woman cocked her head. "Yes. Specific. Please go on."

After another pause, Grove swallowed hard and told the crowd everything.

He told them about the Sun City murders. He told them that the FBI was currently hunting for a "person of interest" who had come into contact with the Mount Cairn remains. He told them everything, and then implored them to keep the information strictly confidential. He told them he had just broken about a half dozen bureau regulations by disclosing details of an active investigation. As he spoke, he noticed rumblings out in the crowd, furtive whispers, worried glances. He figured he had lost about half the room. He figured that maybe fifty or more of them were now plotting their escape, planning to hop on the next flight out of San Francisco. These were, after all, merely academics, some of them still working on their doctorates.

Professor Armatraj, the Indian, was the first to break the uneasy silence. "Am I to understand, you believe this suspect is somehow recreating the mummy record?"

The dusky-skinned professor wore a sedate linen suit and bow tie, and looked like a throwback to old Colonial India, as though he had emerged fully formed from an E.M. Forster novel.

Grove nodded. "In a manner of speaking, yeah."

"Good *Lord*," Armatraj exclaimed, more to himself than aloud.

A sudden eddy of whispers and low voices swirled through the room.

"What does this have to do with archaeology?" a jittery woman in the back called out.

Another voice: "This is not why we came here!"

More voices swelled, and Grove held up his hands in a calming gesture. "Folks, please!" The voices subsided slightly, and Grove took a breath. "I understand your concern. Why don't we take a break? And those of you who need to get back home, or those of you who would prefer not to continue working with us . . . you're certainly free to go. And we thank you. Anybody else who might have further information, or might be able to help us out, we'll discuss this later today, after everybody's had a chance to get something to eat and get some rest."

Finally Grove thanked everybody once again, and asked those who were departing if they could possibly leave their documentation with Agent Zorn.

The exodus began on a rush of voices, squeaking chairs, and clanking coffee cups. Some of the attendees went over to Zorn, who had a stunned look on his face as they inundated him with manila envelopes, file folders, business cards, and loose documents. Most of those present milled their way out the door, then into the gathering throngs in the corridor. A dozen or so lingered.

Maura came over to Grove and said under her voice, "So what now?"

Grove shrugged. "We start going through the materials, see if we can learn anything else from the brave souls who stay with us."

"Y'all certainly know how to clear a room," said a voice to Grove's immediate left.

Grove turned and came face-to-face with Dr. Moses de Lourde. The small thin man was dressed in a brilliant white suit with a red silk cravat tucked neatly in his pocket. He looked like he could be the fashionable author Tom Wolfe's older gay brother.

"I'm sorry?" Grove said to the man.

Professors Endecott and Armatraj stood behind the southern gentleman, listening closely, each looking alternately worried and engrossed.

"I said y'all know how to clear a room, which unfortunately is somewhat akin to the effect I have on my own students," de Lourde said with a smile, offering his delicate, manicured hand. "Moses de Lourde at your service, sir. Professor of Antiquities, Tulane University."

"Pleasure, sir, thank you," Grove said.

"I must say, Agent Grove, I detect the tip of an iceberg in your query regarding the psychological connection between your suspect and the mummy record."

Grove gave de Lourde a weary smile. "Very perceptive, Professor, you got me."

Edith Endecott spoke up then. "I must concur, Agent Grove. You've piqued my interest as well."

Professor Armatraj, who stood next to her, said nothing, but appeared uneasy.

"May I be so bold," de Lourde added, "as to inquire about your initial hypotheses regarding the deeper connections to the neolithic evidence?"

Grove thought it over for a moment, gazing around the emptying room. By that point, Maura and Zorn had both come over to listen. The banquet hall had almost completely cleared out. "Before I answer your question," Grove said finally, "let me pose one to you and your colleagues."

De Lourde gave his head a polite tilt. "Please."

"Would you folks have any interest in some breakfast?"

The southerner glanced at his colleagues. A nod from Dame Edith Endecott and a shrug from Armatraj. De Lourde offered the profiler another grin. "I might be talked into some lightly poached eggs . . . that is, if you would be so kind as to procure a bottle of Tabasco."

Grove smiled, glancing first at Zorn, then at Maura. "I think that can be arranged. C'mon."

He led the five of them over to the door, and they were about to make their exit when a voice rang out behind them.

"Agent Grove!"

Grove froze in the doorway, the others pausing outside in the bustling corridor.

"If I might have a word with you!" said a feeble voice from inside the room.

Grove glanced over his shoulder and saw a slight, hunched old man in a priest collar and coat limping along with a cane, coming slowly toward him. "We haven't had the pleasure yet," the old clergyman wheezed as he approached. "My name is Father Carrigan. From the Jesuit Order of Santa Maria. In Brazil."

"Sorry, I didn't . . ." Grove stammered, not knowing exactly what to say. Behind him, the others huddled in the doorway, listening.

"I'm not an archaeologist," the priest said. He spoke with the subtle rolled r's of a Bostonian, and his wizened face twitched and blinked as he spoke, perhaps the result of a minor stroke. "One of the Brazilians from the university in Sao Paulo told me about the meeting here."

"We're happy to have you," Grove told him, wondering what the agenda was here, why an old arthritic priest would travel all this way.

"This pattern you've been discussing . . . I've known about it for quite some time now."

"No kidding. You an amateur criminologist, Father?"

"To paraphrase the Bard, there's far more in heaven and earth than you've ever dreamed, Agent Grove."

Grove smiled. "I've had some pretty wild dreams."

The priest scowled suddenly. His milky eyes, buried in wrinkles, radiated gravity and sorrow, his neck wattle shaking as he tried to put into words what he had to say. "You are opening the proverbial Pandora's box, Agent Grove, and I'm not sure you're prepared for what will crawl out."

Grove stared at the man for a moment. "Listen . . . Father Carrigan . . . why don't you join us for breakfast? The magazine's buying, and you can tell us what's on your mind."

The priest pursed his lips. There was an air of almost aristocratic dignity about the old man, the way he leaned on his burnished pearl-handled cane, the old tarnished signet ring on his crooked finger adorned with the symbols of some obscure secret society. Finally he gave a nod and said, "That would be lovely, thank you."

There was very little pleasure on the priest's face.

A casual observer—were there any left alive—might notice the first rays of sunlight streaming through the closed front blinds of the Regal Motel lobby, and maybe wonder why the blinds were shut (not to mention adorned with a CLOSED sign) at such a busy time of day for early-bird hunters a week into duck season. They might also notice the deep scarlet drag marks on the carpet leading across the reception area and then around the edge of the counter, as well as the metallic odors of drying blood and rotting meat beginning to permeate the stale air. They would surely notice the tall, gnarled figure standing behind the counter, as still as a dime-store Indian.

He had been standing there for nearly an hour now,

disconnected from the pain gripping his back, staring straight ahead as though in some kind of trance, as though he were an android desk clerk waiting for a customer that would never come. The old Richard Ackerman never would have been able to stand motionless like that for over an hour. He would have folded to the floor in raging spasms within ten minutes, caterwauling at his wife for his Vicodin. But this was the *New* Richard Ackerman, and he had to push this body to its limits because the revelation had finally come.

The lobby sat in silent dust motes except for the faint sound of dripping. And the New Richard kept thinking.

In the Pacific Northwest, there's a bird known as the peregrine falcon. A natural predator, this robust creature has a wingspan of five feet, talons like claw hammers, and an insatiable appetite for mice, smaller birds, even snakes and lizards. Ornithologists have even observed the peregrine attacking its *own species*. And not for food. Apparently the bird is one of the rare species currently in existence that seems to hunt and kill merely for the sport of it.

Way back in the early Copper Age, over six thousand years ago, there was an ancestral species to the peregrine—long since gone extinct—that was twice as big, with a nine-foot wingspan, and eyes like black pearls. This neolithic falcon had an added offensive mechanism of being able to disguise itself, sucking in its torso and feathers until it appeared smaller, weaker, perhaps even injured. In this fashion it would draw its prey into a chase, and ultimately, in a violent turning of tables, it would ambush its pursuer. The hunter would become the hunted, and the falcon would devour its prey with the greatest of ease. The thing inside Richard Ackerman was, in many ways, just like the peregrine. With one exception.

He had only one natural enemy.

The New Richard gazed out at the tawdry motel

lobby through Ackerman's eyes—scanning the room, thinking, pondering, imagining all the men who were searching for him. He kept wondering how to lure the dark-skinned one, the important one, the only one who mattered now, into the chase. *Ulysses Grove.* The name was bitter ash on the puppeteer's palate. But the name also served as a powerful incantation. "Ulysses Grove" was the doorway. But how many victims would it take? What could the New Richard possibly do that would have enough impact to draw the brown hunter into the fray? It would have to be something on a scale much larger than a single killing. Something much grander than two dead cretins in a reeking motel lobby.

Head rotating on its axis with prehensile, almost insectlike jerks, the thing inside Ackerman glanced around the room for the thousandth time, searching for the key, an idea, some way to draw the hunter into the hunt.

The rays of steel-gray, overcast Oregon morning slanted across ratty furniture, refracting wisps of dust and painting the far wall with dull stripes of light. The misty dawn had barely shoved back the shadows, dimly illuminating the blood-streaked lobby. More objects were visible now than before, including the spray of old dog-eared magazines on the coffee table, the spindly rubber plant in one corner, the faded seascape painting on the far wall. The tall man's gaze flitted from object to object. He looked at the flickering TV set, which was now broadcasting some inane program on weight loss, and he looked at the yellowed lamp shade. Finally his gaze fell on the black leather binder lying open on the counter in front of him.

It had been right in front of him all along.

The *register.*

Twitching fingers opened the tattered binder, the old glue crackling. A bloodstained fingertip lightly tracked down the column of names that were scrawled along the left side of the page. Handwritten in the style of old-fashioned roadside inns, the register contained a virtual cornucopia of lonely transients—many of whom, at that moment, were slumbering in the squalid units flanking the lobby . . .

. . . each of them unconscious, dreaming banal dreams, waiting to be sacrificed.

12

A Secret Wrapped in Secrets

Father Carrigan's eyes flared with anger, the teacup trembling in his palsied hand, its contents sloshing over the rim. "Go look in the Vatican library, if you don't believe me, it's all there," he told the table, his feeble voice straining to be heard over the gathering noise in the coffee shop. "These precious discoveries of yours, they've stirred up forces that are best left undisturbed, and it's only because of *hubris*, pure hubris, that these poor souls keep getting dug up." The padre paused for a moment, as though exhausted by the sheer emotion coursing through him. Then he looked across the table at each of the distinguished professors sitting there. "Tell me, Professor de Lourde . . . why would you come all this way for so little remuneration? Why would all these renowned archaeologists travel halfway around the world at the drop of a hat to attend such an obscure meeting?"

Professor Moses de Lourde was about to take a bite out of a small triangle of toast when he paused, the toast poised in midair in front of his mouth, a faint, little, ironic smirk crossing his elegant face. "I suppose, Father," he replied finally, "the reason is good old-fashioned ego.

For a room full of archaeologists, a feature article in a national science publication is akin to waving a slab of raw meat in front of a pack of wild dogs."

Knowing smiles passed among the professors, and even Maura found it difficult to suppress a grin.

The table grew silent for a moment, as Grove sat in front of a plate of cold scrambled eggs and tried to get a reading on the priest, tried to size him up, tried to figure out if he was crazy. The others deferentially stared into their laps, or absently sipped their coffee and picked at their breakfasts, not wanting to agitate the priest any more than necessary. The restaurant, which was a long, narrow assemblage of round tables nestled in the middle of an atrium lobby, was already filling up with early morning traffic. Wait staff bustled. Cappuccino machines hissed and sputtered. Silverware clanked. Grove noticed some of the other patrons shooting glances this way. He could only imagine what this table of eccentrics looked and sounded like to the uninitiated.

So far Grove had gleaned several things. First, it was becoming apparent that the phenomenon of unearthing ancient murder victims with similar pathologies was no secret to much of the world. Factions of historians and scientists had formed around different theories, most of them concluding, as Okuda had, that the killings were ritual based. Second, most experts agreed with Okuda that these victims, in most cases, were probably shamans or healers. They each carried their own version of the "medicine bundle" found on the Mount Cairn Iceman. But what had ignited such a vigorous dialogue at the breakfast table was Father Carrigan's assertion that malevolent events followed the discovery of each mummy, that something metaphysical was released as a result of each excavation.

Professor de Lourde dabbed the corners of his mouth with a cloth napkin. "May I ask the good father what exactly he did during his tenure in Vatican City?"

The old man puckered his liver-colored lips, then raised the teacup with trembling hands, daintily slurping at the brown liquid. His wrinkled visage had turned scarlet in the heat of the discussion, and now his face looked mottled and hectic with burst capillaries. "I was a bureaucrat, a committeeman," he replied at last. "But you would not recognize the committee if I told you its name."

"Try me, Father."

Gray eyes flashed. "*Consilium de Miraculum.* You see? The name would not mean much to any of you."

Professor Endecott spoke up, gazing over the tops of her reading glasses. She had been taking notes on a small spiral-bound pad. "May I ask why you're so certain none of us would know of this group?"

The old man scowled at her. "Have *you* heard of the committee . . . Professor . . . ?"

"Endecott. Edith Endecott. Actually no. I haven't heard of it."

"That's because the committee did not exist."

"Pardon?"

The priest took a haggard breath as though he were crossing a laborious rubicon by explaining such a thing. "The committee did not exist, because it was a secret, but then again *everything* under the Vatican banner was secret, so this was a secret wrapped in secrets."

Grove broke in. "My Latin's not great, but it sounds like, what, 'Committee on Miracles'?"

The priest nodded. "It was a group of clergy, anthropologists, scholars, and antiquarians—all dedicated to investigating and authenticating miracles."

An exchange of glances around the table. Maura County did not look amused. Sitting in front of a half-eaten bowl of granola, she looked at Grove from across the table, and Grove tried to read the expression on the journalist's face. It was an odd mixture of fascination and repulsion, as though all the enthusiasm had drained out of her—the prospects for a juicy article long ago replaced by a gathering dread. Next to her, stirring a packet of sweetener into his iced tea, his cowboy hat sitting on the table next to him, Terry Zorn looked as though he might burst out laughing at any minute. He obviously wasn't buying much of this. Grove, on the other hand, was ambivalent. He felt as though he were on a train that had inadvertently snapped a cable.

Grove looked at the deeply lined face of the priest. "And what kind of miracles are we talking about here, Father?"

Father Carrigan sighed. "Miracles are not always happy ones, Agent Grove. Miracles are not always benign and friendly to mankind. The beneficial miracle is a New Testament concept."

A pause. Grove told him to go on.

"On at least three different occasions, the committee was called upon to investigate the similarities between mummified remains found in the late 1950s in Italy. And later—in the early 1970s, I believe it was—at various locations around Eastern Europe. And finally North America."

Another pause. Professor Armatraj, his eyes gleaming with interest as he daintily sipped his tea, spoke up then: "And your conclusions were . . . what exactly?"

The priest swallowed hard, as though the mere subject matter was draining him. "At first we had no inkling what we were dealing with. We couldn't make heads or tails out of the tattoos and markings that seemed to be common among the mummies. But we immediately saw a connection between the pose—the way the arms were raised—and the gesture of summoning."

Armatraj said he wasn't following.

The elderly priest raised one arm with great effort, the palsy making his brittle tendons twitch. "In the ancient rites of the Church," he croaked, "the practitioner lifts his hand like so. The supplicant does the same. It's a gesture of absorption."

"Define absorption, please," Armatraj said.

The priest dropped his arm, looking exhausted. "Absorption in the sense of a summoning."

Grove studied the old man. "A summoning of what, Father?"

Carrigan looked at Grove as though the profiler had just asked the color of the grass or why there is gravity. "A *spirit*, of course," he said, sounding a bit impatient.

Grove asked him to elaborate.

"I'm referring to the summoning of a *spirit* into one's earthly *body*," the old man explained, his eyes fierce within the folds of his drooping lids. "It's a very powerful gesture. We saw it in every instance, and we came to believe there was a connection . . . between the summoning and the horrible events that were occurring in the aftermath of each discovery."

Now Maura chimed in: "Can you tell us about these events? You've mentioned in passing these horrible things that have happened."

The priest gave her a grave look. "My dear, for centuries the *Consilium de Miraculum* was a virtual seismograph for spiritual activity—both good and evil. In the years immediately following each of these discoveries, the reports of human misery virtually pinned the needle. Especially in the areas around the discoveries. Death and mayhem, even reports of what Agent Grove might call 'copycat' murders. Believe me when I tell you, Miss County, we had our hands full. I'll admit that opinions differed among church authorities . . . but I believed then, as I still do to this day . . . there was a connection to the unearthing of these wretched souls."

Maura thought about it for a moment, then said, "So what happened?"

The priest looked confused.

Maura clarified: "After you came to believe there was a connection—what did you do about it?"

A shrug from the old man. "World politics made it impossible for the church to conduct any official investigations, or to come to any conclusions. People were too busy arguing over who owned the mummies. Everything was done in secret, Miss County, and local authorities were very stubborn, very reluctant to even talk with representatives of the church. The fact is, even my colleagues at the Vatican eventually placed their attentions elsewhere."

The old priest looked down then, fondling the burnished handle of his cane, which stood next to him, propped against the table.

"In time," he went on, "they managed to get rid of me and my crackpot theories. They discredited me, treated me like a senile old man. Eventually they sent me to my beloved South American gulag."

Another pause, and Grove started to ask something else, when all at once he fell silent, noticing something strange across the table. Professor de Lourde, normally jovial and sanguine, had lost all his color. The fashionable southerner sat bolt upright against his chair, his eyes wide, his lips pressed together tightly. It was clear that de Lourde had realized something disturbing.

"You okay, Professor?" Grove asked de Lourde.

"Uh . . . yes," he softly intoned, his voice barely above a whisper.

"Something the matter?"

All eyes were on the southerner now. Face drained, his gaze suddenly haunted and fixed on the middle distance, de Lourde tried to speak, but had difficulty putting what he was thinking into words. Grove felt a cold prickling sensation at the base of his neck. To see the affable, genteel de Lourde like that—suddenly at a loss for words—somehow disturbed Grove more than anything else that had occurred all morning.

"I apologize," he said at last. "It's just that . . . I just had the most diabolical realization."

That's weird, Olivia Mendoza thought as she turned off her rust-bucket Chevy Geo and sat for a moment in the Regal Motel parking lot, staring through the rain-streaked windshield at the entrance to the front office. A plump little Latina with a peroxide-blond flip and rusty brown skin, Olivia wore the trademark baby-blue pinafore of the Mighty Maids Company under her tattered down coat.

It looked as though old Pete Bowden had mistakenly put the CLOSED sign up on the door again. The old bastard had probably been dipping into that "secret" bottle of J&B he kept hidden behind the file cabinet in the back office, the bottle that nobody was supposed to know about. Olivia had stumbled upon early morning remnants of the innkeeper's little "secret" many times before. One time a couple of years ago the maid had arrived for her shift only to find a pair of women's panties hanging from the Mr. Coffee in the front room. Another time she arrived to find Pete Bowden passed out on the floor of the lobby, half naked, his underwear bunched around his ankles. That time it took all of Olivia Mendoza's willpower not to just bust out laughing at the size of Pete's shriveled little pecker.

But this time, the old coot had gone too far. Not only was the CLOSED sign facing out but the blinds were shut as well. And the lights were off. The place looked boarded up, condemned, gone out of business. *Which wouldn't be a half-bad idea,* Olivia thought with a sideways grin, *if I could only find another housekeeping gig in Portland.*

The maid let out a sigh and reached for her umbrella, which sat on the passenger-side floor, buried beneath a pile of Adkins bar wrappers. The rains had let up a little, but still were coming down hard enough to warrant an umbrella. The Geo's backseat was littered with cleaning products and empty cans of Slim-Fast. Olivia Mendoza had tried every fad diet known to man, and her latest fixations were the low-carbohydrate trips, which so far had only served to make her grouchy rather than thin. She grabbed the umbrella, climbed out of the car, wrestled it open, went around to her trunk, rooted out her little plastic caddy full of cleaning products, then trundled through the mist to the office entrance.

At first she thought the door was locked, but then realized it was simply stuck—or maybe *stuck* was the wrong word. It gave a little bit as she tried it, crackling as though something had dried and crusted along the bottom edge. She remembered when her youngest, Ramon, was just a toddler, and the kitchen door of their shotgun flat would get like that—sticky with egg and juice and stewed prunes.

The door finally gave, and Olivia entered the dark lobby.

Immediately she smelled something unusual that she had never smelled in the place before—and if there was one thing Olivia Mendoza was well versed in, it was *odor.* It was a harsh, mineral smell, and it seemed to hang in the airless lobby as Olivia gazed around the shadows. She shook the rain from her umbrella and put it down. The place was a mess, of course, streaked with ink or vomit or God-knew-what-else spattered across the walls and carpet in great smudged streaks. *The old fart's done it this time*, Olivia thought as she looked around the dim room and heard that crackling sound again beneath her. She looked down and her heart started beating faster.

Blood.

That's what was sticking to the bottom of the door, and that's what was currently sticking to the bottom of her white crepe-soled shoes, making delicate crackling noises as she shifted her weight. Blood, for God's sake! Olivia's mind raced for a moment. *Pete Bowden must*

*have gone and gotten himself so drunk last night he took a fall
and knocked his teeth out, or maybe he got violent and finally
took out his sick frustrations on Evelyn with a paring knife, or
maybe there was a fight, yeah, that must be it, but God, that's
a lot of blood even for a barroom brawl, and look at the walls,
and the floor! Maybe kosher salt and club soda would get that
out—maybe—but good Lord, look at the streaks on the carpet—ohmyGod, look at the carpet!*

Olivia dropped the plastic caddy, and cans of disinfectant rolled across the floor.

Something made the housekeeper freeze. There was
a cry stuck in her throat, and her mouth was as dry as
bonemeal, but she stayed planted on those sticky tiles
by the door for a moment, gawking at that blood-
ravaged lobby, trying to get a breath into her lungs. She
made her legs move. She willed her legs to start toward
the front desk, across the room, maybe twelve feet away.
Slowly, convulsively, she followed the drag marks around
the edge of the counter.

The bodies were neatly tucked behind the desk, laid
against the baseboard.

Olivia's hand shot up to her mouth and trembled
there as she stared at the pair of corpses—the thin man
and the heavy woman—carefully arranged in identical
poses, arms raised, ashen faces contorted, gray flesh
marbled with blood the color of tar. The backs of their
heads were cemented to the floor in puddles of black,
glassy, hardened spoor.

Olivia Mendoza screamed then, but oddly enough,
very little noise came out of her other than a hoarse,
mucusy mewl that sounded like an injured bird in its
death throes, as her trembling hand reached out blindly
toward the countertop.

Her fingers found the telephone and fumbled for
the receiver, knocking it off the cradle.

* * *

In the days and weeks to come, much would be made of the speed—or more specifically the *lack* of it—with which the official investigation of the Regal Motel massacre got under way that morning. Normally the Portland PD would be dispatched to handle such a serious violent crime in one of the city's outlying areas. But the motel was located just across the state line, in Washington, so all the jurisdictional complications immediately ensued.

Vancouver, ten miles to the north, was the closest town with any kind of homicide squad, but the crime scene lab had to come from Olympia, nearly a hundred miles away. Initially this caused a significant delay between the time the first patrolman—a fairly green deputy from the county sheriff's department—showed up at the scene, and the point at which the CSI unit from Olympia finally arrived.

Official records placed the deputy arriving at the motel at ten minutes after seven o'clock. He found the maid huddling in her car outside the office, nearly catatonic with terror, unable to utter even the simplest reply to any of the deputy's questions. At twelve minutes after seven o'clock, the deputy drew his sidearm and entered the premises, finding the bodies of the motel owner, Peter Bowden (fifty-three), and his wife, Evelyn Bowden (forty-nine), on the floor behind the front desk. They appeared—to the deputy, at least—to have been dead for several hours.

The deputy immediately called in the apparent "187" to dispatch, and the Vancouver squad was called. The next thirty minutes would become particularly problematic throughout subsequent inquiries for both the sheriff's department as well as the Vancouver PD. For reasons known only to the deputy and the first-on-the-scene detectives, no one thought to check on the motel's guests until sometime after 7:40. Perhaps the problem was the lack of activity anywhere on the property. For the two minutes the deputy was talking to the maid, as well as the five minutes or so he was investigating the blood-spattered lobby—and even after the first unmarked squad car had arrived from Vancouver—nobody stirred in any of the rooms. No faces in the windows, nobody peering out of any of doors. Maybe the investigators simply figured the place was empty. But regardless of the reasons, the first knock on a guest room door didn't occur until exactly 7:42 that morning.

Of course, no one answered, despite the fact that eleven out of the twenty-four rooms were listed as occupied on the blood-spackled register in the Regal's office. Eventually one of the detectives took a peek through a curtained window and saw blood. Doors were broken down and met by coughs and flinches of surprise. More calls were made. Grim instructions went out over the lines, voices constricted with stress. In addition to the crime lab in Olympia, local FBI field offices in both Seattle and Portland were alerted.

By eight-thirty that morning, in the veils of mist billowing in from the Pacific coast, the Regal Motel teemed with somber activity. A kaleidoscope of cruiser lights and emergency flares streaked the sheets of rain with bloody watercolors, attracting onlookers like flames beckoning a swarm of moths. Hikers, duck hunters, third-shift workers on their way home, and mechanics from a nearby body shop—they all huddled in grim fascination under a blanket of umbrellas on the edge of the police cordons. Some of them sat on makeshift chairs, ice chests, and crates. Others chatted nervously.

They all wanted to glimpse a little carnage, maybe get a fleeting look at the victims being extracted from the motel under bloody sheets. But for the next hour and a half, only technicians passed in and out of the rooms: stoic morgue attendants dressed in white hazmat suits, sullen-faced detectives carrying clipboards. Whispers of the unseen abominations passed through the crowd, but nobody outside the cordons really knew what was going on in there. Nobody except the tall, hunched, middle-aged figure standing behind the group of mechanics.

This unidentified man, his long, gaunt face shrouded by the hood of a stolen parka, stood in the rain as though getting soaked to the bone didn't bother him in the least. Nobody paid much attention to him as he lurked there, his head craning to see over the tops of umbrellas.

He had the patience of a sphinx as he watched and waited, paying very close attention to every new investigator who arrived at the scene.

13
Rogue

NEW ORLEANS (AP)—"Old Sparky," as the inmates on Angola's death row refer to the electric chair, was fired up one last time Sunday for the execution of a man who at one time held Louisiana and east Texas in a grip of terror. Convicted mass murderer John George Haig, known to local old-timers as "Dracula," had no last words as he was led down the narrow cement corridor at 11:45 a.m. yesterday to the "processing room."

Haig was read the last rites and strapped into the chair at 11:55. As the second hand on the big regulator clock reached straight-up twelve o'-clock, ten thousand volts passed through Haig's body—thus bringing to a close two epochal examples of Louisiana's living history. The first being the use of the electric chair in state executions—recently made obsolete by a constitutional amendment that goes into affect at the end of next month. The second example being Haig himself.

THE MAKING OF A KILLER

Born in Oxford, Mississippi, in 1935, the son of a Pentecostal preacher, Haig grew up in a world of Old Testament fire and brimstone. Records indicate that Haig got as far as the third grade, then ran away from home and spent the next ten years of his life drifting from town to town, begging and panhandling. Chances are Haig was mildly retarded, although he was never diagnosed as such.

Psychologists tell us that the seeds of homicidal behavior are planted early. And in the case of John George Haig, all signs indicate that the boy was on the road to murderous behavior at a young age. Friends and relatives told tales of animal torture, petty crime, and arson. But the first documented, public display of Haig's strange and violent behavior occurred in 1965 at a traveling museum exhibit popular throughout the South.

Known as the Inman Brothers Emporium of Scientific Oddities, the show had been playing to huge crowds across the bayou area that summer. The main attraction was an actual mummified human believed to be a mound dweller over 2,000 years old—on loan from Tulane University, which had unearthed the find in a bog at Poverty Point the year before.

Eyewitnesses reported seeing Haig acting "in a peculiar manner" around the display case that housed the mummy. Seconds later, Haig had broken the glass with his bare hands and was trying to abscond with the artifact. Security men interceded and saved the mummy. The 29-year-old Haig was arrested and thrown in jail for three months.

REIGN OF TERROR

Upon his release, Haig seemed to vanish into the backwoods. Over the next ten years, most official records lost track of the man, but criminologists have pieced together a time line that paints a picture of spiraling madness and violence. Unsolved murders started piling up in the parishes, baffling investigators.

Random victims were found posed in odd postures, their necks ripped open as though by a wild animal. Traces of human saliva were found in some of the wounds. As well as teeth marks. Rumors started circulating that the killer was some sort of cannibal or vampire—drinking the blood of his victims.

When Haig was finally captured in 1975—from fingerprints found in a gas station bathroom—the number of unsolved murders attributable to Haig had risen to 34. Over the next 18 months Haig was interviewed extensively by a number of experts. The results paint a portrait of a deranged, bloodthirsty lunatic with inscrutable motives.

FINAL JUSTICE

During his trial, Haig revealed much about his twisted psychology, not to mention his modus operandi as a killer. He believed that he was gifted with supernatural powers bestowed upon him at birth by God. He also believed that his true calling was revealed to him on April 13, 1965—the day that he first laid eyes on those mummified remains at the Inman Brothers show.

Over the course of many interviews Haig revealed to psychologists that the "voice of God" had come out of the mummy and commanded him to "perform cleansing rituals until the enemy is found."

"The sacrificial lambs never suffered," he told one interviewer. "They died quickly and painlessly."

The drinking of the blood, which Haig had done on several occasions, was ceremonial, according to the murderer. "So I can live forever."

On Sunday, much to the gratitude of those who remember the horrors perpetrated on Louisiana by this sick individual, this last wish was dashed with a single jolt of electricity.

Professor de Lourde nodded at the screen of his laptop after the others had gotten a chance to skim the newspaper article. "I must confess," he said gravely, "until now, the connection was lost on me."

De Lourde sat on a velveteen and brass chair that was pulled up to a telephone terminal outside the hotel's mezzanine restrooms, his Mac Powerbook connected to the wall jack. The terminal was nestled in a little alcove at the end of a bank of pay phones, and doubled as an Internet hookup—an exorbitant fee charged for each minute of activity. Muzak droned softly, and the faint scent of pipe tobacco flavored the air. Thankfully, it was still early enough in the morning to ensure relative privacy in this little cubby area.

"The enemy . . ." Grove murmured, standing directly behind de Lourde, peering down at the Tulane University home page that displayed the archival strip of news print down the center of the screen. "What's *that* about?"

The others had gathered behind Grove, gazing over his shoulder at the Web site. Zorn stood on one flank, looking skeptical and restless as always, and Maura County stood on the other, chewing her lip nervously, looking as though she might be sorry she had started all this. Father Carrigan was perched on a chair beside Grove, fingering his cane and looking askance at the twenty-first-century technology that he didn't seem to fully comprehend. The other professors stood behind Maura, each of their faces thoughtful and pensive. Dr. Armatraj looked especially engaged by the whole turn of events.

Moses de Lourde gave a shrug, his gaze still fixed on the Haig execution article. "Before yesterday I would have assured you it was nothing but the ravings of an unhinged mind . . . but now, after conferring with all my colleagues and speaking with the good father here, I'm not so sure."

"I'm not so sure of *anything* anymore," Grove muttered, trying to ignore the cold finger on his spine.

De Lourde glanced over his shoulder at Grove. "There's more."

"I'm listening."

The southerner licked his lips judiciously. "The mummy that the article speaks of—the cave dweller?— this was the reason I came here. I was part of the team that originally discovered it."

This got everybody's attention, and Grove nodded at de Lourde. "Go on."

"Well . . . as I told some of the folks last night, I was only thirty-two at the time . . . 1964, I believe it was. I was working on my doctorate in anthropology at Tulane, when I learned about this dig out at the Poverty Point site. Heard they had recovered a mummy from the bog. As Professor Endecott will tell you, human remains that end up in a bog will stay as well preserved as that of any medium, including ice. Am I right, Professor?"

From behind Maura, Edith Endecott nodded her assent. "A lucky break for us archaeologists, I might add."

"Absolutely correct. Anyhow . . . there was much discussion at that time of the *era* in which this alleged victim of ritual sacrifice lived. It was theorized by most anthropologists that the mound dwellers believed they were being punished by their gods."

Grove looked at the southerner. "Punished?"

De Lourde nodded. "Again, it's all speculation, but the world was changing around the first century. Especially in the Middle East. Prophecies were coming true. Christ was crucified, the Roman Empire was beginning its decline. Even in North America, cultures were clashing. The mound dwellers believed that a demonic force was starting to kill them off. Who knows? Maybe it was simply nature at work, an animal, a plague. But it could have been human."

Grove thought about it for a moment. "An early serial killer, you're saying."

A shrug from the southerner. "A stealth attack from an adversarial culture . . . who knows?"

"The *cycle* is what it is!"

All heads turned toward the elderly priest, whose rusty voice burbled like a broken pipe organ. "This is exactly what I'm talking about," he went on, his shredded breathing coming in fits and starts. "The wickedness following each discovery paralleling the evil and misery present eons earlier when the mummy lived and died. Do you see? This is the endless cycle, repeating down through the centuries."

"It would appear there's something to this theory," de Lourde allowed. "If you look at the empirical, even the circumstantial, you'd have to admit there's a pattern."

Zorn finally spoke up: "Excuse me, but that is just grade-A horseshit."

"Terry," Grove warned.

"All due respect, Father," Zorn said, glancing at the trembling priest. "But I've been zippin' my lip through most of this dog and pony show. I think I got the right to put my two cents in." Zorn looked at de Lourde.

"You're talking about one example, okay. One so-called cycle. I mean, let's get *real* here, people. This ain't even *circumstantial* evidence. We got a copycat out there. There's no voodoo in it. There's no—"

"Agent Zorn, if I might say a word," interrupted a soft, accented voice from across the corridor. Professor Armatraj stepped forward, nervously fiddling a handkerchief in his delicate brown hands.

Grove gave the dapper Indian a nod. "Go ahead, Professor."

"The female remains that we recovered from the Italian Alps in 1987 certainly match the pathology," he began, addressing Zorn, mostly. "The fatal wound in the neck, the artificial posture. The mummy was carbondated back to two hundred BC, also a time of much upheaval, as my colleagues will certainly attest."

De Lourde glanced up at the Indian. "You're talking about Locusta?"

"Exactly."

Zorn let out a weary sigh. "I'll bite. Who the hell is Locusta?"

Armatraj looked at him and said, "She may very well be history's first serial killer."

"She was a creator of poisons," de Lourde added, "although I understand she used other methods as well. Strangulations, stabbings. Today we'd call her a contract killer—a hit woman for the empire, if you will. Legend has it she kept a stable of slaves on whom she tested her potions and tortures."

Armatraj nodded. "She also ran a school for 'poisoners.' It was thought that she and her students collectively killed over ten thousand people. The Roman emperor Claudius was probably her most famous victim."

The priest spoke up again, that soft warning wheeze making the hair stand up on Grove's neck: "Locusta the

Sentinel was a historical figure whom the Vatican believes was under the influence of demons, a person possessed by an unclean spirit. This is documented fact."

Zorn was shaking his head. "I don't understand. You're saying these remains were *her*?"

Armatraj raised his slender brown hand. "A *victim* of hers, was the unofficial consensus among my team, and I believe they were correct. Especially now. Now that we have a deeper context."

There was a pause, and Grove said, "Was there something at the other end of the cycle?"

Armatraj took a deliberate breath. "In 1988, less than a year after we recovered the Icewoman from the Alps, there was a scandalous case in Italy. An infamous gangster . . . he suddenly became . . . I suppose we would say the man went *rogue.* Started killing people for the sport of it."

Grove took a deep breath. "Let me guess: the method of these killings was—"

"An ice pick to the neck, the *back* of the neck," Armatraj said, his dark eyes shining. "And he fooled with the bodies afterward, too, posing them. At the time, like Dr. de Lourde, I saw no connection."

Grove was starting to say something else when he noticed a heavyset man in a topcoat and English cap, carrying a sample case, approaching one of the pay phones at the far end of the corridor, maybe twenty feet away. Close enough to overhear this conversation. The fat man dialed a number and started talking. Other businessmen and various early risers were circulating around the mezzanine level beyond the bank of telephones. They were making Grove uneasy.

"Professor de Lourde, I'm going to need you to go ahead and unplug the computer," Grove instructed in a low voice, then gestured toward the far reaches of the vestibule, beyond the phones, beyond the restroom doors, where they could speak in private. "This way, everybody . . . please, just for a second, if you could please come this way."

He led the group over to the far end of the corridor, a deserted area where two upholstered "smoking chairs" flanked a small glass table, and the subdued yellow light from Victorian brass wall sconces shone down on the rich accoutrements with tasteful elegance. The group huddled around Grove, who all at once felt a little bit like the reluctant intelligence officer herding his operatives behind enemy lines where everything took on sinister dimensions—the muffled thrum of Muzak, the low lighting, the perfumed sterility of the Hotel Nikko's mezzanine. Grove's head swam with the silent revelations, his gut tight with icy dread. "Dr. Endecott," he said finally, his voice barely above a whisper, gesturing at the blue-haired woman, "you've been fairly quiet through all this."

She sighed. "The truth is, I'm not aware of any rash of killings following our discovery at Flodden Bog—although the remains did bear the same patterns we've been discussing."

Another pause, another exchange of glances. Grove asked her if it was possible she missed something.

"I don't believe so," she replied after a brief moment's thought. "I'm sure there was crime, there's always crime, but nothing that would match the signature you've described." She smiled then, a strange, crooked sort of smile. "There were people at Oxford who put forth some interesting theories, I will admit that, about the Flodden remains."

Grove looked at her. "Such as . . . ?"

The woman shook her head as though dismissing it. "One of my colleagues, a gentleman named Hartrey, was convinced the mummy had been a victim of the Sawney Beane family."

Zorn asked who the hell Sawney Beane was.

"Gotta brush up on your serial killer lore, Terry," Grove said, not taking his eyes off the Scottish woman. "The Sawney Beanes were cannibals. They terrorized Scotland back in, what, the 1700s?"

"Earlier actually," Professor Endecott said. "Fifteenth century, it was. According to legend, not a brigade could cross the coastal moors without losing at least one of their number to this vicious family of savages. The father was the instigator, moving his family into a cave by the seaside and feeding off travelers. They drank the blood of their victims, and fed the flesh to their children."

"*Jesus,*" Maura uttered.

"By the time of their arrests, they had something like fifteen children, maybe thirty or more grandkids. I understand they all were taken to Edinboro and executed, every last man, woman, and child." The older woman shrugged, looking at the priest. "I don't know if it qualifies as part of any cycle, Father, but it surely has—"

The sound of Terry Zorn's cell phone interrupted the woman with a shrill cheeping sound. "Sorry 'bout that, Professor," he said, digging the phone from the inner pocket of his sport coat. He looked at the caller ID window, then shot a glance at Grove and said, "It's Quantico Dispatch."

Grove watched as Zorn turned and walked away, answering the phone in a low, confidential voice.

"I have a question for the group," Maura was saying as Grove turned back to the professors. "I know we've already beaten this dead horse, but I still haven't gotten a handle on who these people were."

Professor Endecott asked her what people she was talking about.

"The mummies, the victims. I mean, basically we've established there's a pattern there—with the victimology, as Ulysses has been calling it."

There was a brief pause as the professors looked at

each other as though trying to decide who would answer. Professor de Lourde finally spoke up. "For the most part, I would put my money on holy men."

Professor Armatraj was nodding. "Definitely. These were shamans. We know this by the artifacts that were found with most of the bodies, by the tattoos and the bundles."

Grove looked at Armatraj. "The what?"

"*Bundles*, medicine bundles." The Indian made a cupping gesture. "Small leather pouches in which primitive men from poor societies kept supplies, tools."

Grove remembered the fungi that was found on the Mount Cairn Iceman. "Yeah, right, okay . . . I know what you're talking about." He shot a glance at Maura. "They found something just like that in Alaska."

She confirmed it with a nod.

Another pause, and Grove glanced over his shoulder, finding Zorn at the opposite end of the atrium, maybe a hundred feet away, across a wide expanse of lush carpet, standing by a potted palm, illuminated by rays of morning sun slashing down through skylights. The mezzanine bustled. Glass elevators full of early risers rose and fell behind Zorn as he talked intently into his cell phone.

Maura's voice tugged at Grove's attention: "But what I'm still wondering is, what were these holy men doing out in these remote areas?"

"I'm not following, my dear," Professor de Lourde demurred with a confused look on his lined face.

"What I'm saying is, the Mount Cairn remains were found at something like ten thousand feet . . . and Flodden Bog is way out in the wilds . . . we know what these areas were like because of the fossil record. Right? So basically most of these victims were murdered in the wilderness."

De Lourde touched his lip and thought for a moment. "I suppose you're right."

"So what were they *doing*? What were these holy men doing out in the middle of nowhere when they were killed?"

The question hung in silence for a moment as Grove glanced again across the mezzanine.

Zorn was coming this way. The Texan walked with a grim sort of purpose, snapping his cell phone shut, his expression all furrowed with urgency. *Only one thing would make Terry Zorn look like that,* Grove thought, and felt a cold splinter of ice pierce his stomach.

Edith Endecott was saying, "A legitimate question, Miss County, but alas, there's only so much one can learn from human remains."

"Where have I heard that before?" Maura said with a weary sigh.

"Excuse me, folks," Terry Zorn broke in as he approached in a whirlwind of nervous energy, all business, eyes flashing with that weird and sudden urgency. "Gonna have to borrow Mr. Grove for a few minutes."

Grove didn't have to ask why, *he knew,* he knew everything he needed to know by the look on Zorn's face.

Maura County's room was on the twenty-third floor— a single suite with a small lounging area and a breathtaking view of the fog-shrouded Golden Gate Park to the east. She had reserved the room on the magazine's tab in order to conduct private, one-on-one interviews with any of the participants who had interesting stories to tell. Now she found herself standing in the room's tiny vestibule, watching Grove and Zorn over by the immense king-sized bed in the center of the room, arguing with each other about guns and crime scenes.

"We're supposed to be criminologists, Terry, *suits,* we're not tactical, I haven't carried iron in over ten years," Grove was saying as he buckled his suit bag and stowed his few remaining belongings into his attaché.

Zorn's expression flared with anger as he fiddled with a metal travel case on the bed. "This Portland scene is already out of control—okay? Now did you or did you not say you think this perp's a spectator?"

"Terry, c'mon—"

"Did you or did you not say that!"

Grove sighed. "Okay, yeah, I think it's possible he's haunting the scenes, yes, but that doesn't mean—"

"Then you're carrying a piece today," Zorn said, opening the road case, revealing a large handgun nestled in black molded blister pack. Zorn paused for a moment, glancing over at Maura, who suddenly felt like an outsider eavesdropping on some arcane negotiation she had no business seeing—like a child watching two adults argue about sex.

She cleared her throat. "You know what . . . maybe I should wait downstairs."

"No, hey, no." Grove glanced over at Maura. "This is your room, for God's sake, you don't have to leave."

"I've got some calls to make," Maura pressed, backing toward the door.

"No, please—" Grove went over to her and put a hand on her shoulder. "You're part of this investigation now, Maura. I want you to stay."

His touch was so gentle—tender, even—that for the briefest instant, as their gazes met, Maura felt something new pass between them. Something subtle and inexplicable. Like fate, or some kind of chemical reaction. In the heat of the moment, it was fleeting, and later, Maura would wonder if she had merely imagined it, her brain fueled by stress and excitement. She swallowed hard. "Great, great—no problem, the calls can wait."

"C'm'ere, Ulysses, time's burning," Terry Zorn said from over by the bed. He had the handgun out of the case at that point and was clicking open the cylinder. The weapon made a clunking sound, which put a fine layer of gooseflesh along the backs of Maura's arms.

Grove went back over to the bed and took the gun from Zorn. "Haven't been on a range since I was in the army," he muttered, pointing the stainless steel sidearm at the floor and gazing down its barrel. To Maura the revolver looked massive and intimidating, its barrel maybe eight inches long.

"Just like ridin' a bike, old hoss," Zorn said, digging in the case for something else.

Grove studied the gun. "What is this, a .38 Bulldog?"

"Charter Arms .357 magnum Tracker with hollow-point loads, liquid tip."

To Maura's untrained eye, Grove appeared to be proficient—albeit a little rusty—at handling the gun. "Single-action, right?" he asked, easing the cylinder back into the frame and locking it home with a click.

"No, sir, that's a double-action weapon, just point and squeeze. And one shot will stop the hell outta this son of a bitch."

Grove sighed. "Terry, is this necessary?"

"Yes, it's necessary, and watch out you don't shoot your foot off with it, or we'll find your toes somewhere in the vicinity of China."

"That's lovely."

The men spoke very fast, without humor, their nervous tension as thick as a veil drawing over the room. This made Maura all the more uneasy.

"Here, catch." Zorn tossed him a leather harness sporting a holster and a couple of smaller compartments the size of change purses. "Put it on and keep it on."

"Yes, *sir.*"

Then Zorn threw him a couple of smaller objects that looked like tiny metal canisters of ball bearings. "Keep two speed-loaders in the belt, and a box of rounds in your suitcase."

Grove asked Zorn if he had checked with customs about traveling with the firearms.

"We're not flying commercial." Zorn was securing his

own holster-harness over his oxford shirt and tie, checking his own piece, which looked like an automatic to Maura. It was sleeker and made of brushed black metal. "Geisel scrambled a chopper out of Travis Air Force Base."

Grove finally got all the weaponry strapped on properly, then shrugged on his suit jacket. "What's the ETA?"

"Flight time's about an hour, should be back on the ground before noon. Let's move. They're picking us up downstairs in ten minutes."

Maura watched, marveling at how, even now, Grove seemed to maintain his grace under pressure. He still looked meticulously groomed, even after a sleepless night listening to the chatter of a bunch of over-caffeinated scholars. But the seams were starting to show. On his face, in his posture. Maura could see the exhaustion and stress darkening the skin around his eyes, slumping his shoulders.

He came over to Maura and touched her gently again on the arm. "This is a bad one," he said. "They're escalating, and we've got to stop this guy."

"I understand, Ulysses, I completely understand."

"Sorry to leave you with this mess."

"Don't worry about it," she said. "Just do me a favor and be careful."

"Will do." He gave her a quick smile and a pat. "Keep the professors talking, they're giving us great stuff."

"C'mon, partner," Zorn called over his shoulder as he whisked past them and made for the door. "The scene's gettin' old and so are we."

"I'll call you," Grove told her and touched her cheek, just a touch. Then he withdrew his hand very quickly as though second-guessing himself.

She wished him luck, then watched him walk out the door.

For a moment Maura lingered there in that empty room—feeling helpless and small and ridiculous in her one good dress—the echoes of clanging gunmetal in her ears. Then she went over to the door and peered around the corner.

The two profilers were already halfway down the corridor, making their way toward the bank of elevators. Zorn walked a few paces ahead of Grove, mumbling orders into his cell phone. Grove was checking his watch, the tails of his beautiful overcoat billowing behind him.

For one brief and awful instant, Maura County wondered—somewhat irrationally, perhaps—if she would ever see Ulysses Grove again.

14
The Beckoning

They were airborne by ten o'clock, lifting off the tarmac at Travis in a light drizzle, the intermittent gusts goosing the Huey Cobra like breaking waves. The chopper pilot was a 'Nam throwback named Zimmer with a jarhead Mohawk and steroid-rippled arms. He babbled ceaselessly the whole way, his voice blending with the droning roar of the blades, the shifting horizon reflecting off his mirrored aviator sunglasses. Grove and Zorn sat side by side on the gunner's bench—in *front* of the pilot's seat—like two overgrown children in a school bus. Through the grimy canopy glass they could see the world tumbling away in nauseating, glacially slow gyrations as the helicopter bored through the thick, changing atmosphere.

What should have been an hour-and-a-half trip turned into a three-hour thrill ride through all manner of spring weather. First it was the wind. It chased the Huey out of Travis, across the black spires of the Mendicino National Forest, and halfway up the western seaboard. The arrhythmic gales made the rivets groan. Rain lashed the bonnet, and Captain Zimmer had to two-hand the stick for nearly an hour, wrestling with the bucking bronco of an aircraft. Miraculously, neither Grove nor Zorn got sick. They simply spent most of the time giving each other looks, nervously glancing down at the convulsing treetops five hundred feet below them, occasionally grabbing hold of the bench seat's torn leather edging for dear life.

At one point Grove called out over the din of rotor: "You thinking about putting her down?"

"What's that?" Zimmer hollered.

"Flying a little low, aren't ya?" Grove indicated the jagged precipice looming beneath them. It looked as though the landing skids were only inches away from scraping the granite. Grove's gut wrenched with panic.

"That's Mount Shasta, boys, take a good look!" The captain nodded down at the alien planet of craggy tundra rushing beneath them, and as he nodded the entire aircraft seemed to *nod* along with him, yawing to one side like a ship tossing on a stormy sea of air.

"I said, you're flying a little low, aren't ya!"

Zimmer smirked, his mirrored eyes flashing. "It's the only way!"

"The only way for what!"

"For stayin' under the wind!" The pilot cackled. "Used to do it back in the 'Nam, flying Cobras over the Mekong! Scared the bejesus outta the slopes!"

And it went like that for what seemed an eternity, but was, in fact, maybe an hour and a half, or maybe two hours at the most, until finally the wind settled into a steady barrage of rain against the Huey's bulwark. Grove tried to concentrate on the Ackerman case as he sat there stiff and coiled, the safety harness cutting into his midsection, but his brain would not cooperate. A fireworks display assaulted his mind, the shards and shrapnel from his nightmares flashing at him with each bump—shadowy figures on a mountainside, an inhuman wail, an ash-handled flint dagger scraping the ice. Grove could feel the lump of the .357 magnum pressing against his kidney. *What the hell am I doing with this firearm,* he kept thinking, *like I'm John Motherfucking Wayne or something?*

The word *enemy* kept bubbling to the surface of Grove's consciousness. How had de Lourde's article on John George Haig put it? *The voice of God had come out of the mummy and commanded Haig to perform cleansing rituals until the enemy is found.* So maybe Haig was a nutcase who heard voices. But what *enemy* was he talking about? And what was the purpose of the ritual?

Somewhere over the Oregon border, as the chopper lurched and pitched over columns of swaying redwoods, the sky darkened so abruptly it was as though the aircraft had flown directly into a long tunnel. Grove felt the g-forces lift him out of his seat as the chopper dipped, and the light plunged away. Hazard lamps flickered on inside the fuselage. Day turned to night. Voices crackled out of Zimmer's radio, and the pilot started communicating with people on the ground. Then the noise started. It sounded like firecrackers going off. The pilot yelled something, but Grove couldn't understand a word.

"What!"

"Hail!" Zimmer yelled.

Zorn spoke up. "Is that a problem?"

The pilot was gritting his teeth. "Not unless we run into lightning!"

The next forty-five minutes or so were a blur. Grove and Zorn vise-gripped the seat frame as Zimmer fought the stick and commandeered the chopper through the tunnel of black sleet. The ice crystals tommy-gunned against the canopy, and the rotor shrieked. And for the first time during the flight, Captain Elvin Zimmer didn't talk much.

They *did* eventually run into lightning but, luckily, not until the final leg of the journey, just as they were entering Takoma air space. Zimmer managed to put the craft down on the edge of an overgrown auxiliary airfield about fifty miles south of Fort Lewis, and when they finally touched down, the entire Huey creaking like old bones settling, Grove said a silent prayer of thanks. His skull was throbbing, and for some reason, right at that moment, as the heavens opened up above the base, and torrents came crashing down on the idling chopper, he thought of his mother. Which was strange because Grove rarely thought about his mom, but here he was again, thinking about Vida, and all her African mumbo jumbo, for the third or fourth time in as many days.

He remembered how Hannah used to write letters to the old lady, humoring her, asking her about Africa and the old days in the mother country. "You oughtta be inviting that woman over here more often, Uley, she's your mama, for God's sake," Hannah would nag Grove, and he would just shake his head and give his wife mortified looks and absolutely refuse to have anything to do with the old woman and her primitive chicken-bone-and-feathers Nubian nonsense.

Grove shook off the memories as he extricated himself from the shoulder harness and climbed out of the aircraft.

The rain had risen to a full-fledged downpour, lightning strobing and popping every few seconds, tearing across the angry sky like the claws of a great beast. The two profilers splashed through puddles, hustling toward the main hangar holding newspapers over their heads.

"You don't really buy any of that cow pucky, do ya?" Zorn called over the noise of the rain as they jogged along.

"What cow pucky is that?"

"Bad mojo comin' off these mummies? Some innocent S-O-B comes along, gets infected by it?"

"The truth?"

"No, I want you to lie to me."

"The truth is, I'll buy anything at this point," Grove yelled as lightning bloomed again all around them, momentarily turning everything into silent-movie slow-motion.

The bureau escort was waiting for them in the hangar doorway. A paunchy veteran agent from Portland Community Relations named Karyn Flannery, the escort wore a frumpy raincoat and plastic scarf, and had a couple of spare umbrellas under one arm. She looked like a tough little gal, standing there, snapping her gum as the profilers approached, her hard eyes glinting.

"Gentlemen," she said, indicating the far door, which led into a breezeway connecting the main building with the front entrance. "I know you're probably in a hurry to get out to the scene."

Zorn gave a nod at the heavens. "If the goddamn scene's *still there.*"

She gave a shrug as she started toward the door. "Whatta ya gonna do? Washington state in the spring, right? Watch your step, gentlemen."

A moment later they emerged from the building, hunching under their umbrellas as they trotted through the downpour toward Special Agent Flannery's Jeep Cherokee. Zorn sat in the backseat, Grove sat shotgun. Flannery gunned the four-wheeler out of there in a gasp of exhaust vapors.

The thirty-minute trip down to the Regal Motel took them through Cowlitz County, a vast stretch of small towns and protected lands so densely forested the landscape swallowed whatever dim daylight managed to filter through the clouds. Riding swiftly along that two-lane highway, the wipers beating a counterrhythm to Flannery's monotoned rundown of the scene logistics, Grove gazed through the rain-strafed window glass at the passing landscape. He knew he should be taking notes on Flannery's thumbnail scene analysis, but instead he found himself thinking about fairy tales, "Hansel and Gretel" and "Little Red Riding Hood." The dark woods always beckoned in those stories. Had they beckoned to Ackerman today? Was he out there skulking in the shadows?

Flannery was telling the profilers about the discovery of the victims in their guest rooms. Vancouver Homicide had not been certain about the matching signatures until they had started going through the doors, discovering that each victim exhibited the same apparent time-of-death and cause-of-death, and the same bizarre postmortem pose. It was officially the worst mass murder in southeastern Washington State history, and before the Olympia crime lab had even arrived at the scene, the Vancouver chief of detectives had put out a bulletin announcing to all divisions and media outlets that a man who was wanted by the FBI named Richard Conrad Ackerman was probably at large in their area and should be considered armed and very dangerous and very likely unstable. Photographs of Ackerman were ready in time for most of the morning news shows. The details of the murders—including the identities of the victims—were still being withheld pending notification of the victims' families.

The crime lab people found a potpourri in the rooms—hairs, fibers, saliva, prints, the whole enchilada—so much hard evidence that even a first-year law student would be able to seal a conviction. Extra teams of investigators were called in to do canvasses in the area. By noon, extra foot patrols as far away as Yakima and Eugene had been enlisted to canvass rest areas, bus depots, train stations, and airports. That was two hours ago, and so far nothing had turned up. Nobody had seen any strange cars parked around the hotel. Nobody working the third shift at neighboring firms had seen any strange men loitering in the area during the night. It was as though Ackerman had done his evil deed and had simply vanished. Into the dark woods he went. To grandma's house—*hi-dee-ho hi-dee-ho!*

Grove gazed across the Jeep's interior at Agent Flannery, who was squinting to see through the rain as she steered the vehicle around a hairpin. "I'm gonna need you to help us out at the scene, Agent Flannery," Grove said at last, "if you feel up to it."

"That's what I'm here for."

"What time you got, Agent Flannery?"

She glanced at her watch. "Ten after two o'clock. Should be there in five minutes or so."

"Okay, here's the thing: I'm sure Olympia is doing a fine job collecting evidence."

"Yeah, sure."

"We're not interested in that right now, all right?"

"Okay."

"We're gonna be looking at something altogether different at the scene today, is basically what I'm saying."

The woman shot him a glance. "You're going to be looking at something *different* than evidence."

"I need you to understand what I'm saying here, I need your help at the scene."

She chewed her gum a little faster. "If you want me to help you, you're gonna have to be a little more specific."

Grove glanced over his shoulder at Terry Zorn, who sat in the backseat like some millionaire oilman with his cowboy hat in his lap, his bald cranium beaded with rain. "We're gonna be looking at the rubberneckers, ma'am," Zorn told her.

Agent Flannery didn't say anything.

"I assume you got a crowd out there, a peanut gallery?" Grove asked her.

The lady chewed her gum even faster. "You're gonna be looking at the gawkers."

"That's correct."

"Because you think he's still at the scene," she said softly, chewing that gum furiously now.

"He's probably not," Grove said.

"It's just a theory," Zorn added from the darkness of the backseat.

"We're dealing with an organized personality here, Agent Flannery," Grove explained. "It's all about ego with these guys, is what I'm saying."

A searing flash of magnesium light erupted outside, illuminating the corridor of trees, and the lonely highway, and even the interior of the Jeep, as though someone had just taken a photograph of the scene. A volley of thunder followed on its heels.

"Okay, real good," the stocky woman said then, a slight stiffening of her spine against the driver's seat the only sign of any reaction to all this—other than the frantic chewing and snapping of that Juicy Fruit.

Zorn chimed in from the back: "You're gonna be our front line, ma'am."

"Pardon?"

Grove looked at her. "The minute we get to the scene, everybody's gonna want to talk to us, put their two cents in. We're going to need you to run interference. You follow?"

"Yes, sir."

"Gonna need you to buy us some time, keep the detectives away from us while we scope the crowd. Do you understand?"

"I think so, yeah."

"What I'd like to do," Grove went on, "is *appear* like I'm working the scene, but what I'm really doing is working the *crowd*. You see?"

"Got it."

"So what *you're* going to be doing, Agent Flannery, if you're feeling up to it, is bullshitting both sides. Make the crowd think we're finding clues and whatnot, and at the same time you're distracting the detectives and the MEs. Keeping them away from us."

"I can think I can handle that, Agent Grove."

Grove gave her a smile. "I don't doubt it."

Five minutes later they crossed the outskirts of Vancouver and saw the first signs of the Portland metro sprawl sliding past them behind curtains of rain—gas stations, bait shops, convenience stores—all deserted and forlorn in the mean weather. They reached the Columbia interchange and turned west onto the narrow access road that snaked along the river, winding its way through fishing burgs toward the state line.

Soon the first hints of chaos glinted in watery coronas of red and blue light ahead of them like sinister holiday decorations in milk glass. Zorn had said the scene was out of control, but Grove had not expected such a mess. It looked like something Dante might have reported on his journey down the seven circles of hell. At least two dozen sheriff's cruisers were scattered at odd angles along the road, some of them stuck in the mud, rear wheels grinding, fishtailing, and sending gouts of filth in all directions. An ocean of umbrellas undulated along the north side of the road and up along the adjacent rise. Hundreds of onlookers had gathered. The cordon was in complete disarray, huge tails of yellow tape wagging in the rain and the wind.

Flannery reached down under the dash and flipped on her chasers, the red beams suddenly illuminating the Jeep's backwash.

"It's worse than I thought," Zorn grumbled from the back, slamming his cowboy hat down onto his shimmering pate.

Flannery flipped on her headlights, then flipped them off, then on and off, on and off, on and off, as she pulled up to the disintegrating roadblock. A fat man in a hunting vest dashed across the beams of her headlights. Somebody bellowed angrily. A voice crackled incomprehensibly through a megaphone.

"Just play it nice and natural," Grove advised as a trooper in a clear plastic rain poncho loomed outside Flannery's window. She rolled it down and started to say something.

"The hell you think you're going!" the trooper boomed at her.

She sighed and flashed her *federal investigator* tag, and then gave the guy a look that had daggers in it. "You mind if we go in, sweetheart?"

For a brief instant the trooper looked as though he had been slapped, the rain dripping off the bill of his Stetson. Then he waved them on as though everything had been authorized to his satisfaction.

Grove braced himself, feeling the bulge of the revolver under his coat, as Flannery plunged ahead.

Inside the cordon things were not much better. At least a half dozen morgue wagons were fanned out across the shoulder of the road in front of the motel, lights boiling, rear hatches bustling with miserable attendants shrouded in white plastic haz-mat gowns, wrestling slippery apparatuses in and out of the vehicles. The motel's tiny pea-gravel lot, which was littered with plastic garbage bags and drenched bed linen, had flooded to the consistency of overcooked oatmeal. Investigators in sodden topcoats hopped puddles as they circulated, weaving through clusters of patrolmen in yellow slickers. Silver strobe-light flashes from forensic cameras popped at odd intervals, syncopated with the occasional flicker of lightning.

Flannery found a place to park between one of the morgue wagons and a light pole on the far southwest corner of the property. "Let's start with the front row," Grove said, kicking open his door and nudging open his umbrella. "Then we'll move outward from there."

Lightning flickered again as Grove emerged from the Jeep, the cold, clammy breeze engulfing him. He looked at the building for a moment through the rain, through squinting, burning eyes, marveling at the depressing *sameness* of the place. How many of these fleabag roadside motels dotted the American countryside? And why did they all look the same? Regardless of whether they were owned by big franchises or were mom-and-pop shops, like this one, they all had the same neon signs made at the same factory, the same itchy sofa fabrics, the same cheesy color schemes—burnt-orange tiles and olive-green drapes—and the same cheap, papery-thin, interchangeable amenities. The same Styrofoam cups, rust-stained sinks, little stale soaps in paper sleeves, and sour, rubbery odors in the bathrooms.

The loud stench of death merely put an exclamation point on all this inhuman sameness.

Grove glanced over his shoulder for a moment, not too long, just a quick look, just to get a feel for the layout of the crowd. In that brief instant, Grove's studied gaze took in a lot. He saw the heartiest onlookers up front, extending a good city block, pushed up against the edge of the cordons in front of the motel, most of them under umbrellas. Behind them, others were craning to get a better look, spilling across the road, which had been blocked earlier in the morning. The demographics looked fairly homogenous to Grove: mostly male, mostly blue collar, mostly harmless. Hunters, local teenage boys, merchants from up the street. Grove saw a few consumer video cameras getting wet, a few women clutching at scarves against the chill wind.

"Excuse me—you the profiler?"

The voice came from behind Grove. He whirled around to see one of the local field agents approaching, a big guy with broad shoulders in a soaked London Fog. The man's square, mustachioed face was dripping.

Flannery came dogging up behind him. "Sir!" she barked. "Hold on a second!"

"It's okay, it's all right," Grove said with a nod to Flannery, then turned to the field agent and extended his free hand, clasping the umbrella with the other. The umbrella was proving handy, a way to shield Grove's face from the crush of onlookers. "Special Agent Ulysses Grove, Behavioral Science, and that gentleman over there, that's Special Agent Zorn." Grove nodded as nonchalantly as possible toward the cowboy hat bobbing under a flimsy umbrella thirty feet away.

A wet handshake.

And then a rapid-fire exchange, their voices raised just enough to be heard over the rain and noise, but no louder than that:

"I'm Agent Masamore, Portland field office, sorry about the circus here, I'm not sure what else we can glean from this one. Seems like he's flaring out. Already got a six-state search going on. We'll get him."

Grove nodded. "Excellent, great."

Masamore jacked a thumb toward the building. "You'll probably want to speak to the FOS—"

"Agent Masamore," Grove interrupted with an open face and a raised hand, as nonthreatening as possible. "Let me just break in here at this point—"

An arched eyebrow from the stocky field agent. Flannery gazing at the ground.

"Because what we'd like to do is just ease into it, if that's okay." Grove wiped a bead of moisture from his nose. "Maybe start a spiral out here and work our way toward the center of the chalk line."

"That's fine but . . . just so you know . . . we did that already."

Grove kept his expression polite, warm. "We'll definitely huddle with you in a few minutes, probably use a lot of your notes . . . if that's okay."

Special Agent Masamore shrugged, raising the collar

on his coat. A little on the irritated side. "Knock your-selves out—*me*, I'm getting out of the rain." The stocky special agent turned and trundled back across the mushy gravel toward the Regal's office.

Grove watched the agent vanish inside the gaping of-fice door as another bolt of lightning streaked across the sky, flickering white-hot light everywhere. The rain thumped relentlessly on Grove's umbrella as he felt something on the back of his neck. *Somebody's watching me.* The sudden and unexpected feeling bubbled up from Grove's subconscious, and he immediately dis-missed it. *Nervous tension, old hoss, that's all it is,* he thought. *There's a lot of people watching you right now. Flannery is watching, Zorn is watching.* Grove turned and shot an-other furtive glance at the crowd.

Scores of anonymous faces, many of them creased with a lifetime of work and drink and smoke and worry, were compulsively scanning the scene. They were like spectators at a slow-motion sporting event. Grove had studied crowds in the past. He wrote a thesis about them years ago at the academy. He had developed sev-eral theories. One he called the "radiant attention" the-ory, which stated that a minimal amount of interest was required to keep a crowd gathered at a scene. In other words, if one guy seemed interested in something, a hundred other guys would stand there like sheep wait-ing for something to happen. Attention was passed through osmosis.

Another theory Grove had developed came to be known—in his final paper, at least—as the "interest/fre-quency response ratio," which merely meant a crowd re-quired a minimum frequency of action to stay put, to stay coalesced, to stay intact. In the case of the Regal Motel scene, this stimulus was provided by white-suited morgue attendants emerging from guest rooms with bodies in tow. Like lab rats caught in some morbid Pavlovian experiment, the crowd would begin to disperse every thirty minutes or so, their compulsion to leave certainly exacerbated by the downpour, but then another body would be borne from the shadows of a blood-soaked room, and the crowd would snap back into position. Victims were coming out, one at a time, about every forty-five minutes or so—which was, as it turned out, just frequent enough to keep the crowd riveted to the scene despite the inclement weather.

Grove made eye contact with Zorn and gave a slight nod, reaching under his raincoat and into his inner breast pocket. He had brought along a couple of one-sheet bulletins he had taken off-line back at the Hotel Nikko. The letter-sized pages, which were folded in half, had a recent picture of Ackerman in the upper right-hand corner. Grove pulled them from his jacket, unfolded one, and looked at it. Raindrops pattered on the photo of Ackerman, which was rendered in the smudged, shadowy quality of a second-generation copy: a gaunt-faced, graying man with tired eyes and pallid skin. In the photo—which had been provided to the FBI by Ackerman's sister, *not* his wife—he was dressed for a company portrait, clad in suit and tie, and posed against a standard satin backdrop. He was smiling in the photo, but it was a humorless, passport smile.

Even through the inky layers of disintegration caused by multiple copying and faxing, that dead impression behind Ackerman's eyes was apparent.

Zorn was making his way toward Grove, slowly yet steadily moving along the flapping yellow tape. Every few moments the Texan would pause and glance casually over his shoulder at the crowd, registering any changes, noting faces, then turning his attention back to the ground as though he were investigating footprints.

Grove went over and handed Zorn one of the soggy bulletins, and the Texan took it, acknowledging it with a nod, but didn't look at it. "If he's here," Zorn said under his breath, gazing at the ground, "I'm thinking he's gonna be across the street or lurkin' somewhere in the rear."

"Maybe, maybe not," Grove countered, giving the crowd his back. "Remember it's about the *show*, he's putting on a show for us, for our benefit."

Zorn pretended to look at something on the ground, the rain sluicing off the rim of his umbrella. "You gotta balance the ego with the prospects of getting caught."

"That's part of what fuels the fantasy, the thrill of it, what he gets out of the risk."

"You want to take the box seats? And I'll take the bleachers?"

"Yeah, good."

Without ceremony the two profilers turned and went their separate ways. Zorn casually limboed under the cordons and headed toward the other side of the road looking as though he had forgotten something. Grove lingered near the front row of onlookers.

Squatting down and acting as though he were inspecting something embedded in the muddy gravel, he took out the bulletin and looked at the picture in the corner again. The rain had blurred it. Now Ackerman's emaciated face was streaked in distorted tears of black ink. The gaunt visage burned itself into Grove's midbrain as lightning flash-popped again overhead, turning the premature darkness to silvery daylight. *Somebody's watching you again . . . somebody in the crowd is concentrating on you, now, look!*

Grove peered around the edge of his umbrella, and through the veils of rain studied the closest ranks of bystanders. It looked like a working-class Mount Rushmore: a perfect row of chiseled, scabrous Caucasian faces shaded by umbrellas, all eyes fixed and pointing forward, their gazes locked on the Regal's facade. They looked hungry for more carnage.

Grove's gaze traveled down the row of onlookers: guys in orange down hunting vests, teenage boys in shop-worn denim jackets, a bearded biker in glistening black leather, an old geezer in a yellow oilman's slicker who looked like he just stepped off a tuna can label, a portly woman holding field glasses to her eyes, and finally, at the end of the row, a tall man in a hooded coat looking this way.

Gazing directly at Grove.

15
One Shot

The man wore a dark blue nylon raincoat, which bulged slightly in the back, his face obscured by the oversized hood. In the rain, at such a distance—fifty, maybe even seventy-five feet—it was almost impossible for Grove to positively identify the man by his picture. The only things visible within the black hole of that hood were the very tip of the man's long patrician nose and a dull gleam of teeth—either a smile or a grimace . . . or both.

The man made no sudden movements. He looked like a statue standing there in the rain at the end of that long row of onlookers, gazing out of the shadows of that hood directly at Grove. And even as Grove hesitated, looking away, attempting to give the impression that he had not noticed the hooded figure, he could tell in his peripheral vision that the man had not budged, his gaze still fixed on Grove.

Adrenaline percolated through Grove as he crouched there, trying to appear only interested in the weather-beaten gravel. He was still clutching that ridiculous umbrella and that water-blurred bulletin, and for several agonizing moments he couldn't make his brain work, couldn't gather his thoughts, couldn't move. He knew he couldn't get to his gun without alarming Ackerman (and everybody else, for that matter). And he knew he couldn't signal Zorn without spooking the perp.

All at once, he willed himself into a kind of hyper-attenuated hyperalertness that he first learned on the training course when he was at the FBI academy. Back in those days they would send young guys like Grove into this vast fake city hewn from immense particleboard building facades, plywood cutouts, and spring-loaded cardboard criminals, and they would run the poor new-bies through the gauntlet, making them jump at shadows with their little .38 starter pistols—*bang! bang! you're dead!* Much to the section trainers' delight, Grove turned out to be almost preternaturally adept at fake-killing fake targets. But now, a million light-years away from the academy, engulfed by the stench of the real world, Grove found he had to struggle to achieve that same cobra calm.

Crouching in that horrible blood-scented mud, getting drenched by the filthy rain, a calliope of noise swirling around him, he bit down hard, so hard he nearly cracked his teeth. He felt the unwavering reptilian gaze of the tall man in the hood on the side of his face like a heat lamp. And he felt his joints tighten with fight-or-flight panic. *The son of a bitch hasn't figured out what's going on,* Grove's inner monologist marveled, *he doesn't know you ID'd him, he hasn't figured out he's been made!*

Another volley of lightning erupted, turning the scene into a silver photographic negative.

Grove knew at once that he had an opportunity here. If he could continue the ruse—the Academy Award–worthy performance of An Investigator Examining Pavement—he might be able to get his hand inside his coat, and get it around the grip of the .357 Tracker, without giving himself away. If he could utilize the element of surprise, he might be able to pull down on Ackerman quickly and decisively enough to prevent any further violence or mishaps. Of course, this theory was all predicated on the belief that Ackerman had a few brain cells of sanity left in his beleaguered skull. Unfortunately, Grove had no way to gauge the extent of Ackerman's sickness. Right now, all that Grove had was a huge, gangly perp with a touch of catatonia, and a face shrouded in the shadows of an oversized hood, standing stone-still on the edge of Grove's peripheral vision.

An idea occurred to Grove, a way to get to his gun without alarming the killer, and over the space of a mere second or two, the profiler plotted out his actions: He would do it in three steps. One, he would reach down to his outer pocket with his free hand and dig out his small spiral notebook. Nothing out of the ordinary there; nothing that any investigator wouldn't do a million times in a day. Then, two, he would pretend to search for a pen that he didn't have, patting all his pockets and frowning and generally playing the part to the hilt. And finally, three, he would reach into his coat, unsnap the Tracker's holster, and draw the gun out as he was rising and dropping the umbrella and aiming a bead on Ackerman in one fluid motion.

The object of all this physical business was not to give Ackerman any chance whatsoever to react. In other words, to make it nearly impossible to respond. The keys to success were speed and resolve. Which was why Grove started taking deep, steady breaths. Like a golf swing, gun work is all about relaxation and breathing.

Ackerman had yet to move.

Grove began the three-step journey to his gun, becoming hyperaware of the crowd around him. Very few of the bystanders were talking, or if they were, it was impossible to hear their voices above the noise of the rain. Somewhere on the other side of the parking lot, a detective called out for assistance, and a pair of morgue attendants hurried across the lot with a collapsible gurney under their arms.

Ackerman kept staring at Grove.

Grove pulled the little beige spiral notebook from his pocket.

So far, so good. Ackerman had not moved. Grove laid the notebook on the ground, then pretended to search for his pen. He made a big deal out of it—like a stage actor playing to the back row—patting his right breast pocket, then his left, frowning, patting his trouser pocket, then finally reaching into the inside of his coat. His heart was beating so rapidly, he could feel the pulse on the inside of his arm as he frantically worried open the holster. His mouth was dry. His neck palpitated with excess adrenaline. He heard the muffled snap of the safety strap.

He had his hand—moist and hot with nerves—around the grip of the gun when he heard an unexpected cry ring out across the street.

And that was when everything started going to hell.

"Everybody down! Everybody down! FBI! Don't you dare move, Ackerman, you son of a bitch! FBI!"

Terry Zorn hurled across the street with his big black steel Desert Eagle raised and ready, colliding with an elderly duck hunter, sending the old man sprawling to the pavement. The crowd lurched and jerked like a herd of sheep spooked at the commotion, many of them complying instinctively, splashing down into the puddles. Moving in an awkward, tumbling, sideways gait, Zorn held his gun up with both hands in the "weaver" position—the best posture from which to shoot—as he roared toward the hooded suspect.

The tall man in the hood hardly had time to turn, which he did instinctively now, as people careened to the gravel around him.

Roaring toward the suspect, closing the distance to thirty-five yards, then thirty, then twenty-five, Zorn forgot the field procedure that had been drummed into him back in the academy a couple of decades ago. Something had snapped in Zorn's brain a few seconds earlier when he had just *happened* to glance up from the damp bulletin and look back at the motel, and he had just *happened* to see the hooded figure at the precise moment a bolt of lightning had just *happened* to illuminate the landscape enough to light up the inside of that hood, and *there he was*, the motherfucker from the bulletin, standing right there, his gaunt face creased with a cadaverous smile, and it was that *grin*, or grimace, or whatever the hell it was, that lit the fuse inside Zorn and made him drop his umbrella and draw his weapon and sent him charging through the rain full of hellfire and fury, and now he was maybe twenty yards away from the subject with a bead dropped directly on the black hole inside that hood.

Then all sorts of things happened all at once and very quickly.

There was an audible collective gasp, loud enough to be heard across the street, as the front row of onlookers seemed to duck down in unison like a sloppy chorus line, umbrellas tumbling away on gusts of rain. Some of the investigators across the lot instantly crouched down, hands involuntarily reaching for weapons, while others appeared in doorways, already armed and rigid and instinctively standing in tripod positions. Zorn couldn't see Grove but heard a shrill silent warning alarm ringing in his ears as he approached the suspect, the sudden danger registering in Zorn's innards before his brain had a chance to send the news to his legs.

Ackerman had grabbed the closest bystander—the portly woman with the field glasses—and was quietly holding something long and sharp to her neck.

Sudden hesitation threw off Zorn's stride, and the

Texan slipped on an oily patch ten yards away from the suspect. His legs flew out from under him and he fell directly onto his ass, banging into a cowering duck hunter, the impact hard enough to knock the air out of Zorn's lungs. Amazingly, the barrel of that big black automatic never wavered from its trajectory toward Ackerman's hooded face—even as Zorn sat shuddering in pain near the flapping yellow tape.

By that point another weapon had been drawn and trained on the killer.

Ulysses Grove stood in firing position about fifteen yards away, his face taut and dripping, his gaze seared and fixed on Ackerman and the hostage. In that brief instant, Zorn's brain seethed with panic and regret and shame—the realization almost instantaneous as he sat there like an idiot, like a rookie, like a goddamned trainee on the wet shoulder, his spine screaming with pain. He had forced them into a standoff. He had violated about a dozen principles of good tactical work, and now they were faced with a hostage situation because of *him*, and all these thoughts crossed Zorn's mind in a millisecond and then blew apart like leaves in a hurricane—

—because Ackerman had started moving.

Had the killer hesitated another few seconds, the other law enforcement people might have had a chance to get into position for a decent head shot, but there were many aspects working against the cops and feds that day.

The rain—which had obscured everything with a film of Vaseline—proved to be the least of their troubles. First and foremost was the crowd. The gawkers had scattered in all directions at the first sign of gunplay, making it impossible for an average shooter to pinpoint the bad guy. Too many frantic bodies were lumbering this way and that in the deluge, their umbrellas tossing and tumbling on the winds, skittering willy-nilly across the gravel and the road and even the roof of the motel.

Lightning only worsened the effect with its intermittent, raging punctuation of silver tungsten supernovas, retarding movement down to time-lapse, Nickelodeon slow motion—which is exactly what it was doing at the precise moment Grove aimed his revolver at Ackerman (who was roughly ten feet away) and hollered in an even, booming, stentorian voice over the rain, the call of a lion tamer scolding an errant animal: *"Let her go, Ackerman, there's no way out, so don't make it worse! Let her go!"*

Ackerman frantically yet steadily kept backing toward the yellow tape that fluttered on the west edge of the property, dragging the field-glasses lady like a hunting trophy, ignoring her wriggling and mewling, shooting regular glances over his shoulder as though he were an automaton triangulating the distance between Grove and the other armed authorities and the empty forest beyond the property line. It looked as though the killer held a short spear or hunting arrow to the woman's jugular, the slender tail wagging in the rain.

Another violent flicker of lightning lit up the world, and Grove had to squint in order to maintain the killing bead on Ackerman's hood. He could see Zorn back on his feet and in the weaver position just off his right shoulder, and he could sense time slipping away as the other shooters behind him coalesced as quickly as possible on the periphery, the sounds of bolts clanging, rounds injecting into chambers with dull thunks, shuffling footsteps, and a swelling din of frenzied voices. But it was all gelling too slowly because Ackerman was already halfway to the fringe of scrub along the western edge of the gravel lot.

"Don't do it, Ackerman! Don't do it, don't do it, don't do it!"

Grove's finger, moist with flop-sweat, curled around the trigger, and in the space of a single second he saw the worst-case scenario open up before him like a sinister pop-up book revealing its garish inevitibility in his midbrain: the edge of the gravel lot simply ending, without border or garden trim or edging, merely melting into a leprous hill of ironweed and litter now shrouded in gloom and shadow, providing a perfect escape route into the dense wall of birch that loomed just beyond the motel's property line.

Before Grove had a chance to do anything about the situation, several things happened almost simultaneously in the flashbulb strobe of lightning.

The killer made the tactical error of glancing over his shoulder at the woods long enough for one of the peripheral shooters to squeeze off a shot at his hood. Grove was in the process of firing a warning shot when he heard the blast, and it must have been a large-caliber bore because the report was immense, a teeth-jarring boom that rivaled the thunder. It slapped and echoed off the distant hills. The trees above the killer were perforated in a cloud of mist, and Grove's gun suddenly discharged as though touched off by sympathetic vibrations, sending a round into the air in a plume of silver light, and everybody dove to the wet ground, and the killer lurched toward the dark forest, doing something jerky and decisive to the lady.

Grove was on the ground all of a sudden and could barely see the woman with the field glasses collapsing, folding into the dirt ten yards away, her neck breached and gushing blood as black as india ink in the deceptive light of the storm. She convulsed once and then stiffened in shock and imminent death, her hand still gripping those pathetic field glasses as her carotid leaked all over the mire. Ackerman was a blur on the side of the hill behind the victim as scores of firearms—maybe hundreds, it *sounded* like hundreds—suddenly began discharging from all points across the parking lot.

The light and noise lit up the storm. Grove ducked down and covered his head. Zorn dropped to the ground not more than ten feet off Grove's flank. Out of the corner of his eye Grove saw the battlefield firelight—countless yellow lumens popping like phosphorous in the dark. The birch trees boiled. Contact sparks traced across the adjacent woods. The sound had a magnificent ugliness to Grove's ears—nothing like the cowboys-and-Indians fireworks-crackle of the movies. *This* sound was a dirty, metallic pummeling sound.

Ackerman had vanished.

The gunfire ceased.

"We need medical attention over here. Somebody get a doc over here, now, now!" Grove bellowed at the top of his voice, but he could hardly hear it in his own ears, they were ringing so badly. He managed to rise to his feet and lumber over to the field-glasses lady, who was soaked in her own blood, twitching in the mucky puddles of the parkway, her gray face contorted with agony, her eyes pinned open.

Grove dropped his gun and pressed his hand down on the woman's neck to stanch the bleeding, and he felt the fluttering, wounded-bird pulse of the woman's heartbeat, and knew, he *knew*, the lady was gone, she had only moments left. Thrusting his bare fingers down into her blood-clogged throat, Grove cleared her airway and began a futile attempt at CPR as movement and voices swirled all around him. Terry Zorn flashed by Grove, vaulting across the parkway and hurtling into the woods after Ackerman. *"Zorn, goddamnit, wait!"* Grove howled through the rain. *"I told you, we're not tactical!"*

The next few seconds were critical for Grove. He

looked down at the portly woman's blood-spattered face and saw her mouth moving, eyes blinking, no sound coming out of her other than a faint clicking noise in the base of her throat, and Grove's midsection seized up with a poisonous cocktail of rage and misery, because he was looking into that dying woman's eyes, and he saw only pathos there, he saw only the hardscrabble life of a working-class mother with too much eye shadow caking her aging lashes, and now somebody in a white jacket was yanking Grove off the woman, and Grove tumbled backward onto the edge of the gravel, rolling onto his side and clawing for his gun.

Terry Zorn's cowboy hat lay on the ground a few inches away, dented by a muddy footprint, and for some reason the sight of that hat lying there did something to Grove, and he rose up and started lurching toward the forest, the revolver hot in his hand now. He could barely hear the frantic voices of the other investigators converging on him.

Grove ignored all the warning cries and plunged headlong into the woods.

Zorn kept his automatic pointed out in front of him like the prow of a ship cutting through a storm as he charged up that narrow mud path between thickets of spruce and ferns, the rainy darkness enclosing him. He could barely see the bleary shadow of the killer—*sense* was a better word—about twenty yards or so ahead of him, fleeing into the wooded hills, something bouncing around inside the back of that jacket.

Voices pierced the storm. Zorn ignored them, gripping the gun tightly in both of his wet hands, the classic cradle-hold they teach you the first day on the range. He leaped over a deadfall and nearly stumbled, but somehow he kept his balance. His bald head was cold and crawling with adrenaline. His eyes stung. But he kept churning forward through the thickening foliage, his faltering gaze riveted to that ghostly outline of the killer moving through the undergrowth ahead of him.

The path ended, and the forest seemed to close down around Zorn like a black corridor. Rain sluiced down through endless columns of cedar, birch, and hemlock. Lightning flickered, the birch, bark momentarily gleaming in Zorn's peripheral vision like bleached bones.

Ackerman was getting away. Zorn could see the silhouette receding into the deeper growth in the distance, and the Texan tried to quicken his pace, but it wasn't easy now. He was cobbling over rain-slimy rocks and rotwood, squeezing between bottlenecks of branches, moving deeper and deeper into the uncharted darkness of unincorporated Clark County, the steely tendrils bullwhipping at him as he passed.

One shot. That's all he needed. One clean shot and he could drop this sick son of a bitch and save the taxpayers the expense of further investigative hours and legal fees and appeals. And he kept thinking this as he tore through the woods, careful not to slip on the greasy exposed roots or partially buried granite facets. He had two extra nine-round magazines jiggling around in his raincoat pocket, which meant he had a total of twenty-seven rounds—including the clip already seated in the Desert Eagle—which should be more than enough firepower to get the job done. He would go for a head shot. The takedown would settle all accounts, obliterating Zorn's earlier mistake. Tom Geisel would be proud. So would Zorn's VFW daddy back in Tennessee. Even Grove would have to admit that Terry Zorn was a force to be reckoned with.

He kept thinking about all this for quite a while, putting almost a mile behind him, before he began to slow down. He walked a few more paces before stopping.

He was now alone.

The realization slammed through his gut as he stood in a shadowy little clearing shrouded by a low canopy of spruce and a wall of wild undergrowth so thick it looked as though someone had stitched it out of vines and branches. Zorn's heart started thumping. He was drenched. His jacket felt as though it were pasted to his back, his feet swimming in his boots. He could no longer hear Grove. Nor could he hear the voices of the other cops and ATF guys. The only sounds now were the distant, dieseling belch of thunder and the incessant rain snapping against the tamarack leaves.

Wiping the beads of moisture from his bald dome and his eyelashes, then glancing over his shoulder, he squinted down into the river valley from which he had come and realized he had ascended a gradual rise into a densely forested ridge overlooking the Columbia. The molten gray reaches of the river—over a mile away— were visible through breaks in the sumac. Zorn glanced down at his gun, snapping the slide back and checking the chamber, making sure he was operational.

He started up a jagged pitch of limestone. His boots slipped on the moss and he nearly fell backward, grabbing at a hank of branches overhanging the rocks in order to avoid tumbling back down the slope and hitting his head and dying in shame. Finally he made it to the summit of a craggy plateau that overlooked the river.

The rain was blowing profusely up there, and Zorn had to lift his collar and squint in order to see around that desolate clearing. It was the size of a squash court, the ground a rolling mogul of granite and petrified deadfalls. The rocks looked like tiny tombstones sticking out of that seared earth, glistening from the rain. The surrounding foliage and trees formed a natural barrier, behind which windblown shadows danced and swayed.

Somewhere nearby a twig snapped.

Panic sizzled off Zorn's nerve endings, and he crouched

down suddenly, involuntarily grabbing his Desert Eagle with both hands, every muscle in his body tensing up. The hair on his arms stiffened, his scalp crawling. He had just remembered something at the precise moment he had heard the snap of that twig behind him, and the revelation was like a giant lead weight pressing down on his shoulders all of a sudden, taking his breath away, leeching his courage, and squeezing his heart.

It was something he should have remembered from all the profiles, something incidental that now called out to him like the voice of doom on that wind-whipped plateau: the long, slender object bouncing around inside Ackerman's raincoat!

Ackerman had a bow and arrows.

16
The Bottomless Dark

Ulysses Grove heard two noises in quick succession up ahead of him. The first was a muffled cry—so distorted by the noise of the storm and the apparent anguish being expressed that it was difficult to identify the gender. This choked wail was followed almost instantly by the bark of a large-caliber handgun—a watery blast arcing up into the sky and echoing off the decaying thunder like a sonic boom.

The two noises sent adrenaline bolting down through Grove's arteries as he struggled through a thick, strangled copse of hemlocks, immediately quickening his pace, awkwardly slashing at the hanging branches and wiry undergrowth with the long stainless steel barrel of the .357. The woods of the Pacific Northwest are basically rain forests, and this one was no different. The floor was a matted carpet of resinous, mold-slick ferns and moss, which felt to Grove as if he were trying to run on ice skates.

The ATF guys were behind Grove somewhere, yelling at him through the rain, ordering him back, but Grove ignored their muffled warnings and kept hacking through the foliage as he made his way up the side of the rise, slipping on the greasy deadfalls, the gun throwing him off balance. He could see a jagged precipice of rocks up there, perhaps fifteen, perhaps twenty yards away, and he muscled toward it.

The sounds had come from up there somewhere, and Grove homed in on them. He was drenched. His clothes felt as though they weighed a thousand pounds, but he ignored the handicaps and roared toward the source of the gunfire. A moment later he reached the lip of the plateau, a ragged outcropping of boulders and exposed roots shiny with rain.

He climbed over the slippery rim and into a small clearing of scabrous stone.

"Nnnaahhh—"

The sound penetrated the rain, and Grove whirled to his left, his gun stuck out amateurishly in front of him, the barrel dripping and trembling. He saw Zorn keeled over in the mud twenty yards away.

Lightning erupted.

Grove's first instinct was to rush over to his partner, but something stopped him, some deeper instinct, something emanating from deep within his primitive reptile brain, ordering him to *get down, get down, getdowngetdowngetdown!*

Grove slammed down hard onto his belly, an evasive military position that his muscle-memory had dredged up from his days in basic training. He kept his arms outstretched, the gun out in front, pressed against the ground, braced and ready, his arms aching. What the hell was wrong with his arms? Why were they aching all of a sudden?

This is a trap, it's a trap. Do something! Do something now!

Another garbled cry rang out—this one more of a croak, or perhaps a feeble attempt to speak—and Grove realized his partner was dying, maybe bleeding to death, maybe in shock. It was difficult to see any details through the rain. Terry Zorn appeared to be lying supine, his arm raised at an awkward angle, tangled in the weeds on the edge of the clearing. His chest heaved, and his neck looked dark and shiny, as though someone had poured black paint on him.

Grove crawled on his belly across the mossy ground toward Zorn.

Thunder vibrated the air, the ringing in Grove's ears constant now, as he tried to remember the axioms of Israeli counterinsurgency techniques that he had learned in the academy. *You wield the gun like you're pointing a finger at the target, and you focus on the back sight, not the front sight*—or was it the other way around? Grove's brain was swimming with panic.

He reached Zorn and got close enough to hear the watery gasping noises.

"*Ahhh—sssssuuh—*" Zorn was convulsing, his blood-spattered face contorting, something resembling words coming out of his breached throat. He was drowning in his own blood. His neck was punctured all the way through, a broken hunting arrow sticking out of the back, forming a V.

"It's okay, I'm here, I'm here, Terry, take it easy, gonna get you outta here—*Shit!*"

Grove rose to a crouch, set down his gun, reached for the Texan, and tried to cradle the man's head. Blood was splashing in the raindrops. Tributaries of Zorn's life snaked off from his body, seeping into the moist earth. With trembling hands Grove pressed a flat broadleaf against Zorn's jugular in a futile effort to stanch the bleeding.

Zorn's eyes were blinking fitfully in the rain. "*Ahhmm sahrrrrrr—*"

All at once Grove realized that Terry Zorn was trying to say *I'm sorry.*

"Don't worry about it, man, you're doin' fine, gonna get you outta here, you're gonna be okay—" Grove glanced over his shoulder, wondering what the hell happened to the ATF guys. Did they get lost? Grove's voice piercing the rain: "Officer down! Goddamn it, officer down! Officer down up here! Somebody get a goddamn doc up here right now!"

Zorn was trying to say something else, craning his neck, bloody lips quivering. Grove leaned down close, the rain dripping like liquid rubies onto Zorn's face.

"S-sorry," the Texan enunciated barely above a whisper, then let out a ragged breath.

"Terry—"

Zorn deflated like a balloon in Grove's arms, and Grove shook the man. "Terry!"

Nothing.

"Terry!"

Zorn was a stone.

Grove stared and stared at the man's empty cellophane eyes. Emotion flooded Grove, and all of a sudden he did something that field analysts would later deem reckless and foolish and strictly the act of an amateur: he hugged his friend. The embrace didn't last long—the blood-steeped rain was sluicing down between the two men, and Grove's fight-or-flight instinct was surging inside him, stiffening the tiny hairs on the back of his neck—but for that one foolish, amateurish moment Grove felt a tremendous sadness and affection for the Texan. Zorn had been a friendly adversary for years, a casual associate, certainly threatened by Grove. But now, in that single, terrible instant of clarity, the dead man's body still warm in his arms, Grove felt the entire crestfallen arc of Terry Zorn's life coursing through him, the sorrow of it, the father who could not be pleased, the standards that could never be met. Grove's eyes welled. His stomach clenched.

He held his deceased friend for one more brief moment until he heard a new sound emanating from somewhere close by, a sound that defied easy categorization, a sound that penetrated Grove's skull and resonated the strings of his central nervous system like a tuning fork being struck.

Human emotions are slippery. One emotion can present itself as another. Feelings can project themselves inappropriately. On that rain-swept ridge above the Columbia River, Ulysses Grove slammed up against a painful confluence—years of repressing his loss and sorrow over Hannah's death, months and months of losing control over his health and his life and his powers as a behavioral profiler, an endless, painful embrace of a man lost in the line of duty, and that indefinable kernel of preternatural cognition that had been stirring deep inside him. All of it seized up in his gut suddenly and presented itself as cold, metallic rage—rage spurred on by that otherworldly noise coming from the shadows to his immediate right.

He gently laid Zorn back in the mud and slowly lowered himself back into the "trench" position—belly against the ground, arms out front, neck craned. He reached for his gun. The .357 Tracker felt cold and oily in his grip. *Where the hell are those ATF guys, for God's sake?* Grove's hands had stopped shaking. His tears had ceased. The anger steadied him, fortified him. He started crawling toward the noise, his embattled brain attempting to identify it.

It came from the deeper woods along the north edge of the clearing. Grove elbowed steadily toward the wall of spruce and foliage, ready to shoot at any moment. The sound was difficult to place. It was more of a vibration, a gravelly, twenty-cycle *hum*, like air blowing at frantic, uneven intervals through the lowest chambers of a pipe organ, and the closer Grove got to the trees, the more it sounded like labored *breathing*. Maybe Zorn had wounded the killer. Maybe this was part of the trap. Grove didn't care anymore.

He reached the threshold of the forest and rose to a crouch, jerking at every sound no matter how faint, his hands in the weaver position on the gun. The noise had ceased for a moment, and Grove peered through the columns of trees and thickets of vines, expecting an arrow to leap out at him at any moment. He yelled through the rain, his voice sounding bizarre in his own ears, as though it were coming from some one else:

"Ackerman!"

It was black as night in those woods, a world of criss-crossing timbers and rioting undergrowth, so dense it swallowed any remnant of the gray daylight. Grove scanned it over the barrel of the Tracker, backsight blurred, frontsight crisply focused, his arms and tendons as steady as a marble pillar. To his right, something gleamed dully in the ethereal light. Grove blinked away the rain in his eyes.

He finally identified what he was looking at: a sheer plane of rock behind the trees, a natural convolution of granite probably carved eons ago when the Columbia was young and the Iceman was still trudging across the frozen slopes of the Cairns. The weathered face of sediment was obscured by forest and mist, but it clearly framed a deeper shadow in its center—down at ground level—an opening.

A cave.

Grove braced himself. The noise was coming from that black opening. It was snoring and sputtering, a breathy, guttural wheeze echoing from the darkness. Staying very low, both hands on the gun, licking lips, blinking moisture from the eyes, he started toward the cave.

The noise rose as he approached.

Grove reminded himself that he had a double-action revolver with hollow-points in his hands, and two speed-loaders pressing against his kidneys. Even if he were struck in the carotid with an arrow, he would probably be able to squeeze off a few rounds and vaporize the bastard's face. Rage coursed through him, galvanizing him. The mouth of the cave was a jagged seven-foot oval— just tall enough for a grown man to pass. The noise hummed.

For a moment, pausing at the threshold of the cave, heart thumping, rain slanting down, Grove considered waiting for backup. He could linger at the mouth of the cave and cover the exit until the ATF guys arrived to do the cleanup. But as quickly as the thought crossed his mind he abruptly discarded it. What if there was an opening at the other end of the cave? Grove took a deep breath and slipped inside the darkness.

The dampness slithered around him, engulfed him in its moldy chill. The deep, sepulchral snoring rose all around him—the sound of a giant bellows. Grove crouched and inched sideways through the darkness with the gun held out.

Lightning flickered outside the cave, just for a moment, just enough to illuminate the depth of the cavern, and it was *deep*, incredibly deep, the far reaches seeming to vanish in the bottomless dark. About ten feet wide with stalactites of limestone hanging down from the ceiling and walls glistening with slime and guano, the cave was moldering stone, with the fossilized remains of an iron rail long since oxidized into crumbs, embedded in the mossy floor.

Grove had a vague memory of hearing about these mine shafts cut into the sides of hills in the Pacific Northwest. He couldn't remember if they had openings at either end. He couldn't remember much of anything right now but a strange fragment of a nightmare clinging to his midbrain: *a pellet of copper, a bundle of grass, a lizard's foot, a curled tube of birch bark, an ash-handled flint dagger.*

He inched deeper into the cavern, his eyes watering. The odors of ammonia-rot and something else—something so rancid it was almost sweet, like spoiled meat—permeated the air. Grove sniffed. He was about to wipe his eyes when he saw movement out of the corner of his eye.

He whirled.

A shadow blurred across the cave behind him—immediately registering in Grove's brain as *huge, massive,* and probably not human, the way it shambled instead of scurried. The gun went up, finger on the trigger. Grove's flesh crawled. He crouched and listened to the low pipe organ noise rising in front of him like an engine.

Lightning flickered, illuminating the cave for just an instant.

An adult male bear was blocking the opening of the cave, its massive incisors gleaming with drool, its eyes rolled back in its head like egg whites—that subterranean growl like the lowest, longest, deepest bellows of an organ.

In the momentary strobe-light flicker, Grove was paralyzed with primordial terror—his finger frozen on the trigger—as the giant black bear emitted a thunderous roar before gathering its haunches.

Then it pounced.

The .357 went off—two silver flashes in the darkness—blasting tufts out of the bear's ear in midleap as Grove stumbled backward over his own feet. He landed on his ass, the air punched out his lungs and the Tracker knocked out of his hands.

The gargantuan bundle of fur and teeth landed on

Grove, eliciting a garbled gasp—it was as if a small automobile had been dropped on his midsection.

The bear's gaping jaw full of dripping fangs and filthy breath came at Grove's face, and Grove, moving on pure instinct now, summoned all his strength in one last-ditch attempt to pinion his hands against the black glistening muzzle of the rampaging beast.

In the darkness Grove fought for his life: it was like holding on to a fat, wooly, vibrating chain saw, the creature's jagged teeth impaling Grove's hands, the animal's bulk pressing down on Grove's legs, its rear claws gashing the profiler's thighs, stabbing divots into his sodden trousers. A keening shriek came out of the enraged, bleeding bear—a weird, almost infantile sound—bleating out of the chasm of the animal's throat.

Lightning popped again.

In the violent silver flash Grove and the animal were face-to-face when all at once a whispery noise snapped behind the bear and made the animal's head jerk.

Over the space of a nanosecond—before the flicker of lightning subsided—Grove saw the shimmering metallic tip of a hunting arrow protrude from the animal's left eye. The bear deflated then. Noxious air puffed out of the animal, its massive jaws still quivering open. Then it sagged in a heap, a bundle of dead weight pressing down on Grove's torso.

Sudden agony screamed through Grove, and for a moment he couldn't breathe. His hands were numb, ravaged with wounds, a major gash clawed open on his left leg.

He wriggled out from under the bear and rolled across the mold-slick stone, gasping for breath. He struck the wall and sucked air for a moment—all manner of panic coursing through his brain: *The gun! The gun! Get to the gun, you idiot! THE GUN!*

That's when he heard a new noise—a low, percussive

burst of breathing—and Grove realized instantly that this new sound did not come from a beast of the forest.

It came from a man.

A man who now darkened the entrance of the cave, silhouetted by faint traces of lightning.

17
Cruel God

Grove tried to move. His body was sluggish, flooding with cold concrete from the sudden blood loss and trauma, making movement excruciating.

The dark figure started toward a silver object gleaming on the stone floor maybe ten feet away: *the .357 magnum.*

"Ackerman . . . *Ackerman!*"

The shadow continued slowly yet steadily edging across the cave toward the gun.

It was too dark to get a good look at the man, but it was clear he was moving in a strange manner—stiffly, jerkily, as though electric current were running through his tendons. That low, hyperventilating noise emanating from his lips had coalesced into something that sounded like an incantation or a litany in some unidentifiable foreign language.

"Ackerman, listen to me, okay? Listen now, just for a second, focus, okay? Focus and listen, listen, listen—"

Grove tried to scoot backward toward the deeper regions of the cave, tried to buy himself time, but his body was as heavy as a block of ice, slimy with blood. His legs shrieked, perforated by the mauling. His hands were greasy with blood. He could feel his pulse in his neck, and his vision was beginning to blur. Hypovolemic shock can quickly indicate paralysis, disorientation, even hallucinations.

The figure was less than ten feet away, kneeling down by the gun—only inches away from the great, steaming carcass of the dead bear. At this close proximity, Grove could see the man's quiver of arrows hanging off the back of his ragged nylon raincoat, the hunting bow dangling, the hooded face partially obscured in shadow, a pale, creased visage of teeth and crow's-feet. The man's head shivered convulsively as cryptic words spewed out of him very quickly and very softly, echoing in the darkness: "*Aaahhh-baal-sssahh-geeee-utu-utu-ssssuh-hoooolnamm-nin-ssssahhh—*"

Grove tried to say something else, but his words got clogged suddenly when he saw Ackerman pick up the gun. Grove's mind raced: *I'm not going to look away, I'm not, I'm not going to cower for the son of a bitch, he can damn well kill me now, but I am not going to look away!*

Across the cave Ackerman stood up, brittle knees cracking. He raised the gun and aimed it at Grove.

Lightning flickered again, and Ackerman tossed his head in victorious, primal bloodlust, reminding Grove of a wild dog in a feeding frenzy. The cave flashed. All at once the hood slipped off Ackerman's cranium, and for a brief instant the killer's face was visible—a ruined map of wrinkles and leathery skin, eyes shimmering like glass embers.

Grove was gagging on his own blood, simultaneously weeping and roaring: "*Go ahead and do it! Do it already! Get it over with!*"

Something unexpected happened then: in that terrible split second of flickering light, Grove saw the man's face spontaneously transform—the flesh sagging like an air bladder shriveling, all the fire immediately going out of his eyes. The brutal rictus of a grin melted into mortified horror. "Ohhhh—G-Gawd—n-no—" the killer stammered suddenly, trying desperately to communicate something to Grove.

"What! Talk to me, Ackerman, what? What the hell do you want!"

The gun wavered, the tall man flinching as though inner forces were battling over control of his body, and Grove instantly recognized the signs in some deeply buried compartment of his embattled mind: the classic dissociative movements of an MPD, *a multiple personality disorder.* But something deeper, something more significant lurked beneath the realization like a vast, black, underwater leviathan.

"D-don't l-let him," the killer stammered, a tear like a diamond on his cheek, the gun hanging at his side now, eyes furrowed in utter agony.

"Don't let him—what! Do what!" Grove boiled in rage and pain, his legs deadweight, glued to the stone. The dark returned, deeper now. Absolute blackness. Grove gasped for breath, tried to see his assailant.

The broken voice in the darkness: "Don't let him k-kill you . . . y-you're the one he wants . . . it's you . . . it's *always* been *you.*"

They reached the edge of the clearing—two tactical guys from Portland SWAT who had arrived only minutes earlier, as well as an ATF agent from the Olympia field office—at the precise moment another volley of lightning lit up the place. Simms, the older of the two SWAT guys, took the right flank, his assault rifle gripped tightly in his gloved hands, eyes squinting into the flickering rain. The younger gentlemen, Karris, top-heavy with Kevlar and rain-soaked tac gear, took the left, signaling the ATF guy, Boeski, with a quick downward jerk of the fist, to bring up the rear and suppress as needed. Then Simms and Karris, like armored ballet dancers, simultaneously hopped over the stone lip and crouched on the rainy plateau. The downed special agent—the one called Zorn—was immediately visible to Simms, who signaled Karris with a quick, flat slicing motion of the hand. Karris, the less experienced of the two, gritted his teeth in frustration, slamming his boot down on the moss, livid that they could lose the subjects in the woods so easily, the place lousy with tactical operatives, all messed up by the storm and the weird way sounds carry in the woods. But the luxury of feelings quickly passed because they were in a red-zone situation at the moment, and the clenching and pointing gestures from Simms twenty yards away on the windswept precipice told young Tactical Sergeant-Second Class Anton Karris everything he needed to know. Simms had made a quick trundle over to the body and discovered that the one named Zorn was gone, S-O-L, but the other one, Grove, as well as the suspect, remained at large, armed, and judging by the way Simms was wildly gesticulating toward the adjacent woods, both remained dangerously close and hot and immediately threatening. And all this happened in the space of instants—a few seconds, actually—before a piercing noise rang out from the nearby columns of spruce and tamarack, making both officers duck involuntarily down into the muck, their backs up like startled animals, their weapons snapping up into the ready position drummed into their muscle memories. But neither could move because the sound—the clarion noise that bellowed through the rain—was virtually unrecognizable to human ears, and therefore had no precedent in any SWAT manual or training scenario.

The New Richard roared in the darkness of the cave. He had vanquished the last shred of the Old Richard inside him as though shitting out a parasitic bug, and now his victory cry erupted in the dark like a chorus of hellish voices as he raised the weapon and aimed it at the brown man on the floor of the cave.

The first shot sounded glorious, lighting up the cave with a flash of radiant yellow fire.

The hollow-point struck Grove in the hip, gouging a two-inch capsule of muscle and cleanly passing through the meat of his buttocks, imbedding itself into the moldering stone of the cave wall behind him.

Grove let out an involuntary gasp, jerking sideways in a thundercloud of cordite and dust, his body slamming facedown into the corner. The blast had just the disabling effect the New Richard had calculated—a preamble to the ritual he had learned in dreams.

"Get it over with!" Grove moaned on the ground, his face pressed against the cold stone, his tortured breaths raising little puffs of dust in the darkness.

The killer tossed the gun to the ground, the weapon clanging as it bounced across the stone floor. He reached up and, with one brittle movement of his right arm, plucked an arrow from the quiver, pointing the shaft heavenward as though it were a lightning rod.

"Laahhh-nahh-hammmmaahhhhh-nam-silig-akaaaahhh-sssu-zeeee-sahh-mahhhhh!"

The New Richard sang out the dissonant howl of words, secret phrases taught to him in nightmares, and the voice rose and ululated like a mad cantor in a register that strained Ackerman's vocal cords to the breaking point.

Grove, on the ground, in the dark, bleeding to death, face in the dust. He knew what was coming next, he just *knew*, the realization materializing in his brain like a photograph in a developing bath. He thought of Hannah, and then, for a brief instant, he thought of Maura County, and all that could have been. Then he closed his eyes—

—because the iron vise of a hand was around his right arm. The pressure was enormous, as if a machine were grasping him around the forearm. Then a quick, terse *yank* . . . and now Grove's right arm was positioned in the familiar pose.

Next Grove felt the cold pointed tip of the hunting arrow kissing the back of his neck.

Karris saw the granite maw of the cave first—a dull, sandy facade in the jungle of foliage, obscured by sheets of rain and columns of hemlock. A moment's hesitation, crouching down behind a fat spruce, wiping an arm across his wet face, realizing the howling noise had come from the cave, Karris clucked his tongue at Simms, who was duckwalking through the undergrowth thirty yards away. Simms froze. The two tac officers traded frantic hand gestures. Then Karris trundled toward the cave, Simms close on his heels, an Ingram M-10 assault rifle ready to rock, its thirty-round magazine locked. The two officers—their training ingrained—slammed up against either side of the stone doorway. More hand gestures. Deep breaths. Muscles coiled. Wet fingers on the triggers. A lot of information still missing, a lot of questions flashing in their midbrains over the course of that brief instant: what kind of a cave were they about to enter? And maybe more critically: was it one of those old abandoned zinc mines that Karris had read about once—the interminable kind that went all the way through to the other side of the plateau?

Grove opened his eyes in the darkness. *Still alive? I'm still alive?* Paralysis gripped the entire left side of his body, which was wrenched into the telltale position of the Sun City victims—a cruel joke played by a cruel god. His vision blurred, essentially useless in the shadows of the cave. But he *sensed* something happening behind him, something happening to Ackerman. The sound of halted breathing echoed faintly, barely audible to Grove's ringing ears, a deeper shadow trembling in his peripheral vision.

He tried to crane his neck around, tried to see what was going on. He felt as though he were nailed to the deck of a sinking ship, the gravity of pain and blood loss tugging him down into the black depths. Shuffling footsteps echoed behind him. Ackerman was gasping.

Gasping?

Grove made one last heaving effort to lever his head around far enough to catch a glimpse of the killer. Searing hot agony shot down his spine as he peered over his shoulder, the pain forcing a yelp out of his lungs. Finally he managed to get a fleeting glance at the silhouette looming over him with the hunting bow and arrow still cocked in its cross-brace.

Ackerman had frozen—mid-strike—the arrow still poised only centimeters away from Grove's neck.

Tremors bolted up Ackerman's spine, straightening him as though a steel rod had just been thrust up his vertebrae. He shivered and winced. His facial features contorted. One eye began to blink fitfully, his jaw clenching as though high voltage were passing through him. Grove, delirious with pain, wondered if Ackerman's head was going to start spinning.

It was the penultimate thought that passed through Grove's conscious mind before the delicate black membrane drew down over him.

Ackerman began gasping for air, the tip of the arrow wavering away from Grove's neck. The gasping mixed with a moaning noise, an almost musical sound, squeezing out of Ackerman as he staggered backward now. One of Ackerman's big, gnarled hands grasped suddenly at his chest—a purely involuntary action.

On the cold stone floor, in the dark, Grove's last conscious thought before fainting dead away was one of relief, perhaps even disappointment. He had remembered something Helen Ackerman had said, and all at once he realized what was happening, and the realization brought with it an unsettling wave of dread that the course of events were being channeled by nothing more mystical than sheer coincidence and the vagaries of the human circulatory system.

The son of a bitch is having a heart attack.

Grove was unconscious by the time Karris and Simms penetrated the darkness of the cave. A pair of halogen beams pierced the shadows and landed on the profiler, who was slumped in a puddle of blood against the damp stone wall thirty feet inside the tunnel. The great pile of black fur and gristle that was once a bear lay against the opposite wall. By that point the New Richard had shambled away into the black depths of the cavern, dragging his numbed left leg along behind him like a rotted log.

The tactical agents made no immediate moves toward Grove. They didn't even bother making a visual assessment of the fallen profiler's vital signs. Procedure dictated that the officers secure the area first, which was problematic in such a confined space with such an absence of light. Was the bear dead? Apparently, yes. Frantic hand gestures and pinpoint choreography sent both men on a diagonal along either wall, barrels raised, aims fixed, muscles tense, fingers on the triggers, slender shafts of halogen light slicing through the motes of filth, the beams sweeping the empty reaches of the cave. The tac guys paused and listened, and heard no audible evidence of the cardiac arrest case lumbering through the uncharted shadows of the mine shaft.

By then Ackerman had reached the narrower channels fifty yards away—dragging along in a monstrous, shuffling gate that would have reminded Michael Okuda, were he present, of Karloff's mummy. Another moment of searching the darkness, and Commander Simms finally felt satisfied that the apparent struggle of a few moments earlier—and whatever had precipitated that god-awful howling sound—had dissipated. Another hand gesture sent both officers over to the profiler. It didn't take them long to discover that Grove was still clinging to life. Neither Simms nor Karris had much medical training, but they knew enough paramedical procedure to recognize that Grove had lost a lot of blood, was probably in shock, and was indicating a very weak, very slow pulse-ox rate. They knew that the next few minutes were critical if they wanted to save the profiler's life, so they improvised a makeshift gurney out of a pair of flak vests and a couple of collapsible reachers, and they got Grove's limp form onto the fabric as quickly and gently as possible, then dragged him out of the cave, leaving a leech trail of blood on the stone while simultaneously making emergency calls on their headset radios and bellowing at the top of their lungs for assistance from the idiots still nosing around the deep woods along the periphery of the hill.

By the time Simms and Karras emerged from the mouth of the cave, the woods were alive with SWAT guys, fanning out through the undergrowth, scanning the rain for a ghost. A pair of Olympia PD officers with tactical training rushed over and helped with the "package" while Simms called for the closest evac chopper and Karras wrestled jury-rigged pressure bandages around Grove's mangled neck and midsection.

Grove remained unconscious through all of this—his mind manufacturing its own secret tumult—and all the noise and vibration of four untrained rescuers jostling his body could not penetrate the storm in his brain.

18

A Hole in the Picture

"No!"

Grove awoke in a paroxysm of sweat and aching muscles. His head jerked on the pillow, his arms flexing against the metal rails of the hospital bed, making the hardware creak. His hands were heavily bandaged, a diastolic pressure clip pinching his right forefinger.

He slammed his head back down on the bed and lay there for a moment, winded, as if he had just run a sprint. He crackled all over, as if he were wrapped in cellophane, and half his body felt as though it had been amputated. He swallowed his panic and licked his dry, chapped lips. He gazed around his darkened room and realized he now lay in some kind of subterranean cavern or catacomb, his bed pushed against the stone wall of some forgotten tunnel that stretched as far as he could see in either direction.

What kind of hospital was this anyway? You would think they could afford some fluorescent lights, maybe a few chairs. Hell, this place didn't even look like it had indoor plumbing. Grove swallowed acid and took deep breaths in a futile attempt to ease the terror that was suddenly constricting his heart. He gazed around the tunnel and realized just exactly what he was seeing. The moist stone walls, leprous with mold and decay, rose maybe ten feet over Grove's hospital bed. Dimly illuminated by faint torchlight, the ceiling was capped with gray stalactites of human bone. Skeletal feet and brittle gray icicles of femurs and knuckle joints dangled down from the rotting sediment overhead.

To Grove's immediate right stretched a row of mummified human remains, each embedded vertically in the wall, emulsified like sardines in files of human sarcophagi. Emaciated hands and shoulder joints stuck out here and there. Partially fossilized skulls lay congealed in rotting limestone, their empty eye sockets gaping up at the nothingness. At their feet, nestled in little crumbling baskets, were desiccated offerings. Grove recognized the powdery remains of *injera* bread, Sudanese beads, *katanka* stones. Icons from Grove's childhood, from his motherland. The sight of them pierced his soul, flooded him with sorrow.

He closed his eyes. He could hear a terrible sound in the darkness, and he knew it was coming for him. *Faint, shambling footsteps*—approaching with a monstrous certainty that touched some inchoate nerve ending at the base of Grove's skull. He kept his eyes shut, willing the vision away. *Please. Please not yet, not now.* The footsteps were nearing him, the rancid-sweet smell of the tomb in Grove's nostrils. He opened his eyes and saw the figure in the dark blue nylon raincoat emerging from the depths of the tunnel.

It was maybe fifty feet away now, coming for him, and it was no longer human. Its long, cadaverous face—still obscured by that oversized hood—had transformed into a masque of putrid, rotting death. The long patrician nose had curved into the monstrous ulcerated beak of a demon, the dull gleam of its teeth elongated into eldritch fangs. Grove was paralyzed because the thing in the hood was lifting its arm toward him, a black skeletal hand jutting out, inviting Grove to clasp it in supplication, to make contact, to touch it.

No, not yet, not now!

The deep, guttural voice that growled suddenly from the depths of that horrible hood was like the shifting of tectonic plates: *You're the one!*

Grove slammed his eyes shut then, slammed them as tight as rivets welded shut by his tears.

Now unfamiliar noises filled his ears. Watery beeping noises, metallic clicking sounds. He heard a breathy noise like a bellows breathing in and out, and finally he found the strength to open his eyes again.

All at once he found himself in an ordinary hospital room, his pulse racing, his chest rising and falling rapidly. He lay back against the pillow and breathed through his nose, struggling to calm himself, struggling to steady his heart rate and get his bearings back.

At last he managed to glance around his bed: he now lay in a small private room with rubber drapes drawn across its single window. The only illumination came from a bank of pilot lights and indicators next to his bed. The soft ticking of a pulse-temp monitor provided the only sound. Grove turned his head far enough to glimpse a digital clock on a bedside cart: it said 4:07. Judging from the stillness and the dark, it had to be a.m.

He found a Call button on the end of a cable hanging off a bed rail, and awkwardly pressed it with a bandaged thumb.

A moment later a nurse swished through the door. Fluorescent lights stuttered on, making Grove jump, making his eyes pound.

"Mr. Grove, good morning," the nurse said as she approached the bed with the nubs of a stethoscope in her ears. A plump, graying woman in a white uniform, she gently placed the contact on Grove's sternum and listened intently.

"Not to be melodramatic," Grove croaked in a rusty voice, "but what day is it?"

"Tuesday the seventeenth, you've been here going on forty-eight hours."

"Terrific. And 'here' is . . . where? Portland?"

"Olympia General. The great state of Washington. How do you feel?"

"I'll get back to you on that."

The nurse pondered the monitors for a moment, taking readings. She reached under the bed's carriage, then flipped a switch that elevated the head. "The doctor's on his way down. Been having some wallopers the past day or two, huh?"

"Pardon?" Grove felt the bed raising him into a sitting position, and found his midsection set in concrete.

She looked at him with a wan smile. "Bad dreams?"

"Um . . . yeah." Grove let out a sigh. "A few." He remembered only fractured moments over the last two days. He remembered waking up in the chopper only minutes after the confrontation in the cave, glancing over his shoulder at the storm clouds falling away from the belly of the aircraft. He remembered falling in and out of consciousness as he was rushed through the harsh light and noise of the trauma center. He even remembered familiar faces hovering over him in recovery—Tom Geisel, Walt Hammerman from Justice, FBI Director Louis Mueller. They had muttered their comforting words, awkward and stiff, inhibited by the politics and protocol of the situation. Grove had made futile attempts to stay awake against the tide of Percocets and lingering shock, but mostly he had slept. For two days. Slept and occasionally awoke to experience horrible hallucinations. Ordinarily Grove would have written off such hallucinations to simple blood loss, hemorrhagic shock, and oxygen starvation. But over the last two days he had come to believe there was a deeper dimension to his visions. He had come to believe the visions were not merely being generated by his own nutrient-starved brain but were coming from *outside* himself. Organic, self-determined, telekinetic—whatever the source, it didn't matter. They were messages meant to penetrate Grove's psyche. He had never believed in the paranormal, and to some extent he still didn't. But skepticism, when faced with the irrefutable, turns to madness. That's why, as he groggily returned to the living that morning, he was so damn rattled.

"There's our star patient."

The voice rang out from the doorway, shattering Grove's ruminations. The white-jacketed doctor was stunningly young—barely out of his twenties—with a thick shock of moussed hair. Approaching the bed with his furious smile and metal clipboard under his arm, he looked like a young insurance salesman about to give Grove a pitch on the benefits of term over whole-life.

"How ya doin', Doc?" Grove had sketchy memories of seeing the youthful face hovering over him, partially obscured by a sterile mask.

"I should ask *you* that question. Take a deep breath, please, and hold it."

The doctor's stethoscope was cold on Grove's chest as Grove dutifully breathed in and out. The profiler's right side was still fairly numb. His groin tingled from a hasty shave in surgery. His throat was sore, and his hands were stiff and cold under all the gauze and white tape. He had pressure bandages around his waist that bulged on his right side. The rest of him was covered with an assortment of butterfly bandages.

Grove looked up at the man-child doctor. "What's the prognosis, Doc? Am I gonna live or what?"

The doctor smiled at him. "Somebody up there likes you, my friend."

The Sacramento Northern Pacific Railway runs along the attic of America like a calcified, forgotten length of plumbing, the fossilized tracks rotting in the earth. Once in a great while a freighter will trickle down the central line with a load of iron ore, making very few stops, passing through the pockets of civilization like a ghost ship in the night. In the wee hours of Wednesday morning, just such a train made an emergency stop outside Eureka.

The engine—a backward conglomeration of loose bolts and greasy platforms—hissed and sputtered to a standstill in the pitch-darkness, disgorging a soiled little man in filthy dungarees. The engineer's name was Jurgens, and he hopped off the runner and into the cinders with the practiced nonchalance of a lifelong railroad rat.

Jurgens marched along the length of rolling stock, tapping his hickory switch against the couplers like an elephant tamer. The problem was the subtle tics he had felt in the curves, the slight weight displacement in the middle boxcars. He suspected hobos. The old-style stowaways had all but vanished in recent years, but lately young street kids from down South were riding the rails, smoking crack or pulling tricks or doing whatever ne'er-do-wells do, and Jurgens had been told by the yard manager that he had to keep the cars clean.

A noise in the darkness yanked at Jurgens's attention, and he picked up his pace to a jog.

Something stirred in the second-to-last boxcar, the Quaker car, the one with the broken hasp and gaps in the slats, and as Jurgens approached, he saw litter trailing off in the darkness along the rails. Shreds of newspapers and food wrappers. Jurgens's heart started thumping, and he wished he had brought along something more substantial than a whittle branch, something like a crowbar or maybe a shotgun, because he saw the blood then. It looked black in the moonlight, splattered across the trash and looping over the dull gleam of iron rails.

"Who's there!" Jurgens barked.

The two kids in the boxcar had been dead for some time, posed in the style of supplication that scholars had been pondering over the ages. But Jurgens would not see their bodies for several moments. He was too preoccupied by the blood-spattered litter on the ground along the gravel rail bed, and down the craggy embankment along the tracks.

He knelt down and picked up one of the ribbons of newspaper. It was speckled with a mist of blood. The headline said PROFILER KILLED IN THE LINE OF DUTY. Underneath the text was a formal portrait of Terry Zorn. Another photograph showed a second profiler who'd been wounded in the shoot-out, but most of the picture had been torn out. Jurgens tossed the shred of paper aside and picked up another. Here was the late edition of *USA Today* showing the two profilers. Grove's face was missing. Another one showed the exterior of the Regal Motel—police cars scattered across the ravaged parking lot—and an inset of the two FBI profilers, the shot of Grove with a hole where his face should be. Another one, dotted with drying blood, Grove's face missing.

Another, and another, and another. Each with Grove's face torn out.

19
The Fabric of Dread

The good news, according to the doctors, was that the bullet had missed all of Grove's major organs and arterial branches. It could easily have killed him if it had struck his femoral artery, or paralyzed him if it had chewed through his lumbar. It was apparent to Geisel and the guys from the bureau's Department of Professional Responsibility that the shooter had gone for a disabling shot instead of a kill-shot, probably in order to make Grove more manageable for God-only-knew-what. Grove's other injuries—mostly the results of the mauling—were essentially superficial. The deepest bite wound in his thigh, which had caused severe vascular injury, had bled mostly *into* the deep facia muscles. The resulting hematoma was enough to cause major shock and delirium. For a while the doctors had been worried that Grove would lose the use of his left hand due to a deep bite wound in his wrist, but luckily the trauma center in Olympia had one of the country's top plastic surgeons. Physical therapy started almost immediately. Every few hours Grove would get out of bed and shuffle around his room with his IV drip-stand like a limp dance partner squeaking along beside him. Considering the extent and profusion of the wounds, he was moving around pretty well. Apparently he had emerged from the incident in fairly decent working order—*physically*, at least.

Zorn's death had sent ripples through every division of the FBI, Justice Department, and Washington State Internal Affairs agencies. The fact that bureau profilers were not traditionally assigned to tactical work was pointed out to Grove repeatedly over those horrible seventy-two hours of recovery. Zorn had an ex-wife and two grown children back in Texas whom Grove had not known about. Much was made of Grove's and Zorn's legendary competitiveness and animosity. Captain Ivan Hauser of the Los Vegas Violent Crimes Unit had made statements about the two profilers being at each other's throats in the desert the previous week.

Terry Zorn's memorial service was held that Tuesday afternoon. Grove heard about it from one of the OPR guys who had come to the trauma center to take a statement. According to the Texan's wishes, the affair was a small family ceremony. His body was cremated, and his ashes were given to his children. A fund was set up at Quantico for donations to the Zorn family's chosen charity—the Big Brothers of America. Grove had five thousand dollars wired from his account to the fund.

Friends and colleagues of Special Agent Terrence Zorn were not the only ones galvanized by his death. The Washington State Bureau of Investigation—one of the country's crack investigative agencies—took the debacle in the river woods personally. They mobilized their state-of-the-art SWAT group, as well as every sister law enforcement agency in the state, in an unprecedented manhunt to take down the fugitive Richard Ackerman. As of Tuesday evening, the subject was still at large, but reports had been flooding the transom all day. A suspicious individual had been seen at a service station by a mining company rep. Ackerman's nylon raincoat had been found in a rest stop bathroom near Vancouver. The authorities were worried about the subject fleeing via the rail system or airliner, but so far none of the surveillance at any of the depots or terminals had turned up anything. They would find him eventually. Everybody knew it. Especially the coordinator of the manhunt—Commander Harlan Simms of the Tri-State SWAT Complex in Portland. It was Simms who had dragged Ulysses Grove from that abandoned mine shaft, and it was Simms who had glimpsed the shadowy figure of Ackerman as the cardiac arrest was setting in.

All this macho enervation only served to curdle Grove's spirit and psyche. He felt no vengeance roiling in him, no need to get back to the hunt, no bloodlust to bag Ackerman. He felt only dread. Barren, desolate, incapacitating *dread*. For himself, for the human race, for the world. It was the kind of pathological emptiness to which FBI profilers were supposed to be immune. But there it was—suffocating Grove in that hospital room like a veil drawn over his face.

Maybe all the obscene violence and banalities of evil that Grove had cleaned up over the years had finally taken their toll. All this hoodoo about Grove being the "one," the one Ackerman had been after—it was all part of the fabric of Grove's private dread now. He simply wanted to crawl into a hole and die. He didn't want to talk anymore. He didn't want to give any more statements. He didn't want to open any more wounds. Perhaps that was why he was so disconsolate when the nursing staff finally allowed Maura County, who had flown in from San Francisco at her own expense, into the ICU.

She came to his room around six-thirty that night.

"Oh my God, look at you," she uttered, peering around the edge of the door, then gingerly padding into the room. She wore her trademark faded jeans and denim jacket, and carried a brown paper grocery bag full of goodies. She came over to the bed and put the sack down on a nearby rolling cart that was cluttered with the remnants of his half-eaten cafeteria dinner.

"Oh my God, oh my God," she said as she leaned down over him, putting her arms gently around him.

Grove was unable to hug her back. He simply could not do it. Physically, emotionally, he had nothing left for her—and she sensed it immediately. There was the briefest moment of hesitation, then she backed away with a stung look on her face. "They said downstairs you're going to be okay," she said, busying herself with the paper sack. "That's awful about Terry, just awful. I brought you some things. I know, I know, I shouldn't have done it, but I couldn't resist."

"How goes the twilight zone?" Grove asked her, propping himself up against the canted headboard.

"I sent everybody home. Although Professor de Lourde and Father Carrigan are still lurking around the Bay Area somewhere, making everybody nervous with their campfire stories." A flurry of awkward business with the bag and a strand of hair in her eye. "I brought you some junk food, magazines—you know—the usual hospital effluvium." She laid a can of peanuts, a few candy bars, and a spray of magazines across his lap.

"You didn't have to come all the way up here, you know."

"That's what friends do, Ulysses. They visit their friends when their friends are in the hospital."

"I do appreciate it."

A pause, fiddling with the hair. "Is there something wrong? Did I do something?"

"No, no . . . it's just . . . the Percocets they've been giving me . . . I'm a little loopy."

She sighed and glanced around the room for a place to sit. She found an armchair, dragged it over to the bed, and plopped down. "I understand he had a family?"

"Zorn? Yeah . . . a little *estranged* but yeah."

She shook her head. "Horrible."

"We'll get the guy. Don't worry."

She looked at him. "I heard he said something to you, something in the cave."

Grove shook his head. "Schizophrenic babble. But how the hell did you know about that?"

"Word gets around the media, somebody bribed one of the field agents in Portland."

"Christ."

"So you're leaning toward this guy being just some nut job with a fixation on the mummy?"

Grove looked at her. "What do you mean?"

"I'm just wondering if you buy any of that stuff from the conference—cycles of murder, something being unleashed when they dug up the mummy?"

Grove looked away, letting out a pained breath. "Who knows what's inside this guy's head? I don't believe in evil spirits. In a way, I believe in everything. And in nothing. It's hard to explain."

"Any idea when you'll be released?"

Grove gave her a shrug. "Couple of days, I don't know. I'm walking pretty well."

"You sure there's nothing wrong?"

Grove managed a smile. "There's nothing wrong."

"Nothing I said or did?"

"Relax, kid. This guy goes down, you're gonna win the Pulitzer."

Maura shuddered a little. "I just want him caught. God. I never dreamed my little article would lead to . . . *Jesus.*"

"It's all right." He reached over the bed rail and patted her shoulder with his bandaged right hand. "They'll catch the guy, and you'll write your article, and everything will be okay. You'll see."

"What about us?"

Grove took a pained breath. He didn't know what to say. His mind had gone blank.

"Ulysses, it's not a proposal . . . we just talked about getting together when this was over. I just wondered . . . you know. I don't know what I'm trying to say. This is probably a totally inappropriate time to—"

"I don't think it's a good idea," Grove blurted, cutting her off.

She looked down almost immediately. "Um . . . sure. You're probably right."

"It's not your fault, Maura, it's something I gotta work out for myself," he said, his words sounding wooden and hollow in his own ears.

She managed a smile. "It's okay. You don't have to dissemble for my benefit." She sounded rueful all of a sudden. She looked away when her eyes began to fill. "I'm a big girl, Ulysses. I can handle it. Believe me."

Regret stabbed at Grove's gut. "Maura, don't take it personally—"

She raised her hand, looking back at him, her expression hardening. "Please. I'm all right with it. I presume you don't mind if I still care about you."

Grove smiled. "The feeling's mutual, kid."

There was a brief silence, the beeping of the pulse-ox monitor thundering in Grove's ears.

Maura finally broke the silence: "You going to join the manhunt when you get out?"

Grove sighed. "Me? Naw . . . I'm hanging up my magnifying glass."

She stared at him. *"What?"*

"I'm quitting the bureau, taking early retirement."

"You're shitting me."

Grove gazed across the room. "No . . . I'm done. Maybe Terry was right. I'm burned out. Haven't cleared a case in years. Glory days are over."

"Have you told anybody about this?"

"Not yet. You're the first. Quite an honor, huh?"

"Ulysses . . . why?"

"Why not?"

"Why *not?* Why *not!*" She got up and started pacing around the room. "For starters, *you're* the one who tracked down Ackerman. Remember? I mean . . . come on. You're the *guy*. You're the—"

"Easy now."

"I'm just saying . . . okay, it's none of my business . . . but it seems to me you're quitting at the peak of your powers."

"Is that right? Did you know they're laughing at me back in Washington? In the Hoover Building I'm a big joke. Terry was right."

"Ulysses—"

"This whole Sun City case, where it ended up, the mummy, the nonsense about ancient cycles of evil. It doesn't matter that it led us to Ackerman. It's unseemly. You see? The whole case has become a bad joke."

Maura strode back and forth across the foot of the bed for a moment, thinking, chewing a fingernail. "You're sure all this doesn't have something to do with me and that *Weekly World News* piece?" She pointed at the spray of magazines on the bed. "Ulysses, I didn't talk to anybody from that rag, and even if I did, I wouldn't have—"

"What are you talking about?" Grove looked down at the magazines. "What article?"

She gaped at him for a moment. "You haven't seen it?"

"Seen *what?*"

"Oh, Jesus." She stood there for a moment, staring, clenching her fists. She came back over to the bed and rooted through the magazines she had brought, mumbling, "I thought maybe you'd just laugh at it . . . I even brought along an extra copy for you, you know, just for laughs. Now I'm feeling like I've really screwed things up."

Buried under the weekly magazines—*Time, Newsweek, Esquire, Entertainment Weekly*—was a black-and-white tabloid with garish forty-eight-point letters at the top reading THE WEEKLY WORLD NEWS. Grove plucked it from the pile and took a closer look. The headline screamed J-LO'S BUTT IMPLANTS EXPLODE!—GAL'S DREAMS OF A BODACIOUS BEHIND BURST AS DOCTORS BOTCH SURGERY! Grove had seen the rag many times in line at the supermarket, occasionally picking it up for a few grins while he waited on an especially slow cashier.

At the bottom of page 1 was a box labeled EXCLUSIVE: BEHIND-THE-SCENES PHOTOGRAPHS OF A MONSTER HUNT. Grove glanced at the minimal copy, which yammered with purple alliteration about "Ulysses Grove, the mysterious manhunter from the FBI, and his mystical methods." A few lines farther down the page, the article crowed about "a monster on the loose, possessed by the spirit of an ancient mummy." But it wasn't the copy that bothered Grove. What bothered him was the accompanying photograph, rendered in grainy paparazzi-style shadows along the bottom corner of the page.

Up until now, Grove had somehow managed to avoid being photographed by the tabloid press. Now he stared at a telephoto shot of himself and Maura in front of the Marriott Courtyard in Alaska, at the precise moment that he had asked Maura to go out on a date. In the picture, Grove was smiling awkwardly, sharing some intimate conversation with the young journalist.

They looked like lovers.

"Okay . . . great, just great," Grove muttered.

Maura County looked as though she had something else to say, but instead turned away and gazed emptily at the overcast light glowing behind the shaded window.

Michael Okuda felt like a street urchin, skulking in the alley behind Olympia General Hospital. He thrust his hands deep in the pockets of his ratty cargo pants, hunching his shoulders against the chill spring wind.

Dressed in a denim jacket, frayed at the collar, his silky onyx hair tufted and cowlicked from restless sleep, the young scientist could easily be mistaken for a crank addict waiting impatiently for his connection. In reality, that perception was not far from the truth. Okuda *was* a drug addict, and he *was* waiting to purchase a sort of contraband substance, and he *had* been tormented by a series of "connections" over the last few days that had sent him on an unexpected journey north to Olympia, Washington, where he was acting like a common street punk.

"Hey!"

The voice came from the depths of the alley, near the hospital's service entrance. A beefy black orderly in a stained white uniform and hair net was striding toward Okuda with an angry scowl on his face. He carried something in a hazardous-waste baggie.

"You got it?" Okuda asked, shivering from the wind.

"Thought you were gonna wait in the damn car," the orderly grumbled as he approached. "I could lose my job, dawg. Somebody see us."

"Don't worry about it."

The orderly handed over the Zip-Loc bag. "C'mon, let's see some Benjamins."

Okuda paid the man—two brand-new hundred-dollar bills—then gave a quick nod. The orderly turned and jogged off without a word. Okuda stuffed the Zip-Loc in his pocket and hurried toward the mouth of the alley.

Okuda's pockmarked Toyota Tercel sat idling across the street. Two elderly gentlemen sat in the backseat, like owls, silently watching Okuda approach. Okuda slipped behind the wheel, then handed the Zip-Loc bag over the seat-back to Professor Moses de Lourde.

The southerner, garbed in his elegant white ensemble, pursed his lips as he looked at the blood-spotted gauze. "'They have washed their robes and made them white in the blood of the lamb,'" he muttered.

"Shouldn't we just talk to Grove about this first?" Okuda asked somewhat rhetorically.

De Lourde waved off the question. "No reason to bother the man until we've got something more than just a theory."

"You're sure this is enough to get a sequence?" asked the old priest sitting next to de Lourde.

Okuda assured him that it was enough, then put the car in gear and pulled away.

20
Uninvited

The figure stood silhouetted in the doorway, outlined by the fluorescent lights of the hospital corridor. At first Grove thought he was seeing another vision. The swish of the opening door had awakened him, but words had yet to be spoken.

Even in shadow the figure looked so familiar: a woman, standing there in the doorway as silent and still as a doe. The long graceful curve of her neck, the pile of hair, the pear-shaped curve of her matronly hips—all so familiar. Grove tried to call out but for some reason could not coordinate his lips. He gazed over at the clock and saw that his afternoon nap had stretched into evening.

There had been one interruption earlier that day— at around three o'clock—when the young doctor had stopped by to remove some of the bandages and examine Grove's hip. The prognosis had been excellent, and Grove was informed that he would be released the next morning. But now, flexing his bare hands, sitting up against the headboard, blinking away the grog of sleep, he felt completely disoriented.

"*Mtoto tamu,*" the woman said, lingering in the door-

way, tilting her head with a regal quality that pierced
Grove.

"Who is it?"

"*Mazazi hapa huku.*"

The words were familiar—Bantu or Swahili—and the
voice, that velvety voice plugged right into Grove's central nervous system like an ultrasonic whistle jolting
through a dog. Grove sat up straight. "Mom?"

The fluorescent overheads stuttered on as Vida Grove
stepped tentatively inside the room and stood there for
a moment, her elegant brown hands clasped in mortifi-
cation, her long, handsome face furrowed with worry.
"*Hivi . . . kwa hiyo a kutisha,*" she uttered softly.

Grove swung his bare legs over the edge of the bed,
quickly covering himself. "In English, please."

"So frightened, I was . . . so frightened," she uttered,
putting her hands to her mouth, then shuffling over to
him with the broken grace of an aging ballet dancer.
She put her arms around him, pulling him into her
bosom, and he didn't move, did not even raise his arms.
He breathed in her smell—Estee Lauder and bacon
grease and cigarette smoke—and he recoiled from it.

Vida backed away. "Your friend says you were hurt
badly," she said after standing there for a moment. She
wore a long, tunic-style African dress known as a *maa-
sai*—the linen dyed vibrant shades of scarlet and indigo—
which hung loosely off her spindly limbs. She had a
little paunch belly, and her cigarettes hung in a pouch
that dangled from a leather strap around her neck. The
smokes bounced against her sagging breasts as she ges-
ticulated frantically. "Your friend says you been shot,
chasing this evil man, you need surgery."

Grove looked at her. "I'll live. What friend?"

Vida glanced nervously over her shoulder.

Another voice drifting in from the hallway: "It was
me, it's my fault." Maura County stepped into the room,

her denim jacket buttoned to her throat. She looked sheepish and a little defensive. "I know it was none of my business, but I thought somebody should call her."

Vida started to say, "*Mtoto*—"

"How the hell did you find her?" Grove wanted to know. His gut burned, his scalp tingling with anger. Sorrow and regret—even fear—easily curdles into rage. "I never even mentioned her."

"That night in the Marriott lobby, you said your mom lived in Chicago."

Grove rubbed his face. "Jesus Christ."

"I called Tom Geisel, ran it by him, asked if it was okay if I called her."

Grove looked at his mother. "I'm sorry you came all this way for nothing."

The elder woman looked confused. "For 'nothing'? For nothing I come here? I do not understand."

Grove shrugged. "As you can see, I'm gonna be fine, I get out tomorrow morning."

Vida touched the rail on his bed as though she were absorbing his pain. "When your son is hurt, a mother comes, this is just the way that it is."

Grove shook his head. "Okay . . . you're right. Thanks for coming all the way out here. But I'm fine now. Really."

Vida looked at the journalist. "He was this way even as a child."

Maura smiled. "Why am I not surprised?"

"He would fall down, get in a fight, I would try and comfort him, and he would push me away, just push me away—"

"All right, Mom, that's enough—"

"Never wanted any help."

"Enough!"

The volume and intensity of Grove's voice stiffened both women into silence, and held the room for several moments in awkward stillness. Grove turned his face away. Vida gazed at the floor. Maura stood there, flabbergasted by this unexpected display.

Finally Maura broke the silence: "I thought she had a right to know, Ulysses. She's your mother."

Grove shot an angry glance at her. "You have no *idea* who she is, and you have no idea who *I* am."

Maura looked away as though punched in the gut.

Vida cocked her head defiantly at her son, her great pile of gray, woolly hair looking almost regal. "*Mtomo*, I come here only because—"

"Look, I don't want to offend you," Grove interrupted, searing his gaze into his mother's huge, sad eyes. "But I don't need any magic charms or chicken bones or rain dances—I'm fine. All right? Now if you don't mind, I have to rest. Thank you for coming. I appreciate the effort, but right now what I need is some time alone."

After a long, agonizing silence, Maura gently took the older woman's arm and ushered her out of the room.

The Irving Potok Center for the Analysis of Forensic Evidence—known among law enforcement insiders around the Pacific Northwest as the CAFE—is the Home Depot of police laboratories. The squat brick building, which is located on a busy street corner in Seattle's Pike County market district, offers hair, fiber, blood-type, and DNA analysis to everyone from U.S. Government agencies to junior college biology classes. And just like its retail counterpart, the CAFE is open twenty-four hours a day and always busy.

Its dank lower level, with its cramped warren of CRT cubicles, regularly bustles with pathologists and assistant medical examiners gathering evidence for some bureaucratic headache they're trying to soothe. Once in a great while, the CAFE will get an academic—an archaeologist or a geologist looking to authenticate a specimen. But never in their entire eleven-year history have the lab personnel seen such a strange and motley little threesome huddle in one of their basement cubicles, awaiting the results of a DNA test.

"Here it comes," Michael Okuda said, nodding at the screen. The Asian sat in a swivel chair, shaking with dope-sickness, his hair askew, his eyes drawn and bloodshot. Professor Moses de Lourde stood behind him, arms crossed against his natty double-breasted white suit. Father Carrigan stood farther back in the corner, leaning against his cane.

The first sequence flickered on the screen, a checkerboard of black and white stripes that resembled a very complicated retail bar code.

"Now this is, what, the Iceman's DNA?" de Lourde wanted to know.

Okuda nodded, staring at the computer. More bar codes flashed across the screen—the headings and keys mostly numerical. Okuda had to correlate them with a guide he had been given by a lab assistant. His vision was bleary and he had to blink away the nervous tension. His trembling worsened. Finally he saw his vague suspicions confirmed in a pulsing brushstroke of glowing cathode ray light.

"Lord have mercy," Professor de Lourde commented as the final sequence sputtered and typed onto the screen, the blue-green light reflecting off Okuda's and de Lourde's faces: two wholly different matrices superimposing over each other like a colony of insects falling into perfect luminous rank and file.

"Holy shit," Okuda muttered under his breath as he gaped.

It had seemed like such a non sequitur when it had first occurred to the young Asian, like such a reach. But the translation of the Iceman's tattoos had sunk a hook into Okuda. *En-nu—en-nu-un*—loosely translated as "Protect us while We protect them." At first Okuda had figured it was simply a comfort-prayer, like "Saint Christopher, protect us," but after de Lourde and the priest had started babbling about these "feelings" they had about Grove, and the cycle of evil, and elliptical histories, Okuda had started seeing all sorts of alternative meanings to the words. All of which had led him *here*, to this damp, subterranean lab, and the converging stripes of light and dark on the computer screen.

"We've got to talk to him about this," Okuda said at last, feeling a twinge of guilt, as though he were sifting through another man's fate with the carelessness of a transient rifling through a garbage can.

"The blood is secondary," a voice murmured behind Okuda. Father Carrigan was staring at the floor as he spoke to no one in particular, his deeply lined face creased with solemn regret. "The blood is not what is most important."

De Lourde turned to his new friend. "And what is most important, Father?"

The old man looked up and uttered in a deathly soft voice, "What is important is the summoning."

They sat in a blue cigarette fog, two incorrigible smokers hunkered down in a deserted ham-and-egger across the street from Olympia General Hospital.

Vida Grove held her L&M between slender brown fingers and puffed daintily from it, as though she were sipping medicine. "He was not even supposed to *be*," she said with a wistful nod of her magnificent gray head. "I never told Ulysses this, but he was never supposed to *be*."

"I'm sorry, I'm not sure what you mean," Maura said. She sat across the booth with a cup of coffee and an untouched cruller in front of her. She felt wrung out, drained, ridiculous. But now she listened closely to what the elder woman seemed to be about to confess.

"When I was just a young girl," Vida began, "and I was—how do you say it, *with* him? With Ulysses?"

"Pregnant?"

"Yes, there were problems, the doctor told me, I had the diabetes, six months carrying this baby, and they told me I would probably lose the child."

Maura nodded. "That must have been terrible. You were a single mother, right?"

Vida waved away the question. "My husband remained in my life long enough to give me the child, and then he was gone like a ghost."

"Oy vey."

Vida dragged on her cigarette. "I would not accept this news, however, that I would lose the baby. I went to a seer—"

"A what?"

"A *seer*—a Sudanese man who lived down the street, a shaman. This man was a healer, and he told fortunes, and he helped other Africans. I know it sounds strange, but I would not accept this news that my baby would die and I went to the seer and asked him what I should do. I will never forget that morning I went to his home. He had me down into his basement, where it was dark, with beads across the doorway, and I sit down in front of his brazier—"

"Brazier?"

"It is a ceremonial fire, very full of magic, like what you call—what is it, *incense*? In a Catholic church?"

Maura gave her a nod. "Right, right."

"And here I am sitting there, this frightened girl, six months along, and this man, his eyes get very big, like his face is very surprised, and perhaps frightened even, and I am saying, '*Washiri*? What is wrong?' And he says, 'This baby of yours is very special. And he will be a prophet, and he will walk with great leaders.'"

Vida paused then, casually exhaling smoke and snubbing out her cigarette in a scorched foil ashtray sitting next to a bottle of congealed ketchup.

"I just want to know whether my baby will survive," she went on, "and what I can do to save my baby, but this seer is telling me my baby will grow up to be a great man, and will walk across the dimensions. I cannot take it anymore and I ran out of there. I ran."

"What happened?"

"It is difficult to explain but it was a kind of—what is the word?—a *turning point* for me. I took herbs and I did a ceremony every night. I prayed for my son to be born healthy, and I tried to *believe* he would be born all right, and he was. He was small but he was all right."

Another pause, and Maura noticed the African woman's eyes were wet.

Maura touched her hand. "He turned out okay, I'd say. You were a good mother."

Vida let out a dry, bitter laugh. "That is not what Ulysses would tell you. It was really my fault that he hated me so—"

"That's ridiculous."

"No, you see . . . my boy always wanted one thing: to be an American. To have friends and be a normal American boy. But the words of that seer never left my memory. Not once. I suppose I was too . . . *something*. Maybe I raised the boy too . . . 'African'? To be different in this American culture, it is a sin, and kids can be cruel, very cruel . . ."

Her voice trailed off then, and she gazed out the dirty plate glass at the deserted streets wet with rain. Maura let the subject slide.

Maura broke the silence at last. "I hate to say it, but I think I've kind of fallen in love with your son."

Vida nodded and said she was aware of that.

"How did you know?"

"I am a woman."

And with that the subject was closed. And then they

talked about nothing in particular for a while, just small talk, and finally Maura said, "I have to go back to work, back to San Francisco."

Vida seemed disappointed. "You will say good-bye to Ulysses?"

Maura managed a downtrodden smile. "Already did."

They paid their bill, got up, and walked to the door. Outside, the rain had lifted, but the air was shot through with dank electricity. The two women hugged and said their good-byes, and then walked in separate directions.

Maura glanced over her shoulder only once at the sad, elegant matron wandering off into the night. And for a brief moment, Maura wondered if she would ever see the woman again. She thought not. She felt as though *her* role in this drama had ended.

She would soon learn, however, how wrong she was on both counts.

21

Everything Is a Ritual

At some point in the lowest chasm of the night, Ulysses Grove had another vision. His third over the course of a single, tumultuous week. This time there was no hospital bed, no tether to reality.

This time he was the Iceman, and he was suffocating. Buried under tons of snow. Gasping for air. Convulsing. Dying. And all he could see was a black, serpentine object in the ice above him, burrowing down toward him.

At first he thought it was a snake. Blurred by layers of snow and slush, pulsing with horrible, malignant life, the dark object wormed its way closer and closer, until Grove started screaming. He tried to turn away from this terrible thing coming for him, reeking of menace, infected with disease and evil.

Shuddering in his death throes, lungs heaving, his body numb and useless, Grove let out a howl of terror as the object broke through the ice only inches from his face.

The hand was ancient and blackened, the hand of a mummified corpse, and it beckoned to Grove, tempted him: if only he would grasp it, accept it, surrender to it. Touch it!—

—and that's when he was literally jolted back to the here and now.

He jerked forward in the darkness of the hospital room, a paroxysm of gasping and shuddering. It took him a moment just to catch his breath, and another few moments to realize he was crying. The tears had already left salty tracks on his face and soaked the collar of his cotton gown, and he fought them for a moment. *What is wrong with you!*

But the more he fought those tears, the more he realized that this vision had revealed something important. Something critical about the mummy, and the connection to Ackerman, and, most importantly, what Grove would be expected to do in order to stop the killing. Which was the saddest part. It was too late. Grove was finished. Someone else would have to live out this destiny.

Someone stronger than Grove.

He lay there for a moment, letting go of his emotions, letting the tears sluice through him, the whispery noise of his bitter, breathless weeping filling the empty room. It went on for some time, the IV drips and monitors unhooked and shut down, the silence absorbing the noise . . . until finally Grove realized his sobbing was not the only sound in the room.

At first it sounded like an electronic *hum* just underneath the noise of Grove's sobs, but the more audible it became, the more Grove listened to it . . . and the more he listened to it, the more his cries dwindled. Before long he had stopped weeping altogether, and now he simply tried to breathe, his respiration hitching and hyperventilating like the chugging gasps of a frightened boy. He listened more closely to the humming sound and realized it was another voice in the room with him.

"Wha—"

A shadow hovered over his shoulder, and he recoiled from it, jerking back with an involuntary gasp. The shadow cooed softly then, an arm appearing out of nowhere, settling gently on Grove's forearm.

He looked down and saw the ashy brown fingers of his mother on his arm, and he realized Vida was in the room with him. He had been hearing her voice in the darkness, softly humming an African lullaby, comforting him.

"Mom?"

"It is all right now," she whispered. "I am here, Uly, I am with you."

His eyes adjusting to the darkness, Grove saw his mother on a stool next to the bed, illuminated by a slender thread of moonlight seeping under the blinds. She leaned over the rail and put a slender arm around Grove's shoulders. And her touch, the warmth of it, momentarily stirred a cauldron of contrary emotions inside Grove—shame, loneliness, regret—until the feelings all burned off like a flame kissing a pool of denatured alcohol.

Grove felt another tide of sobs rising in him, and he let it come.

He leaned over and cried in his mother's arms. He cried for all the years of vague hostility toward his mother, all the years of resentment, of betrayal, of misdirected anger. Vida held him and went on humming her tender lullaby. Soon she was singing softly, slightly off-key, in a smoky voice—and the song penetrated Grove's sorrow, and he recognized it: an old Zambian lullaby called "Mayo Mpapa," a folktale that teaches children about the protection a parent provides a child:

"Mayo mpapa naine nka ku papa
Ukwenda babili kwali wama pa chalo,
Ndeya ndeya ndeya no mwana ndeya
Ndeya no mwana wandi munshila ba mpapula,
Munshila ba mpapaula

Iye, iye, iye yangu umwnaa wandi
Yangu umwana wandi mushila ba mpapula."

("Mother, carry me.
I will care for you one day.
It's not good to be alone in this world.
Mother, carry me.
I will carry you one day
The way a crocodile carries its young on her
back.")

When she was done singing, Vida held her son in the silent darkness. Grove was still. He felt changed somehow, like the remnant of a fuse that had burned out.

At last, he got out of bed—

—but the moment his bare feet hit the floor the dizziness and pain washed over him, and he had to grasp the bed rail for purchase. The dizziness passed. He took a deep breath and shuffle-limped—very slowly—over to the switch panel, then turned on the lights. Then he managed to painfully shove an armchair around to the other side of the bed so that his mother could sit more comfortably. Grove's injured hip throbbed, and his face tingled as his tears dried. He sat back down on the bed very carefully.

They talked then. Well into the predawn hours of the morning. They talked and talked. About the old days in Chicago, about the old neighborhood and old relatives who had passed away. They laughed at certain things, and they got very quiet at others. At one point, Vida held her son's hand, and Grove made no effort to pull it away. It was as though he could see clearly for the first time in his adult life.

Eventually the conversation circled back to their troubled relationship.

"I'm sorry, Mom," Grove said at last. "I'm sorry for a lot of things. I should have—"

"Please, Uly," she interrupted. "Do not ever say you are sorry." She smiled when she saw his puzzled face. "There is no need for apologies, because this is the way that the spirits meant it all to happen."

Grove smiled back at her for a moment, then his smile faded slightly as he wondered what else the spirits had in store for him.

After his talk with his mother, Grove took two Vicoden and slumbered for nearly four hours while Vida sat in the corner of the room, reading, watching her son sleep. And for that brief interlude, as the dawn lightened the window behind the blinds, that hospital room felt as safe and sane as any room had ever felt in the history of Grove's stormy life.

When he finally awoke, shortly before 9:00 a.m., his body felt oddly replenished—albeit still very sore. His hands had most of their mobility back, but were stiff, and the wounds along his torso and upper thighs had swollen and tightened. Every movement brought a twinge of deep pain, and the dizziness had worsened, but he felt strangely energized.

He said good morning to his mom, then carefully climbed out of bed and prepared to be released. For old times' sake Vida helped him get dressed. Grove grinned to himself as she laid his jacket—still in its plastic dry cleaner's bag—on the foot of the bed just as she had laid his flour sack dashikis on his little trundle bed a million times when he was a kid. She also carefully positioned his briefcase, which had been retrieved from Special Agent Flannery's Jeep Cherokee, next to the pillow. Grove took another painkiller and pondered the briefcase for a moment.

He debated about what he should do with the contents of the attaché—the .357 Tracker still in its holster, the speed-loader belt, the Palm Pilot, the notebooks, the battered tape recorder, the gloves (both rubber and white cloth), the case folders, and the old Polaroid Land Camera. The tools of his trade. He never wanted to see them again. He was done with them. He reached down and flicked the case open.

The lid crackled.

Inside the attaché, among the hardware and notebooks and electronics, Hannah's lucky key chain was nestled in its little cloth pouch, wedged behind an elastic pocket. Grove rooted the pouch out of the case and opened it. The talisman was burnished from years of nervous fondling. Grove looked at the tiny magnifying glass—a hairline crack zagging across it. He ran his fingertip across the leather spindle, gently brushing the embossed word: SHERLOCK. He wondered if he should give it to Maura County.

Something sharp stabbed at his heart.

Maura County. Had he given her the big brush-off merely to protect her . . . or was he afraid of something? He could not stop thinking about those tiny flecks of gold in her pale blue eyes, or that goofy, whiskey-cured voice, or that swanlike curve to her neck. Had he rejected her for heroic reasons . . . or was he simply afraid that he would fall in love with someone other than Hannah? Which was ridiculous. Hannah would have kicked his ass all the way to Sunday.

All at once Grove made a decision. He would change his life. Today. He would go and find Maura, and he would get her back.

"What is next?" Vida asked, standing near the doorway, wringing her skinny brown hands as though she had read his thoughts.

Grove put on his sport coat and carefully shot his sleeves, looking at himself in the mirror—ever the fashionista. "Some unfinished business, and then I'm quitting. I'm going home and I'm going to sleep for a week."

"That is good, a boy needs his rest."

Grove smiled then, snapping the briefcase closed. He went over to his mom and took her by the arms. "And as soon as possible, I'm going to come visit you in Chicago, so you better get that pot of Harissa stew cooking."

Vida's smile could have powered Commonwealth Edison for a week.

Everything is a ritual for an African. Even a fallen, assimilated one like Grove.

After receiving a clean bill of health from Dr. Man-Child and being released from Olympia General, Grove hailed a taxi and traveled to the nearest post office. He proceeded to meticulously, ceremoniously package his FBI investigator shield in a small priority mail carton. He addressed it without notation or explanation to:

Chief Thomas Geisel
Section BSD-1333
Federal Bureau of Investigation
J. Edgar Hoover Building
935 Pennsylvania Ave. NW
Washington, D.C. 20535

When the package was ready, Grove waited in line, thinking about Maura and what he would say to her. He wanted to start over with her, start clean. He wanted to court her the old-fashioned way. He imagined taking her to a coffeehouse in San Francisco, some beatnik place, and listening to her life story. He finally reached the head of the line, and when the next window opened up, he limped over and decisively shoved the package across the counter.

Good . . . now there was one last thing to do.

22

Reunion

The cab was waiting for him outside the post office, the meter still ticking, running up an enormous bill. Grove didn't care. He stiffly climbed into the backseat, still lugging his suit bag and briefcase. Letting out a pained sigh, he told the cabbie to take him to the airport.

The driver made the trip in record time. Before entering the terminal, Grove dismantled the .357 in order to avoid detection, putting the pieces in his briefcase, then putting the briefcase inside the suit bag and checking it with a red cap at the curb. Without his bureau tin, he was a civilian in the eyes of security.

The flight to the Bay Area left on time and barely lasted an hour and a half.

On the ground in San Francisco, Grove rented a car at the airport and drove through a steady mist, using a map he had gotten off-line in Olympia. It was just after five o'clock, and he hoped that Maura would be home.

Grove couldn't remember ever paying an unannounced visit to somebody like this—anal-retentive criminologists simply did not do such things—but somehow it seemed appropriate that day. He still wasn't sure what he was going to say to her. He planned on going with his gut, apologizing to her and maybe even telling her that he loved her. He could tell her about his epiphany, about his reconciliation with his mom. No . . . maybe not. Best to keep that to himself.

Maura lived north of the city, across the Golden Gate Bridge, up in the hills of Mount Tamalpa. Grove had to consult the map twice—once when he was stuck in rush-hour traffic on the bridge, and again, as he wound his way up the slope north of Sausalito.

He reached Corte Madera around six o'clock and started looking for Maura's place through the rain-beaded window glass of the Avis sedan. He could see the suburban sprawl of Marin County in the distant hills up ahead like cave dwellings tucked into the gray-green ocean of redwoods.

A sign loomed in the fog on his right: PLAZA DE MADERA - 1 MI.

He sensed something not quite right the moment he reached the cul-de-sac that bordered Maura's salt-grayed condo building. Maybe it was his natural paranoia—acquired from years of entering chambers of horror. Or maybe it was a simple case of flop sweat, the tension of dropping in unannounced, not knowing exactly what he was going to say. But whatever the cause, the hair on his arms and neck stiffened as he pulled his car over to the curb behind Maura's rust-bucket Geo that she had described in casual conversation with Grove a week earlier.

Grove recognized the bumper sticker as pure Maura County—REAL WOMEN DIG FOSSILS! The car's driver's-side door was hanging open.

He parked and got out of his car. The air was clammy and fragrant with the smell of pines and the wharf. He lifted his collar, then struggled up the narrow gray wooden steps, his hip humming with constant pain now.

He needed another Vicoden. The stairs ended at Maura's door—number 1C.

Her entrance was the only one on the south side of the building, and when Grove knocked on the hardwood jamb, the rapping noise sounded hollow and dead in his ears. As though he were knocking on a tomb. He waited. He knocked again. Nothing stirred inside the silent condo.

Grove leaned down over the edge of the porch, stretching over a low tangle of eucalyptus to see inside a gap between the blinds and the front window. One of his stitches popped under his jacket. His heart jumped.

"Jesus!"

He whirled around almost involuntarily, his brain seizing up with panic—the pain forgotten now. He scanned the deserted property. All at once he felt naked and impotent without his shield, without his gun, without his bureau tag.

He trundled back down the wooden steps to his rental, tore open the back door, and clawed the .357 pistol out of his suit bag. Crackling through his brain like a dissonant counterpoint: *Maybe it's nothing, maybe it's nothing, maybe, maybe—*

Back up the steps to the door. His spine twinged, his wounds completely numb now. He knocked again on the door. Harder this time. "Maura, it's Ulysses! You there? *Maura!*"

Nothing.

Grove wrenched open the screen door, then slammed his three-hundred-dollar Armani shoe against the inner door. A cracking sound and pain erupting in his hip, his stitches tearing. The door held. Another kick and the door gave, and then Grove was inside the condo.

The blood shouted at him. It was everywhere. The shock made him crouch down. Made his testicles contract. Made his pupils dilate.

The atmosphere in the cluttered condo was empty and electric—as though the dust motes had frozen in midair.

Grove gaped everywhere at once, not seeing much of anything other than the slash marks.

"Maura! Maura!"

His cry slapped back at him off the desecrated walls, then died.

What was he doing? He swallowed hard. He tried to think straight: *Calm down and look at the place, look at it, that's what you do, you look and you see things, you reconstruct what happened, so do it now, reconstruct, RECONSTRUCT!*

He quickly scanned the modest living room with its exposed brick and hardwood floors and framed posters of Johnny Rotten and Jane Goodall, and he saw the signs of a struggle, an overturned lamp shade, an upended coffee table, books strewn across the place. The blood on the walls formed crude handwritten words that made no sense yet made terrible sense.

His gaze lingered on a newspaper on the floor, spattered with blood. It was the *Weekly World News* with the article about Grove and the Iceman. The photograph in the bottom right-hand corner clearly showed Maura County's face, now speckled with deep scarlet red.

All at once a series of realizations flooded Grove, and he stood there with his gun in both hands, sticking out and shaking, his heart slamming. *Oh my God, oh my God, don't do this to me, don't do this!*

There were other rooms to check.

Grove sucked a deep breath and shuffled sideways, his gun still raised and twitching as though he were in a war zone. Through the closest doorway. Into the kitchen: the refrigerator was open, a carton of eggs broken across the tiles. Not much else.

In the bedroom Grove found more writing on the walls—that same nonsensical uggah-buggah language—

and the furniture in disarray. But no body. Thank God, there was no body.

Thank God.

By the time he checked the bathroom and saw the medicine cabinet door hanging open and all the tiny bottles shattered in the sink, he became convinced that Ackerman had done this, the motherfucker had found Maura through the article, and had come here and kidnapped her and he was probably torturing her at this very moment if she wasn't already—

No! Grove bit off the thought and stood in the bathroom doorway for a moment, the gun still cradled in his hands, his lungs heaving.

The worst part, the part that nearly choked the breath out of Grove, was the fact that all this was probably done for *his* benefit. It was a sick, scrambled message to *him.* Ackerman wanted *him.*

"Don't do this to me !"

Grove's primal scream shook the air, shook *him,* nearly popped a blood vessel in his head. He was out of breath and stood there for a moment, shaking, trying to figure out what to do next. Call the cops? No. The local bureau field office? No way. Not yet. Not until he could get a handle on this, get a handle on himself, on his emotions.

When it was painfully obvious that he was alone in the mortified condo, he eased his grip on the gun and let it fall to his side.

23
Cold Linkage

He paced the living room, limping back and forth across the front window, trying to engage his investigative instincts. Before he called the crime lab in, before he turned the place into a circus, he had to get it fresh, get whatever he could get. Finally he went back over to the front door.

Careful not to arouse any suspicions from nosy neighbors, he slipped outside, then descended the narrow steps. The cool, moist air on his face was a hideous taunting slap. He went over to the car.

He dug the briefcase out of the suit bag with trembling hands. His tools were in there—he needed them now. He needed them to think.

Back up the steps. Back inside. The clunk of the dead bolt sealing him in that horrible silent mess.

The writing on the wall disturbed him the most, fixated him the most. He couldn't bring himself to think about Maura's blood loss. The realization swam around like a shark beneath the hectic currents of his consciousness—that was *her* blood up there, across the floor.

There was a lot of it.

Most of the writing was illegible—slash marks, smudges,

and splatter patterns—but some of the words or fragments of words scrawled like crimson ribbons across the
plaster molding and baseboards strummed a familiar
chord inside Grove: *un una gu susa unna se enu un enuna*—

—the same diphthongs and sibilants that had spewed
out of the rotting mouth of a madman in a cave. Nonsense words? Crazy bullshit or something important?
Grove's mind was an engine revving impotently, seizing
up without oil, without the lubricant of calm.

Settle down, settle, come on, think.

He should take some pictures of the scene. That's
what he should do. He knelt down on one of the stained
Persian rugs and shoved the gun behind his belt. He
fumbled with the clasps on the attaché.

He froze.

The briefcase was vibrating. It felt as if bees were in
there in a frenzy. And for an insane instant Grove actually was afraid to open the case.

Then he remembered why the case vibrated once in
a while and opened it up, holding it precariously on his
knee, hands still shaking.

His phone was telling him it had at least two stored
messages waiting. It buzzed like a hair clipper. Grove
picked it up and tossed it across the room.

The phone bounced against the wall but didn't break.
It slid under the couch.

He fumbled for the rubber gloves. Awkward moments
stretching them onto his wounded hands. He was bleeding. The attaché tipped and one of the spiral notebooks
tumbled out, dropping to the floor.

"Goddamnit!"

He hurled the briefcase across the room. It flipped
once and skidded upside down across the hardwood.
The contents spilled across the floor—the Blackberry,
the notebooks, the tape recorder, the cotton gloves, the
case folders, the Polaroid camera, the lucky charm in its
little pouch.

Grove put his face in his hands and swallowed the urge to scream.

A noise made him jump.

His cell phone was trilling under the sofa.

Grove took deep breaths. Swallowed acid. Girding himself. Something cold and sharp stabbing his gut. Intuition again? *You should answer the phone.* A bitter, ironic voice deep within him: *It's Ackerman calling, you idiot, he's watching, you've got to answer it!*

Rising to his feet, he managed to lurch across the room to the couch, bend down, and retrieve the phone. It vibrated in his gloved hand.

"G-Grove," he croaked into the cell after thumbing the Answer button.

The voice was shrill and familiar: "Ulysses, Jesus, we've been trying to reach you for hours, it's Mike Okuda, where have you been?"

"Who?"

"Michael Okuda, from the Schleimann Lab. I'm sorry, it's just that we've made this amazing—I don't know what you would call it—*discovery*, I guess. Hello? You still there? Can you hear me?"

Grove could barely speak. "Who's *we*?"

"What? Oh, um, I'm sorry, I'm talking about me and Professor de Lourde, and Father Carrigan, from the conference, from Maura's meeting."

Grove said, "What do you want? I have to go, I have a situation—"

"Look, I know we're kind of out of bounds here, but we had to be sure, okay, before we went down this road, all right, so . . . look, I'm not making any sense. Father Carrigan had a theory. So we got a sample of your blood from the hospital, and we had a sequence done on it—"

Grove gripped the cell phone hard enough to crack it. "You *what*? You *what!*"

"Ulysses, listen to me. It's the *same*. It's a perfect match to Keanu's DNA. Did you hear what I said? Hello?"

"Wh-what?"

"I know it doesn't make any sense. But the DNA never lies. The fact is, you're a genetic descendent."

Grove was paralyzed. "A what?"

The voice crackled: "A genetic descendent—of the *mummy*, is what I'm talking about."

Grove said nothing. A pang in his hip made him sniff back the urge to scream.

"You have the same DNA, Ulysses. Which sort of brings me to Father Carrigan's theory. Are you ready for this? Ulysses?"

Grove was staring at the floor—at the clutter of investigative tools fanning out from the fallen, overturned briefcase.

"Ulysses? You there?"

Grove could not speak. All he could do was stare at the upended briefcase.

The spiral notebooks lay there, cryptic ballpoint doodles slathered across their covers, the Blackberry Palm Pilot lying cracked open like a dead beetle, the cotton gloves spidered here and there, the good luck charm in the corner.

The linkage suddenly engaged in Grove's brain like a pulley clasping on to a roller-coaster car.

"He was hunting somebody," Grove uttered under his breath, his voice barely audible as he continued to gaze at his personal effects on the floor.

The voice in his ear: "What did you just say?"

Ulysses said very softly, "He was an investigator. Just like me. They all were. The mummies—they were hunting killers just like me."

After a long, long pause, Okuda's voice crackled: "How the hell did you know that?"

24

Legacy

Grove's ability to make cerebral leaps was legendary among bureau insiders. His brain seemed to be wired visually. When he was barely two months old, Vida noticed his acuity with shapes and colors. Then came the visions, which Grove shared with no one. But he knew—even at an early age—that they were more than mere hallucinations. In the military, he scored off the charts on the requisite psych exams—thematic apperception and symbol-image-symbol. His visual acumen reached its apex in the midnineties. He caught Keith Hunter Jesperson after staring at a happy face sticker on the wall of a truck stop restroom. He led authorities to Anatoly Onoprienko after gazing at a wedding ring on the finger of a prostitute. He never explained the macabre shadow-plays that danced before his eyes at those moments. He never told anybody at the bureau about his visions. How could he? But he found himself using them. He used visions and dream images as the mathematician uses equations. As the wizard uses runes.

Standing in that blood-spattered condominium, staring at the contents of his briefcase strewn across the hardwood floor, his wounds burning and itching furiously, Grove experienced another visual epiphany.

All the loose ends of the past months swam before his field of vision like a graphic animation of swirling DNA strands spontaneously reconstituting themselves— the dizzy spells that accompanied each crime scene, the strange familiarity of a Copper Age mummy, the recurring vision of inhabiting the body of a neolithic mountaineer, the inexplicable behavior of Richard Ackerman, and the insane ramblings of an eccentric Jesuit priest. In the half-light of the condo Grove saw the spilled contents of his briefcase morphing like items carved out of candle wax, melting and reforming, taking the shape of ancient artifacts that he had seen arrayed across an examination table at the Schleimann Lab.

A ballpoint pen became an onyx arrowhead. A spiral-bound notebook became a curled tube of birch bark. Cotton gloves became bound hanks of dried grass. A Palm Pilot became a lizard's foot, and a .357 magnum revolver became an ash-handled flint dagger. Finally Grove saw in the gloomy stillness the last item transmuting: an old key chain that Hannah had given him for luck, a powerful talisman, changing into a saber-toothed medallion on the end of a leather thong—a prehistoric charm to ward off evil. One medicine *bundle* transforming into another.

"Ulysses? Ulysses! Are you there?"

The tinny sound of Okuda's voice rattled in the cell phone's earpiece. Grove didn't move for a long time, didn't say anything, didn't even avert his gaze from the items spilled across the floor, which had suddenly changed back to their prosaic selves.

"Hello? Hello!"

Grove hurled the cell phone against the wall, shattering it, the shards and fragments bouncing back at him. A flake of plastic got stuck in his dark hair. He wiped it away, then sniffed back the pain in his hands.

He went over to the sofa where he had laid his weapon. He peeled off his rubber gloves and tossed them aside. His brain was a furnace. He snatched up the gun and checked its cylinder. Six rounds. He shoved the gun down the back of his belt. Then he went over to the corner where the lucky key chain lay. He picked it up. Put it in his pocket. Grabbed the folder with Okuda's topographic maps and diagrams, and stuffed it inside his jacket.

Then he went over to the phone mounted on the wall near the kitchen door.

A handkerchief over his hand to preserve any prints. Then he punched out 9-1-1. When the local emergency operator came on, Grove spoke clearly and rapidly, "Listen to me very carefully because I'm going to say this only once—"

"Sir—"

"I said listen to me very carefully, and if you miss something, use the transcript tape. Okay, now I want you to send a unit, a CS lab tech, and somebody from the local bureau field office—"

"Sir, I'm going to need you to—"

"Listen to me or I will hang up, and I will see that you go before IAB and probably lose your job. Now what I said was, I need you to send these units to the following address, 2217 Madera Drive in Corte Madera, and the door will be open, and it is now the scene of an apparent kidnapping. Now do your fucking job!"

Click!

And then he was on his way across the room. *Bang!* The door bursting open. Into the chill sea air. Down the narrow, weathered stairs. Around the front of the sedan. Wrenching open the door, slipping behind the wheel. He repositioned the .357 around his hip so that it wasn't pressing against his bandage, then started the car.

Gunning it out of there, he roared away in a thundercloud of exhaust.

A casual observer, perhaps peering through the curtains of an adjacent condominium, watching Grove boom away, would very likely conclude that the man seemed to know exactly what he had to do, and where he had to go to get it done.

PART IV

THE SUMMONING

"On the path that leads to Nowhere I have found my soul."

—Corrine Roosevelt Robins

25

Blood and Turpentine

Long after the Sun City case had been relegated to the annals of law enforcement legend—not to mention the tawdry pages of yellow journals and sensationalist tabloids—Grove's flight would be much debated, fervidly analyzed and argued over. The truth of the journey was much simpler than history would have people believe.

The truth of the matter was that Grove did not *flee* the scene in Corte Madera in any way—although *technically* he was no longer an agent of the law, thus making his disappearance problematic for the bureau, the Justice Department, and their legal representatives. In the inevitable civil cases that followed, Tom Geisel argued under oath that Grove was simply pursuing unfinished business—acting, as always, in a consultative capacity. The urgent nature of the trip was officially played down. The portrait of Ulysses Grove painted for the courts was one of a methodical perfectionist. No mention was made of his visions, or his relationship with the hostage, or his unorthodox presentations to the bureau brass, or even how he had drawn his conclusions that Ackerman had returned to Alaska, to Lake Clark National Park, to the place where he had first encountered the Iceman.

The truth is, the reality of those frenzied twelve hours after the discovery of Maura County's savaged condominium—during which time Grove consumed a grand total of eight codeine tablets—would be difficult to explain to a court.

Grove proceeded directly to San Francisco International that evening, and got lucky. There was one remaining flight to Anchorage about to push off from the Jetway at 7:41 p.m., and Grove convinced the desk clerk that he had urgent government business up there, and he needed to be rushed through security. His gun had been safely tucked into his luggage, and he flashed an old bureau business card that he had found in his wallet. They let him on at the last minute.

He had no way of knowing—at least, with any degree of certainty—that Maura County was still alive, or that Ackerman had retreated to Alaska. At the rental car place outside the airport, he made one hasty phone call to an old friend who worked at FBI headquarters in Washington, and asked if anything had come through the wire room—or the wire rooms of field offices in San Francisco, Portland, Seattle, or Anchorage—which had the aroma of Sun City. Normann Pokorny, Grove's friend in Latent Prints, reported that there had been dozens of calls, maybe even a hundred or more throughout the day, regarding sightings or suspicious behavior that smacked of Ackerman. But Tactical Commander Simms and most of the field office managers working in the Pacific Northwest had pretty much discounted the majority of the calls as either pranks or dead ends. Grove had asked Pokorny if there were any calls that were being taken seriously, and Pokorny had said he only knew of two. One was from an Oregon state trooper who had spotted a sign painter's van that had been reported stolen speeding north on Highway 5. The trooper had subsequently lost the van. But later, a call had come in from the Royal Canadian Police in British Columbia, reporting a vehicle matching that description breaking through a roadblock on a northern provincial highway.

It didn't take long for Grove to triangulate the information, a luminous arrow slashing across his mind-screen—the kidnapping in San Francisco, the trooper's discovery on Highway 5, and the roadblock in British Columbia—forming a straight line toward Alaska. But even without the eyewitness reports, Grove probably would have returned to the great rugged North, the scene of the original crime, because he believed that Alaska was the only place on earth where he had any chance of resolving the case. And there would have been no way to explain that to anyone—especially bureau personnel—without appearing insane.

Grove was painfully aware that he was violating every procedure in the book by not calling in the feds, by leaving the scene in Corte Madera, by going on this insane trek across hundreds of miles on sheer intuition. But he also had the epiphany. He knew what the Mount Cairn Iceman had been doing on that mountainside six thousand years ago. Perhaps he knew what *all* the mummies had been doing.

Hunting killers.

Grove now believed that each of the mummies had been ambushed somehow in the heat of pursuit. Perhaps the killer had doubled back on them. The pose was still undetermined. Grove could not make much sense of Father Carrigan's theory that it was a "summoning." But that didn't matter anymore. Grove believed that there was only one chance to save Maura. One chance to bring this thing to a close. One chance.

Something that would never be known to the bureau's Office of Professional Responsibility—or any of the reporters, journalists, or hacks writing about the case in the coming years—was that Grove never once doubted his theory. Never once second-guessed himself. Even sitting in that small, prop-driven airliner with its engines roaring so loudly that the single flight attendant had to shout to ask if anyone wanted a bag of peanuts. He never once considered that he might be wrong.

The night flight to Anchorage can seem endless to the uninitiated. For five excruciating hours a turboprop aircraft bumps and pitches and yaws on a northwestern vector over the black sky above Vancouver, then banks north across the wilds of the Cariboo Chilcotin Coastal Range, then skirts the western edge of British Columbia, and finally crosses the endless black Pacific Ocean before beginning its descent into Alaskan air space over the Aleutian Islands.

Strapped into a seat in the rear of the business-class aisle, Grove hardly noticed the passage of time.

He was in a zone now, studying maps that Okuda had prepared for him, ignoring the burning pain down his side and along the tendons of his mangled wrists, ruminating over Maura and praying that she was still alive.

She fought against the currents of her *own* black ocean, struggling to lift her face above the waterline, to gasp a lung full of air, but it was very difficult, very difficult, and she figured instead she would just give up—instead of living, instead of fighting, she would just sink into the cold, empty depths.

Some distant, buried part of her psyche realized that she was not in the sea at all. She was actually in a vehicle. She was actually lying facedown on the cold, corrugated floor of an Econoline panel van in her underwear, her hands bound behind her, her elbows and breasts and tummy stuck to the floor in a drying puddle of her own blood.

Eyes adjusting, she found herself in the cargo hold of a stolen van as it rattled along a mountain pass with a madman at the wheel and her blood gluing her to the floor. She felt herself sinking deeper and deeper into the void. She knew she was going to die. A part of her marveled at the fact that she had survived this long, had remained semiconscious this far. A part of her wondered if her captor knew exactly how long she would survive.

The madman seemed to have it all planned—the way he had surprised her at her apartment, the way he kept her bound yet conscious through most of it. She felt like a lamb being dressed for slaughter. The way he had nipped her fingers and her scalp to get the sacrificial blood, but avoiding any major arteries. And the way he had kept gibbering.

She recognized some of the words, the ancient tongue—Sumerian—and she knew something else. She knew who this creature was, and what he was capable of, and she knew he would probably sacrifice her. But now, as she drifted toward death, one of her last conscious thoughts was: why all the travel? Where was he taking her?

She was trying to come up with an answer when she heard the sirens.

At first they came from a great distance, as though from a dream, and she had to strain to hear them. They almost sounded like a nursery of crying babies—which was silly, but that's exactly what occurred to her—*whaaaaaa-whaaaaaaa-whaaaaaaa*. Was she imagining the sounds?

Part of her problem was the shock, and part of her problem was the cold. She was shivering, approaching the final stages of hypothermia. She just wanted to go to sleep forever. She could't hear very well, but there was something about the way the van was rumbling now, picking up speed, swaying and rocking violently, that told her those sirens were real, they were real, and they were closing in.

They were coming for the madman.

She blinked and swallowed and moved her head, coming awake on the floor of the van, enervated by the sounds of hot pursuit. She could see very little: the walls covered with filthy drop cloths, the scattered paint cans, some of them open and overturned—the rainbow colors of paint, the thinner and linseed oils mixing with her blood, a strange marbeling effect in the seams of the icy steel floor.

The van took a sharp corner and she rolled. The glue of dried blood ripped at her flesh. *Bang!* She hit a wall, eyes filling with stars. She choked. Ears ringing. The van was pitching and fishtailing now, apparently trying to elude the caterwauling sirens—*whaaaaaa-whaaaaaaaaaa-aaaaaa!*

She lay on her back. Braced herself on a side panel. Her hands were numb and blackened with drying blood. She tried to hold on. The ride was getting bumpy now— engine roaring, chassis shuddering over rocks or pot-holes or logs or something.

The sirens faded.

Had he lost them? The van took a hairpin, and she slid backward toward the rear hatch doors. The van was climbing a steep grade now. Another turn. A steeper grade. Where the hell was he going? She tried to hold on to the floor. Where was he taking her? She could smell something faintly in her nostrils—pine? Dead rot? The mountains? Was he taking her into the mountains?

The mountains—why were mountains so important? She couldn't remember. Couldn't think straight. Couldn't see. Couldn't breathe. The van was slowing down. The sirens were gone. Silence gripped the cargo hold. The gears began to grind. The van stopped.

Footsteps dragged awkwardly outside, coming around the vehicle.

The rear doors jumped open.

Maura County tumbled out onto the snow-crusted pavement. The impact of her bare flesh on the weathered asphalt popped like firecrackers in her skull. A gasp escaped her lungs. She lay there for a moment, shivering in the darkness, trying to breathe, her nude body numb, her hands still bound behind her. The sky was shrouded with skeletal pines, branches like supplicating arms, clawing at the black clouds. The madman towered over her like a monstrous, shadowy Gollum.

She closed her eyes. She knew her days were about to come to an end. She would be sacrificed to some esoteric god—her blood the medium, her corpse the message. *What a fitting way for a science journalist to check out of this world: her own spoor transubstantiated into messages from beyond.*

In those final moments, waiting to die, Maura's mind ridiculously cast back over the years of failed romances. She had never even gotten on base with anybody. How pathetic. The tear on the side of her face burned in the cold wind, and she thought of Grove.

She would connect with him, perhaps, only in death—how perfect. At least she wore her good Bali bra and panties. Her mother always said, Never be caught dead in bad underwear. Maura sobbed in the darkness on the ground, and waited for a cold razor to take her pain away.

But the blow did not come.

Maura opened her eyes and saw the monster standing near the gaping doors of the van. His face was buried in shadows. Unreadable. There was a flash—a yellow spark from a butane lighter—then a flame leaping across Ackerman's face. He was grimacing in pain.

His teeth shone like maggots.

He held a soda bottle half-full of yellow fluid, its rag of a wick burning orange. It looked like a makeshift Molotov cocktail. He casually tossed it over his shoulder. It landed inside the paint-saturated van, clattering across the steel floor and puddles of blood and turpentine.

Maura started to crawl away. Ackerman whirled and vanished into the trees.

Maura managed to get halfway across the blacktop lot before the van erupted.

Primary access to Lake Clark National Park is by small aircraft or boat. The hundred-square-mile preserve is a trailless wilderness, riddled by lakes and rivers, forming one of the largest salmon fishing grounds in the world. At night, approaching from the air across the Cook Inlet, the mountainous region appears to rise out of the ground like a great black temple. The horizon to the north seems to draw the jagged range up into the void of space in a seamless carpet of vaporous clouds.

Riding in the shotgun seat of a small Piper Cub airplane retrofitted with pontoons, which had been contracted out of the Mount Redoubt Ranger Station only minutes earlier, Ulysses Grove was the first to see the incongruous dot of light on the fabric of blackness below the aircraft. *"The hell is that?!"* he yelled over the bellowing engine.

"What!" the pilot hollered back at him. A skinny, weathered man wearing a gray uniform, down vest, and yellow goggles, the pilot was a deputy with the park police.

"There! Down there!"

Grove pointed at the pinprick of brilliant yellow light twinkling in the darkness of the trees, and the plane lurched slightly as the pilot glanced through the side window down at the landscape three hundred feet below them. Sure enough, there was a smoldering ember in the blackness near the northwest corner of Bristol Bay.

"Looks like a goddamn fire!" the pilot yelled over the thrumming din.

"A fire!"

The pilot yanked the wheel, and the plane banked to the north, the g-forces sucking at the fuselage. *"Haven't had one of those in fifty years or more!"*

"You got a twenty on that?"

The pilot shrugged. *"Looks like the Mount Cairn Ranger Station!"*

Grove nodded.

The scene of the crime.

Taking long, bracing breaths, Grove withdrew deeper into himself.

26

A Little Slice of Hell

Grove asked if the pilot could put the plane down anywhere near the fire.

The pilot reached up. Thumbed a button on the overhead console. A narrow lid flipped open with a laminated park map on the back of it. *"Upper Bristol Lake's pretty close!"*

"Let's do it!"

The pilot shot another glance out the side vent. *"It's pretty narrow down there!"*

"Do it!"

The pilot took a deep breath. Wiped his face with the back of his hand. Then yanked the stick. The plane immediately banked steeper.

Grove felt the bottom of the aircraft fall out from beneath him, the vague horizon tilting, the engine screaming. He felt himself slide toward the door. An involuntary clutching at the handgrip on the opposite side of the cabin. Muscles and tendons flexing. His stomach lurching. Acid reflux. Wounds throbbing.

The trees rose toward them, opening up, revealing the north branch of Lake Clark. The water got closer and closer. Looked like a mile-long sheet of black glass reflecting the jagged shadows of the Chigmits to the south and the west. And that yellow, luminous bruise on a field of black, refracting off the lake—bloating, pulsing, a fifty-foot tongue of fire obscenely licking the sky.

The water levitated up toward the belly of the airplane until . . . *bang!*

The pontoons kissed the surface, and the cabin jerked, and the plane rattled, and Grove bit down hard, nearly cracking his molars. The engine whined and complained noisily as the pilot wrestled with the stick, struggling to keep the craft from sideswiping a rocky outcropping. It took several frenzied moments—as well as a quarter mile's worth of lake—to finally brake the plane.

When the engine finally sputtered off, the silence was a tremendous weight pressing down on the aircraft.

"Sir, if you could stay in your seat for a moment, I'll get us over to the dock," the pilot said, climbing out of his seat and grabbing a small oar.

Grove used the time alone to steady himself. His pressure bandage inside his jacket was stiff. Inside his leather gloves his hands were raw from the cold. He flexed them. The documents were folded lengthwise in his inner pocket. His brain was full of fractured impressions, and he tried to organize them. He tried to focus. *The fire's for you, old hoss, so don't blow it. You got one chance, one opportunity to get this right, so let's go.*

The plane bobbed and slid sideways as the pilot couched on the pontoon, rowing them over to land. Water lapped against the floats. There was a bump, and then the sound of the pilot's voice. Something about waiting there for an escort, and the head of the Anchorage field office.

Grove climbed out of the plane and stepped onto the weathered dock.

Dizziness washed over him. He fought it, grabbing a

piling for purchase. The darkness was huge, the sky enormous. The cold wind buffeted him, clawed at his face. He buttoned his overcoat, lifting his collar. The bulge of his .357 felt reassuring on his wounded hip.

"Excuse me! Sir! Where you going?" The pilot's voice rang out as Grove strode across the dock. "Sir? Sir!"

Grove was already crossing the adjacent gravel lot. He could see the glow of the fire over the treetops to the north. Maybe a quarter mile away. His heart thumped.

The pilot called out again, but Grove ignored the warnings and kept limping along.

He found an access road at the northwest corner of the lot and followed it, using the radiant yellow glow against the belly of the sky as his guide.

Seeing a place you've only read about can be disorienting. It can also be a revelation. Grove had studied the ranger's journals, the police files, Detective Pinsky's twenty-four-hour report, and the lab's documents. They all described the trailhead at the base of Mount Cairn—the place where the Ackermans had first appeared with the Iceman's remains—in similar fashions: a beautiful, sylvian switchback on the edge of the woods, with a quaint, little log ranger shack and a stunning vista of the snow-capped summit rising to the north.

But what Grove found that night as he rounded the corner at the top of the paved trail was nothing of the sort.

The carcass of an old panel van sat near the trail head, sputtering and billowing black smoke out its gaping rear doors. At least a half dozen emergency vehicles crowded the clearing with chaser lights boiling. The air stank of noxious gases, and was tinged a garish purple from all the bubble lights, an ugly little slice of hell.

Grove saw mostly park police, state troopers, and local

evidence-techs running around, yelling at each other. Presumably the bureau had not yet arrived, the gravity of the situation not yet apparent. Grove was certain that Geisel and his men were on their way. Judging from the phase the fire was in—dwindling flames and a fog bank of smoke already permeating the park for miles—the feds would be here soon.

That was when Grove noticed the ambulance on the other side of the clearing.

His heart jumped. There was a light on inside the rear hold, a pair of paramedics administering CPR to a patient laid out on a gurney.

"FBI!"

Grove's voice was hoarse as he staggered through the chaos, flashing his out-of-date investigator card to anyone who showed any interest. Oddly, nobody seemed the slightest bit fazed by Grove's presence.

The rear door of the ambulance was ajar, and Grove peered in to find one of the paramedics—a heavyset Hispanic in a stained white uniform—working on Maura County. "C'mon, c'mon, c'mon, lady, c'mon," he kept murmuring while he rhythmically nudged her chest—*one-two-three-four-five*—then leaned down and breathed more air into her lungs.

"Oh, Jesus, Jesus!"

Grove stood there gripping the door frame, unaware that he had even spoken, gaping at Maura's wounds. Seventy-five percent of her battered, partially nude body was bandaged, much of the gauze soaked in her blood. The paramedic kept working on her. *One-two-three-four-five. One-two-three-four-five.* Grove looked away, his brain seared with emotion.

He prayed then.

He prayed to an obscure god that was a mishmash of his African heritage and own private cosmology. Until that moment, in fact, Grove had not even been aware of this god's existence in his imagination. But now it materialized out of the murky shadows of his subconscious.

The sound of a cough pierced his praying, and Grove looked up.

Maura County was moving. She was alive. Her body shuddering, convulsing, she gasped for air—a fine mist of her own blood spraying across the paramedic's uniform. The paramedic gave her a shot of something, then felt her neck. He nodded at his partner. "Got her back," he said. "Got her back, man, got her back."

Grove pushed the door open.

"Hey!" the other paramedic called out as Grove climbed onboard. "Who the hell are you?"

Grove crouched and shuffled past the paramedic, nearly knocking the IV stand over.

He went down on his knees, put his arms around the journalist. Laid his forehead on her shoulder. The paramedics tried to pull him off, but he held on to her. Her flesh was cold and smelled of alcohol and copper. Her breathing was steady. She was going to make it.

Grove's voice was so soft it was nearly inaudible: "I'm so sorry, I'm sorry, so sorry . . ."

They finally managed to tear him away.

They got him back outside the ambulance, and the big Mexican paramedic stayed with Maura while the other one—a younger man with a punkish blond crew cut—tried to make some sense of what was going on with Grove. "Sir, I'm going to need to know who you are," he said.

"FBI," Grove said.

"Yeah, okay, so—"

"Ulysses Grove, FBI, Behavioral Science Unit." The tears on Grove's face dried in the icy wind. "Please go take care of her, please."

"Um . . . yeah."

Grove was backing away. The paramedic let out a

puzzled sigh, then shrugged and went back to the ambulance. Grove turned and took a few shaky steps.

Then he paused, standing there on unsteady legs directly in front of the smoldering Econoline van.

The dwindling flames blurred in his wet eyes. His throat burned. Teeth clenched. The other cops were too busy to notice—or even care—that a strange man who claimed he was from the FBI was standing in their midst, gazing balefully at the burning vehicle.

Grove gazed over his shoulder at the ranger cabin twenty yards away. It sat under a canopy of spruce boughs, buried in shadow, the fire reflecting off its single little framed window. Grove took a deep breath. The empty shack was waiting. The mountain was waiting.

Grove knew what he had to do.

The ranger cabin had a single-cylinder Yale sand-cast dead bolt. Grove had studied breaking-and-entering techniques at Quantico, and had honed his knowledge of locks to a fine edge. Like many other field agents, he had the picking abilities of a good second-story man.

He snapped the lock in under five seconds.

He sought two things in the dark, airless confines of the shack—and he found both of them. First he needed a trail map of the south face of Mount Cairn. He found one in a Lake Clark park guide under the unfinished wooden counter that faced the door. He tore out the map page, folded it in half, and slid it into his back pocket.

A noise outside made him jump. One of the sirens had squawked suddenly. The ambulance was pulling away. Taking Maura away.

Thank God.

Grove searched the deserted shack for the second item that he needed—something to wear on the mountainside. Boots or a down coat or a sweater. *Something.*

Again he got lucky: of the three individuals who regularly worked at the Mount Cairn trailhead station—Grove saw their names on the counter, printed on table tents—two were female, one male. Apparently the male ranger was a bit of a slob.

Under the work desk in the rear Grove found a stash of *Maxim* magazines, old greasy White Castle sacks, and a gym bag. Grove opened the bag with shaking hands.

Inside was a pair of well-worn all-terrain boots, the blond suede uppers worn down to a scorched, shit-brown color. They were a couple of sizes too small, but Grove managed to squeeze his blistered feet into them. There was also a sweat-stained fleece vest and a large nylon windbreaker with the park ranger insignia on the back. A coil of nylon rope lay on the bottom of the bag, as well as a few miscellaneous pieces of climbing gear—rusty carabiners, an ice ax, crampons, and boot gators.

Grove hurriedly changed into the outer wear—shrugging off his Armani sport coat—while the voices and flames and bubble lights and radios crackled in dissonant chaos outside. Grove's hands were still trembling as he checked the .357 magnum. He had twelve rounds left. Six in the cylinder, six in the speed-loader on his belt.

It took him an inordinate amount of time to zip his vest and outer coat. His fingers would not cooperate—the cold and the stitches making him fumble. Finally he got it. He shoved the gun down the back of his belt, secured the speed-loader, buttoned the windbreaker, and put on a stiff-billed ranger cap. He made sure he had his maps—the trail guide and the ancient overlay map that Okuda had prepared for him—easily accessible. His lucky Sherlock key chain was bulging in his pants pocket.

Starting for the door, he hesitated for a moment, pausing in the darkness. He pulled out one of the maps and looked down at it.

He went back to the desk. There was a large blotter scrawled with doodles, and a cup with pens and pencils. Grove plucked one of the felt-tip pens out of the cup and kelt down. He thought of the Iceman then as he laid Okuda's map of Mount Cairn on the floor.

What horrors had the little shaman stumbled upon six thousand years ago on that glacier?

Grove looked at Okuda's map. The young Asian had absently marked the corner with a doodle of his own. The familiar balloonlike shapes of the Iceman's tattoos.

Grove lifted his right pant leg, exposing the flesh of his leg. Then he carefully drew the symbols on his skin in the exact same position as the Iceman's markings:

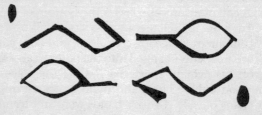

When he was done, he tossed the pen away, lowered his pant leg, rose, and went over to the door. He paused one last time in the shadows.

Protect us while we protect them.

Then he slipped out of the shack.

The cold and noise and shifting lights assaulted Grove's senses. He sniffed it away. Swallowed hard. Then hobbled quickly toward the tree line.

Nobody saw him fade into the copse of Sitkas and birch trees to the north. And nobody saw him circle back around toward the trailhead on the other side of the smoking van.

Safe in the shadows, just beyond the reach of the flashing blue lights, he found the little red flag on the end of the wire stick that marked the beginning of the summit hike.

He limped past the flag and started up the side of the mountain.

27

The Keyhole

The first leg of the Mount Cairn summit route winds through a dense forest of spruce. In the deepest pit of the night these woods are absolute black. Hiking at this time of night is strictly prohibited.

After nearly forty-five minutes, Grove was still maneuvering his way through this frigid darkness at a fairly steady gate, considering his injuries, his breath showing in delicate plumes of vapor.

The crackle of his boots against the crust of snow echoed in the silence. There was still quite a bit of snow on the ground for mid-May, and as Grove wove his way through the trees, he wished he had a flashlight. There appeared to be recent footprints in the snow ahead of him, but they'd been badly distorted by the wind, and were almost gone.

In the absence of a trail, the tiny red flags sticking out of the six-inch padding of snow were the only signposts marking the route.

Grove could hear his wheezing breaths like thunder in his ears. His side ached, and his chest throbbed. He could feel his pulse in his wounds. The altitude was working on him already. He was light-headed, and his breathing was getting labored. *Think of Maura ravaged and bleeding, think of the innocent victims, think of Zorn, make the anger work for you.*

He expected an arrow to leap out of the blackness behind the spruce at any moment. He reached into his windbreaker and found the beavertail grip of the .357. Without breaking stride, he unsheathed the weapon, brought it out, and held it at his side while he trudged along.

For some reason that he did not yet fully understand, he found himself thinking of Father Carrigan's mad rant at the Hotel Nikko a few days ago. What had the old man said about the position in which all the mummies had died?

It's a gesture of absorption . . . a summoning . . . the summoning of a spirit into one's earthly body.

Grove felt as though he was doing just that. Alone on this godforsaken mountain. Trying to draw out a madman. Trying to *summon* the son of a bitch out of hiding. Following two parallel routes in the darkness—one modern, one ancient—their trajectories aligning like crosshairs, like two identical strands of DNA.

In the darkness ahead of him, another miniature red flag materialized out of the snow.

Grove went over to it and paused. The snow had deepened. It was up to Grove's shins now, making each stride an arduous challenge. His feet had lost all feeling. The trees had thinned. The air had thinned. His breath bloomed. He looked up and saw the chaos of stars overhead, as brilliant and impassive as the dome of a planetarium.

He felt as though he were about to leave the earth's atmosphere and emerge into deep space. He tried to catch his breath. Tried to focus. His wounds thrummed with pain. He pulled out the two maps and studied them in the ethereal silver light.

His hands trembled as he tried to focus on the concentric lines of blue and black ink on the yellowed vellum paper. Comparing the two routes—the one the Ackermans had taken, and the one the archaeologists had reconstructed for the Iceman—Grove came to the conclusion that he was nearing the point that the two paths met. *The burial place of the Iceman.* Grove's leg tingled underneath his trousers where the felt-tip tattoo had dried: *Protect us . . . while we protect them.*

A noise made him jerk.

The map fluttered to the snow and the gun came up instinctively, like a jack-in-the-box, both his hands on it now, eyes pinned open like shiny medallions in the dark. Something had moved ten yards away. Grove pointed the barrel at it.

A flash of skin in the darkness, and Grove fired three quick blasts, the muzzle flashing three times in the darkness—*bam! bam! bam!*—the gun bucking hard in Grove's ruined hands, the bullets crackling through the dwindling foliage like paper ripping.

Then silence.

Ears ringing in the ensuing calm, stars spangling his vision, Grove managed to lumber through the snow toward the clearing ahead of him with the gun still raised and scalding hot in his icy hands. He'd gotten just a glimpse of something rolling across the ground in the muzzle flash.

Something twitched in a shadow to Grove's left. He glanced down at the scabrous white surface of the snow, and saw the animal. It took a while to even register in his mind. He stared and stared at it, his panting breaths puffing white vapor in the darkness. The thing stared back at him with empty feral shock in its beady little eyeballs.

The bird, twitching in its death throes, choking on its own blood, was enormous. The size of a ten-gallon hat, with gray mottled feathers, gouged and scorched from one of the blasts. Grove recognized it from a photo in the guide he had studied on the plane. *A willow ptarmigan*. The park was crawling with them. Grove felt as though his chest was about to burst. He peeled off his gloves so he could better feel the trigger.

He was aiming the gun at the poor creature's cranium when he heard another noise.

It came from the vast ice fields above him, beyond the tree line—from the white tundra where the oxygen-starved atmosphere kills all the trees and deforms the undergrowth into twisted abominations sticking out of the snow. It came on the wind like a whisper, and Grove's genitals shrank. The hairs on his body stiffened like metal filings in a magnetic field.

Somebody had called his name in an unearthly voice. A voice without tone or humanity—like the icy snap of a sulfur match tip.

"Ullllysssseeeeeeees."

Grove swallowed his terror and climbed through the snow, up the steepening slope. Moonlight shone down through the thinning boughs. His boots sank with each footstep, making cracking noises like parchment tearing. He could see the threshold of the tree line just ahead of him opening like an archway into an ancient white ruin.

The park guide calls it the keyhole—a clearing of shriveled saplings and undernourished Sitka spruce. The keyhole ushers hikers into the higher, alpine elevations where the base camps are established for technical climbs. Past visitors have rhapsodized about its scenic beauty.

When Grove reached the clearing and got his first glimpse of the vast moonlit ice field, his heart nearly stopped. The late-stage moon shone down on the glacier like a klieg light—illuminating an uncharted planet bordered by great white craters and dunes. The black granite tower of Mount Cairn's summit rose to the north.

A delicate strand of boot prints stitched off into the distance like sutures across the snow.

Grove let out an involuntary gasp, and the gun came up with a jerk.

In the distance, something like a hundred yards away, at the point where the boot prints stopped—the precise same point that the mummy had been found one year earlier—Ackerman stood shin-deep in the snow. His face still obscured by that dark nylon hood, he was a mere silhouette: facing this way, his hunting bow at his side, an arrow clutched in his hand.

In the distance all you could see inside the hood were yellow teeth.

28

Trapdoor

C'mon, c'mon, you idiot, shoot him! For Christ's sake, fire the gun, you got three chances, the gun's rated for four hundred yards or more, c'mon, C'MON!

Grove aimed the gun.

C'mon, c'mon, c'mon!

He fired. Once. Twice.

Shit!

The flashes bloomed silver in Grove's eyes, the booms vibrating the thin dark membrane of night air. In the distance Ackerman jerked, startled by the noise. Then he spun and hobbled away, his gangly arms working furiously as he cobbled over the snow toward a gigantic buttress of rock to the east.

Missed him! Goddamnit, missed him!

Grove lunged across the clearing, the gun still cradled in his numbed, frostbitten bare hands. Lungs heaving, brain screaming—*don't let him get away, not now, so close, SO CLOSE!*—he fixed his sights on the silhouette fleeing in the distance. The wind howled through the canyon. Somewhere to the south a falcon shrieked.

As he charged across the ice field as fast as his failing

legs would allow, Grove felt the vastness opening up before him like a desolate planet.

They call it the Chikilna Glacier Highway—an immense slope the length and breadth of five football fields, bordered on either side by jagged hills and buttresses of stone slathered with permafrost. The edges can be treacherous. Giant plateaus of snow loom like waves frozen in midcurl over deep crevasses. Footing can give way without warning, and deep trenches can appear out of nowhere, with the slightest shift of wind direction.

Ackerman had vanished over the edge of a stone buttress two hundred yards away.

Grove hurried toward the buttress. It was too dark to see what lay beyond those giant rocks, but the predawn glow on the snow diffused the light into a sort of dreamy, purple radiance. Grove's brain swam with panic as he scanned the horizon for any sign of the killer. *One round left in the gun, one round left and then six in the belt!*

His ranger hat flipped off into the wind. His hip ached and panged as he approached the buttress, his boots sinking deeper into the snow. It felt as though his legs weighed a ton. As though a nightmare were gripping him in slow motion as he churned through the drifts.

All at once Grove's brain flashed on the fragment of a vision, a genetic memory, another manhunter's final assault on a mountain thousands of years ago: *The wind sluices down the dark corridor of skeletal trees. It whistles past the shaman like a banshee howling in his ears. He takes one step at a time, his grass-netted boots sinking into the snow up to his knee. His feet are numb, and he can barely see his hand in front of his face as he climbs the crevasse. He's almost there. He must keep going, he must, he must—*

A noise snapped Grove out of his daze.

It sounded like a gasp or a yelp, piercing the cold darkness behind the buttress somewhere. Grove immediately dove to the ground. He landed on his hands and knees in eighteen inches of snow, eating a mouthful of ice, tearing more stitches, setting off fireworks of sparks in his field of vision.

The gun went off.

The watery blast, muffled by the snow, popped in Grove's ears, the bullet ricocheting off a nearby boulder, chewing a chink of ice from the rock. The sonic boom echoed down ghostly chasms in the distance.

Grove's hand, buried in the snow, completely without feeling, was still welded around the grip of the gun.

He crawled behind a boulder and brushed the snow off the icy stainless steel barrel. Heart racing, he levered the hot cylinder open. Smoke whistled out of the chamber and into the wind. He dumped the empties. The little brass casings bounced into the snow.

Grove reached inside his coat. Found the speed-loader. Pulled it out and slammed it into the cylinder. Something wrong. Jammed? No. The speed-loader was frozen. Frozen! The bullets cemented in there like ice cubes.

Another noise, and Grove jerked around. No ammo. Naked! Naked!

He rose to a crouch. Then turned. *Think! Think!* He circled around the back of the boulder. *THINK!* Pulse pounding, eyes stinging in the wind, he formulated a plan. *Toss something across the front face of the buttress . . . then crawl over the top and surprise him!*

Grove crept as quietly as possible around the rear end of the buttress, then paused, taking a deep breath. Then he hurled the useless gun as hard as he could at the leading edge of the plateau thirty yards to the north.

The gun made an unholy clang and clatter as it struck the jagged stone.

Moving as quickly and silently as possible, Grove scaled the buttress, then frantically searched the magenta shadows for Ackerman. *Where the HELL is he? WHERE THE*

HELL IS HE? Grove crawling on hands and knees. Searching, searching ... until suddenly, there was a crack, and Grove felt the buttress give way beneath him like a great trapdoor.

It happened all at once, a loud shifting snap as his right knee broke through a layer of snow, and the ledge collapsed suddenly on one side. And then Grove was sliding backward. Toward the face. Sliding out of control. Crying out. Sliding, sliding—

—clawing at the ice now—

—until he slipped off the ledge.

29

Black Eternity

At the last moment Grove's bloody fingernails dug into a crack in the crust like grappling hooks. His body flopped and banged against the side of the crevasse, and he hung there suddenly. Hung in midair. His paralytic, frozen fingers hooked into a fissure. *Don't look down, don't look, don't do it, don't!*

He looked down.

The crevasse plunged into black eternity below him. A million years of glacial ebb and flow. An endless dark chasm hungry to swallow him.

The wind lashed at his back. He tried to lift himself back up over the ledge, but his wounds would not allow him to. Pain shrieked in his pelvis, his ribs, his skull. His body swayed in the mountain gusts like a deadweight.

Nobody will ever know how long he hung there, alone, in the gelid drafts over that black chasm. It might have been a single minute. Or it might have been much longer. Grove would never know.

In that icy, unforgiving wind, time had jammed like a broken clockwork.

He knew he was going to die, but he could not escape the feeling that he had one last task to perform. One last piece of unfinished business.

Hanging there by his numb, frostbitten fingers, Grove kept hearing his mom's soft lullaby of a prayer playing over and over again in his traumatized brain like a fever dream, in rhythm with his gasping, hyperventilated breathing:

"Ndeya no mwana wandi munshila ba mpapula,
Munshila ba mpapaula
Iye, iye, iye yangu umwnaa wandi
Yangu umwana wandi mushila ba mpapula."

("It's not good to be alone in this world.
Mother, carry me.
I will carry you one day
The way a crocodile carries its young on her back.")

Tears burned his eyes, and he was about to give up, when he saw two things almost simultaneously that kept him holding on for one more terrible moment.

Dawn had come.

The first rays of brilliant, unadulterated alpine sunlight sliced through the gloom, painting the side of the mountain in violent slashes of blood-orange. The jagged face of rock around Grove turned luminous. Ice crystals scattered the light into silver sparks.

Then, in that unheralded appearance of morning, a hooded shadow slithered across the stone surface of the east face. It was tall and rangy, and came from an outcropping above Grove. An arrow protruded from a bow, aimed directly at the back of Grove's neck.

"*It is yourrrr timmmmmmme.*"

Barely audible above the gusts, the unexpected words reached Grove's ears like sympathetic strings being plucked. The revelation vibrated through him. *It is your time.* Four simple words, wheezed in a mucusy, feral baritone, raveling together in Grove's brain, making sense of everything: the beast had lured him here to this precipice, this terrible fate, just as it had lured so many man-hunters down through the millennia.

The realization nearly knocked Grove off the side of the mountain, but he held on for one last millisecond, long enough to twist his head around and look up into the face of absolute desolation leaning out over a crag of rock.

In the putrifying sunlight, Ackerman's face was par-tially visible inside the hood. A pointed chin, an ulcer-ated beak of a nose, one visible eye luminous with demonic energy. The face looked as though it had been dead a long while—probably ravaged by stroke or car-diac arrest. It was the color of frozen black cinders. "Your timmmme," the monster hissed as he drew the arrow back, taught against the bow.

Grove slammed his eyes shut.

A gust of wind, and then—*twannnng!*—the noise followed by a sharp slashing pain just above Grove's left shoulder blade. It was as savage as the bite of a rabid dog, and it nearly knocked Grove off the mountain. But he held on, held on with everything he had left, his frozen fingers wedged into that fissure. The pain raged down his side, penetrating his innards like a hot poker, as another sound wrenched his attention to his left.

He caught a glimpse of the arrow tumbling down the side of the glacier, tossing and turning end over end on the wind currents, then vanishing in a puff of white powder. The wind! Thank Christ, the wind had thrown the arrow off enough to only graze him!

A low, guttural growl came from above, and Grove tried to look up when his fingers suddenly slipped.

"Aahhhhh!"

He bounced against the rock, then dangled there in the wind, hanging by one hand now—*one, weakening, numbed hand!* Gasping for breath, vertigo choking him,

heart pounding, windburned vision blurring, he tried
to look up. The gusts rose again, clawing at him, yanking at him. Time running out. His icy fingers slipping.

The thing that was once Richard Ackerman, only
inches away now, leaned out over the ledge. He reached
for a second arrow. His face was clearly visible in the
pale sunlight now. It was an abomination of a face, not
really a face at all, more like a fleshy effigy, deformed by
evil, eye sockets sunken like a rotten gourd, pupils glowing phosphorous yellow with some inextricable, parasitic will.

Grove looked up at Ackerman—looked *through* the
human eyes, into the demon's eyes, into the abyss. And
the abyss looked back. And Grove managed to lift his
free hand—his posture and position taking on a decent
approximation of the position in which all the victims
had been found. One hand raised to the heavens. *The
summoning.*

The demon paused, cocking its distorted head in
confusion. *What is this?*

Grove was offering a trembling, frostbitten hand,
begging for help. The great manhunter, begging for his
life! The demon savored Grove's last thoughts: *Please
don't let me fall. I will take your hand. Please. I will take your
hand, I will surrender to it if only you'll help me.*

The Richard-Thing grinned, then reached a long,
emaciated, blackened hand over the ledge.

Grove reached up with his last scintilla of strength
and grasped the hand of evil.

30
The Aperture

"Come into me!" Grove howled with his final breath, and all at once the demon stiffened like a marionette charged with a million volts of electricity. The distended mouth dropped open for a moment, its rotten maw gaping impossibly wide, emitting a hellish shriek that shook the glacier like a depth charge . . . and then the black entity flowed into Grove.

In that single terrible instant, very little of the transference was visible to the human eye.

The only external evidence of the absorption was a spontaneous change in both Ackerman and Grove as if the two were on opposite sides of a great balance: Ackerman collapsed, and Grove inflated like an artificial rubber doll hanging in midair, the two frozen hands still clasped in paralytic symbiosis.

The thing that entered Grove was a black, poisonous banshee. Grove convulsed. It felt as though a *second* skeleton were unfolding inside him, its bones made of obsidian, its marrow extracted from hell. Grove's brain trembled with garbled soliloquies, Sumerian gibberish, horrible images popping and flickering—centuries of murder, ceaseless cruelties, rivers of human blood flooding the land, crashing in crimson tidal waves against the flimsy ramparts of men. And that's when Grove played his final card.

He let go.

He plummeted nearly three hundred feet, his arms and legs flailing, his body convulsing and seizing in free fall like an insect in its angry death throes. The cry that came out of him was not of this earth, the Doppler effect changing pitch as he plunged, a demonic bellow that deepened into the sound of a hellish, enraged, baritone aria.

The profiler landed in a capsule of snow with a muffled *fuhhhmmp!* that echoed faintly off the great steeples of rock and ice.

Then there was nothing but silence.

At the top of Mount Cairn's east face, Ackerman lay dead, his savaged brain released at last.

Hundreds of feet below, Grove lay buried in twelve feet of soft pack. The newborn sun slanted across the impact site. The crater was in the shape of a bat. Or an angel. Depending upon your point of view.

Clinically dead under all that snow, yet clinging to the last embers of life, Special Agent Ulysses Grove felt a tremendous pressure at the base of his brain stem as he lay suspended in his white tomb of ice.

It was an all-consuming impulse, a terrible compulsion that snaked through the tributaries of his circulatory system and kept him alive far beyond the limits of human survival.

It was the urge to kill.

Epilogue
The Cabin

"All is change; all yields its place and goes."
                                        —Euripides

Voices. In the dark. Muffled by the snow. Crunching sounds of machinery. Shovels. Helicopter rotors vibrating the glacier. Getting closer. Closer.

Then a single male voice rang out as clear as a slap, shot through with urgency: "Found him! Over here! Let's get a medivac down here stat! *Stat!*"

The womb of snow trembled.

He couldn't move. Like the mummies of Anubis he had to wait in silent stasis for the course of mortal events to discover him. He felt a distant stirring in his chest. How long had he been under the snow? Seconds? Minutes? Hours? Millennia?

The darkness cracked open. Daylight pouring in. Gloved hands brushing away layers of powder.

Eyes barely functioning, he could see the rescuers now: a half dozen men in ATF parkas digging him out of his cold white tomb. A paramedic with a trauma box— portable defibrillator, oxygen, traction splints, inflatable antishock trousers—burrowed down into the drift around him.

A gloved hand reached down and grasped him by the lapel of his frozen jacket.

"He's alive! We got eyes blinking! Get the telemetry radio down here!"

The digging quickened. Radios crackled. Voices yelled. The snap of an ammonia capsule by his nose. Through glazed eyes he tried to see the medic.

"Agent Grove? Can you hear me?"

He could not speak, could barely breathe. When did he fall? Only a few minutes ago? More men were working on him now. Pain seared his shoulder where the arrow had grazed his nape. Tremendous pressure on his chest now. A gurgling sound coming out of him. Cables looped across his legs. The medic—a young black man wearing a chopper helmet and goggles—fiddled with defib paddles. "Got a flat line! Gonna shock him! Everybody clear—clear! Okay, clear!"

Whap!

The jolt stiffened him, arching his back like a scorpion, and he gasped.

"Got it back!"

The snake slithered up through his brain, through his autonomic nerve center. The puppeteer took control of his tendons and muscle. The medic was still working on him, oblivious of the awakening, doing something with a hypodermic, when the snake struck.

"Jesus Chrahhhh—"

Grove's hands, blackened with frostbite, wrapped around the paramedic's neck.

The young man let out a garbled cry, which only fed the thing inside Grove. Slender, dark, frostbitten fingers tightened around the poor medic's Adam's apple with the force of an iron drill press.

The medic turned ashen, his gray tongue protruding, delicate threads of saliva puffing out of him on convulsive squalls of coughing. And deep within Grove's brain, cocooned in a sheath of blackness, the real Grove watched in horror like a man bound and gagged in a dark room, watching a snuff film unspool on a distant screen. His hands were operating with a will of their own, lustily strangling the life out of the young man. Orgasmic pleasure spurted through Grove as the medic's eyes bugged, and it was horrible, and wonderful, and terrifying, and erotic, all at the same time.

Others descended on the scene. Grabbing the New Grove. Prying his frozen fingers off the medic. The pinch of a needle in Grove's arm—a heavy sedative coursing into him. The puppeteer raged, a terrible bellowing scream coming out of Grove as the drug pressed down on him.

His body flopped in the snow for a moment, stringers of blood staining the whiteness, arms flailing, spine seizing up, as the drug spread through him. Movements slowing. The light dwindling.

Slowing.

Dwindling.

Until finally . . . darkness descended.

One week after Harlan Simms and the joint tactical force from Alaska saved Ulysses Grove from the crevasse on Mount Cairn, a young woman passed through Washington National Airport unnoticed by most of her fellow travelers. She wore jeans and a denim jacket, and she walked with the aid of a metal cane. Her milky blond hair was pulled back in a tight ponytail, and she held an unlit cigarette in anticipation of exiting the non-smoking area.

Outside the terminal, she immediately lit the cigarette and hailed a taxi.

In the daylight, her wounds were more visible. Most of the bandages had come off the previous day during her brief visit to a clinic in San Francisco, but there were still scattered butterfly bandages across her arms, her left cheek, and under her blouse. She'd been through endless interrogations and interviews over the last week. She'd been told there would be scars. Some of them would likely be unseen, *psychic* scars. But for all practical purposes she was expected to fully recover.

That's not what she was worried about. Her own well-being was not what was making her nervous as she climbed into that airport cab, shoving her overnight bag across the rear seat and giving directions to the driver. She was worried about Grove. In awkward conversations over the past week—with both Tom Geisel of the bureau and Michael Okuda of the Schleimann Lab—Maura had learned the broad strokes of what had happened to the profiler.

Apparently the tactical force had arrived at the Mount Cairn trailhead only minutes after Grove had embarked up the side of the mountain. They heard gunshots, and minutes later found Ackerman near the original burial site, dead of cardiac arrest. Not long after that, they found Grove buried in the snow, barely alive, ribs broken, a lung punctured, a deep wound in his neck where the arrow had grazed him, severe hypothermia threatening his life. Evidently, a hypothermic individual can appear dead—even diagnosed as clinically deceased—and still be revived.

But the problem wasn't physical. They managed to save Grove's life—his wounds were surprisingly minimal thanks to the cushion of snow that had stopped his fall—but for some reason he had slipped into some kind of bizarre psychosis. Geisel wouldn't—or couldn't—say much about it. And Okuda seemed to have vanished off the face of the earth. Maura learned later that Okuda had gone into a drug rehab program after being so shaken by the bizarre turn of events. But everybody was being tight-lipped and secretive about Grove, as though he had become some kind of classified state secret. Even Vida was fairly cryptic over the phone. She told Maura that Grove had been moved two days ago to a remote cabin owned by Tom Geisel on the Shenandoah River about seventy miles west of Grove's home in Arlington.

En route, riding in the back of that rattling airport taxi, passing the verdant hills of former Civil War battlefields, Maura braced herself for what she might find at the cabin. She didn't care anymore about the paperback rights to the Sun City story or her imminent promotion at *Discover* or all the raving and gushing old Chester Joyce had been lavishing on her at work.

She just wanted Grove to be okay.

At that precise moment, as Maura was brooding her way across the lush Virginia landscape, the final stages of an ancient rite were occurring in the woods west of Leesburg.

In a cedar-planked room, its windows shuttered and closed off from the forest around it, three individuals had been sweating over the bed of a fourth for nearly forty-eight straight hours. By the afternoon of the second day, working without a break, eating and sleeping in shifts, the three practitioners finally saw a change.

Vida had been hovering over her son, waving a smoking hank of ceremonial wheat, droning in Swahili the word for "out," when it happened.

"Nge—nge—nge—NGE! Nnn!"

Grove jerked forward suddenly on the bed, the padded ropes and creaking frame barely containing him, his skivvies ragged with blood and bile, his neck wrapped in the bandages.

Father Carrigan, who had been standing at the foot of the bed, calling out the familiar Catholic litany of exorcism—"the archangel Michael commands you!"—suddenly reared back in surprise, his glass vial of holy water flying out of his hand and shattering against the knotty pine wall behind him. Professor de Lourde, standing in the far corner of the room with a small, breadbox-sized digital video camera, his finely tailored dress shirt wrinkled and soaked through with perspiration, suddenly gaped, jaw dropping.

The video camera slipped from his hand, falling to the floor, its lens cracking, which unfortunately made the documentation of what followed impossible.

And what followed was a miracle.

Or at least that's what ran through Father Carrigan's mind as he watched the transformation. On the other side of the bed, Vida stared wide-eyed at the change, interpreting the phenomena quite differently. In that amazing instant, she believed the gods had come down and helped her son perform the most powerful magic she had ever witnessed. In the far corner of the room, over the course of that same astonishing moment, Professor Moses de Lourde—ever the academic, ever cynical—instantly formulated a *third* opinion: he thought they were all crazy, and they were all seeing things. But that was part of the deal the threesome had struck when they convinced Tom Geisel to let them bring the psychotic Grove here to this remote cabin. Whatever happened, whatever the results, the three friends would all bring their own perspective and culture to the task of exorcising the demon inside Grove—Vida's African mysticism, Father Carrigan's Catholicism, and de Lourde's benevolent skepticsm. But now, as they all watched the phenomena unfold, not a single one of them was certain of what they were seeing.

The body on the bed—blackened, scarred, and savaged by demonic possession—had suddenly and spontaneously jerked upward into a semisitting position . . . and then something extraordinary happened. A *second* body—an astral body that appeared initially as pure white light—tore through the flesh of the first like a

butterfly ripping out of its chrysalis. This *second* Grove
lurched forward across the foot of the bed and tumbled
to the floor.

Then, just for an instant—an instant that would
never be verified by video, and would never truly be believed by anyone who was not present that day—there
were *two* Groves in that cabin: a blackened husk of the
man on the bed, and a glistening, damp, exhausted version sprawled on the warped oak floor. And that's when
the final change occurred.

The shell of the man on the bed began to dissolve
before their eyes, the sound of an alien wind moaning
through the cabin like a dying beast. The figure blurred
and undulated for a moment, like a sculpture made of
smoke, then began to whirl off the bed, a column of
noxious gas, rising and swirling upward, penetrating
the ceiling and then vanishing on a faint, torturous
shriek.

Thunder rumbled suddenly outside.

Vida ran over to her son, kneeling down and taking
him in her arms, as de Lourde and Carrigan both lurched
instinctively over to the window. Through the grimy
glass, they could see the gray sky above the treetops roiling like a cauldron. A black whirlpool—as deep and
opaque as squid ink—shot upward from the roof of the
cabin, darkening the horizon like black skeletal fingers
clawing the heavens. De Lourde gasped, and Father
Carrigan prayed.

Lightning crackled and veined the sky, and the rains
started.

The sound of the rain was like a salve on the cabin,
and de Lourde and Carrigan turned back to the room.
Vida was still holding her boy. Grove had sagged in her
arms, clad only in his boxer shorts and bloody bandages.
He was still semiconscious, and he looked a little delirious. But he was alive, and he was whole, and he was back.
He closed his eyes and clung to his mother and tried to

breathe normally again. Nobody said anything for quite some time.

The blessed sound of the rain filled the cabin.

From that day forward Grove would hold on to a single memory of the exorcism. Alone inside the dark prison of his mind, shrouded in blackness, watching his own body flail and convulse, he had suddenly seen another hand reaching for him through the darkness, a familiar hand, a woman's hand. It pierced the fog and reached down for him with graceful, slender fingers, inviting him to accept it, surrender to it, grasp it. A gold wedding ring shimmered on one of its fingers.

Hannah's hand.

It was not the power of Father Carrigan's litany, or Vida's ritual, or even de Lourde's steadying presence that yanked Grove back to reality. In the end it was something far more intimate and secret that had ripped him from the moorings of evil, tearing him free of that terrible doppelganger. Hannah had come for him, her lovely caramel-skinned hand reaching across the years of grief.

And Grove had gladly followed her out of the shadows.

Hours later, after the storm had passed and a certain calm had returned to the woods, Vida's dusky face appeared in the doorway of the cabin's back room. "You got a visitor, *mwana.*"

Grove sat in a bentwood rocker near the window, a country quilt across his lap, a pair of aluminum crutches canted against the jelly cabinet next to him. He had been absently paging though a Geisel family photo album, enjoying the simple, mindless pleasure of looking at pictures of grandkids at Thanksgiving dinners. Now he looked up and smiled at his mother.

"*Wanawake?*" he said.

Vida's face broke into stunned delight. "Yes, it is a woman. *Jinsi gani?*"

Grove grinned. "Um . . . *labda* . . . *labda yumkini?*"

Vida chortled. "We will have to work on your Swahili. It is Miss County."

Grove rose, put the crutches under his arms, and shuffled over to a little oval mirror above a porcelain washbasin. Every labored breath brought a dull ache from his punctured lung and broken ribs. He wore a fresh undershirt and jeans, but he didn't like his reflection: his face looked terrible. Like a brown rag that had been wrung dry. The bandage around his neck was stained a ghastly yellow. *You really look like hell, old hoss.*

He sighed and slowly made his way out the door.

Maura was waiting on the porch, staring out at the old gnarled chestnuts that stood sentry on the edge of Geisel's property. The rain had lifted. The sun had broken through the gray clouds here and there, and the air smelled of pine and wet earth. But the distant horizon still hung black and laden with portents—as though the evil had diffused into the atmosphere only to start its long reconstitution.

Maura whirled around when she heard Grove's crutches creaking behind her.

"Um . . ." Grove started to say and suddenly fell silent when their eyes met.

"Yeah . . . so." Maura stopped short as well, looking as though she had a speech planned but couldn't put it together. She took a step closer.

"I'm okay," he said. "And so are you, it looks like."

Then the crutches fell to the floor—

—and they hugged.

It was a full-on homecoming embrace. And they said nothing. They simply hugged each other for agonizing moments. And Grove breathed her in as she held him upright. He could smell for the first time in what seemed like years. She had a distinctive scent—wintergreen,

smoke, some kind of powder that Grove couldn't identify. He breathed it in and held her in the calm of that
clapboard porch.

At length, Maura pulled away and retrieved the
crutches, positioning them back under Grove's arms.
Then they sat down next to each other. On two wooden
Adirondack chairs canted toward the swaying shagbark
trees. Maura was the first to break the silence. "Ulysses,
I don't know what to say."

Grove looked at her, saw that her eyes were moist.
"You don't have to say anything."

"I'm glad you're okay."

"The feeling's mutual."

"Ulysses . . ." She paused again.

"What is it?"

She looked at him. "When you said you didn't think
it was a good idea for us to . . ." Another pause.

"Look, Maura, I was . . . confused. I was messed up."

"No, you see, the thing is . . . you were right."

Grove studied her wan face. "Maura—"

"No, I mean it." She licked her lips, measuring her
words. "Your world is not . . . it's not my world."

A long pause.

Regret stabbed at Grove's heart. He could hear birds
somewhere a million miles away. He started to say something else, but instead simply put a hand on her arm
and patted her tenderly.

There would be time for more words, perhaps time
for starting over. But right now it felt much better just
to sit. Which they did.

They just sat there and didn't say a word and watched
the ebb and flow of the breeze, wondering how long
this respite from the darkness and turmoil would last.

Because it never does.

Don't miss Jay Bonansinga's next electrifying thriller . . .

TWISTED

Profiler Ulysses Grove must confront a serial killer with a personal vendetta on his agenda, as a vicious storm ravages the Gulf Coast.

Coming from Pinnacle in 2006.

More Books From Your Favorite Thriller Authors

Thrilling Suspense From
Wendy Corsi Staub

All the Way Home	0-7860-1092-4	$6.99US/$8.99CAN
The Last to Know	0-7860-1196-3	$6.99US/$8.99CAN
Fade to Black	0-7860-1488-1	$6.99US/$9.99CAN
In the Blink of an Eye	0-7860-1423-7	$6.99US/$9.99CAN
She Loves Me Not	0-7860-1424-5	$6.99US/$9.99CAN
Dearly Beloved	0-7860-1489-X	$6.99US/$9.99CAN
Kiss Her Goodbye	0-7860-1641-8	$6.99US/$9.99CAN

Available Wherever Books Are Sold!

Visit our website at **www.kensingtonbooks.com**

BOOK YOUR PLACE ON OUR WEBSITE
AND MAKE THE
READING CONNECTION!

We've created a customized website just for our very special readers, where you can get the inside scoop on everything that's going on with Zebra, Pinnacle and Kensington books.

When you come online, you'll have the exciting opportunity to:

- View covers of upcoming books
- Read sample chapters
- Learn about our future publishing schedule (listed by publication month *and author*)
- Find out when your favorite authors will be visiting a city near you
- Search for and order backlist books from our online catalog
- Check out author bios and background information
- Send e-mail to your favorite authors
- Meet the Kensington staff online
- Join us in weekly chats with authors, readers and other guests
- Get writing guidelines
- AND MUCH MORE!

Visit our website at
http://www.kensingtonbooks.com